Praise for Kat

"Both deeply moving and edge

Berlin Letters is an eloquent reminder of the brutal totalitarianism of Soviet Communism and the unsung heroes who fought to tear down the Iron Curtain and free Eastern Europe."

—Beatriz Williams, *New York Times* bestselling author of *The Summer Wives*

"*The Berlin Letters* is a thrilling read that has it all: secret codes, espionage, and a fascinating glimpse into the world behind the Berlin Wall. Katherine Reay always delivers well-researched historical fiction with a perfect blend of heartwarming characters and fast-paced action. Fans of historical spy novels are going to love this enthralling read!"

—Madeline Martin, *New York Times* bestselling author of *The Keeper of Hidden Books*

"Surrounding the Cold War and the fall of the Berlin Wall, Reay's action-packed novel is told in dual-narrative form between a daughter with a rebellious streak and her father's buried secrets. A story of hope and resilience, *The Berlin Letters*, is a thrilling story full of intrigue, espionage, code-breaking, and at its core, loyalty and humanity. You won't be able to put it down!"

—Eliza Knight, *USA TODAY* and international bestselling author of *Starring Adele Astaire*

"Both a gripping tale of espionage and a moving portrait of a family ripped apart, *The Berlin Letters* offers readers a fascinating glimpse at a fraught period of all-too-recent history and the people caught in the crosshairs of geopolitics who chose, each in their own way, to fight back."

—Jennifer Thorne and Lee Kelly, co-authors of *The Antiquity Affair*

"In her nail-biting latest . . . Reay builds an immersive world behind the Iron Curtain, full of competing loyalties and a constant, chilling sense of paranoia. Readers will be enthralled."

—*Publishers Weekly* for *A Shadow in Moscow*

"This book is a consummately rendered and captivating espionage account of the Cold War, told from the perspective of two sympathetic and admirable women . . . Filled with surprise twists and turns, and ultimately uplifting and inspiring, I found this superlative novel an enduring gem. Five stars!"

—Historical Novel Society for *A Shadow in Moscow*

"Rich with fascinating historical detail and unforgettable characters, *A Shadow in Moscow* deftly explores two female spies who will risk everything to change the world. Katherine Reay eloquently portrays the incredible contributions of women in history, the extraordinary depths of love, and, perhaps most important of all, the true cost of freedom in her latest stunning page-turner. A story that will leave readers examining what they hold most dear and positively brimming with hope, this is an important, timely tour de force—and a must-read for anyone who has ever wondered if just one person can make a difference."

—Kristy Woodson Harvey, *New York Times* bestselling author of *The Wedding Veil*

"Katherine Reay's latest has it all—intrigue, twists and turns, acts of bravery and sacrificial love, and an unforgettable Cold War setting with clever, daring women at the helm. An expertly delivered page-turner by a true master of the craft!"

—Susan Meissner, *USA TODAY* bestselling author of *The Nature of Fragile Things,* for *A Shadow in Moscow*

"This riveting story of two female spies operating in Moscow during different eras has everything you could ever want in a novel—suspense, intrigue, compelling characters, exotic settings, deep insight, and gasp-inducing plot twists. A word of advice: clear your calendar before opening *A Shadow in Moscow*. Once you start, you won't be able to stop until you regretfully reach the last page of Katherine Reay's masterfully written novel."

—Marie Bostwick, *New York Times* bestselling author of *Esme Cahill Fails Spectacularly*

"Spellbinding. Reay's fast-paced foray into the past cleverly reveals a family's secrets and how a pivotal moment shaped future generations. Readers who enjoy engrossing family mystery should take note."

—*Publishers Weekly* for *The London House*

"*The London House* is a tantalizing tale of deeply held secrets, heartbreak, redemption, and the enduring way that family can both hurt and heal us."

—Kristin Harmel, *New York Times* bestselling author of *The Forest of Vanishing Stars*

"*The London House* is a thrilling excavation of long-held family secrets that proves sometimes the darkest corners of our pasts are balanced with slivers of light. Arresting historical fiction destined to thrill fans of Erica Roebuck and Pam Jenoff."

—Rachel McMillan, author of *The London Restoration*

"Expertly researched and perfectly paced, *The London House* is a remarkable novel about love and loss and the way history—and secrets—can impact a family and ultimately change its future."

—Syrie James, bestselling author of *The Lost Memoirs of Jane Austen*

"The town of Winsome reminds me of Jan Karon's Mitford, with its endearing characters, complex lives, and surprises where you don't expect them. You'll root for these characters and will be sad to leave this charming town."

—Lauren K. Denton, bestselling author of *The Hideaway*, for *Of Literature and Lattes*

"In her ode to small towns and second chances, Katherine Reay writes with affection and insight about the finer things in life."

—Karen Dukess, author of *The Last Book Party*, for *Of Literature and Lattes*

"Reay understands the heartbeat of a bookstore."

—Baker Book House for *The Printed Letter Bookshop*

"*The Printed Letter Bookshop* is both a powerful story and a dazzling experience. I want to give this book to every woman I know—I adored falling into Reay's world, words, and bookstore."

—Patti Callahan Henry, bestselling author

THE BERLIN LETTERS

Also by Katherine Reay

A Shadow in Moscow

The London House

Of Literature and Lattes

The Printed Letter Bookshop

The Austen Escape

A Portrait of Emily Price

The Brontë Plot

Lizzy & Jane

Dear Mr. Knightley

NONFICTION

Awful Beautiful Life, with Becky Powell

The BERLIN LETTERS

A COLD WAR NOVEL

Katherine Reay

The Berlin Letters

Published by Harper Muse, an imprint of HarperCollins Focus LLC.

Library of Congress Cataloging-in-Publication Data

Names: Reay, Katherine, 1970- author.
Title: The Berlin letters: a Cold War novel / Katherine Reay.
Description: [Nashville]: Harper Muse, 2024. | Series: A Cold War Novel | Summary: "Near the end of the Cold War, a CIA code breaker discovers a symbol she recognizes from her childhood, which launches her across the world to the heart of Berlin just before the wall comes tumbling down"-- Provided by publisher.
Identifiers: LCCN 2023039223 (print) | LCCN 2023039224 (ebook) | ISBN 9781400243068 (paperback) | ISBN 9781400243075 (epub) | ISBN 9781400243082
Subjects: LCSH: Cold War--Fiction. | Berlin (Germany)--Fiction. | LCGFT: Thrillers (Fiction) | Spy fiction. | Novels.
Classification: LCC PS3618.E23 B47 2024 (print) | LCC PS3618.E23 (ebook) | DDC 813/.6--dc23/eng/20231012
LC record available at https://lccn.loc.gov/2023039223
LC ebook record available at https://lccn.loc.gov/2023039224

Printed in the United States of America

23 24 25 26 27 LBC 5 4 3 2 1

PROLOGUE

Monica Voekler

EAST BERLIN, GERMANY

Sunday, August 13, 1961

The jangling telephone broke into her dreams.

As Haris climbed from bed with a groan, Monica felt the cool air touch her skin. Today would be another hot day, but it wasn't hot yet. It wasn't fully light yet. It was too dark for calls or climbing from bed. Too dark for anything but sleep.

She sat up and looked to the clock, but she couldn't separate its black hands from the room's deep grey.

Was it Luisa?

Monica lifted her chin and closed her eyes to listen. After recently moving from her crib to a "big girl bed," their three-year-old daughter had been getting up and wandering the apartment at night. Haris often found her curled up fast asleep in the hallway, or nestled under the kitchen table, or, most terrifyingly, tucked near the toilet.

Monica disentangled her feet from the covers as another ring reverberated through the apartment. Haris shuffled into the kitchen, grumbling, before he lifted the receiver from its cradle. His tense, urgent tone emerged barely above a whisper.

Her husband walked back into the bedroom, all shuffling gone. Haris reached for his pants, thrown over the room's only chair, and pulled them on with such haste, he lost his balance and dropped into the chair. It scraped against the hardwood.

"What's the matter? Where are you going?" Standing now, she grabbed the clock and held it close to her face: 4:00 a.m.

"Potsdamer Platz. It started there late last night, and it's almost completed."

"Another riot? What's completed?"

"Not a riot, but I hardly know. A barricade of sorts. Koch called it an *Antifaschistischer Schutzwall.*"

"What is an anti-Fascist protection barrier?" Monica's head felt muddled. "How can you have a physical barrier to an ideology?"

"That's what I'm going to find out. Koch wants an article for the afternoon edition. General Secretary Ulbricht called him personally. Whatever this is, it's been in the works for some time. Thousands of soldiers flooded the city last night to construct this thing. That takes coordination and planning."

With pants pulled above his narrow hips and still working the buttons on his shirt, Haris stepped toward her and dropped a kiss atop her head. His dark hair, though short, was still ruffled at the crown from sleep. "Go back to bed. I'll be back soon. If I don't make it before you leave for lunch, tell your parents I'm sorry."

"As usual then?" Her tone came out sharper than she intended. His face was so close she could look up and see a muscle flicker in his jaw, clenched against reacting, no doubt.

"Don't." He sighed. "Not this morning."

"At least try to come for lunch." She reached for his hand. "It's been over a month."

"If they wanted to see us, they shouldn't have moved away."

"Not again." She climbed back into bed and pulled the covers up around herself. "Everyone is moving away, Haris. We should at least consider it."

While not mathematically true, it felt true. And it was concerning. Haris learned the numbers at the newspaper and had repeated them to her. She suspected he regretted that slip, as it bolstered her position rather than his own, but there was little he could do about that now. Besides, it wasn't as if she hadn't noticed. Everyone had noticed. Last month alone more than thirty thousand *Deutsche Demokratische Republik* citizens had come through Berlin's Soviet Sector, commonly called East Berlin, then crossed into one of the city's western sectors—most often the American one—and left forever. Haris's newspaper, *Neues Deutschland*, didn't print that number, of course, but that didn't make it any less real. The paper also hadn't printed that the DDR had lost a full 20 percent of its population since 1949. Yet that was real too.

"No, Monica. Our lives, our work, it's all here." Haris exited the room, calling back over his shoulder, "And I'm not getting fired over a luncheon with your parents."

Monica curled against her pillow and hoped for another hour or two of sleep before Luisa awoke. Their ever-present quarrel wasn't worth losing sleep over.

Haris had not returned by midmorning.

Monica fed Luisa breakfast, bathed her, and played dolls with her to pass the time. Then at eleven o'clock she dressed her daughter in her best dress, loaded her into her pram, and maneuvered them both out their building's front door, down the few stairs, and onto Rheinsberger Strasse.

It was a beautiful summer morning. One full of rare sun. A perfect day to walk the several blocks to the American Sector—West Berlin—rather than take the S-Bahn.

After a few steps, Monica noticed a strange hum in the air. More people traversed the street than on a normal Sunday. They walked quickly, anxiously. Some carried trash bags. Some carried suitcases. And while those moving in haste were mostly traveling her direction, others were walking more slowly with tears and stricken expressions—walking toward her, past her, and away from the train station and border crossing.

Border crossing.

Monica shook her head. It was hardly a border. There were signs, "You are now leaving the Democratic Sector of Berlin," to mark one's steps from the Soviet to American Sectors and a few bored guards who might comment occasionally, but nothing more. In fact, a few close friends lived on Bernauer Strasse, a unique street in which the building was in the Soviet Sector but the sidewalk right outside the front door was in the American. Those friends simply walked out their doors without nodding to any guard at all.

Life passed between the sectors with hardly a pause—along with telephone lines, electricity wires, train tracks. In fact, one could live in one and work in another, and many did. The Soviet-backed SED government didn't like its citizens earning and bringing Western currency into the Soviet Sector, but there was little they could do about it. It was still one city, after all. Berlin.

It was true, however, that the border had been more problematic in the past. Monica remembered the year 1949, during which the Soviet Union decided to close off West Berlin from the West altogether. Nothing could arrive by road or rail to the American, British, and French sections of the city without passing through a hundred miles of DDR territory. They were left with only two fly routes, but the West proved indomitable. Using those two fly zones, they dropped all needed provisions into the city by flying planes over it every thirty-one seconds for an entire year. The DDR finally had to cave because they were the ones hurting—they needed raw goods from the West.

Monica knew people left, of course, thousands of them, but she wasn't entirely sure why. Other than the fact that she missed her parents, she did enjoy her life in East Berlin. Like Haris had said, their lives were good. Work during the week occupied her. And though she hadn't chosen that job, she did enjoy it, and the rest of her time was filled with her daughter, her husband, evenings with friends, and Sunday lunches with her parents.

She paused with her hands clutching the pram's handlebar as a government announcement blared over the neighborhood's emergency loudspeakers. It was the same announcement she'd vaguely heard from inside their apartment several times already.

". . . Bornholmer Strasse, Brunnenstrasse, Chausseestrasse . . . The border between East and West Berlin has been closed."

Closed? She looked around, expecting others to react with equal incredulity. *A city can't be closed. There are no barriers to close.*

No one reacted with surprise. They simply hurried on.

Monica smiled at her daughter and continued toward the border crossing. It was ludicrous. A mistake. She turned the corner onto Brunnenstrasse and jolted the pram to such an abrupt stop Luisa lurched back.

With wide eyes the three-year-old pulled herself upright. "Mama?"

"Shhh . . ." Unable to pull her focus from the sight in front of her, Monica reached down and handed Luisa her sewn doll that had fallen forgotten into her lap.

Straight ahead and across Brunnenstrasse at the Bernauer Strasse corner, Monica counted a dozen guards dressed in the green uniform of the German police, the Volkspolizei, and a couple more dressed in the MfS grey. Whatever this was, it required both the VoPo and the Stasi. Each of the VoPo carried a machine gun slung over his shoulder. The sight was so shocking, it took her a moment to shift her gaze from the men to the mass behind them.

Barbed wire coiled in large loops across the street.

Monica felt, rather than saw, a man stop beside her. She glanced over. He reminded her of her father with his grey hair and his formal felt hat pushed low onto his brow. His eyes narrowed as if he was thinking or simply trying to see more clearly.

"What's happened here?" she whispered.

"They did it. They finally built their prison." The man scrubbed his hands across his eyes. It looked as if he hoped the action would wipe away the reality in front of them. His eyes widened in alarm when it didn't, and without another word, he turned around and shuffled away.

Monica stepped forward. Her parents had moved only a couple months before and only a few blocks into West Berlin. Surely she could pass through for a luncheon.

A full ten meters from Bernauer Strasse, a guard waved and yelled to her, "Get away. Go back."

"I'm having lunch with my parents. They live just down to the left." She blinked and corrected herself. "Across that, then to the left."

The young soldier turned to follow her pointed finger, as if he, too, might see her parents' new building on the other side of the tangled wire. Her eyes dropped with her finger, and she noted cans scattered across the pavement. Tear gas cans. She remembered them from the 1953 riot at Potsdamer Platz.

She hadn't been there that day when the Soviet tanks rolled in, but she'd seen cans still scattered across the plaza a week later when she accompanied Haris to gather details for a huge newspaper assignment, his last in a series of articles covering the now-infamous June 17 protest.

What had horrified her that day fascinated Haris. They'd just started dating, and his attitude was one thing that drew her to him.

Soviet aggression terrified her but not Haris. She'd tried to learn from his confident and cavalier demeanor but never had.

Even now, seeing Soviet guards a block away, long-dormant memories of her family reaching Berlin in 1945 crept near the surface. Memories of the June Potsdamer Platz riot too. Her father had been injured that day. Merely crossing the plaza to reach home, he'd almost lost his leg in the crush as Soviet tanks bore down on the protesters.

Haris held no such fears. The Potsdamer Platz riots had been his big break at *Neues Deutschland*, and he saw the Soviets, the protests, and his opportunities in a different light. *"Sometimes a forceful message must be sent."*

Haris and her father barely spoke following those published articles and the awards and promotions Haris received because of them.

Monica took a sharp breath to draw herself from her reverie to the situation at hand. She faced the guard. "They'll worry if we're late."

"The border is closed. No one crosses." Another soldier joined him. This one was older, and while approaching, he looped his arm around his Kalashnikov and gently rested his hand near the trigger.

Monica stepped back. He stepped forward.

She spun Luisa away and raced home. The pram bounced over the uneven pavement, some of it not fully replaced and smoothed since the war. The jagged terrain made Luisa laugh. Monica, however, did not laugh. As she took in the people around her, she began to see what was happening. They were trying to breach the wire and escape or, barring that, they were trudging home in defeat.

She stopped at the S-Bahn station and reached out to a woman trudging down the steps from the platform. "Is the train crossing over?"

The woman's eyes were wide and red. Her lips trembled as she answered. "It is closed. The sign says the last station is Rosenthaler Platz. If you look, they cut the wires." The woman waved her hand up and behind her.

Monica could see the severed wires above the tracks hanging loose.

"They pushed us back with clubs."

Without waiting for more, Monica continued home, yanked Luisa from the pram, and, leaving it on the street, dashed up the three flights to their apartment and their telephone. The dial tone was normal. She dialed Haris's office at the newspaper. No one picked up. She dialed her parents. The line went dead. She dialed again. And again, the line went dead.

Monica gathered Luisa, handed her a cookie, descended the stairs, and dropped her into the pram once more. This time she headed north toward Strelitzer Strasse, a quieter street that also crossed Bernauer Strasse into West Berlin. At the corner she again found a mass of barbed wire, but with only two guards protecting it.

Across the street, her parents, Gertrude and Walther, and her younger sister, Alice, frantically waved to her.

She ran forward and the guards turned her direction. "Get—"

Monica cut the young guard off with a smile. "Please. I'm just talking. I'm only—"

He turned away before she finished. At first she thought he didn't want to engage with her. Then she noticed a commotion a block away on Brunnenstrasse. It looked as if a child, a young boy about five years old in blue shorts, stood alone near the guards in the center of the street. Shifting her gaze in the direction of each guard's focus, Monica saw what she surmised were his parents calling to him—from across the wire.

The boy ran to the barricade, only to be thrown back by the guard. The parents started wailing across the street, the mother keening in her husband's arms. As if deaf, the VoPo did not turn toward the mother. They kept their attention fixed to the east, on the boy and on the gathering crowd. Twice more the child tried to run. Twice more he was captured within the guard's grasp and slung back.

With no one watching them, Monica's parents, along with Alice, joined her at the barricade. Monica almost reached out to her father, needing his reassurance that all would be well. If her father said something was true, Monica believed him.

"What's going on?" She spoke to him alone.

"West Berlin is surrounded. In one night. We are on an island now, fully separated from the DDR and from you. They're calling this an 'anti-Fascist protection barrier,' and claim it's necessary to keep unsavory Western influences away from their pure ideology. They want to keep you and all DDR citizens in as much as they want to keep us out."

His words struck Monica as familiar, almost identical to Haris's description hours earlier.

"The agreement was to divide the city but to always allow its citizens to move freely between the sectors," her father continued. "But it was never written, never codified. Only assumed. And now too many people are using East Berlin as their escape hatch into the West."

His voice sounded weary and defeated but not surprised. Monica felt that same childhood assurance she had growing up. Her father would know what to do.

"What should I do? What's going to happen?" she asked, fully expecting him to smile and ease her fears. *"Wait a few days,"* he might say. *"All will be well."*

Instead Father shook his head. "I don't know. I doubt America or Great Britain will risk going to war over this, over us. During the blockade they dropped food, but they never pushed the Soviets to let up. Instead the Soviets gave up. That's very different. No . . . They won't fight for us."

"But will it come down?" Monica pressed for reassurance. "People work across the border. Families are divided. They can't leave us like this."

Father didn't give it to her. Mother looked away. Alice bit her lip, tears running down her face.

"What?" Monica reached out again. The barbed wire snagged her wrist. She snatched her arm back as blood flowed in a thin line to her elbow. Her mother pressed her palm firmly against her mouth, eyes full of tears and fear.

Father shook his head again. "A few minutes before you arrived, a VoPo called out that this is permanent. He said their plan is to fortify it within the coming days. To make it not a wire border but a physical wall. It's not coming down within days, Monica. Perhaps not even within months."

He stepped forward. The barbed wire reached no higher than his midsection. His voice dropped to a whisper. "Remember who your husband is and who he works for, Monica. He serves the State. He loves you, but you must be careful. This barricade changes everything. They will need to sell this to the people of East Berlin or there will be protests within the Soviet Sector far worse than Potsdamer Platz in 1953. The Party will need its mouthpiece."

While her father had never stated it so plainly, Monica knew it was true. *Neues Deutschland* was East Berlin's top and best-funded paper because it was the Party's paper. And Haris was its star reporter.

Monica glanced toward Brunnenstrasse again. One of the guards picked up the crying boy and carried him away, while another threw a tear gas canister into the growing crowd. People scurried and smoke blurred the scene.

It carried an acrid scent on the morning's soft breeze, and it was so thick she could barely see the happenings only a block away.

They could barely see her.

Without another thought, Monica wrenched Luisa from her pram, and after hugging her fast and tight for the briefest moment—so fast her daughter didn't cry out or react—she lifted Luisa high and thrust her over the barbed wire. Luisa's leg caught and her cry pierced the air. Red filled Monica's vision.

It took only an instant, yet it felt like a lifetime. Images stacked upon each other. The scream. The crimson flash from Luisa's small thigh blooming across her nappy, her dress, and down into her white sock. Father's eyes, wide and scared, then determined as he stumbled forward to seize his granddaughter, catching her under one arm just as her small legs neared the pavement.

In a single motion he scooped Luisa up, pressed her tight against his chest, and turned his back to the VoPo, who now moved their direction.

Monica realized her father was bracing himself and trying to protect his granddaughter from bullets. She understood he fully expected to be shot for what she had done. She pressed her hands between two jags of twisted wire and pushed the top loop down just far enough to stretch her leg over. She knew she'd be cut, but she didn't care. One jump and she'd be with her daughter. Safe.

"Stop or I will shoot." The soldier's call filled the air and saturated every cell within her. Monica fell back paralyzed. He had not called out in German. He had called in Russian.

The breeze that had felt warm moments ago now felt cool against her skin. She looked at her arm. The line of blood had mixed with a sheen of sweat and her whole arm was stained pink. She thrust it behind her back so as not to draw a connection between her arm and her daughter's leg, which was sending an ever-widening pool of blood across her father's white shirt and trousers.

But the guards didn't notice because they didn't look to the west. They didn't spare Father a glance. They kept their focus solely on her. She backed away. "We are only talking. Please. Please." She kept backing away despite willing her feet to stand rather than retreat. In her periphery she saw her father run off down the street. Her mother and sister stood silent and frozen across the wire.

"Get back now. I won't say it again."

Monica stepped back, again and again. Her eyes remained fixed upon her mother and sister. No one spoke aloud, but Monica felt the waves of terror and panic wash between them. She stumbled and realized she had backed up and tripped over the street's curb. Her father and her daughter were gone. Her mother and sister still stood silent and in shock by the barricade. The VoPo didn't speak to them or even acknowledge their presence. Their eyes remained fixed on Monica.

She pressed her palm to her mouth to stop the sobs churning up from her gut. She turned and stumbled up the curb, heedless of her bleeding arm, and ran back to her apartment without another look behind. She saw nothing. She heard nothing. She felt nothing. She had left the pram abandoned by the barbed wire.

It was dusk by the time Haris returned home. Afternoon clouds had turned the evening light to a leaded brown with touches of a sad, almost mournful pink rather than the bright oranges of the previous week. The browns, greys, and dusty pinks made the apartment feel even more forlorn, quiet, and empty.

Monica could tell Haris felt it as soon as he shut the door behind him. Rather than look to her, sitting near the door at their kitchen table, he glanced around the kitchen, down the hall, and even out the windows, as if in search of the source of the disquiet.

No lights were on. No happy noises of play or dinner. His searching finally ended and he settled his gaze upon his wife. "I thought you might be out. The pram isn't in the lobby. Why are you sitting in the dark?"

He flipped the switch. The white ceramic fixture bathed their small kitchen in a yellow light. It felt aggressive, glaring. Monica closed her eyes and wished for the darkness.

"Where's Luisa?"

Monica didn't open her eyes. She didn't speak. She couldn't speak.

She felt Haris drop into the chair across from her. "Your arm. What happened—? Monica, look at me. What happened? Where is Luisa?"

She opened her eyes and stared at him.

Haris blinked in recognition of some unspoken horror. "Monica?" He pulled back, his hands reaching across his chest and gripping his shoulders so tight he seemed to fold in on himself. His thumbnails turned red, then blanched with the pressure.

She wanted to feel sorry for him. She wanted to say she was sorry. She wanted to—

She did nothing. She said nothing. She felt nothing.

"Monica?" His voice cracked in the middle of her name. "Speak to me. Tell me . . . What have you done?"

CHAPTER 1

Luisa Voekler

ARLINGTON, VIRGINIA

Friday, November 3, 1989

While seemingly complex, codes, ciphers, cryptograms, or whatever you choose to call them, are deceptively simple. Once you crack them.

In reality, only a few in the history of code breaking—at least that I'm aware of—were truly ingenious. The Enigma cipher? Undeniably impressive. It had billions of permutations. Thank goodness there was a brain like Alan Turing's around. The Great Cipher, or Grand Chiffre, was also brilliant. But it was too unwieldy to be truly utilized. It employed fourteen hundred numbers that meant all sorts of different things—words, phrases, or even references to other codes. But if one can't use it, how brilliant is it? I mean, who is going to lug a huge book around to translate a Grand Chiffre code? No one on a field of battle, that's for certain.

So for ease of transmission and translation, most ciphers are based upon some form of shift, substitution, or transposition. Furthermore, a coder rarely varies his or her approach. I suppose that's a bit of hubris on their part, or they simply do what they know best. But it does mean that once you crack a coder's go-to method, you've got them. Their codes unfold easily and then you get a nod from your boss and a round of celebratory drinks with your coworkers at a Friday happy hour.

At least that's how it works for those of us on Venona II.

No one outside this office knows about Venona II. Heck, the first Venona Project, which ended nine years ago, is still classified and will remain so for the foreseeable future. We were only briefed on it because we are picking up where those brilliant women left off. After thirty-seven years of deciphering Soviet codes from World War II into the early Cold War, the Venona Project shut down and its record became the stuff of lore. It's truly impressive—they discovered Kim Philby, Klaus Fuchs, Soviet infiltration of the Manhattan Project, Julius and Ethel Rosenberg, and so much more.

We only hope we can do so well.

Four of us analysts are on Venona II, and everyone—excluding me—works on Cold War codes. I'm still stuck on World War II. Not that it's a status thing to move on to the next "war." It just feels to me like World War II has been covered. If those smart Venona Project women didn't uncover it already, can it really be that valuable? Or relevant any longer? Yet it undeniably is, so I spend my days on Third Reich ciphers spanning from 1939 to 1945. And I shouldn't complain. Just this summer I unlocked the names of two previously unknown Nazi guards from Auschwitz, and both are now poised to stand trial for "accessory to murder" for 200,000 and 180,000 deaths respectively.

It's those victories, along with some impressive finds during the early Cold War era, that keep CIA Deputy Director of Analysis Andrew Cademan funding Venona II as a small line item on a hidden budget sheet in an off-site office. We have to be off-budget and off-site because, just like the original Venona Project, we sometimes uncover a few of our own turned traitor. That's a dark day around here and, unfortunately, there have been a few of them.

"*We matter*," Andrew says at almost every weekly meeting. "*Our wins and the accountability we provide matters.*"

That said, working here is not where I expected to be, and sitting at a desk basically solving puzzles is not what I expected to be doing. Not by a long shot. After college, when I took the Foreign Service Officer Test and applied to the CIA, I aimed to be an agent, an operative under nonofficial cover if I proved so worthy. It was a leap, but it was the dream too. Granted, my desires probably outstretched my skills, especially after consuming a steady diet of John le Carré books, old episodes of *The Avengers*, and James Bond movies throughout my teenage years. But I was so sure I could cut it, that I wanted that life, and that I could keep all those secrets safe while doing good in the world, that I experienced a bit of tunnel vision.

I got in. I got close. Then one day, I got cut. I made it all the way to covert training at the Farm, and I didn't lose my asset, I didn't shoot a civilian in a fictional village or in simulated attack, and I didn't do anything wrong that I could discern. I simply got called into the field operator's office and was reassigned to Andrew Cademan's division, at first in budgeting no less, with no explanation given. No one gives or gets those in the CIA.

That was the hardest part. Not knowing what I'd done wrong.

That's not true. The hardest part was the pitying looks, comments, and hugs my peers gave me as I packed my duffel. Every person in my class wanted to know what happened, and when I couldn't tell them, they acted like I'd caught a contagious virus. They offered their tepid condolences while backpedaling lest they catch it too.

Only Daniel Rudd gave a crap. Only Daniel pursued me to talk, digest, even rage if I wanted to. But I didn't want to be pursued. I wanted to hide away, lick my wounds, and forget I ever tried to reach so high. After a month, he gave up and simply vanished.

I worked five years in budget analysis for another of Andrew's groups until he started Venona II a little over two years ago. While I don't miss calculating and reconciling costs, I am a little tired of sitting at a desk and culling through the past with a fine-tooth comb and a microscope.

I—

I need to stop complaining . . .

It's been a long week.

I rub my eyes so hard, gold flashes in the red behind my lids. It's just after noon, but I've been poring over a batch of communiqués from 1945 between a commander in the Soviet Red Army and some low level in the Third Reich based out of Berlin since 7:00 a.m. The Nazi spy's code name was HEMPKE, and he had something to prove. The man conveyed everything in hopes of pleasing the Soviets, but it's nothing new. And it's horrific how he minutely detailed every atrocity the Nazis were committing as they knew their end was drawing near.

Berlin bombed. Berlin in flames. Hitler working to destroy his own people before they were captured. Hitler hanging people in the streets. The Red Army advancing. The pillaging. Rapes. Wreckage. Senseless cruelty and savage destruction. HEMPKE gave details but no names—nothing the Soviets probably wanted or needed—yet I've been deciphering HEMPKE's sycophancy for almost six months.

I'm worn out. Worn out from slogging through the worst humanity offers. I'm also sad. Sad for the world that it ever happened. And sad for my family who was there.

My grandmother, my *Oma*, never talks about the war or the years right after it. It's as if she would like me to believe nothing existed before I came to live with my grandparents when I was three. Then the world became all cheek pinches and wholesome cooking. And while he was alive, *Opa* wasn't much better. If fear or worry over the past ever flitted through their expressions, they made sure to wipe them clear before looking my direction. But after spending these months with HEMPKE, I finally understand my grandparents and those fleeting glances, clenched fists, and occasional trembling lips. I'm also beginning to understand my ever-missing, often-icy aunt Alice a little better too.

I knew, for instance, that Oma worked as a rubble woman—one of the thousands forced to haul away the rubble from city streets and plazas—upon her arrival in Berlin in 1945. She and Opa, with their daughters, came to the city expecting to find sanctuary but found devastation. Stalin arrived in Berlin, well before the rest of the Allies, and wanted his Soviet dream built immediately. So while he was stealing away machinery and shipping it to Moscow, he was also clearing the rubble to build opera houses, movie theaters, cabarets, and more. And the work to effect this seemingly instant transformation—much done before the Western Allies landed just four months later—was truly backbreaking and brutal. Hundreds of women died from strain, malnutrition, or abuse.

The goal of all that, my Opa once commented, was to control the people through the culture. You own the culture and you own everything about the country.

That's the kind of stuff HEMPKE describes. He conveys secrets about a regime that tried to mandate every aspect of life and culture and was willing to annihilate it all when it lost to a new regime starting to establish an equally pervasive and brutal control.

That's what has made this week so hard. Usually I don't get involved. I don't care what the messages contain so much as I care about the methodology to crack them. That's my job. Crack the codes and pass the intelligence along for the decision-makers to decide what to do with it. But HEMPKE has snuck into my subconscious and into my dreams, and now, just picking up a new sheet of his coded messages to work on makes my heart race as dread creeps like a tiny spider up my spine.

I rub my eyes again.

A tap on my office door brings my hands down and my head up.

Carrie tilts a half step from stumbling across the threshold. Always in motion, that one, and being eight months pregnant has not helped her balance. Being eight months pregnant hasn't helped her fashion sense either. Today she wears a huge royal-blue dress covered with multicolored polka dots. I almost make a clown joke. Almost. It would backfire anyway. Outside pregnancy, Carrie has a far greater fashion sense than I do. I'm a quiet Ann Taylor type to her more Princess Diana / Sloane Ranger style.

"I'm not talking to you."

"Why?" I laugh because Carrie is clearly talking to me.

"You didn't say I'd cry. I made Teddy take me to the movies last night, and I ended up crying past midnight."

I'd recommended that new movie *Dead Poets Society* to her. But not for a Thursday night and not to attend with her husband. "I told you to see it during the day. I specifically said that. I even said we could go tomorrow or Sunday."

Carrie lowers herself into my one spare chair. "I wanted to get out. We never go anywhere anymore, and Teddy has to work this weekend."

"I'm sorry you ended up crying. What did Teddy say about the movie?"

"He said you're on movie probation and that if Kenneth went with you to see it, he's lost all respect for him." Carrie blinked. "I didn't mean to say that."

I lift my hands in surrender. As Carrie knows, but perhaps her husband does not, my ex-boyfriend Kenneth has been gone for over a year, and there hasn't been anyone serious since. My last prospect, if I could call two dates a "prospect," telephoned before our third date to say it "wouldn't work." For some reason, no one seems to enjoy my Oma grilling them when they call or inviting them in for food when they pick me up for a date. The fact that Oma answered the phone that night and relayed his "wouldn't work" message rather than letting him deliver it himself kind of made his point.

There's only one guy I've ever met who could possibly endure my present living situation, but as I said, I vanished on him, so when he vanished on me a month later, I felt vindicated rather than devastated.

I shake my head to push away Daniel and every other man, and smile my appreciation for Carrie's discretion. It's actually nice her husband, Teddy, doesn't know how pathetic my love life is.

I'm well aware of it.

"Don't do that." Carrie wiggles an unpainted fingernail at me like she's drawing a circle around my face. She gave up perms, highlights, and nail polish, too, when she became pregnant.

"You'll meet someone. Just like in the movies." She adds that last part with saccharine-sweet sincerity. She feels I rely too much on rom-coms for my romance lately and am not "putting myself out there" enough. Again, I'm well aware.

I direct us back to the movie. "Did you at least like it, despite the tears?"

"I didn't expect it to be so sad. It's set in the fifties. Everything was nice in the fifties."

"Really?" My voice arcs at her strange and misinformed logic. "I can't help you if that's how you view history."

"But I do need your help." Her voice loses all teasing tones.

I straighten. "What's up?"

Carrie swings her hand behind her and pushes my office door closed. She then pulls a single sheet from the manila folder she'd been resting on her lap. Without her saying a word I know this is a cipher or a code she's struggling with because we don't ask each other for help. Except for sometimes when we do. I study the page while she talks.

"It's a new batch. I'm calling them the Berlin Letters."

We often name batches of correspondence. Each coder, and therefore each missive, message, note, or letter, has a personality. So they each deserve a name. HEMPKE is part of my Ground Zero batch because that's basically what the Nazis on the way out and the Soviets on the way in made Berlin: their Ground Zero.

"There are about twenty of these. I just started them last week, but I've got nothing, and I want my desk cleared before I go on maternity leave next week."

"Why does it matter? It's not like they're going anywhere. They're not operational."

"It wasn't the movie last night," Carrie confesses. "I'm obsessing over these and I can't sleep. Please. I want my desk clear, Luisa. I can't explain it. I just need it."

The manic tension in her voice vibrates, and I drop my focus to the page. "Okay then. We'll clear it."

She shifts forward in the chair, leaning her forearms on my desk. "I can't get my mind past what I expect to see."

I smile, but I keep my head down and my gaze on the page. It's a statement we constantly make to each other. In our line of work, you must leave your expectations behind and deal with what's in front of you. How else will you discover what no one wants you to see?

The top of Carrie's photocopy marks it as a message out of the German Democratic Republic, the GDR—or the DDR as an East German would call it—on September 14, 1945.

I glance at her. "You're working World War II?"

"No. That's first contact. The Berlin Letters run from September '45 to July '61." She looks to my desk. "You?"

"Andrew says I'll work World War II for the foreseeable future. I'm still on Ground Zero."

"That poor spy probably thought he was changing the world."

"Saving his neck by offering an excess of nothing, more like." I let my eyes go fuzzy and my mind drift to semiblank. It's how I approach any coded message for the first time. I absorb what is on the page without reading or thinking about the words. When explaining my method to Carrie for the first time, I described it like peering at one of those dotted pictures in which you can only see the airplane or the cow when you widen your eyes. Then out of a field of random red and green dots, you spot a cow eating grass.

Nothing comes to me. No letters stand taller or wider than others. I discern no pattern to the arrangement of spaces and lines. I don't note any errant marks. I start counting out the letters to find an inconsistency with sentence length or structure. Nothing.

The words also form coherent sentences. They're boring but sensible. That means it's not a shift, pigpen, substitution, or modulo shift. And it's a cipher, not a code. I shake my head. "Ottendorf? Using letters rather than numbers. It's been done."

"I wondered. But it was sent to us, which would mean an East German and a CIA officer would need to own the same edition of the same book in the same language. Not impossible but unlikely, cumbersome, and risky. And . . ." Carrie taps a finger on the first sentence. "It doesn't read like a book cipher using letters."

"I vote for an acrostic." I slide the paper back to her.

"Duh." She pushes it back to me. "But you tell me what. I've tried the first letter of each sentence, third, fourth—"

I cut her off. "We'll get it. Are you sure there's anything here? We've had innocent correspondence misfiled before." I read the letter aloud in its entirety, paying close attention to the words in both the German on the page and their English translations as I move through it.

"I envy you that. I'm so slow."

I don't reply and Carrie doesn't expect me to. She knows full well that German was my first language and that's the only reason I'm better at it than she is. She also knows I love translating it—it's a part of me I always hid growing up as Oma constantly chastised me for speaking German outside our house. "*You don't know who will hold it against you.*"

While she was and remains absolutely paranoid on many levels, Oma wasn't entirely wrong about that one. In a society terribly afraid of the Soviets and the nuclear terror they could rain down on us, people often mistake German for Russian. Americans, on the whole, aren't multilingual and can be a little culturally myopic. So we pretty much only spoke German at home. Regardless, my fluency is still not enviable, especially as Carrie speaks and translates five languages with ease.

She's right. The sentences are stilted. Odd even. And terribly mundane. But they make sense, both individually and collectively. Like her, I quickly tag the first letter of each sentence, the last, and a few in between. I'm stumped.

"Maybe let me see the original?" Although we work with

photocopies we can mark up, the originals often hold details that carry significance.

Carrie huffs and hauls herself upright, waving her hand as she exits my office. "I knew I forgot something."

She returns and drops the letter on my desk while I pull my hair back in a scrunchie then grab my magnifying glass. My eyes are fine, but one wouldn't believe how small some of the signifiers can be in a coded message. One time, it took 10x magnification for me to see a single blue dot in a Nazi communiqué that unlocked months of ciphers.

I twist my chair to lay the paper on my light box, which sits on the credenza beside my desk. I start at the top and scan every paper fiber through the magnifying glass. Nothing.

Then I notice a single tiny dot mark above an *S* in the second sentence. A dot that in the photocopy looked like dust from the machine.

"Here." I wave a hand to Carrie. "Come see."

She leans over me and I point to it with the tip of my pencil, careful not to mark the page.

"Find out if that's got any significance. I bet that's it. And here." I point to another above a space in the second paragraph's first sentence. "He's using the spaces too and switching between paragraphs?" I lean back. "Crafty bugger."

It was true. Within three paragraphs Carrie's Berlin Letters coder had switched from an acrostic to a telestich to a mesostich cipher. Which, while sounding cool, simply means he used the first letter of the sentence to build his acrostic, or code, then in the next paragraph used a letter in the middle of the word, then in his third paragraph he built his codes from the last letter in the word. He was dexterous, and Carrie might not get all twenty letters cleared by her maternity leave.

Carrie sighs. "I swear I looked at all this." She reaches around me to slide the page off the light box.

"Wait." I grab her wrist as my eyes travel to the page's bottom-right corner. "What's this?" I point to a mark. I compare the photocopy to the original. Carrie had cut off the bottom of the page when copying it.

"The infinity sign? It's just that, I think. It's on all the Berlin Letters. Once I translate these, I'll know if it has any significance, but I doubt it. It feels like a signature rather than part of the message to me." She rolls her eyes. "I know. I'm not to make assumptions."

But this time I don't tease her. My mind is elsewhere. "It's a signature. He's saying he could be anyone. Anyone doing the right thing. An everyman."

Carrie pulls back. "What?"

I blink. I feel caught and shrug in a way-overdone dramatic manner to deflect her attention. I'm suddenly fifteen again, and though way too old to be reprimanded by Oma for sneaking a cookie before dinner, I'm about to be reprimanded. "At least that's how I'd sign them." I wave my hand as if my musings can't matter. "Were they mailed? Do you have the envelopes?"

"These weren't mailed. This is the closest one to a full letter. Maybe it was passed within a book. Most of them are scraps, probably stuffed into lighters, pens—you know the stuff they used back then. I assume the messages were passed from the Soviet Sector to the American before the Wall went up. The last one is dated the month before, July 10, 1961."

Carrie sweeps out of my office with a thanks, and I sit weightless, floating. I know that symbol. I've seen it once before and I've never forgotten it. It was that small and just as discreet. Drawn on the corner of an envelope.

One of my grandfather's envelopes.

CHAPTER 2

WASHINGTON, DC

Friday, November 3, 1989

"You are my girl of infinite possibilities."

I was eight years old when I handed my grandfather the envelope and pointed to the small sign in the corner. "Opa, look, it's a tipped-over eight."

Rather than answer, he asked, "Did Oma see this letter?"

I shook my head.

"Probably best." Opa winked. "This can be our secret." He tapped the envelope's corner. "It's not an eight, *Mäuschen*; it's the symbol for infinity. Infinity doesn't mean endless or simply eternal. It means there is nothing lacking. It is all-encompassing. Complete. Self-determining. We are that when we do the right thing. Everyone can be that, and this man is becoming that. You, dear one, you are my girl of infinite possibilities. You will be that too."

He kissed the top of my head as if certain I had understood every word he'd said, rather than simply, "*You are my girl of infinite possibilities.*" He then left me alone in the kitchen and closed the door to his study. I never saw the envelope again nor another like it.

Although I haven't thought about that conversation in years, it comes back to me with the vivid clarity of making this morning's coffee. It struck me then as it strikes me now. Opa was telling me something. Something far beyond my abilities to understand, but something so fundamental and important it needed to be said nonetheless. *Complete. Self-determining. Nothing lacking. Everyone.* I understand those words better now. I've failed to live up to them, but I understand them.

And here is the symbol again all these years later. It doesn't feel like a coincidence. It feels like a secret. A truth hovering out of reach that somehow has eluded me but has always been present. Carrie's cipher, that symbol, that scene days after my eighth birthday—something has happened, was happening, is happening . . .

Oma. Opa didn't want my grandmother to know. That means she still may not know. Or might she?

I cancel Friday drinks with work friends and steer my car toward home. How will I get answers with Opa gone? The drive from Arlington into DC's Cleveland Park usually takes twenty-six minutes. I'm undone at minute thirty-nine. Opa, my solid rock, feels like shifting sand. Unable to draw a full breath, I crank my window down for more air. I roll it shut again against the chilly November evening as goose bumps prickle my skin.

I turn the dial and scroll through radio stations, trying to distract myself with snatches of songs and white noise. I finally land on Cher's "If I Could Turn Back Time." I would if I could—to almost a year ago before Opa died. I miss him—I miss what I thought he was and what I believed our relationship to be.

I drive too fast down our block of Quebec Street Northwest and, pulling myself from my fog, catch a surprised and stern look from Mrs. Peterman. It's warranted and I wave an apology as I tap the brakes. Several new families on our street have young children. I grew up here, in this house, and what once seemed old, staid, and boring is quickly changing. A neighborhood with older

German families, grandchildren stopping by only on the weekends, looks more youthful and refined these days with planted annuals along front walks, swings hanging on freshly painted porches, and young kids running across the streets. I love seeing the kids. They make our little corner of DC a more hope-filled and brighter place.

I pull into the driveway, pass the house, and park in front of our detached garage. Striding across our small backyard, I note Oma has worked in her "garden" again today. If one can call the mess of dirt within her five raised beds a garden any longer. Since Opa's death, nothing has grown there.

I pause. Something about Oma's bleak garden convicts me. My heart contracts with the realization that I've doubted Opa on the basis of Carrie's Berlin Letters mixed with a memory. A memory of a mere moment twenty-three years ago that may be nothing more than my imagination. I let it consume me and I've trusted that, more than the grandfather who loved and raised me. More than the grandfather who, in his last months of life, helped his wife plant a garden just to see her smile as the flowers bloomed.

I've emotionally betrayed the caring man who loved me best all my life and the man to whom I would never deny anything. When Opa asked me to return home to care for Oma after he died, I said yes. I didn't pause. I didn't think. I simply said yes. After all, they gave up everything—including their homeland—to raise me well and in safety after my parents died. I owe it to Oma to be here, and Opa had a right to depend on me. It's my privilege to contribute to the bills, the upkeep, anything and everything Oma needs. That's what our family is and what we do, and yet here I am looking at him, at her, and even at this dead garden with suspicion.

I stall and take in the shriveled plants. I lift a wilted leaf from the tangle of other wilted leaves. *I know how you feel, little guy.* When moving back in with Oma, I didn't think it would feel so hard some days or that it would end my social life, my sense of independence, and my love life—all of which, quite honestly, have become as colorful and vibrant as this garden. And those feelings, all negative, almost condemning, made this afternoon's downward spiral all the more slippery.

I drop the tiny leaf and it falls among the tangle once more. I look to the house. It's later than I expected to arrive home, and the light has already changed. Yet no outside lights are on, nor any inside either.

I close my eyes to calm my breathing, my heart, my anger, and my fear. It doesn't work, so I do the next best thing: I open them once more and step forward.

There are questions to ask.

I climb the three wooden steps and a squeak reminds me I need to tighten all the boards here and on the stairs outside the side door tomorrow. Since I moved back in, it's what I do on Saturdays. All the little things Opa did in a few spare minutes after work now take study, concentration, and whole weekends for me to accomplish. Even then, the results are often substandard.

I swing open the unlocked screen door and find my grandmother in the kitchen. She has a mug of tea pressed between her hands and sits staring out the side window.

"It's too dark in here, Oma." I flip the switch. "And can we shut the door? It's growing cold with the sun gone."

"Is it?" She rouses herself and clucks her tongue at me. "Don't give me that sad look. I was simply resting. There's nothing wrong with slowing down and taking account of your day." Her English still carries a thick German accent.

"I see you were in your garden today."

"You call it a garden?" She scoffs. "I churned it all up again. I planted a fall crop in August, just like the book said, and nothing sprouted. I'm trying again with oats and peas next week. It will supposedly keep the soil healthy over the winter and nourish the spring seeds."

"That's a great idea." I infuse my voice with an enthusiasm I don't feel. The summer before Opa died, Oma's garden brought them both incredible joy. But since he died last winter, nothing has bloomed except Oma's frustration and despair. And I don't see that changing. I don't see us changing.

Oma smooths her apron down her skirt and I'm cast into her past. Not one I experienced, but one I sense still lingers about her. She dresses much the same as I expect she did when making my mother and my aunt dinner all those years ago in Germany. The same dark colors, and always an overlaid apron. She steps to the refrigerator. "Dinner will be ready soon and your aunt—"

Before she can say another word, creaks sound on the stairs above us and my aunt Alice calls down, "It's clear. It just took one round of Liquid-Plumr and a pot of boiling water."

I look to Oma.

"My bathtub was draining slowly."

"Why didn't you tell me? I would—"

"It's okay, Luisa." Aunt Alice pauses in the doorway with Oma's large soup pot in her hands. It's in that moment I sense the odd humidity of the room. The warm wet clashing with the cool air from outside. "You shouldn't have to take care of everything."

I give her a tiny nod, unsure of how to reply. Alice is only thirteen years older than I am, but we've never been close. I don't sense animosity from her, but no love either. Simply indifference.

"Are you staying for dinner?" I hear the thread of hope in my voice and swallow hard to bury it. One would think it would have died after years of being rebuffed. I'm embarrassed it hasn't.

"Of course she is." Oma clucks her tongue again. "It's been too long, and here I am gathering wool."

Alice smiles at me, small and knowing. We both know Oma is about to launch into motion. Alice steps forward to offer help, but before she can say a word, Oma flaps a hand at her and tells her to sit at the table, then another hand flails in my direction, and she tells me to wash up.

Alice drops into a chair, and I head to the downstairs powder room to wash my hands. I gave up offering to help Oma cook soon after I moved back home last January and began to simply thank her in March. I actually started to appreciate the time it gave us together in May and the opportunity it gives us to see Alice. She comes by more since Opa died. I think she, too, worries about Oma. Not that she's ever said anything to me about it.

When I return to the kitchen, Oma is a tornado of activity. I look between her and Alice, sitting at the table, unsure about where I'll be more welcome. When Oma notices me, she shoos me away. I drop into my usual seat at the table and sit silently across from my aunt.

"How's work?" I ask her after our silence stretches to awkward.

"It's good. I have a good class this year."

Alice is a first grade teacher.

I shift around for another innocuous topic and, finding none, land on the one thing that has filled my mind since lunch. "I was thinking about Opa today."

Oma throws me a glance before returning to sauté her onions while simultaneously stirring her beans. "You were? So was I. Alice too. That's why she came." Affection and loss fill her voice, the loss still carrying a hint of rawness.

I look to my aunt.

"The power went out at school today. I couldn't help it." She smiles.

Opa was a really good electrician.

"I was thinking about all the stories he told me and all those letters he wrote," I add.

Oma turns from the stove. "He loved those. He worked so hard on each of them. I never understood his passion for those silly scavenger hunts. All around the house. Such a mess you two made."

Her soft expression tells me she sees him in her memory, probably humming and penning his treasure hunts.

"Around the neighborhood too." I laugh because those were good times. I want to rest in them.

My Opa was my greatest champion, my best friend, and my true north. If Opa said something was right, it was right. Wrong, and it was wrong forever. He was a masterful storyteller, a font of sound logic and practical wisdom, and the best creator of scavenger hunts and riddles I ever knew. I often suspect I'm so good at my job because of all the childhood games we played. And when he said I was his girl of infinite possibilities, I believed him because I believed in him. His words made me, despite my natural inclination to duck and hide, invincible.

What happened to that girl?

"You kept all his stuff, right? I don't mean his clothes, but his books, letters, things he loved?" I gesture to the converted porch off the kitchen. He called it his study, but it was his sanctuary, where he kept his books, papers, pictures, and sports memorabilia. He was relaxed in that room, and tucked into his favorite armchair, he'd tell me the most wonderful stories. If the tale he spun wasn't about a sports hero, it was a fairy tale. The true German kind, Brothers Grimm stuff, with heroes, swords, dragons, and witches, that ended in true love and peace but got pretty gory along the way.

Oma hasn't entered the room in the past year other than to clean it, and I haven't had the courage to ask if I can use it for myself. So it sits. A silent monument to the man our lives revolved around.

Oma pauses and lifts her head, like a deer smelling fear in the air. She, too, glances to the room. "Why you ask this?"

Her English skips and I know she's a heartbeat away from switching the conversation to a new topic and the language to German. She feels safe within her mother tongue. It's the language of home. "*Was ist los?*"

What's going on?

"Nothing." I stick to English and peek to Alice. Her face is blank. Does she feel that the tension in the room just shifted, or does she not care? Either way, I'm on my own.

"I just wondered." I push up from the table and cross the kitchen for a glass of water. I need something to do. I need to soften my focus. "Remember those letters he used to write me as a kid? Did he write you letters too?" I offer the last question to Alice.

"No. That wasn't a part of Papa he shared with me, not—" She presses her lips shut and simply shakes her head. "No."

"Do you remember your thirteenth birthday?" Oma twists from the stove again and waves her spatula at me. "He spent weeks making up those coded clues. You ran all around the neighborhood before finding your bike in the Petermans' garage. Then we went to see *Willy Wonka and the Chocolate Factory* at the cinema. You sang all the way home."

"How do you remember that?" My mind drifts to chocolate, Oompa-Loompas, their song, and Veruca Salt's *"I want it now, Daddy!"* before I stop short. "That was it. That was when he started coding messages for me, creating ciphers I had to crack rather than riddles I needed to solve."

When I was twelve he wrote,

> You need me for lunch, not for dinner.
> In the box Oma's best is always the winner.

His riddle sent me to Oma's bread box where I found a pack of colored pencils.

But days before my thirteenth birthday, Opa handed me a card with a coded message. That code led to another and another. For two days I raced around the neighborhood until the final message appeared my birthday morning,

> Vlr'ii dl cox lkzb ver cfka jb fk geb Mbqboplkp' dxoxdb

It took me almost the entire day to decipher it: *You'll go far once you find me in the Petermans' garage.*

Now I know it was a Caesar cipher, a simple three-shift backward A-to-Z code, but back then it was the toughest mystery I'd ever encountered.

"He was so proud of you. He was sure he was helping you develop your 'little grey cells.'" Opa was also an avid Agatha Christie fan.

"He wrote you codes?" Alice's voice is small and tight.

"Whenever he wanted to hide a gift or reveal something special, I had to jump a hurdle, solve a code, or tackle a challenge." I glance at Oma, including her in my answer. "I had forgotten because he quit when I went to college."

It's true. The game simply died away with my childhood, as did the memories. I carry my glass of water to the table and sit down. I peer up to find Alice's darker eyes settling on me, but she says nothing.

My mind casts back to Carrie's Berlin Letters. Were my Opa's riddles and codes truly games? The question feels dark, but as much as I want to push it away, I cannot. My grandparents, both so straightforward, trustworthy, steady, and practical, suddenly feel mysterious and complex. Solid ground once again shifts and I lose my bearings. Because I know. I know with a bright certainty that I saw that symbol on an envelope when I was eight. I know it was the exact image—size and structure—of Carrie's infinity symbol this morning. And I know that flash wasn't an illusion but rather a glimpse into something real, and secret.

"Luisa?"

I look up, sensing this isn't the first time Oma has called my name. "Did you say something?"

She is standing next to me holding two plates. A plate has already been set before Alice.

I reach up to take mine from her. "I'm sorry. I was lost in thought."

Oma laughs again. "See? It's not so hard to do, is it?"

"Opa again. I was just thinking about all those messages." I set her plate, then mine onto the table. "Oma?"

She settles in her chair, then focuses on me.

"Was Opa a spy?"

CHAPTER 3

My jaw drops.

I didn't mean to ask that. It was the worst thing I could have done. Because if I dislike secrets, prevarications, and complications, I learned it from Oma. She hates them more. Opa too. Lying and shading the truth in any way was not allowed growing up. Even when Oma asked Opa that proverbial question, "*Do I look all right?*" before they went out for dinner, only honesty was offered in reply. "*You have looked better.*"

My eyes still widen remembering that one.

And while Opa had a sense of humor about my childhood, when I wiggled around absolute truth after I broke something or disobeyed, Oma did not. She was and remains the epitome of a "yes is yes" and a "no is no" person. She is straight lines. She is narrow judgments. And she can tighten her eyes and hold fast to a grudge like no one I know. I expect her to snap at me and am surprised when she doesn't. I shift my gaze to Alice, who sits staring at me like I've grown a second head.

I toggle my attention between the two women. How alike they are and so different as well. Alice is definitely a younger version of her mother with the same square jaw, straight nose, and deep-set dark blue-grey eyes. Her hair also holds early hints of grey at the temples. How many years will it be until it turns fully white like Oma's?

Neither answers me. Alice lays down her fork and drops her hand into her lap. She looks to her mother, as do I. I expect Alice to say something, but she doesn't. I sense she's waiting for Oma to answer me and share what she does or does not know. But, like Oma, she doesn't laugh, scoff, or deny it. She simply sits.

I watch Oma process my question and realize how little I understand her. I have lived with my grandmother for twenty-eight years, minus college and the few in my apartment after graduation, and she remains a conundrum wrapped in a mystery. Her sense of duty is unquestionable, but her soul—feelings, thoughts, desires—is beyond me. Even now, watching her and waiting, I can't tell if she's angry, relieved, annoyed, or even wondering herself at my question.

The moment stretches interminably, but I can't break it. Oma does not dismiss or chide me, and a shiver travels to the tips of my fingers.

I glance to Alice. Nothing. I finally I venture out, "Oma?"

"You watch too many movies. I tell you they play with your imagination." Her tone is brusque; her color rises. She points toward the living room, and I have a hunch she's envisioning the new VHS player I gave her for her birthday.

Really I bought it for me and her birthday was my excuse. Oma doesn't watch movies, but I thought she might and we could enjoy them together. But her response, "*Your father loved the cinema*," killed that notion. Bringing up my father is Oma's code for expressing her disapproval, though I've never understood why. Growing up, neither Opa nor Oma talked about my father. In fact, they did anything and everything to avoid mentioning his name. If I begged for a family story, I might be offered one from when my mom, their older daughter, was young. But I never got one about my father and rarely even one about my mother after she met him. If I pressed, I'd simply be told that both died in a car accident when I was about three and that was that—with the implication that my father was to blame. That was, according to both my grandparents, all I needed to know about the man.

"Your Opa fed that silliness," Oma continues, bringing me back to the present. "He told you too many stories. All those riddles too. They put your head in the clouds. They—"

"I'm sorry, Oma," I interrupt. I wave my hand as if wiping the air and the question away, because she'll continue this diatribe all through dinner if I don't derail her. I look to Alice, who sits watching us both. "I'm sorry."

Alice shrugs as if I haven't ruined her dinner, only Oma's and mine. Yet her hands still rest in her lap.

Oma looks between us. "Enough of this. Let's eat."

Without another word we three silently eat a dinner of baked pork chops, carrots, and beans cooked too long. They've lost their bright green color and mush rather than snap when I bite down.

After dinner Oma clears the table and shoos us away again when both Alice and I offer to wash the dishes. I have hurt her feelings. I have doubted Opa. I'm thirty-one years old, and my Oma can make me feel five. I open my mouth to apologize again, but it dies in my throat. I can't say it. I have already apologized twice. It should be enough.

"I need to get going." These are Alice's first and only words since dinner began.

I wave my hand to her. "No, please stay. You two go in the living room and chat and let me finish the dishes."

Without answering me Alice crosses the room and kisses her mother on the cheek. "I'll call you next week."

Oma pauses, hands still gripped on a plate, and leans toward her daughter. "And you will come for Thanksgiving."

"Of course I will." Alice pulls her into a hug, looping her arms around Oma's shoulders. "I'll bring the pies too."

"You make such good pies." Oma smiles and, as Alice straightens, she drops a kiss on her daughter's forehead.

I've ruined the evening—one of the few times my aunt comes to visit. I stand in the center of the kitchen feeling like I'm six again, when Alice moved out and never came back. I expect her to walk right past me like she did back then, but she doesn't. She pauses and grips my forearm. She squeezes gently. "You're okay. Don't give up."

I blink and open my mouth to ask her meaning. I lift my hand to pull her back. But before I do anything, she's down our hallway to the front door and gone without another word or look back.

I face Oma again. She's still scrubbing an already sparkling china plate. I stand in futile silence as she finishes, wipes her hands down her apron, then removes it and hangs it on a hook by the back door.

"I am tired tonight. I will go up to bed." She crosses the room and pauses in front of me. I kiss her cheek just as Alice did moments before. "Don't stay up too late, Mäuschen. Get a good night's sleep."

I close my eyes. *Little Mouse.* I am forgiven.

I lean against the counter and listen to the sounds of her walking down the hallway, turning up the stairs—the third stair from the top creaks loudly—and entering her room. The door shuts softly. I drop into a kitchen chair once more and ponder the glaringly obvious truth before me: Oma never answered my question. The woman who approaches everything straight on skirted around me. That alone is interesting, but what it implies is concerning.

I let my mind drift back to Opa's final days. He was given the cancer diagnosis in spring, and by late summer a year ago, it was clear the treatment wasn't working. By last Thanksgiving, we started preparing ourselves to say goodbye. And by Christmas we were saying it. He called me into his study right before New Year's and asked me to move back home. That was also when he handed me the manila folder in which he'd placed his obituary, his funeral arrangements, and an outline of all his financials.

"Opa?" I was shocked and a little horrified.

"Your Oma is strong in many ways, but those will be too hard for her." He pointed a craggy finger at the file. "Turn to the insurance. There's some that will pay down the mortgage, but it's an old house. There will still be costs, and—"

"I'll take care of it. All of it."

"I know." He sighed with obvious pride. "You handle budgets for the government; you can handle this." He chuckled. "Well . . . keep our budget balanced."

"Opa." I moaned. He was constantly teasing me about the government's inability to land anywhere but in the red and my inability to fix the problem. As working in budgets was still my cover story after moving to Venona II, I took each jab in stride.

"She'll be lonely, Mäuschen." All teasing vanished. "She'll never say it, but your Oma will be very lonely." He paused then and I remember how his color changed. "There is something more I must tell you." He paled further and his skin took on a waxy sheen.

I jumped from my chair and knelt in front of him. He smelled of peppermint oil and pipe tobacco. "Whatever it is, don't worry about it. I'll be here for Oma as long as she needs me. Forever."

I gripped his hands. They were cold and their frailty surprised me. The hands that had fixed my bike, helped me build a birdhouse, taught me to change the oil on my first car, and even how to rewire an outlet were past the ability to do any of those things. Past the ability to squeeze my fingers.

He shook his head and opened his mouth to speak.

But I launched ahead and cut him off. "Come, let's get you to bed." I helped him out of the chair and up to his bedroom. He died a couple days later.

Now I sense I misread that moment. As it comes to mind with almost accusing clarity, I know I did. What would he have said if I hadn't interrupted him? By trying to make myself feel better by making him feel better, had I kept him from sharing a last wish? A last request? Did he shake his head not because he was cold and tired but because I was talking over him and interjecting like I always did? And is it too late to find out? I think of the last question and sit pondering the answer.

Opa was a meticulous man. He moved his family from a small village in the far east of Germany to Berlin in 1945 and morphed from being the only electrician in his village to becoming one of the most sought after in Berlin. I gather he built a highly successful business from always being on time, having the right tools on hand, and executing his work flawlessly and quickly.

And here in DC he was no different. He kept up with six full days of clients a week, kept his papers and billing orderly, shelved his books by author within subject, and aligned his pens at the end of every day at the edge of his desk. And he made up codes, ciphers, and riddles for me to solve; he read me stories and made up other stories for me on a daily basis too. Trailing back through the years, I realize he was far more complex than I'd given him credit for.

I cross the kitchen and enter his study. In almost a year, Oma hasn't changed anything inside. Five black pens sit perfectly straight at the right edge of his desk. As there is no dust on the desk, I figure she lifts the pens weekly and sets them back again just as he would have wished. The beauty of her gesture brings tears to my eyes.

This is it. I turn slowly within the room. This is the place where Opa would hide something important. It's a simple room. There is a desk with drawers on either side, bookshelves line the interior wall that backs against the kitchen, and photographs and windows line the other three. It's a converted outdoor porch with few hiding places.

I pull out each desk drawer, studying its depth and width, and don't find any inconsistencies that would denote a hiding place. I look to the bookshelves and discern they are all the same depth. I tap against their backs and the sound is solid, wood against brick. No hiding places there either. I open a few of the thicker books. They are all real.

It takes me only a half hour to sort through his files and the few boxes resting in the corner. As I said, Opa was meticulous.

I then glance to the floorboards and remember this room opens underneath the house. I return to the kitchen and grab a flashlight from the drawer by the back door. Now I'm crossing a line. What I've done so far can be laid at the doorstep of curiosity. If I take this flashlight outside and open the crawl space beneath the house, I am doubting Opa's integrity, his honesty, his very soul. And that will be hard to explain to Oma if she catches me.

I carefully and quietly open the back door. Oma's room is right above the kitchen. I jump over the back three steps to avoid their telltale creak.

I am committed.

A thorough scan under the house reveals nothing but cinder blocks and wood chips. There is no box, safe, or built-in compartment Opa could access from above. He was handy that way and that's what I would have built.

I pull myself to standing and chuff a quiet laugh. Although it feels forced, it also feels good. Maybe Oma wasn't avoiding my question. Maybe she was speaking the truth about my imagination getting the better of me. It occasionally does. I return to the kitchen, drop the flashlight back into the drawer, and grab my bag from the hallway floor to head upstairs myself.

My imagination makes me pause at the entrance to the living room and flip on the light. This house is as straightforward as my grandparents. Bungalow style, built in the 1920s, it is clean with few built-ins, which means few hiding places. But I scan them all. The living room holds a couch, two chairs, bookshelves with no cupboards beneath, and a large chest. And I know the contents of that chest: Opa's scrapbook, Oma's Christmas linens, cloth place mats for the dining room table, candles, and a stack of broken picture frames Opa and I were supposed to glue back together. That's another thing I could do to help Oma tomorrow.

I flip off the light, round the corner at the front of the house, and peek into our family room. It's the same. A charming, snug room with wood paneling beneath the chair rail, white walls above, and stained, not painted, molding. It's in this cozy front room that the offensive VHS player sits in the cabinet beneath our Zenith television. Maybe that's what I'll do tonight—watch that copy of *Ladyhawke* I picked up at Blockbuster last evening. I have no desire to chase my friends down. I have no desire to laugh, make small talk, and opine with them over my nonexistent love life. After a few drinks, they always land there.

A movie alone may be just what I need . . .

Because something is pulling at me, like a thread that, rather than drawing out an answer, is opening an ever-widening hole.

~

I climb the stairs, skipping the third from the top. I don't want to let Oma know I've got no better plans tonight than staying home and "getting a good night's sleep." It feels a little pathetic that at thirty-one, I'm still being admonished by my grandmother not to stay up too late. More pathetic is the fact I'm obeying her.

I click on the light in my bedroom and groan at what I see. I moved back almost a year ago and I still haven't removed posters from high school. I could now—I've got plenty of time tonight. But I won't. I won't because it means I'm staying. It means I'm stuck here. And while that's ungrateful and unfair, it's also true. I promised Opa I would take care of Oma no matter what, and he was right—she needs me. She needs me for chores on the weekend, to sort and pay the bills, to contribute funds to meet some of those bills, and for company. She has few friends, and those she does have still enjoy the companionship of their living husbands. She has discovered evenings can become very lonely times. I have too.

But at the very least, Barry Manilow and Shaun Cassidy should go. I pull off the edges of each poster, pushing away my sense of defeat, and roll them up. I drop the rolls into my trash can. I almost laugh as it hardly helps. John Travolta and Olivia Newton-John still dominate the wall next to my closet. I flop on my bed and concede defeat—I will always be at most sixteen years old within this room.

Feeling a little lost and a lot nostalgic, I drop to the floor and sweep my hand under my bed. The box is still there. I pull it out, smiling at *My Treasures* penned with colored markers on top. Years of notes lay inside. Dried flowers, friendship bracelets, notes from friends, notes from boys who were friends and became more, and a few from those same boys who broke my heart, asking if we could be "only" friends once more. Why I saved those breakup notes I'll never know . . . Reminders of love won? Love lost?

I dig deeper and find the riddles and coded messages Opa created for me. He was quite inventive really. After that first three-shift cipher for my thirteenth birthday, he moved on to substitution, transposition, and even a Vigenère for my sixteenth birthday.

I pull out a random note. It's the Vigenère that employed my name as its key word. The note translated read,

> **Happy Sweet Sixteen! You are growing up too fast. Please stop. Your gift is in the garage. But you must look hard.**

That was an exaggeration. I didn't have to look hard at all. My gift was a baby-blue 1965 Chevrolet Impala that Opa and his best friend, Mr. Holbein, spent a year refurbishing in the Holbeins' garage. It was the absolute best birthday gift ever!

I close my eyes. *This is why I am here.* Opa and Oma gave up everything to move to America for me—to give me a better life—and they denied me nothing that was in their power to give. This realization also answers why I saved all these riddles, codes, missives, and even the breakup notes. They're part of my life. They are the moments that made me laugh and cry, love and learn. They made *me*.

And that is why Opa never would have destroyed that letter I saw at age eight, or any others that came before or after. His own "Berlin Letters," as I now think of them, would have been too important to him. The man cut newspaper clippings and pasted them into a scrapbook. If he did that with articles published in the press, there is no way he would have destroyed private and personal correspondence. And there was also the element of secrecy about them—Opa didn't keep secrets from Oma. At least, I never thought he did. Now I can't decide if I'm imagining things, I'm a fool, I'm tired, or I've been too close to the largest tree in the forest to notice the thousands surrounding me.

With equal measures of curiosity and dread, I open my bedroom door and stand in the hallway. I can see across the U-shaped space into the hall bathroom, into the entrance to my aunt Alice's old room, and Oma's shut door at the top of the U.

If Opa wanted to hide something, truly hide it away, he would not attempt it in Oma's domain. Therefore, I can dismiss her bedroom, bathroom, and closet. Aunt Alice moved out when I was six years old and her room has stood empty for twenty-five years. It's a possibility.

I push open her door a few inches more to enter, hoping the hinges won't give me away. They don't. Opa kept everything well oiled and running smoothly. I absorb the space. I haven't stepped within this room or even thought about it in years. It's a time capsule. Just like my room but from an earlier era. There's a stack of spiral notebooks on the built-in bench beneath the window, an old Westclox alarm clock on the bedside table still keeping time, and a massive Rolling Stones poster covering the wall above her twin beds. Considering the band formed in '62, I stand impressed with my aunt's taste. She was an early adopter of what's become "classic" rock and roll. I run my finger over the bedside table. While I haven't been in here in years, Oma has. It's dust-free too.

I open all of Alice's desk drawers. There's no need to look for secret compartments as I did with Opa's desk because this one isn't solid and a hundred years old. It's small, utilitarian, and probably came from one of our many family garage sale hunts. I check under the bed and in the closet. There's nothing other than some old clothes in dingy colors hanging on the top bar. I don't think of the sixties as being a particularly dingy-colored decade. Maybe not full neon like today, but still bright and even flowery. Then again, I'm thinking of America. I often forget that while I grew up here, Aunt Alice did not. She was an angry seventeen-year-old German teenager when we came to America in 1962 and probably dressed in the same clothes she arrived in for the two years she lived with us. One year of high school and one year at a community college and she was gone. First to George Mason University, then out into the working world.

I tap the walls. I study the floorboards. I run my fingers along the door trim, the window trim, and the baseboards. I'm acting like a crazy person. Am I seeing conspiracy in coincidence? I tiptoe back to my room and shut the door. I put on my pj's and grab the *Ladyhawke* tape off my desk. A desk not unlike Aunt Alice's. Small, wood, three drawers—cheap and perfect for a middle schooler. It's another item that keeps my room locked in time. Looking at it now, I can't imagine sitting in that small chair at that cramped desk and actually getting work done.

As I turn, my eye catches the corner of my rug and another flash of my childhood snags me. This memory is a funny one—a good one—and all mine.

When I was about ten, Oma made the most glorious chocolate cake. A true masterpiece of at least six layers with thick chocolate icing and coconut between the layers. We each got a slice for dessert and were told not to touch it until the next night. But after school the next day, I couldn't wait. I'd been thinking about that cake nonstop. So when I got home and no one was around, I grabbed a slice, and the second I tipped it onto a plate, Oma's car pulled into the driveway. Rather than abandon the cake, I ran to my room and hid it in the most secure place I knew—under a loose floorboard. I'd discovered the opening a few months before and had hidden notes from Spencer Velasquez, the cutest boy in the third grade, in there.

I thought the cake could rest there for a few minutes while Oma came to check on me and tell me to get straight to my homework, but she called me downstairs instead. She asked me to put the groceries away, clean the carrots, help make dinner, and do the dishes afterward. By the time I was alone again, I'd forgotten all about my hidden cake, especially as I'd gotten a huge slice for dessert in thanks for being such a good helper.

Three days later my room was swarmed by ants. Thousands of them. They were everywhere. Oma freaked out and ran screaming from the room. She was reeling, like in the chaos of a massive cyclone. I stood stunned, illuminated by a focused lightning strike. The cake!

While she was off gathering her mop, detergents, and pesticide, I lifted the floorboard and almost threw up at the writhing mass within my secret spot. But as horrible as that was, getting caught in a lie was far worse. I dove my hand in, grabbed the plate, and threw it and the cake out the window into the side yard. I'd barely dropped the floorboard back in place before Oma returned. While she attacked the mysterious infestation, I snuck into the side yard, retrieved the unbroken plate from a hyacinth bush, washed it, and returned it to the kitchen cupboard.

The ants never returned and Oma never found out.

Feeling nostalgic, even though I never hid another object in that spot, I pull back the rug and drop to my knees. The board lifts as easily and silently as I remembered it did. It's still the perfect hiding place. Nearly ten inches in depth, it runs about a foot by two feet and is framed by floor beams. As I resettle the board back into place, an incongruence catches my eyes. White, not wood. What book did I hide inside that has lain long forgotten?

I reach for it, but rather than slide toward me it slides apart. Pages splay across the subflooring. Not pages. Envelopes. Stunned, I drop into a full sit on the bedroom floor.

The infinity symbol marks the upper left corner of each envelope.

Opa's letters.

CHAPTER 4

Haris Voekler

EAST BERLIN, GERMANY

Sunday, August 13, 1961

"Haris, did you know?"

It is the first question—the only question—Monica asks when I come home. She wants to know about the barbed wire. I can't answer her and I certainly can't tell her it won't be barbed wire for long. Word is already circulating about what those coils will become. A true wall. A cement barricade. Yet even today, the looped barbed wire was effective. It did its job.

I am angry, exhausted. I've been on the streets or in the newsroom for fifteen hours straight today without stopping for food or water, and I want a moment of peace. Just one. When I stepped into our apartment, a horrid chill filled me as my wife asked her question again and again and I asked mine. It's a painful volley between "What have you done?" and "Did you know?"

In some respects, yes, I did know. Something electric has filled the air this summer. Something is wrong, so something had to change. The DDR is hemorrhaging citizens. Although we closed our borders like all other Soviet Bloc countries, we have—we *had*—a unique "escape hatch" through Berlin the others did not. Yet did I envision a "wall" or have any idea such a thing could happen? Never.

But to the victors go the spoils of war—that's how we got divided, both our country and our city—and that's how we got our wall.

After all, tensions didn't start this morning. The Western Allies broke apart our land at the end of World War II. They took the land to the west and, in May 1949, established the Federal Republic of Germany. The Soviets took the east and, months later in October 1949, established the Deutsche Demokratische Republik. They also broke apart our city. Although Berlin is situated in the center of the DDR, France, England, the United States, and the Soviet Union each took a section, and the treaty granted unfettered access between them.

The Soviets managed their section very differently from the others, and soon it alone was dubbed East Berlin. France, England, and the United States informally mixed their sections together to form West Berlin. Well, France didn't quite cooperate with the others.

Anyway, it quickly became known that any East German or DDR family who wanted to leave the Eastern Bloc simply needed to travel to East Berlin, then either walk, hire a taxi, or hop a train across the line into West Berlin. The Volkspolizei might ask for one's papers or inquire about one's business, but it was nothing more than that. Merely the delay of a few minutes and a few questions. So they came—and they left. From 1949 to today, over three and a half million East Germans came to the Soviet Sector, walked across a line, and disappeared.

"No." I finally answer after our third volley of "Did you know?" and "What have you done?" I force myself to calm. I'm on the verge of yelling at my wife, and I am not a yeller. Yelling, any loud noise, always upsets her.

I take a deep breath. "I didn't know, Monica. Not anything specific. But something had to be done. You know that and you'll see. It'll be temporary. Just until people understand."

"Understand what?"

"What we're trying to do here. That we're creating a new and better way to live."

"No." Monica's voice grinds out low and guttural. It surprises me. My wife is kind, gentle. And while she holds opinions and defends them, she's never argumentative or unreasonable. We talk. We compromise. But this word brooks no discussion. It forms an impenetrable barrier between us, more formidable than any wall.

I sink into the chair across from her, almost believing that if I can convince her I am right, she won't confirm what I can't bear to suspect. I keep my eyes on her so as not to search for our daughter. I reach for Monica's hands. She yanks them off the table and away, as if I am a monster set to devour her.

"Monica, stop. It's for our protection." I speak in the same tone I use on Luisa. It is high-pitched and placating. It feels weak and passive. I drop my voice. "Once people realize the Socialist Unity Party is doing the right things, they'll see, and the wall will come down."

"They'll see? They'll fall in line? They'll no longer get upset that the Party is stealing our freedoms and caging us in like animals?"

"That's your father talking," I bark back. *Remain calm.* I press my lips tight against a further outburst and sit back, but I can't stop myself from crossing my arms as a hard stone settles in my stomach. First her parents ruin us and, tonight, my wife defends them.

She leans forward, as if to attack. Monica never attacks. "Leave my parents out of this. They saw this empty future you want and they left."

"And destroyed us in the process," I shoot back and jump to stand. My chair tips over behind me, startling us both. I right it, then scrub a hand over my eyes, gripping my temples so tight I feel as if I might push through the soft skin at the edge of the bone. I need to get a modicum of control. I didn't intend to say that.

"What do you mean?" she whispered.

"It doesn't matter. Where is—"

"No. You finish that."

I sigh and slump back in the chair again. I've been out all day, and this isn't the fight I want. But we've skirted around the fact for over a month that Monica's parents and her little sister were among the twenty thousand to walk from the Soviet Sector to the American last month. We've skirted around the fact that such actions carry consequences for those left behind. Defection always carries consequences.

"I won't get another promotion, Monica. I won't get access to the best interviews anymore. In fact, I'll be cut from any top-level stories and marginalized until I am nothing. Today, for instance, I was stuck on the street chasing first-line reporter stuff. Your parents ruined our futures, our job prospects, our respect. Your job won't go anywhere either. You'll be demoted again and again."

"Mine's not going anywhere anyway." She flicks out her hand. She is a typist, and a good one, at a shirt factory and she likes her work. But before I remind her of any of that, she continues. "And you? You're their top reporter. Best propaganda master they've got."

I blink. I have never heard such derision, bordering on hatred, from my wife before.

We have a good marriage. A good family. A good life. Everything I wanted for us, when we first married, happened. Through brains and ingenuity we got to a good place. Sure, there was a hiccup—a big one—last month when my in-laws defected. But I remain sure that with time and effort, I can overcome even that. I can win back the paper's approval, the Party's approval, anyone and everyone's. But this? Monica's disdain? Where did we go wrong?

I shake my head and try to explain more clearly so, perhaps, she will finally understand. "The Stasi, the Party . . ." I let my breath out long and slow. "When you reach a certain level, you can't have contact with the West. No friends and certainly no family over there. It's disloyal. It threatens everything we're trying to accomplish here. Today, for instance, another reporter got the interviews with Ministers Honecker and Krenz, General Secretary Ulbricht, and other Politburo members. People who a couple months ago were inviting me to their private dining rooms and asking me to write articles about them. Not propaganda, but real articles. I can only hope that, in time, I'll be able to win—"

"They must be terribly weak to be so easily threatened."

"Enough." I slam my hand on the table. The sting feels good, but it startles me as well as her. "Enough." The word falls again, soft and sad between us. "Where is Luisa?"

"Gone."

Tracing a crack in our kitchen table with my finger, I cling to my fantasy a moment longer. "Get her back. Call up Joyce or Rebecca or whoever's apartment she's playing at and get her back. We should eat dinner as a family tonight."

"She's over your anti-Fascist barricade, Haris. So if you are wrong and it doesn't come down soon, she'll be gone for a very long time."

With that, Monica pushes up from the table, walks into our bedroom, and shuts the door. I stare at the door, one thought filling my mind. *I can get her back.*

I live with that illusion for two weeks. I write letters to my in-laws, Walther and Gertrude, but get no replies. I set pen and paper before Monica and demand she write to them. She refuses. Writing is our only option, and such a weak one at that. Telephone lines have been cut.

I then throw myself into my next plan. The barrier can be good for our people. Once we get the planned economy settled and we mold people's expectations and work ethic, we will prove to the world that our way is better. So every day I pour my heart and soul into sharing that plan, promoting it, and outlining its benefits across the front page of the paper. I work without food, without sleep, to share the good news of our wall, our protection, and the clean purity it provides for our city. Because if we all believe, really believe and get on board, then we won't need the barrier at all—and Luisa can come home.

But every day it gets harder to believe the barricade is temporary. On August 27, hundreds of trucks and bulldozers haul in prefabricated concrete sections. The looped wire becomes a wall. They also start clearing a "Buffer Zone" so citizens can't approach the final barricade. Within a couple weeks some areas along the wall are stripped within three meters. Trees, houses, parks, even cemeteries get bulldozed over and plowed under. In other areas it is more than three meters. Hundreds of meters. Rumor is that the Brandenburg Gate and our church, the Church of Reconciliation, are going to be "trapped" within this new Buffer Zone.

"You can't do this!" By mid-September I reach the end of me. I rage at Monica. "Get her back! She's my daughter too."

My wife says nothing. In that single day, my open and affectionate wife, my best friend, confidante, and lover, became a stranger. Her silence and obstinacy surprise me, anger me, flummox me. All I can surmise is that on August 13, she left me as decisively as Luisa did. And it's only now I recognize that she didn't leave me so much as she left herself. Monica is absolutely paralyzed with fear.

"I can't do this, Monica, without you. I need your help." Tears well in my eyes. I refuse to let them fall.

"There is nothing you can do. Nothing I can do. They're in

charge. They've always been in charge." She shakes her head at me like I am a child and slow to understand. "You can't see that. Everything you have the State gave you. You think it is your ingenuity, your smarts, but they created you, will use you, and nothing is your own. Your demotion, merely because your in-laws moved a few blocks away, should have proven that to you."

"Is this what you think of me? What you've always thought?"

"No. But only because I didn't mind the future they handed us after I met you. The past didn't hurt so much then. You were brighter than their darkness, but I was a fool. I forgot who they are."

I sit stunned with no reply. It isn't the first time I've heard such words about my future, but it is the first time in many years Monica has even obliquely referenced her past.

As for my future, I heard as much a few days after the wall went up. I was at a friend's apartment for beers after work. He took a long pull on his bottle, then leveled his eyes to mine. Felix looked hawkish. He always did when he got serious.

"Don't be so arrogant you can't see it. You're smart and you liked the future they handed you, but they handed it to you, Haris, just like they've handed one to me and they will to our children. What if Luisa doesn't end up as bright as you and gets sent to *Producktionsarbeit* after tenth grade and placed on a factory line in Leipzig?"

"That won't happen," I scoffed. "She's smart. She'll make it to University."

"I'm not willing to take that risk." Felix said nothing more. We simply drank our beers in silence until his wife said their dinner was on the table.

The next day, August 16, I heard that Felix and his entire family had stepped out their front door and into West Berlin.

They could do that. The Matherns lived on Bernauer Strasse.

It's a unique section of the wall because the buildings on that street sit directly on the border line between the West and the East. If you lived in one of those buildings and stood inside your doorway, you were in East Berlin. If you took one tiny step onto the sidewalk, you were in West Berlin.

The wall doesn't go around those buildings. It can't. It goes right up next to them and between them, but not in front of them. So on that first day, and for a couple after, families simply opened their front doors and walked away.

On August 17 the Volkspolizei started nailing those doors shut.

It must have been around then I asked Monica the question that had plagued me for days. "Why didn't you go? Eight hundred people got across the barrier that first day. Guards have even been arrested for helping some."

"I heard his voice. He spoke . . ." Monica put a trembling hand to her mouth.

I stepped forward to comfort her, but she drew back. She didn't need to say anything more. I knew. Whoever it was, he spoke Russian.

Something cracked inside me. And although I was angry, I also loved her very much and I hated seeing her in pain. It led me to tell her something on the 19th I wasn't supposed to share . . .

We heard stories of successful escapes at the newspaper, but we were never to report on them. We weren't to talk about them at all. Only the stories of captures were to be reported or relayed. But I knew of one.

"The Knittles jumped from a second-story window on Bernauer Strasse today."

Monica gasped and tears sprang to her eyes. "Rebecca is nine months pregnant."

I held out a hand. "It's all right. I heard they sent a note to the fire department and there were nets to catch them."

I stood at our kitchen counter watching her wring her hands in a dish towel. "And the Radishewskis were moved from No. 2 to No. 10 today as well. The VoPo are moving people and bricking up the windows. They'll move the Radishewskis again soon. But . . ." I stared at her. "Their windows aren't bricked yet. Get a letter to your parents and go."

"And you?" The flash of hope in her voice tore through me.

"I can't, Monica. I want to for Luisa, but then I would be giving up on all I've worked for and believe we can accomplish here. This, all this, is for her." I pressed my fist into my chest as if that force, that pain, could quell my doubts. "But you can't live here anymore. You must know that."

We didn't talk about it again, but each night that week, as I unlocked our apartment door after work, I expected to be met with empty darkness. I craved it. Yet Monica was there every night, and I knew fear was still stopping her.

Finally, as she sat across from me at the kitchen table and met my eyes three nights ago, I killed any hope left within her.

"You have to stop thinking about crossing the wall now."

"I've tried. I keep getting closer. It's just there are so many guards. I—"

I cut her off. "I'm sorry, but don't—" I reached out for her but dropped my hand before I touched her. She had not welcomed my touch in two weeks.

"Don't what?"

"Don't go anywhere near the wall anymore. Don't go that direction at all." I took a breath, then delivered the final blow. "A shoot-to-kill policy went into effect today."

"And this is temporary? For our benefit?" Her skin turned grey and her spatula clattered to the floor.

I couldn't reply. Because I couldn't bring myself to question the Party and the plan.

But now . . .

Secretary Walter Ulbricht was smart when he built the wall. Of course, he had everything meticulously planned. Within days it became clear that even before permission from Moscow was granted, he'd secretly stockpiled barbed wire and created the concrete slabs outside the city to avoid notice. He had also mapped the wall to sit two meters within the Soviet Sector. As not a millimeter sat on US, British, or French soil, he determined they would have little to say about it. And he was right.

US President Kennedy took four days to make a statement.

British Prime Minister Macmillan said nothing of note.

No one would go to war over Berlin.

Then today, in defiance of the treaty that divided Berlin in the first place, VoPo guards demanded US diplomats show their identification papers to cross into East Berlin. The US finally balked.

I reported on their bad behavior in the news because it's the right of any sovereign nation to secure its borders. Foreign citizens, diplomatic envoys or not, should always have to show identification papers and deference to another nation. But I did not report that after questioning a soldier, I learned the diplomats refused to comply because the US views East Berlin not as a capital of a sovereign country but still as a Soviet-occupied territory. Officially the Americans have never recognized the DDR and have been operating since 1949 accordingly under the treaty that guarantees free and unfettered movement. The paper's publisher, Dietrich Koch, made it clear we were not to report this insult to our autonomy and national identity in the paper.

The Americans took their umbrage further. When the VoPo guards refused to stand down and demanded, once more, to be shown diplomatic papers, the Americans rolled ten M-48 Patton tanks with guns uncovered to the border crossing. With tanks aimed at both East German and Soviet soldiers, the Americans again asserted their right to unrestricted access into East Berlin.

As *Neues Deutschland*'s new top reporter is laid out with a cold, Koch calls on me. Racing to the border crossing the Americans call "Checkpoint Charlie," I can hear the tanks rumble from a block away. Black smoke billows and fear bombards me, a dark, pervasive shadow I have not felt since childhood when Allied bombs rained down on Berlin. I dread what might come next.

Ten Soviet T-55 tanks come next.

The border crossing looks surreal and feels harrowing. Reporters and soldiers, on both sides of the wall, stand for sixteen hours as the twenty tanks face off not one hundred meters apart all through the day and night. Every one of us fears the instant our city will be destroyed once again. Only this time, with nuclear weapons available to both the Americans and the Soviets, we will not survive. Berlin—always in the midst of one war or another—will be Ground Zero for nuclear destruction.

I pace all night, unable to stand still or sit. I am shredded and shaking as I hear a US tank engine roar to a higher pitch. It pulls back this morning. In reply, one Soviet tank does the same. Then slowly, one by one, the other eighteen tanks follow suit.

"Kennedy backed down." Dietrich Koch stands grinning when I finally stumble back to the newsroom this evening. "Write it up for tomorrow's paper. The October 28 headline will be a victory call for us."

"What did we concede?"

Koch chuffs. "Soviet General Secretary Khrushchev simply agreed to unhindered access for US diplomats. They don't have to show their papers like before. It's hardly anything. But it proved Kennedy isn't interested in a war here. He even stated Berlin wasn't 'vital' to US interests. Don't write that up, though. Just publish our win. Our win, Voekler, not any concessions."

"Of course."

Koch returns to his office and opens a bottle of vodka. Several other men are already there. I can tell a couple are members of the Soviet State Security, the KGB. They have a look about them. Watchful. Secretive. In command. They are toasting and congratulating themselves on this supposed victory. The Party, the Stasi, the KGB, Moscow, the decision-makers—they are the victors. Not us. Not Berlin. In this one moment I realize all Monica says about me is true. All Felix said was true too. I live a life they control. I have only the future they grant to me. Nothing is mine. And nothing ever will or can be.

I accepted that I wouldn't get access to the best stories for a time after my in-laws defected because I thought I could win Koch over or back, or whichever direction it was that meant I moved forward. But I can't. I can't because I am a pawn. We are all pawns. Pawns of those men in Koch's office toasting their victory.

But they weren't there. They didn't stand all day and night with legs cramped and stomach clenched, watching soldiers on either side of that barricade stare each other down with fingers hovering over their triggers and hatred burning in their eyes. One move. That's all it would take. One finger and one trigger. One reflexive twitch and a gun would fire. And this time, what began with gunfire would have ended with nuclear bombs. Berlin, which has survived for centuries, would be wiped from the global maps forever.

And what's worse—the Americans are right. I see that too. We truly remain a Soviet-occupied territory. Nothing gets done without instructions from Moscow. Yet even they won't be bothered if we are destroyed. We came close today. What about tomorrow?

I write up exactly what is expected of me.

But I drift in a whole new and terrifying direction as I trudge home, exhausted yet oddly determined. And as I pour myself another shot of vodka, I decide that tomorrow will be in my hands and I will find a way over the wall.

For my wife and for myself.

CHAPTER 5

Luisa Voekler

WASHINGTON, DC

Friday, November 3, 1989

I pull the envelopes out by the handfuls. A cursory count reveals close to a hundred splayed across my floor, each with the sideways infinity symbol penned where the return address should be printed.

Could they be related to Carrie's Berlin Letters? She said her batch ended July 1961 and it was 1966 when I saw Opa's envelope, one of these envelopes. Could the writer be the same person? If so, it can't be Opa. He was here. Was he the recipient? Was he always the recipient, even in Germany? Was he a courier?

My mind reels and none of these scenarios please me or fit within what I know of Opa, Oma, my life, or who I believed our family to be. And if these are part of Carrie's Berlin Letters, then they are related to a CIA matter, and as a CIA officer, I have to turn them over to my boss, Andrew Cademan. That concerns me too.

My eyes land upon a Dr. Scholl's shoebox through my open closet door, and after I grab it, I drop the envelopes inside and toss the box onto my bed. It feels like I've trapped something dangerous. My heart is pounding into my throat, and I'm seconds away from hyperventilating.

I have definitely trapped something dangerous.

"Stop." I say the word aloud, using it as a verbal cue to shut down the cacophony in my head and deal with what's in front of me. I open my window and lean out into the cool night air. The action reminds me I need to haul the winter storm windows up from the basement. Another Saturday chore that must be done. The mundanity of the thought catches my breath. Life was much simpler five minutes ago.

Perched against the windowsill, I stare back at the box sitting on my bed. *Call your boss and explain the possible connection.* It's the right and safe approach. Or I could hide the box under the floorboards once again and forget about it. Never open the hiding spot again.

It takes less than a second to admit the impossibility of that idea. And if anyone ever did find out and somehow the letters made it to the CIA, the matching symbols connecting Carrie's work to these letters are enough to raise a lot of questions.

Bottom line: I need to do the right thing.

I vacillate and a quarrel erupts inside me just like in the movies as to what that "right thing" actually entails. The angel on my right shoulder admonishes me not to even look at the letters until I turn them in to Andrew on Monday morning. Take the high ground. Be innocent and aboveboard. On the other hand, it's hard to believe that a tiny devil is perched on my left shoulder encouraging me to open them and just find out what I'm dealing with. After all, that's innocent too. If they aren't related to Carrie's work, no problem. And if they are related to Carrie's work, I do have clearance and I am qualified to examine them. So technically, I could do both and still be right—I could look at them and turn them in to Andrew on Monday.

Right?

I step toward the bed and pull out the topmost letter. I can't not look. After all, I searched all night to allay my threads of doubt, not to confirm them. One peek and my doubts could still be allayed. These could simply be innocent letters from a long-ago friend and putting an infinity symbol on correspondence was in vogue in the 1960s. It was the thing to do. Like hearts over an *i* or *j* when you're a lovesick teenager. I almost laugh. The mental gyrations I'm conjuring to justify what I'm about to do are extraordinary. Integrity, I shake my head, teeters at the cutting edge of a very slippery slope.

But this is Opa. The man who loved me best. The man I loved most. The man who taught me to see what's in front of me, without bringing my expectations, perceptions, and subjectivity to the matter. He's the one who encouraged me to study applied mathematics at William & Mary. He was so proud when I landed my job with the "Labor Department" managing budgets.

So many times I wanted to tell him the truth, even that my skill with numbers extended to puzzles, codes, and ciphers, but I never did. I didn't because I'd signed numerous confidentiality agreements, and he taught me that too—your word is your bond. You never lie. You never cheat. You never steal.

And not just with material things. You never steal answers, ideas, credit, or acclaim. You do your job and your duty and that is enough. He would never be part of something secret. He would never lie. And peeking at one letter will prove it.

Tapping the letter against my palm, I recognize one and only one truth: if I'm wrong and Opa was involved somehow and I have to hand my grandfather over to Andrew Cademan and the CIA, I need to know why.

So any way I look at it, I am opening these letters.

I drop the one clutched in my hand atop the others, then pick up the box and cross the room to my desk. I sift through the stack in search of the earliest postmark. It's what I would do at work. I would work from the earliest and from the outside in, assessing all available information in the order it's presented.

October 20, 1964, is the earliest postmark I find. I open the stiff envelope, sliding my finger along the back seam line. Time and humidity have resealed it. I expect the letter inside to be equally stiff, as if read only once, but the page is worn and soft. Stains—the edge of a coffee ring?—darken one corner. The letter was thoroughly handled and, perhaps, returned to the envelope only when the review of its contents was exhausted.

October 19, 1964

Dear Walther,
While you made it clear you never want to hear from me, you need to know Monica passed away on October 8th. I am sorry I did not write immediately. No matter what you've done, you deserve to know. I was upset. I was lost. I was angry. That's the truth of it. I am still upset. I am still lost. I am still angry.

These past years have been hard, and the last few months unendurable. Monica was always fragile, but it was clear to me, that first night after she passed Luisa to you, she gave up. Past ghosts, terrors, whatever you want to call them, stole her away, from me and from life. Then you took our daughter to America. I am not sure you understood the joy Monica experienced seeing Luisa daily, even if from a distance and across the wall. Once you moved away and that daily lifeline was gone, nothing was left for her here. I was not enough and, in many ways, I became the enemy.

She grew weaker. I know you noticed that beginning even before you moved to America. She left your letters on the kitchen table sometimes. Even from two blocks away, across the wall, you noted she was growing thin and you were worried. If true, then why didn't you stay? Why didn't you keep our daughter here? Was earning more money so important to you?

I'm sorry. It's too late for that now, and it does no good. Monica stopped eating much after you moved away and caught cold after cold. About a month ago, her bronchitis turned to pneumonia and she could not beat it.

There is enough blame and pain to leap over this wall and span the ocean. I'm not writing for that. I'm writing to tell you of my wife's passing. Despite what you think, I loved her. I always will. As I love my daughter.

I don't want Luisa to imagine me here as I am now. I don't want her to know I couldn't get across the wall, that I couldn't get her mother to her despite trying desperately. I don't want her to know how I've destroyed our little family.

Please let us both be dead. I don't mind what you tell her. I simply ask that you free Luisa from your anger toward me and tell her both her parents died. I cannot imagine Gertrude has ever been able to say my name without disdain and disgust, and I can no longer blame her for that. I am not what I was, and even I don't regard my former self with equanimity.

Also, please call Luisa *Mäuschen* occasionally. It was my nickname for her, and in that name, I can pretend she will hear me say "I love you always" and know that it is true.

One more thing . . . Before Monica died, she told me an interesting story that Alice shared with her during one of their long afternoons together. It lifted a veil and answered many questions. Give me a chance. Time has changed me,

Walther. Pain has changed me. Write back to me as only you can. And if I can read your words, I ask you to accept my replies.

Your son,
Haris

Mäuschen. "Little Mouse."

I drop the letter and push up from the chair, sending it toppling backward onto the floor. The noise feels deafening in the silence of the house and in the blank that's invaded my mind. Without picking up the chair, I drop onto the edge of my bed, eyes still glued to the pages resting on my desk.

Haris is my father's name. But my father is dead. He and my mother died in a car accident in 1962. That was the impetus for the move to America. There was nothing left for my grieving grandparents in West Germany. They wanted a better life for their remaining daughter, Alice, and their granddaughter. They couldn't take the pain of years of war, destruction, rubble in the streets, decay all around them, and the deaths of two more of their beloved. That's what Oma said. That's what they told me. That's what they've always told me.

Mäuschen was Opa's nickname for me. He said he made it up. He told me it was his and only his. He said it so often and with such affection, Oma eventually adopted it around the time I was ten.

I believed them. About all of it. I mourned my parents with them. I am—was, until a moment ago—still mourning them. I quit asking questions so as not to remind my grandparents and cause them pain. I quit asking, Did my mom have long, pale blonde hair before I did? Was it curly too, or was her hair straight? Were her eyes just as blue? Did she like olives and chocolate and cloud-filled rainy days? Is my chin from my dad? Which movies did he like? Where did he work? What did he do? What did she do? How did they meet?

I stopped so that maybe for a moment, a minute, or a month, my grandparents might forget how much they lost and how much they hurt.

It was all a lie.

A breeze blows through the open window. The air has grown beyond cool to cold. Too cold. I shut the window and pull on a thick sweater and take comfort in its instant warmth. I then set the chair right again and drop into it. I stare at my fingers. My nails are blue. Is it shock, or is it truly that cold? I can't tell. I can't think. I stare at the letter. I stare at one word. *Haris.* I run my finger over his signature as if it, across time and space, can form a connection between us. Haris Voekler. My father.

My dad? I taste the word in my mouth. I chew on it. I've never thought of him that way because I never knew him and couldn't know him. He was right—or is he still alive and that means he *is* right? My Oma never could say his name without a tinge of disapproval. That was another reason I quit asking about him. I didn't want to know what he'd done wrong or why he wasn't loved. Because that could mean if I was too much like him, I might not be loved too.

"Before Monica died, she told me an interesting story that Alice shared with her during one of their long afternoons together. It lifted a veil and answered many questions. Give me a chance."

What chance? What did my mom share?

As the questions billow up, I realize I am staring at the answers. Opa did write back. Obviously. He gave my father—I test the word *dad* again and find myself pulling back as I don't know him yet.

But Opa did. Opa gave him that chance and they corresponded. And by the number of letters resting atop my desk, they wrote each other for years.

I page through the envelopes again, this time sorting every postmark into chronological order. My fingers move fast, my brain faster, as if there's a ticking clock over my shoulder.

There most definitely is.

Oma will awake in the morning, and there are words to say and questions to ask. Monday will come quickly, and depending on what is within these letters, I will have to talk with my boss about them. There's no denying that identical infinity mark on each and every envelope.

Once the envelopes are in order, I stack them carefully in the box and pull out the next one.

January 4, 1965

Dear Walther,

I'm ashamed at how long it took me. Before, I thought I was smart. Everything takes longer now. Granted, it's hard to stay positive and keep up with work each day. I am overly tired. Nothing feels the same without Monica.

Haris

Five sentences only?

I read on. The next letter. And the next. After that emotional first letter, the subjects become mundane—the weather, his walks to work, his musings on plants, bugs, and all the construction going on around East Berlin. He writes about his wife. He writes about me.

I soon notice my father writes of nothing significant and of no one in particular—other than those of us gone. He rarely mentions his friends, anything significant about work, or what he truly thinks about the world around him. If anything, he sounds like a cheerleader for the GDR. Maybe he was. Maybe he is. But he can't write.

I always got the impression from Oma and Opa that he worked in words somehow. Oma even let slip he went to University, which I gather was a big deal. Not everyone in the GDR is given that opportunity. You don't just apply. You're vetted, selected, and funneled into certain courses and a state-mandated curriculum. But my father's field must have had nothing to do with actual writing because his sentences are simple, stilted, and his punctuation is all over the place. He makes sense, but barely. The letter about weeding his garden is particularly odd.

> And Ive grasped top hold.

What does that even mean? Is he talking about weeds? Carrots? It verges on nonsense. With no apostrophe. Or is it existential brilliance?

After about the fiftieth letter, I drop my head to my desk. Why hide nothing? Why lie to me all these years? Because it was a lie. In a letter from 1979, he asks Opa to tell me the truth—that he is alive, that he loves me and thinks of me every day, and that what he's about to do he does for me.

That's when my heart's pace picks up and beats so loud I can physically hear it. I read on and on, eagerly searching for what he was about to do, what he did do, but other than odd sentences that were clear answers to queries from Opa, nothing strikes me. There is no change in the randomness of his subject matter or in his tone. The only curious thing is a change in his handwriting.

In some letters it's fast and frantic, as if my father is rushing. In others it's slow, straight up and down, and methodical, as if telling about his walk or his cup of coffee is the most vital information he can convey within his lifetime and it takes time and care to pen the experience properly. The only consistent elements of the letters are two things—their randomness and their persistent questions about me. In every letter Opa is peppered for details and I am showered with love.

I think back to Carrie's missive. The sentence structure of her letter was different. The subject matters were more relevant to, well, anything. Her Berlin Letter spy was more creative, complete somehow. He was adept, skilled. He is not this man. He is not Haris Voekler. But the symbol? Is it possible her letters and mine are unrelated?

I want to believe that. As hard as it is to believe Opa and Oma lied about my father all these years, at least the lies might end there. Maybe they thought they were protecting me. Maybe they thought they were in too deep with the lie and they'd lose my love, my faith, and my trust if they shared the truth. I don't know. I can ask Oma tomorrow, and while that will help, I'll never get the answers I want. Because I want them from Opa. I want to know why *he* lied to me. Why *he* didn't trust me enough with the truth. Or maybe he did and that's why the letters are hidden here, in a place I might find them.

With a long, soul-depleting sigh, I give up. It's past two o'clock, and if I'm going to get any sleep before Oma wakes at six, I need to try now. Never a good sleeper—actually I've been a horrific sleeper my whole life—I might snag an hour or two if I'm lucky.

Gathering the scattered letters from across my desk, I carefully stack those I've opened in chronological order. They may not be interesting or revelatory, but they are from my father. I set down the pile and reach for the last envelope. Like turning to the last page of a book, I want at least one answer to close my night.

Is he still alive?

The letter is dated December 3, 1988, and I expect it arrived just before Opa passed away. It's the same, nothing new and nothing surprising, other than my father caught a cold on the S-Bahn. A woman sneezed on his fingers, he wrote. Again, strange. And that's the end.

In the morning I'll read them all, then figure out how I can get an address for a man behind the Iron Curtain in East Berlin who didn't have the foresight to put it on his envelopes. I should at least let him know Opa passed away, that I've read his letters, and that—even though we've not seen each other in over twenty-seven years—I love him too.

I run my fingers through the stack, glancing at each page, ready to call it a night when I notice it. An inconsistency or perhaps a consistency. A tiny dot appears above the third letter after the first comma in the second paragraph. It looks like an ink skip—like the one I saw on Carrie's page.

I can't breathe.

I sift through the letters again, looking not at the words but at the ancillary marks. They are tiny, but they are present, never above an *i* or a *j*, never above an *o* or another vowel that requires a diacritical mark. And in German there are lots of those. But the dots aren't there. They are centered over consonants or spaces. They are precise and they are the size of a pinhead. One random dot per paragraph or per letter, and not necessarily on the same counted letter or space each time. It varies. As does the page. In some I find marks on the first page, some on the second or the third. One is on a fourth page of a letter filled with nonsense.

I open my desk drawer and paw through the childhood chaos

inside. Beneath a couple of filled spiral notebooks, I find an old and empty one with a drawing of Holly Hobbie on the cover. The page lines are super wide, and I suspect it's from elementary school. I tear out the only used page, on which I scribbled my 1969 New Year's resolutions, number one being *Talk to Billy Boswell*, and place a blank page before me. Dang, that boy was cute. I forgot about him, and I never did smile at him, much less talk to him.

I go back to the first letter—the first letter after my father asks Opa to give him a chance.

January 4, 1965

Dear Walther,
I'm ashamed at how long it took me. Before, I thought I was smart. Everything takes longer now. Granted, it's hard to stay positive and keep up with work each day. I am overly tired. Nothing feels the same without Monica.

Haris

It's basic, but the message is there.

I B E G I N

I next find the line that bothered me a few minutes ago. "*And Ive grasped top hold*" has a tiny signifier, a dot above the *d*. It's the third letter at the beginning of a sentence. At work I'd start my count there—and so I do. Nothing. I count spaces as well as letters in my next attempt and realize the code exists within one sentence rather than across, which is why it's so odd.

D E A T H

Two variations on acrostic ciphers. And just like Carrie's Berlin Letters, a quick perusal reveals he's using several patterns within each letter.

My mind reels. To write a cipher—any cipher—that actually makes sense in its original form is challenging. It's why substitutions are more often used. They can be complex and that is their beauty. But it's also obvious to anyone who sees one that there's a message encoded. But a sophisticated and changing acrostic is . . . extraordinary.

I cast back to one of my first questions, one I thought I'd already answered: Could my father be Carrie's Berlin Letters spy?

As quickly as I ask, I dismiss it. Carrie's first missive to the CIA was in 1945. The last was dated summer of 1961. While my father could've written the '61 text, as he would have been twenty-nine at the time, I doubt he was penning anything so sophisticated in 1945 at the age of fourteen. Not only that, Opa wouldn't have had to teach him anything. The "I begin" would have been nonsensical. Did Opa train him to do this? *"Write back to me . . . And* if *I can read your words, I ask you to accept my replies."*

I page through the letters again, certain that each one contains a hidden message within. Some letters are several pages long. I can't even fathom what opinions or intelligence might be embedded.

I lunge from the chair and dash out of my room, down the hallway, and into the bathroom. Losing my dinner is one way to deal with this. I slump against the wall and stare up at the little flowers that dot our bathroom wallpaper. They're so little, so pretty, so simple. Just how life felt only a few hours ago.

I push myself up, brush my teeth, and head back to my room.

There will be no sleep tonight.

CHAPTER 6

Saturday, November 4, 1989

I'm slashed. I'm pulled apart. I'm bleeding. I'm—

"Wake, Mäuschen. Wake up."

I hear Oma from a great distance, but I'm falling. The earth is shaking, lights flickering.

"Now. Wake up. You are screaming again."

I open my eyes. My neck hurts and won't straighten. I reach up to rub the base of it with stiff fingers. I lift my head from my desk and take in the light, the letters, my room, and Oma's pinched face.

"You are clammy." She presses a dry, cold hand to my forehead. "Why are you sitting here?"

I shift away as if slashed again. The chair scrapes against the floorboards, catches, and almost sends me tipping over.

"What's wrong?" Oma looks back at my desk. She studies it before sifting through the pages with the same hand that was just measuring my temperature. Every instinct cries out to snatch the pages away. I don't. I sit and I watch her face, not her hands.

"What is this?" Her face is open and curious.

"You tell me." Heat rises within me, and it takes me a heartbeat to recognize it as anger. I wasn't raised to be angry. I'm not an angry person. I'm practical, pragmatic, but not angry. It's unfamiliar, yet warm and emboldening. "You lied to me. You and Opa lied to me. All my life." I point to the letters.

She is no longer touching them. She has stepped back. Her arms now wrap around her body. Her brow furrows in question.

"Haris Voekler is alive. These letters to Opa? They're all from him." The sentence rests between us.

"That can't be. Walther got a letter. An official letter. He told me they died. He would never lie to me." She looks back to my desk. "You are mistaken."

"I'm not, Oma, and the last letter is dated December 3, 1988, right before Opa died. They wrote each other for years."

She steps to my bed and sits. She pales and my heart softens. She isn't lying now and perhaps she never did.

"They were from Haris?" Her voice rises in both question and confusion. "Those white envelopes he hid from me?"

"You knew about them?"

"I saw a few before he could whisk them away." Oma lifts a shoulder and drops it as quickly. "I trusted Walther, and sometimes, most times, it was best back then not to ask questions or pry, even of those you loved." Her eyes widen with a sudden revelation. "Monica?" She lunges forward as if ready to attack all the letters at once. "Is my daughter alive too?"

"No." I hold out my hands and she drops back down to the bed. I'm ashamed of myself now. That spark of hope, instantly bright and snuffed out just as quickly, breaks my heart. "That part was true. My father wrote his first letter to tell Opa that my mother died. He told Opa to lie to me and say he died too."

"She died in a car accident?"

I understand her question. Like me, she wants to know what's true, what's a story, and who made it up. Like me, she's searching for solid ground on which to stand.

I shake my head again, taking this from her too. "He never mentioned a car. He wrote that after she gave me to you and we left for America, she gave up on life. Her health got worse and worse, until she caught a cold that turned to pneumonia and she couldn't beat it."

Oma closes her eyes. Tears stream down her cheeks.

I shift my chair closer and sit with my knees touching hers. "What did he mean by that? About her giving me to you?"

Oma covers her mouth with her hand. At first I fear she's going to change the subject and put me off as she has done so many times in my life. But a second sense tells me that's not what's happening, and despite it being the hardest thing I've ever had to do, I must sit still and keep my mouth shut. Oma is struggling. Some secrets, I expect, only rise to the surface with pain.

"We were awakened on Sunday morning, August 13, 1961, by shouts in the street. Everyone was yelling that we were locked in. Soldiers were everywhere, and people were throwing rocks. The DDR, in a single night, had enclosed the western sectors of Berlin and cut us off from the rest of the world."

I hadn't thought of it that way, but she is right. I, like the rest of the West, focus on how the Wall keeps East Berlin hostage behind the Iron Curtain, but West Berlin—entirely surrounded by the GDR—became and remains an island within a Communist sea.

Oma continues, "We dressed and went to the street your mother usually walked to come to our apartment for Sunday lunch. We had moved from the Soviet Sector to the American weeks before for Opa's work. Monica and Haris, and you, could not move with us." She presses her lips together. "Haris would not move."

There it is. The tone she uses whenever she mentions my father. Now I understand. He wasn't responsible for the accident. He was to blame for not moving the few blocks that would have saved us. Again, I tamp down my questions. I can't risk stopping her story.

"She wasn't there. You weren't there. But there was this horrible barrier of barbed wire. There must have been thousands of meters because it looped in circles and stretched for kilometers, across the whole city, surrounding it. Your Opa said to walk away. The guards were watching us. On both sides. The American soldiers looked as lost as we did. And the VoPo had guns and they threw tear gas canisters, not at us, not at the young men throwing rocks from the American Sector, but at their own people who approached the barricade from the east."

Oma touches a hand to her forehead as if she's trying to either draw up the memories or tamp them down. I wait.

"We walked a block north, where it was quieter, and we waited. It felt like hours, but we didn't know what else to do or where to go. Then we saw Monica. She was pushing you in your pram and I wanted to run to her, but Walther held me back. We approached the wire slowly so as not to draw attention to ourselves. She did the same. The guards were focused on another family, a child, I think, who was separated from his parents. I will never forget the mother's cries."

She sighs and it catches midbreath. I suspect she's hearing that mother right here and now, despite the years and miles.

"Walther wanted to be calm, but your mother could not be so. I knew my daughter. She was terrified, paralyzed in a way I hadn't seen since she was a child, and I—" Oma stops and a fierce expression crosses her face. One I have never seen before. It is almost frightening in its intensity. Then it is gone. "She knew their inhumanity. Their cruelty and brutality. As I did."

For the first time since Oma started talking, she meets my eyes.

Hers are now clear and the anger is gone. Only a profound sadness remains. "She threw you over the wire to Walther." Oma shrugs. "I don't think she even understood what she was doing. Her eyes were vacant. But she did it. She did what I couldn't do for her years before. She saved you. At least, that's what she believed she was doing."

"You didn't believe that?" I couldn't understand or navigate the undertones in Oma's story.

"I did. Then she tried to push down the wire and step over too, but a Soviet guard stopped her. He merely yelled and she fell back. I stood there unable to help her, and Walther had you. You were bleeding so he had to run away so they wouldn't know. She backed away. Alice and I stood there as she ran away."

Oma is openly crying now, and without thinking about it, I rub the long scar along the outside of my left thigh. She has always told me that before Opa tore out the yard's overgrown rosebushes, a thorn snagged me when I was four.

"Yes. That was the barbed wire." Oma gestures to my leg. Her gaze lifts and finds the desk again. "What does he say?"

"I hardly know. I just found the letters last night."

Oma looks around my room. "Walther left them for you? Here?"

I nod.

She covers her mouth again, and the tears pick up their pace, running in rivulets down her cheeks and over her hands.

"I'm sorry, Oma." I drop to my knees in front of her. "I thought you knew. I thought you'd lied."

She nods and pats my shoulder. "You must think me so foolish to never know what my own husband was doing."

"I don't. Never." And I didn't. I grew up in this house, and while it was loving, undercurrents flowed that I could never name but always felt. I always assumed it was simply the generational divide between us, the differences in our worlds—we were oceans and ideologies apart—but it was secrets, fear, sadness, and perhaps even regret.

I reach up and pull Oma into a hug. "I'm sorry."

"We will talk." She squeezes me once and leans back. Although it's not unexpected, it still stings. Oma is not a hugger. "I came to tell you I have coffee and oatmeal ready. I must go check that it hasn't burned."

I push off the floor to stand and step back, creating that distance between us I know she finds most comfortable. "I'll be right down."

I sit for a moment, listening as Oma moves across the hall and down the stairs. The third one squeaks as usual. I close my eyes. It's so simple, so regular, the cadence of our daily and weekly lives now. Over the past year, along with the mundane, I've learned to reseat a toilet into the bathroom's tile floor, fix a disposal by cranking it backward from underneath with an Allen wrench, and patch nicks and dings within plaster and drywall before painting them so well the lines don't show. We have created a workable rhythm.

But this . . .

I look to my desk. I can't do this. I can't process this. The bare reality that my father is alive is one thing, but the stark reality that he's been writing to my grandfather for twenty-four years is another. And then there's the dangerous reality of the hidden messages buried within the letters. A couple I read in the morning's wee hours have international implications—such as the backroom deals with the Soviets that undergirded Ulbricht's New Economic System starting in 1963—and even though long past, it means that on Monday morning, I *must* hand the letters and, therefore, both my father and my grandfather over to the CIA.

Oma's right. This requires coffee and oatmeal.

I walk out to the hallway, and after a quick bathroom stop to wash my face and brush my teeth—and take a few deep breaths—I'm ready for that next step. Food and facing Oma again. There are still questions to ask.

I walk down the stairs, swing around the newel post like a slingshot, as I've done since I was a kid, and head back to the kitchen. A glow catches my eye as I pass by the living room. The smell of a winter's fire reaches me and I backtrack, surprised Oma has built one in November. The weather hasn't dipped below the fifties at night yet, and a glance outside tells me the sun is shining, promising another warm day.

I stare at the fire, my brain not fully firing yet. Oma enters the living room from the dining room's swinging door. She doesn't notice me. She pulls open the bottom drawer of the room's only chest and hauls out Opa's large scrapbook.

My heart softens. Like me, Oma needs reassurance. Reassurance about who and what Opa was. And that's where we will find it. Opa loved his scrapbook and was diligent about noting the important markers of his life and ours within it. There are his few baby pictures he brought from their village to Berlin in 1945, then across the ocean in 1962; pictures of Oma taken with black-and-white film, cooking, cleaning, even raising a hand to swat him away; photos of me throughout my childhood, along with poems I wrote and certificates I won. My college diploma sits within that book too.

Then there are the newspaper articles. Opa carefully cut out and taped within his scrapbook a whole bunch of articles about East and West Germany. He'd read them to me so I'd know where I had come from, where he had come from, and where my parents had died. It sounds morbid, but it wasn't. It always felt like he was inviting me into another story, almost a fairy-tale world of dangers, dragons, sorcerers, and evil forces, so by understanding the world of his real and tumultuous past, I might better appreciate my opportunities. He also wanted me to understand and respect history.

I step forward to apologize again for throwing so much at Oma and so quickly. I want to offer to sit with her and page through the beloved book. But before my foot falls in a single step, she rips out several of the book's front pages and throws them into the fire.

"Noooo!" I scream and sprint across the room.

The pages land upon the edge of pale yellow flames and flash into a bright inferno. Photos curl and page corners turn to ash as the fire quickly moves from their edges to their centers. Without thinking I shove my hand into the flames to snatch them away. Everything is burning. I drop the pages on the hearth, striking at them to pat out the flames.

I feel Oma beside me. She's pulling at me, swatting my head, and screaming in my ear. I try to tip into her to push her away, but the world falls black. It's closed and stifling. I'm flattened on the hearth, and it takes me a moment to realize she's covered me in a blanket and has thrown her body over me.

I push at her. "Oma . . . Oma . . . You're crushing me." The wool is thick and I can't breathe.

The pressure releases and light floods my eyes. I look to the pages first and, miraculously, almost half of each remains. I then look to my hands. They are black with soot and they sting. Oma grabs my arm and together we stumble into the kitchen. She thrusts my hands under the faucet and turns on the cold water. The soot washes away, revealing bright-pink skin with patches of red and white. That's when the throbbing pain starts.

"You are lucky you didn't catch fire. That was stupid. Stupid. What were you thinking?" German pours out of her as she twists my wrists under the water, making sure the water drenches and cools every part of my hands.

"Me? Why were you burning Opa's scrapbook? How could you do that?" I yell back with equal vehemence but in English. I try to pull away, but she doesn't let go of my wrists.

"Stay." She yanks my hands back under the water. "Let me see what you've done." She leans over the sink to get closer to my hands.

A few blisters have bubbled up on the pads of my left fingers and a series of small blisters across the palm of my right hand. Although everything is throbbing horribly, she is right. I am lucky. Nothing looks worse than a minor second-degree burn. The skin is ugly and mottled, but it hasn't burst. It's still there. How that is possible, I have no idea.

"Your sweater could have caught fire. You could've—" She stops as if what she was about to say is too horrible to speak aloud.

I look down at the loose, loopy wool sweater I'm wearing. It was Opa's favorite, an old worn one with Oma's sewn patches at the elbows and with arms so long they roll at my wrists. She's right. And the reality of that, rather than the pain, brings stinging tears to my eyes.

She puts an arm around my shoulders and squeezes as we watch the water wash over my hands. After what feels like a super-long time, she turns off the tap, wraps my hands in a clean bread towel, and ushers me to our kitchen table. She lays my hands out on the towel, then reaches up and, with the pad of her thumb, swipes at the tears falling down my cheeks. With no words she leaves the kitchen. I sit, fully knowing where she has gone and what she'll bring back.

Oma pulls her chair close to mine and opens the jar of her

homemade ointment. The very one that, I was told, went on my thigh after the thorn tore it. The same ointment that has soothed every cut, scrape, burn, blister, and even a few heartaches. After all, a light massage on the back of your hands or your neck with Oma's salve can heal and soothe even the harshest breakups.

Lavender, rosemary, and the rich, sweet scent of honey perform their magic once more, and I am five, seven, ten. I'm any and all ages because there was never a time in my life that Oma didn't care for me when I was hurt. While she may not be a hugger, she is always there and always willing to go wherever I need her to be.

She gently applies a blob of ointment to each blistered finger. She then smooths the salve over the bright pink, unbroken skin of my palm with a featherlight touch. "You will be fine."

"It hurts," I whine. I hear my small, scared voice. All my anger is gone.

"Burns hurt the most." Oma squeezes my shoulder and leaves me again. I listen to where she's going, afraid she'll return to the living room to finish the job she started. Instead she comes back with a glass of water, a bottle of Bayer, and gauze. She taps two aspirin into her palm, and I feel guilty for suspecting her.

She sits again and stares at me. "I won't burn the book." She raises her palm holding the aspirin and gestures toward me to open my mouth. I obey, and she drops both aspirin onto my tongue before she lifts the glass of water to my lips.

"It's hard for me to remember sometimes," she says to my hands as she starts to wrap each in gauze.

"Remember what?"

"That we live here." She gazes at the kitchen and out into her backyard garden before she returns her focus to my hands. "And that secrets, some secrets, maybe all secrets, aren't so dangerous. They don't get you arrested or killed."

Once finished with my hands, she rises and pours us both mugs of coffee. I wonder how I'll drink mine, but I don't say anything. I wait for her to continue.

"I never asked what your grandfather was up to in Berlin when we arrived after the war or here when those envelopes would come and he scurried off to his study. I didn't want to know. I didn't want to carry his secrets. What if, when questioned, I let something slip? I couldn't risk that because I never wanted any of them to touch you. But he is gone now, and I thought all that was gone with him. It was over. And the thought that something more, something in that book could harm you—" She purses her lips. "I am sorry, but I can't take any more. I want it all gone. But—" She looks up at me. "It's not over, is it?"

"I'm not sure. Maybe. I don't know. But you don't need to be afraid, Oma. This isn't East Germany and it's not back then."

She offers me a small, almost indulgent smile. "Maüschen, you know nothing of fear, and I am glad of that, but I am and will always be afraid."

"My father's letters don't seem intent on harming anyone." I press my lips shut because that may not be true. There's a lot I don't know yet.

"Your father . . ." She sighs, more like huffs really. "Monica never could listen to reason over that one. She fell in love with Haris the moment they met. He was . . ." Oma closes her eyes for a heartbeat, then opens them to look at me again. Their grey-blue hue looks fierce and bright like winter ice on a lake. "He was very charming, smart, charismatic. He was so full of energy and ideas. He was also sold on the Soviet dream. He was their puppet."

"She loved him." I hear the smile in my voice and the wonder of it fills me. It's the first positive thing I've ever heard about him, and it starts a whole movie reel of loveliness. At their first meeting he wore a turtleneck, very avant-garde for 1949, and she wore a wide skirt with maybe a poodle on it, saddle shoes, and a red ribbon tying back her bouncy blonde ponytail. Granted, the image is a lot like Sandy and Danny at the beginning of *Grease*, but it feels right. It's a bit of my own romantic fiction, as I suspect with about half of Berlin reduced to rubble at the end of World War II, life was a lot tougher, greyer, and tenser than *Grease*'s Rydell High. Yet that statement is the first and only glimpse into my parents' emotional landscape, from Oma's point of view, and it's a lifeline to me. "*She fell in love* . . ."

From the letters I have already discerned that my father loved my mother very much. There was unbearable pain between them near the end, but he talked about their beginning a bit too. And I get the sense that the pain was made all the worse by its stark contrast to those earlier years. After all, no one can hurt you as much as someone you love.

Oma continues and I don't interrupt again because, through this story, she is telling me exactly what scares her and precisely what she fears I'll find in Opa's scrapbook.

My father.

CHAPTER 7

The letters consume me.

Oma offered little information over our coffee and oatmeal, and I didn't push. Instead I ate and listened to her stories. Snippets really and most not at all flattering of my father. But they provided some of my first insights into Oma's life as a young mom and my mom's childhood. Oma's pain was so obvious and the gulf between our worldviews and experiences so vast, I realized how little I've appreciated her perspective. Her weary eyes and pale coloring soon told me she'd been pushed to her limit in recalling such times—and I was faring only slightly better.

Now she clears our bowls and my mind turns to my bedroom. I'm anxious to return and find myself so focused on what awaits me that her kiss to my forehead surprises me. Without a word she then opens the back door and heads to her "garden." Her raised beds of churned earth. She is determined. Her best friend, Mrs. Oltolf down the street, told her gardening had worked wonders for her after her husband died. And since she and Opa started one the spring before Opa passed away, Oma can't conceive of other choices to manage her grief. Gardening, despite these momentary setbacks, will yield wonders for her too. She is sure of it.

Watching her go, I better understand and respect her dogged determination. A woman who cleared rubble from the streets for months on end and raised her girls in a bombed-out apartment for almost a decade with three other families, all while working at a manufacturing plant that had been stripped of its machinery, is not going to let a few mercurial seeds defeat her.

I, on the other hand, do not head to our small backyard as I often do to help, nor do I go to the garage to find a hammer to fix the back stairs. My hands wouldn't be able to handle the work, regardless. I turn the other direction and head toward the living room.

The burned three pages held pictures of my grandfather as a child along with a small picture of his own parents. His parents stood in starched clothing with stiff expressions. How long did they stay still to create the image? The mark on the back of the photo, which once read *November 1899*, is burned away. The glue that secured the photographs to the pages is also gone, and the pictures lay loose from much of their mounting at odd angles, charred and partially melted. While I am sad Oma has ruined them, I suspect they are not the reason she tried to destroy this book. It holds something else.

I leave the pages and gingerly pick up the scrapbook with my right hand. My palm hurts as I flex my fingers to grip it. So rather than hold it there, I tuck the scrapbook beneath my left arm and head up the stairs to my room.

Resting both myself and the book on my bed, I carefully turn through it page by page. I've seen everything before. Pictures, mementos, articles. There is nothing new. Nothing surprising and certainly nothing dangerous. I finally flip to the last page, noting how it rises up from the back cover, and find the "something else." Four unopened white envelopes, each with the small infinity symbol drawn in the upper-left corner, sit wedged into the book's binding. I surmise Oma did this. She tucked the letters that kept coming into Opa's book, as my father didn't know he died.

I close my eyes. Why is nothing easy?

I carry the letters to my desk. As much as I want to read them, I suspect they'll tell me more of the superficial nothings each of the other letters reveal on the surface. To find what I want to know, I need to decipher them. And to do that, I must continue like I always do—from the beginning without skipping a single step, or a single letter. I set the four new ones aside.

Oma pokes her head in hours later with a plate of cheese, crackers, and apple slices. "You didn't come down for lunch. I thought you might be hungry."

Her tone is soft and conciliatory. Two aspirin slide into my field of vision, and the throbbing heat within each hand reaches past my focus and seizes my attention again. I pick up the aspirin and take them with the glass of water Oma sets there as well.

"What do they say?"

I glance at her. She is not looking at the letters. She is studying my decryptions.

I slide them away from her, fully aware of the duplicitous role my job places me in. If I was really an accountant for the Labor Department, as both my grandparents have believed for years, then I would share these with my Oma. But as a CIA officer who knows these letters are somehow related to an ongoing assignment, I cannot. There are signed agreements forbidding that. There are signed agreements forbidding lots of stuff I'm doing right now.

"I'm sorry, Oma. But I don't have the full picture yet."

She nods and steps away, seemingly satisfied with my answer. She then notices the scrapbook on my bed. She steps over to it and sits on the edge again as she did earlier. I turn my chair sixty degrees to face her.

"I'm glad you stopped me." She runs a finger over the book's worn cover. "I would have regretted it, but it wasn't the letters in the back. Not just the letters." She presses her palm against the cover. "There may be other secrets in here. Secrets I'm not sure I want to face. I was angry. I still am. He lied to me. To both of us. We left that life and he carried it with us."

She's right. Opa's scrapbook is full of newspaper clippings, lists, notes he tucked inside the book, and who knows what else. She's right about Opa too. He lied to both of us for years.

"Why'd you put those four letters in the back? Why not throw them away?"

"They were important to him. I knew that much. It's hard to discard anything someone we love valued." She smiles and it's not so sad this time. A little mischief lurks at the edges. "Until they make you mad enough." She lifts her chin to my desk. "What does Haris say? Not your notes. I see you are working on something, but does he ever mention my daughter?"

"He does." I reach for a letter. "This one is dated April 28, 1971, and he writes about how hearing birds chirp is his favorite sign of spring because it reminds him of Monica."

"She loved birds. She used to stop walking or playing and lift her head with her eyes closed just to hear them better."

I sit silent for a moment envisioning my mother. Young, blonde, blue-eyed, with her head tilted up listening to the birds in peace. It's a lovely image, and I let it replace the one I've held since this morning, the one Oma gave me of her eyes so terrified they became lost and vacant that long-ago Sunday.

Oma stares at me and I know she wants more. I offer what I can. "He's the one, by the way, who started the lie. He asked Opa to lie to me about his death. Not to you, specifically, but to me so I wouldn't miss him or worry about him, I guess. But he also constantly writes about things he wants Opa to tell me. The birds, for instance. He wanted me to know how much my mom loved the birds so I would remember her when I heard them." I set down the letter. "I'm sorry Opa didn't. I would have liked to have known that growing up. I'm sorry he didn't share it with you either."

"Me too. Does Haris still write for the paper?"

"He's a reporter?" It's both a question and an answer. My father wrote about submissions and interviews, but he took for granted that his audience knew what he meant. Opa did, of course, but I did not.

"Haris was, maybe still is, the Party's propaganda mouthpiece. He was the chief reporter for *Neues Deutschland*, the Party's newspaper, before we left." Oma's derision seeps into her tone.

"I don't get the impression that he's left his job, but he doesn't sound like he's the top guy. He's mentioned a man named Manfred once or twice, praising his stories and work. I get the sense this Manfred is the paper's top guy. In fact, I thought my father was support staff or something."

I fold my lips in, taking a pause to test my next words in my mind. I disregard the small voice telling me to stay quiet. "He changed, Oma. You should know that. The letters reveal that even if he started out as the Party's mouthpiece, he wasn't for long. He changed a great deal."

"Haris?" Her eyes widen.

"Haris Voekler."

She nods, digesting the information rather than agreeing with it. "I'll leave you to it." She crosses to the door and turns back. "Will you let me know?"

"If I can, yes."

She shuts the door and I return to my letters.

I keep on. 1971. 1972. 1973 . . .

Each letter uses an acrostic cipher. That doesn't change. Coders like what they like and stick to it. But my father does show remarkable dexterity within the acrostic format. He switches up his pattern by paragraph, and he selects such outlandish numbers no one could guess—who uses the twenty-seventh space after a period in a letter that only has five sentences that long in a three-page letter? And often he doesn't signify the key letter at all until deep into the narrative. No censor in the Soviet Bloc countries could or would catch any of these codes in the time allowed to them. They had and still have to clear thousands of letters daily. He was clever. Too clever. Because I know the patterns he favors and deciphering them is still taking me an extraordinarily long time.

The content changes as well. His first letters after my mother's death in 1964 are angry and questioning. He's bereft and lost and starting to dip his toe into an alternate ideology. He's afraid to commit and name or comment upon the injustices he sees around him. He's slowly waking and constantly asks Opa to confirm or deny his new insights. I wish I had Opa's side of the correspondence. I can't imagine what he wrote in reply or the wisdom he offered.

Another couple years and my father is more confident. He and Opa have clearly drawn closer as well. The change in tone conveys a level of trust, camaraderie, and respect that has grown between them. The few jokes and gentle teasings I catch signal they might have even become friends.

By the midseventies my father's questions, mourning, and loss morph into a passion and purpose. He's angrier at the strictures he witnesses around him, the increased work quotas and security intrusions, and he starts to more openly share secrets and political maneuverings within the Soviet-backed Socialist Unity Party. He shares details that could get him arrested.

By the late seventies his letters go further. I find *Honecker. Liar. Building Stasi. Total control* buried in a letter after Erich Honecker ousted General Secretary Walther Ulbricht from office in 1976. After that, Honecker, along with Economic Secretary Günter Mittag and Stasi Chief Erich Mielke, pretty much ruled the country unfettered until—well, a few weeks ago.

There's also one section in a letter about *Ostpolitik* that would certainly get him in trouble if decoded. He explains how Catholic Pope John XXIII's sort of get-along-to-go-along approach to Catholic life behind the Iron Curtain proved an absolute failure for religious freedom and autonomy. Instead my father shares how it allowed a whole host of KGB and Stasi spies into the Church's upper echelons, both across the Iron Curtain and within the Vatican itself. The Stasi, he writes, was thrilled with their stupendous success.

Throughout the entire day—mine measured in hours, his spanning years—I meet Haris Voekler. I laugh with him, cry for him, and even get really annoyed at some of his decisions. There was a trip in 1978 to a train station, the Tränenpalast, that he knew would cause problems. Yet he still went. The next day he got called to the main Stasi headquarters for questioning but was smart enough to twist the conversation and get himself out before the questioning landed him in deeper danger. It was a daring gambit as the Stasi are renowned, even on this side of the Iron Curtain, for ferreting out every secret and uncovering the smallest lie.

Then as I decipher a letter from 1982—one so dangerous I'm having trouble digesting it—I realize Oma is right. No matter the time or the place, some secrets can get you killed.

I set down my transcription of the 1982 letter and stare at it. Handing these letters to Andrew at the CIA is no longer a question; it's a necessity. This is apocalyptic stuff. I take a deep breath. Should I go on? Can I go on?

After another sip of water and an apple slice, I convince myself I must. It's not Monday yet and I am secure here. The information is secure and I am, technically, authorized to do this work.

Additionally, I will do the right thing at the first reasonable moment I can do it. Until then, I get to spend this time with my father, because after talking with my boss, I won't be allowed to. These letters will be in the CIA's hands—Carrie might be assigned to double-check my work—and I, as his daughter, will be deemed too close to the subject matter to be involved in any way. The debrief on this letter alone will be excruciating.

Every third time I tell myself this, I almost believe my own rationalizations to continue. Every second time, my conscience tells me to call Andrew Cademan at his home right now and ask for a meeting. But I can't bring myself to lift the receiver off its base.

Yet I can bring myself to understand Oma's feelings. If you believed everything the Socialist Unity Party did was wrong, the propaganda my father served up would be upsetting, not to mention deceptive and harmful. Several of his letters make me laugh at how easily he couches his true and evolving opinions beneath mounds of Party cheerleading. Cheerleading that flows so easily, it must have at one point been true. On the surface his early letters are love letters to Communism, the DDR—that's what he calls the GDR—General Secretary Ulbricht, the Party, and even Stasi Chief Erich Mielke.

What my father accomplished in these letters is brilliant. By the late 1960s he is able to craft two letters on opposing ideological planes that exist seamlessly together. I can almost hear his voice.

I certainly sense his charm and charisma as he waxes eloquent about all that is good and right in the DDR. Only the slant of his letters, the racing of the ink across the page, or the crash of his words into each other give a hint at the tenor of the subject matter I'll find beneath. There his charisma and charm drop away. There he is all business. And the business is brutal.

But as the letters arrived nonstop for twenty-four years, it means the censors never glimpsed behind the curtain. The irony makes me smile. They must have loved him. Reading on the surface, he was—and perhaps still sounds like—a true "company man." I glance to the new pile of four letters I've set aside, wanting to get to the end of the story. But I do not. I stay right where I am in the early 1980s.

During these years he befriends a young man named Manfred. Early on, almost reading between the lines, I sense my father was demoted because of my grandparents' move to the American Sector and then, a year later, to America itself. Manfred gets hired in the late 1970s, and with close ties to the establishment, he gets all the best stories. At first my father is wary of Manfred, and although tasked to help him in any way possible, he keeps the young reporter at arm's length. Then in the late 1970s, a friendship grows. There are a few comments to Opa, probably in answer to direct questions, that lead me to believe it becomes a warm and trusting relationship. But after the 1982 letter, I get a feeling in the pit of my stomach that I'll never hear about Manfred again. It almost brings me to tears.

I meet my mother in the letters too, at least the woman my father loved and remembers. Oma said my mother didn't really know what she was doing when she passed me over the Wall. She was full of fear, even terror. But my father describes it very differently. In a 1965 letter I find,

> One might say she died the day she gave you Luisa. Yet in all her strength and fury, in all the sickness and waste that came after, she never regretted breaking her own heart.
> Or mine.

There was no code beneath those sentences. Just my father sharing my mother with Opa.

In other letters he described her as quick and kind, melancholy and haunted at times, but with a laugh that could light up a room. He talked about how her exterior persona of accommodating and friendly, while absolutely real, hid beneath it an armor stronger than steel. She'd been refined in a crucible so hot, she was impervious to bending toward evil or deception. He also wrote he could never take her for granted, as she was the better, stronger, and purer of the two of them and he knew it every day of their lives.

It takes me a few letters to recognize it, but when I do, it makes me smile. He never buries his thoughts of my mother within codes. In every passage dedicated to her, she stands on the page, in full view, as if she's his most important subject. She shines alone.

She isn't in every letter, though. In the sixties I find her in about every third. In the seventies every fourth or fifth. I'm in the eighties now, and she shows up more sporadically. Was it because these letters were his only place to truly mourn her at the beginning, or because she was the genesis of his conversion and now that it's complete, he's on to the work he must do? In the eighties I get the sense my father knows exactly who he is and what he's about. And the horrific costs he'll pay if caught.

Also—not in code—he asks about me. In 1965, barely a year after his initial appeal to lie to me about their deaths, he questions the wisdom of his request. But, still unsure of what he thinks or believes about it, he doesn't recant until 1977. That's when he begs

Opa to tell me the truth and tell me how much he loves me, thinks of me, and dreams of the day he can hold me in his arms.

I have to pause then. The sense of loss and emptiness, unnecessary and unfathomable, swamps me. I feel heat rise within me, within my core and not merely my hands. I want to rage at Opa and the lies he kept while admonishing me that no lie should ever stand. I push the pain away. After all, it does me no good. Opa isn't here to account for anything he did.

I work on, wondering if some comment from my father's side of the conversation will shed light on Opa's choices, but I find nothing on that point. Though I do find Opa shared my life with him. My father wrote, "*My sense of balance was terrible as a kid. It took me three months to learn to ride a bicycle,*" in reply when Opa must have told him how I stayed steady my first push down the street, and "*I wish I could see that medal for math. Her mother was good with numbers. I am so proud of her,*" after Opa wrote him that I won a math competition in the seventh grade.

I only recognize how much time has passed when the sun slips from my window. I've been at it for eleven hours, and I've traveled through nineteen years, landing in 1983. I push to stand and stretch my back. I'm awash with questions, my hands are throbbing, and my vision is blurring. It's five o'clock and Oma will start preparing dinner soon.

I gingerly fold the letters and place them within the shoebox. Although I believe Oma expects to keep her word and will not try to destroy the letters or the scrapbook again, I can't risk it. I'm not sure the need for truth outweighs the specter of fear yet.

I slide the box, the scrapbook, and my Holly Hobbie notebook into the hiding place beneath my floorboard. I open my door. My eyes hit upon Aunt Alice's door. I turn back into my room, grab my handbag from the floor, and head down the stairs. I walk to the back of the house, and sure enough, Oma stands in the kitchen.

"I'm making—" She stops and points a spoon at my handbag. "Where are you going?"

"I'll be back soon. I need to do something." I step forward and kiss her cheek. "Save me some dinner."

Her eyes tell me my reassurance hasn't reassured her, but I'll deal with that later. Right now I need answers from the one person who not only might have some but might actually—if pressed—give them to me.

Aunt Alice.

CHAPTER 8

Haris Voekler

EAST BERLIN

Monday, October 19, 1964

They're both gone and I am alone.

Monica never got Luisa back and I never got us over the wall.

It's been three years, two months, and six days since I held my daughter.

It's been one week, four days, and six hours since I lost my wife.

I thought October 27, 1961, our end point. I thought Berlin and everyone in it would be decimated that day, and I'll never forget the bile in my stomach, the swirl of regrets that filled my brain, or the sheer panic that gripped me. In my naiveté I thought that day would bring down the wall. I thought that if others saw, as they certainly did across the world, how close the wall could bring us to global destruction, it would come down.

"*Cooler heads will prevail,*" as my father once said.

I guess I should have known better. He said that as Hitler rose to power, certain those "cooler heads" would settle down the fanatic quickly. They didn't.

So rather than wait, I tried my best to find a way over, under, or through. I used every contact from work and every informant I'd cultivated to secure an escape. First I said it was for a story, hoping one connection could lead me to another and another. No one would talk to me. No one would help. I then implied it was for me. I was crossing from loyalist to dissident. Still no one would talk.

I switched tactics and talked to Party insiders about weaknesses in the wall over dinners and over beers, searching for an inflection point. But there were no discernible weaknesses. Several people accused me of trying to trap them, of being an *Inoffizielle Mitarbeiter* or, as they are commonly called, a *Spitzle*. A Stasi snitch. One contact, one of my best confidential informants, beat me up when I pressed him too far. Another turned me in to the Stasi. They, fortunately, believed I was setting a trap for a story. But I lost momentum after that, as that ruse could only work with the Stasi once.

It was urgent, however, so I did not give up despite my diminishing chances for success. Eight hundred crossed over that first day, then only six hundred more within the following two weeks. And once the prefabricated concrete blocks were raised, making the wall two meters high, the VoPo started coiling the excess barbed wire into the Spree River, effectively cutting off that last avenue of escape.

By November that year, all buildings along Bernauer Strasse were cleared and much of our old neighborhood too. We were moved back, a block east of our old building on Rheinsberger Strasse so they could increase the width of their "Buffer Zone." In our new home I could no longer pass my daughter's room, trace my finger along the green crayon line she drew near her bed, and try to convince myself she'd be back tomorrow, tomorrow, tomorrow . . .

But emptying the buildings wasn't enough. Another shorter wall was built to the east to define the Buffer Zone. It's formidable now. At some places it is over ten meters wide with a sand strip to catch footprints and a trench of metal shards to tear a runner to shreds—

that's only if he or she makes it past the electrified trip wire and auto-firing guns. And if anyone gets through all that, they then face the reinforced two-meter-high wall at the western border.

Peter Fechter and Helmut Kulbeik tried. In August of '62 they dashed from their construction site and made it through the strip to the final wall. Helmut rolled over the wall's top lip as shots flew around him. Peter, only seconds behind, was shot reaching up. He dropped like a stone, and the world watched and filmed him as he bled to death against the wall's east side. American troops stood helpless on their side; VoPo stood too nervous to approach and save him on ours.

That's when I realized no one was going to help us—ever.

Then the worst came. Walther was moving to America and taking our daughter with him. For money.

> Dearest Monica and Haris,
> It is hard to write this, but I must find more work to care for your daughter and for mine. Luisa and Alice deserve better than the life I can provide for them here. We plan to move to America soon so I can find more work.
> I am sorry.
>
> Love,
> Papa

Before that note arrived, Walther and Gertrude brought Luisa every single day to a park just across the wall. Standing on a rise, Monica could see her daughter during every lunch hour, and I could stand there marveling at her growth and abilities on the weekends. In a single year tentative steps up the slide's ladder turned confident and her run grew strong. Luisa's baby-ness fell away, and a long-legged beautiful girl of four emerged.

At the end of each playtime, Walther would instruct Luisa to wave to Monica. While Monica never waved back, because it was illegal to do so, she always made a motion with her hand against her heart as if capturing Luisa's love to savor it until the next day.

That note got Monica to finally write her parents. She wrote one letter, two, three . . . She kept posting them day after day, even though that very next day—even before Walther's letter arrived—Luisa was not at the park. They had vanished in a single day.

"They're packing. It's been a busy week. They'll be back soon," she told herself and tried to convince me. "Tomorrow. They'll be back."

But they didn't come back.

After a week of "tomorrows," all Monica's letters arrived in our postbox marked *Return to Sender*.

I changed my tactics after that. I no longer mattered, and if I was the problem, I'd cut myself from the equation.

I sought a way out of East Berlin for my wife alone. She would never survive without those lunchtime viewings of our daughter. And I needed to hurry. Monica wasn't eating. She wasn't sleeping. She wasn't working. And despite all the pain between us, I loved her. I love her still.

"You need to go to work." I knelt at her side of our bed one morning. "They're enforcing the *asoziales Verhalten* laws, you know that."

Two weeks without work and one could be declared "criminally unsocial" and arrested. If Monica didn't want to be thrown in jail, she needed to work. Not only were work records diligently documented, but every office, factory, and jobsite had a Stasi snitch, if not an officer on duty, ready to turn people in. After a week, she did pull herself from bed and report to work, but she still didn't eat well and she slept poorly. She wore herself down until chills overtook her, colds came upon her, and finally pneumonia seized her.

After work this afternoon I wander farther northeast than my daily travels usually take me. I don't want to go home. It's a colder and even lonelier place now. I also need to assess work across the city for an assigned article. The government is building a whole new planned community north of Alexanderplatz, outside the old city. Koch wants a series extolling the design, engineering, and construction to run in the paper over the next week.

I stop in the Marienkirche on Alexanderplatz to rest. I am tired. And the day is cool, cloudy, and windy. Few people are out walking and the church is quiet, empty.

I look across the empty expanse. To be expected on a Monday, but I suspect it was just as empty yesterday as well. Few people attend Sunday services anymore. I don't. Then again, I can't. Our church, the Church of Reconciliation—what an ironic name—sits abandoned within the Buffer Zone. But that's not why others don't attend. We, as a people, have moved beyond the crutch of religion by the highest percentage in the Soviet Bloc. Only 5 percent still choose Marx's "opiate of the masses," and even the mighty Catholic Church bends to our will. I didn't say that outright in an article I wrote on the subject last month, but I was encouraged to scoot as close to that truth as politically prudent.

It seems three years ago, Pope John XXIII started a policy of Ostpolitik to increase diplomatic relations between the Church and Soviet Bloc nations. According to the sources I interviewed for that article, Ostpolitik has definitively served the governments over the Church, and it has allowed our intelligence services greater access within the Vatican and our policies a greater infiltration into their homilies. Rather than allowing the Church a modicum of freedom from the State, the State has all but swallowed the Church. At least here in East Germany.

I sit and breathe deep, letting my eyes scan the expanse of the sanctuary. It's a beautiful space. The most beautiful I've seen in a while. Funny, only sitting here in the church do I recognize what's being lost. Beauty. The new neighborhoods are full of tall and identical cement structures that have been built in the last several years, but with little style in their design and little grass and greenery between them. They are not beautiful.

And in the older neighborhoods, the bombed buildings are not being reconstructed in their original fashion. If not left in rubble, the new additions are uniform, cement, and uninspired to say the least. In fact, any outside ornamentation is far more likely to be removed rather than repaired. All the work on those buildings takes little time and it's only a little more time before they start to crumble once more.

I miss beauty.

I miss my wife.

I miss who she was and who I once was in her eyes. The day we met I was a young University student secure in my own brilliance, my plans, and the rewards to which I felt entitled. I was comfortable with my future. I even thought I'd fashioned it. Then I stepped into my department's administration office and a beautiful receptionist took me to task.

"These are my signed forms for next term." I laid them on the counter and turned away.

"You're too late. They were due yesterday." She pushed the papers toward me without raising her eyes from her typewriter. One hand continued to pluck at the keys.

"Professor Forek only signed them this morning." I slid them her direction again.

"You'll need to go back and have him sign this now." She slid them back, along with a new form.

After one more attempt on my part, she looked at me with eyes so fierce I backed away. "Stamping these forms may seem like a menial task to you, but it's what I do, and as everything must be stamped, it makes me your most important person. You should stop annoying me." She narrowed those pale blue eyes, and they morphed from sky to stone. "Or would you rather continue this argument?"

I gulped, took all the forms back, including the new one, and was lost.

I wasn't lost because she put me in my place—many bosses and professors had done that—but because it was personal for her. I was annoying her. I had affected her, and she felt an individual injustice and refused to back away from it. Her individualism felt unique, even dangerous, like a hot flame that drew me in. I wanted to know what she thought, felt, believed, and had endured to become refined into such a sharp glow. I wanted to know if her skin felt as soft as it looked, if her hair smelled like flowers or citrus, and I needed to know if I could bring out that fire again and again, but for me rather than against me. She was a challenge, a mystery, and, within a year, my wife.

I didn't know then that much of that fire had been born of pain. Unspeakable pain.

That last night when I took her hand, it was cold and her eyes were clouded. We both knew she was dying. The doctor had come, and there was nothing more to do. She was slipping away, of her own accord. Her fire dimmed the day she gave up Luisa and extinguished the day Luisa didn't show up atop that old rusty slide. And I couldn't find a way out. I couldn't save her.

"I'm sorry," she said. I assumed she was talking about Luisa.

"It's done. We can't dwell on it every moment of every day." But, of course, we could and we did.

She continued as if I hadn't replied. "I couldn't make you see. I'm sorry I went about it the wrong way. You are smart, and someday you will see. I trust that."

Then she told me what Alice had shared with her about their father. Walther was a simple man of quiet opinions, sent to apprentice with an electrician at the age of fifteen, a man who once did his job well in their little village along Germany's eastern border and then grew his business once he'd moved his family to Berlin. He worked hard and he listened well. That was his true gift. Walther listened rather than talked. I didn't appreciate that gift when we lived only blocks away. I was young and eager to quarrel, show off, engage, and prove myself smart. So I dismissed my new father-in-law. I undervalued him. I quickly stopped paying him any attention at all.

How little I saw.

"He's a spy, or was. He started when we moved here to the city in 1945. Alice says he stopped in July when they moved to the American Sector," she whispered in my ear.

My eyes widened. I pulled back in surprise, even anger, that I'd been duped, our country betrayed. I instantly thought I needed to report it. But to whom? And what would it cost me? I made a list of steps in my head.

"Don't worry about that. He's out of reach now." Monica smiled, as if she could read my thoughts, and all my imaginings careened to a halt. She reached for my hand and drew me closer.

I peppered her with questions, feeling disgust and betrayal, as if I'd taken a bite from a sour apple. "Is this why they moved to West Berlin? To the United States? Did he spy for them? What did he do? What did he tell them about me? About us?"

She didn't answer and I ran out of steam. I dropped my head

onto the bed. I felt foolish and stunned and hated the way both left me feeling vulnerable and exposed.

"Letters." She laid a hand on my head. "Write to him. He will help you."

"Help me do what? I don't need anything from him."

Monica closed her eyes. She tried to sigh, clearly exasperated with me, but it rattled and led to a coughing fit. Once she lay back down, I was calm again.

"Help me how, Monica?" I pressed a hand to her cheek. I could feel her slipping away, but I needed her. I needed her to live. I needed her by my side. I needed to find what we once had. I did need help, but not from her father. From her.

But Monica was gone.

One week and four days later, I sit in this church and visually trace the drawings of its famous fifteenth-century fresco, *The Dance of Death*. I still need help. But I'm no closer to knowing what kind. I feel pulled outside myself. Stretched thin. Everything I once wanted and believed in sits tarnished, shifted out of focus, and simply wrong. There is no other word. I go to work each day. I come home each night. I eat. I sleep. And I am simply wrong.

I walk home. It's dark out now and the city looks dead. There are no streetlights. No lighted signs like the ones I see blinking in the West. It's quiet too. No laughter rings out in the neighborhood, even though it is a mild fall evening. Winter will be here soon, but it's not here yet. People should be out and about. Yet they are all hidden away. We are a silent, dour, hidden people now.

Once home, I open Monica's bedside table drawer. I thread the necklace I gave her on our wedding day through my fingers, letting the small ruby catch the light. I sort past a few books, several letters, and some pictures of Luisa as a baby. With a kiss to each photograph, I set them aside and dig to the bottom of the drawer to find stationery paper and envelopes. It's time to learn what I don't know and, maybe, to ask for help.

October 19, 1964

Dear Walther,

While you made it clear you never want to hear from me, you need to know . . .

CHAPTER 9

Luisa Voekler

WASHINGTON, DC
Saturday, November 4, 1989

I ring the doorbell, then back up two steps and down Alice's first stair. I almost laugh, but it strikes me as pathetic so I don't. My instinctual actions perfectly encapsulate my relationship with my aunt Alice. I looked to her as an older sister, a second mother, chased her all the time, and tried to pull her close. Yet her coolness always kept me simultaneously backing away. I needed her as much as I wanted her, as I felt the distance between myself and my grandparents and thought she could bridge it. After all, I was their granddaughter, never their daughter.

Or perhaps it was the experiential gap I felt between us. Enrolled in preschool, I learned English with no accent within months. I quickly learned colloquialisms and attitudes, too, that Opa and Oma made me feel were too fraught with difficulty, even wrong. I was an American in a German home. I couldn't name it as a kid, but I felt it and I instinctively sought a friend and ally in Alice. I found a void instead.

"How did you know?"

Her tone doesn't surprise me, but her question rather than a hello does.

"About what?" I wave my hands. She's flustered me. "I came to talk to you. May I come in?" I look past her into her open doorway, willing myself into her home, silently begging her to invite me in.

I return my focus to my aunt, who's staring at me. A mixture of wariness, exhaustion, and sadness are painted in bold strokes across her brow, her cheeks, her eyes. They are darker than mine. More grey than blue. Her hair is darker too. She wears it chin length, brushed straight, which makes my longer blonde hair feel frivolous somehow. American and large despite it being my natural color and lacking any of those popular perms or bleached highlights. And yet how she stares at me isn't condemning. I can't describe it other than sad.

Alice tilts her head within her home and steps back, inviting me in. She shuts the door behind us and, without speaking, passes me in the narrow hallway to lead me to the back of her town house. I inhale the most amazing smell—fresh, bright, savory, and comforting. I follow her to her kitchen.

We are about the same height, five foot seven in socks, and build, thin almost narrow, and, I now note, we walk the same too. How much more do I have in common with this taciturn aunt I rarely see? I have painted a picture in my mind of straight lines and hard edges, but watching her move, I sense I've missed her essence.

I shift my attention to her home for clues.

She lives in a row of town houses off Duddington in southeast DC. Her front door and hallway skirt the right side of the house rather than opening in the center. One room opens to the left. It is warm and inviting, with a thick cream carpet, a plush couch, and deep armchairs. Bright pillows are nestled within every seat's corners. Her bookshelves are full to overflowing with stacks on the floor in front of them. There's a sense of movement in her living room as if she's just been here, searching her stacks for the perfect weekend story.

Her kitchen, centered across the back of her home, surprises me too. The cabinets are dark wood and the walls a cheery robin's-egg blue. The bright white trim is clean and fresh. And the one wall filled with at least twenty framed pictures and letters, drawn by little hands with love, is a chaos of color.

That Alice is a first grade teacher is another detail my mind has never been able to absorb. She's clearly a beloved one as well.

She gestures to the table. "I was about to sit down to dinner. Have you eaten?" She reads my face. "I won't eat you, Luisa. You can relax a little."

I bite my lip and nod. Then I pull out a chair at her table and sit. "What did I know about?"

"Papa." My eyes widen. She holds up a hand. "Give me a minute to get the soup and we'll talk. I made minestrone." Her voice breaks midsentence, and I realize she's as nervous as I am. It's so unexpected I don't interrupt or push. I sit silent and watch her take large bowls from her cabinet and ladle them full of soup.

My familiarity with minestrone soup goes as far as a Campbell's can mixed with water. Oma is a traditional German cook and would not appreciate someone bringing Italy into her kitchen. I study the room. "Are these from your students?"

"A few over the years." She turns and points to one in the top corner. It's a good drawing of her, I think, standing next to a young boy in sunshine, with what looks to be a puppy. "The boy who drew that is a famous artist now. He had a solo show at some New York gallery last year." She smiles at the picture and a rose tint infuses her cheeks. "He invited me."

"Did you go?"

She shakes her head, almost in embarrassment at being caught pondering something lovely. "Nein. Nein. I wouldn't know what to do in that world." She crosses back to her toaster, slides in a couple slices of white bread, and soon returns with a plate of toast. She then places a broad bowl before me. The soup looks even better than it smells. There are beans, pasta, sausage, greens; I smell fresh black pepper, fennel, and garlic. I close my eyes and let the steam envelope me.

I open them at Alice's laugh. "You look like you haven't eaten in a while."

"Not much today and rarely something that smells this good."

I am not a great cook. Not even a good cook. When living alone, I mostly ate those TV dinners with the foil covers when not out with friends. Now that I've moved back home, Oma cooks and would be offended if I tried.

Alice raises a brow. "Mama does cook things a little long."

I smile, as does she, and a connection forms between us. She drops into the chair across from mine and hands me a spoon.

I reach for it and sense Alice noting my hands.

"I burned them this morning," I offer.

"I'm sorry. Can you manage?"

"Carefully." I set the spoon between my fingers. The palm of my right hand curls with pain, but it's not as bad as I expect. I successfully spoon up a bite.

Alice blinks her approval and I see the teacher in her. The warm look disappears as fast as it arrived. "Now, tell me, how did you know about Papa?"

"I'm not sure I do. This weekend I found some letters, about a hundred actually. From my father to Opa."

"Haris? He's alive? What about Monica?"

My heart sinks and I shake my head. Just like Oma, Alice bursts with hope. It makes me wonder at the pain and sadness they have both carried all these years.

"So that part was true." She sighs. "The car accident?"

"No. She caught pneumonia and died in 1964."

"Her health was always fragile." Alice meets my eyes. Then her gaze skitters away as if she's revealed something she shouldn't have. "She was strong in many ways, but fragile too." She takes a deep breath and lets it out slow and long. "So Haris? He's still in East Berlin? Is he still reporting for *Neues Deutschland*? He must be fifty-eight now."

It never occurred to me that Alice knew what my father did or what age he'd be now. I never thought about it. Of course she did. All these years and I never thought to ask her about him.

"What could he possibly write to Papa in a hundred letters? They barely spoke when stuck in the same room."

I shrug, working out what to say, but before I do, she adds, "They're coded, aren't they? Papa taught Haris to spy."

I feel my eyes widen and my jaw drops.

Alice gulps. It makes no noise, but her throat almost convulses with the effort.

"I guess I should go first after all." She lays down her spoon and sets her hands on either side of her bowl upon the table. She presses her palms into the wood, just as Oma did this morning to the scrapbook, and I sense she's grounding herself and gathering courage.

"It's my fault. I should have told you long ago. I should have apologized." She states the words simply, plainly, and adds nothing more.

"What do you mean?"

She swallows hard. "I did this. I ruined your life. I killed my sister." Alice's eyes shine with unshed tears. "You look so much like her, you know, and you could've known her too. Seen her across the Wall. Written her letters. At some level you could have known her."

I feel myself cool. I blink to bring myself back to the present and tell my body to wake up and not faint. I press my lips shut so as not to interrupt.

"When you were born, Monica had hope. She adored you and you gave her that. Her hope didn't die when she passed you to us. It almost grew, for you. Every day she stood on that mound with a smile. Rain or shine. Every single day while you played at the park. But that wasn't enough for me and I ruined it all. I took you away from her and that killed her."

Alice continues to tell me the story of a young girl, full of rebellion and anger. A seventeen-year-old who had been a baby in 1945 as her family fled west to Berlin. So while her parents and older sister remembered the horrors of racing in the midst of the Red Army's surge to Berlin, she carried no visceral fear of the Soviets and remembered no pain from those months. That journey, however, scarred the other three, she said, forever.

But what scarred Alice, and made her angry and fearful, was the Wall. She hated it and she hated the deprivations, limitations, and strictures the Soviets imposed. She was furious she was separated from her older sister, her best friend, and her hero.

"I couldn't talk to Mama the way I could talk to Monica. She was eight years older, but she understood, she listened, and she loved me. I'd come over to your apartment every weekend, and we'd play with you, laugh, and chat all day long. Haris was fun too. He didn't talk much to Mama and Papa, but he talked to me. He took me seriously and used to give me all these books to read, and he treated me like an adult. Even after we moved to the American Sector, I still saw them that month. I crossed to the East as often as Monica crossed to the West. But on that Sunday morning, I looked across that wire and she was a world away. I thought only of me and what I'd lost, and I was heartbroken. Then she threw you to Papa and it was a gift, a part of her.

"I loved having you live with us. I tried to be everything to you she was. You cried most of that first week, but not when I tucked you in bed with me. I held you for a whole week and you started smiling again. And we took you to the park every day. Papa even made sure it was during my school lunch hour so I could be there too and see Monica across the Wall."

I set down my spoon as well. I can't process the kind of love Alice is talking about. I don't remember anything but cool indifference from her—ever.

"Nein," she says, using the German word again. "Eat. You must eat. I can't do this if you're watching me."

I pick up my spoon and take a bite. I can no longer taste the soup, but I obey.

Alice continues, "I joined a tunnel crew. It started with some University boys I knew, and I told them I'd help if Monica could be on their escape list. They added her right away, and we worked every spare minute of every day. We did it too. We dug all the way into East Berlin. Over ten meters right under Bernauer Strasse. But when we pushed through the floorboards of the newly vacated buildings, we were hoisted out by five Stasi. Four of us were seized, and I later heard another died as they attached a fire hose and flooded our tunnel with water."

I can't keep up the pretense of eating any longer. I set down my spoon, and this time Alice doesn't notice. She tells me of the deal she made.

After hours of interrogation, bright lights, and no water or food, she secured her freedom by agreeing to spy in the West for the Stasi. She tells me of the commitment papers she wrote in her own hand and signed. She tells me of the codes they outlined for her and the meeting places they designated. And she tells me of the horrors of the *Jugendwerkhöf*, the juvenile correction and "reeducation" camp they threatened her with if she didn't comply.

The soup sours in my stomach. And just as I am about to push up from the table to go throw up, she lands her last line.

"But I knew what Papa did and what he was, and they did not."

I sink back into my chair. "What do you mean?"

"He tried to hide it, but I was curious. I spied on him, I followed him, I paid attention. Quiet, serious Papa was a spy for the Americans." Alice's eyes glow with a momentary pride before she banks it and settles back into her story.

"After they arrived in Berlin, he gained a reputation for being a good and honest electrician. The government hired him for lots of jobs, and he used that access to install listening devices in Party buildings, even at Stasi offices, while doing the work. I now know they're called wiretaps and bugs, but I didn't know that then. I knew enough to appear compliant, however, to the Stasi and get out of that interrogation room as fast as I could. They never thought to ask about Papa or my family, but they could have. I don't know if I would have had the presence of mind and courage to stay silent if they'd picked up on that secret."

She reaches a hand out to me, then pulls it back. "That's what was my fault, Luisa. Papa moved us here to save me, to keep *me* safe. He didn't need more work and we didn't need more money. As soon as I got home, I pulled him out of our apartment and we went for a walk. I told him everything the Stasi said, did, and threatened. When we got back, he must have reached out to the Americans, because within a day, he'd lied to Mama, wrote a note to your parents, and we were on a plane to here. He took you from your parents to save me."

"And that was right." My head might be full of words and images, but one does shine through. It was right for my Opa to save his daughter. There was nothing else he could have done. Whatever happened after. "Alice, I couldn't be with my parents anyway. Don't forget the Wall. You didn't keep me from them."

"I did and I've never been able to look at you without feeling shame." Tears fall down Alice's face. "For Monica, seeing your smile and watching you grow was enough. I took that from her. My life for hers. And within a couple years, they allowed families to visit for an afternoon. So you see, I did ruin it all."

"One afternoon a year." I scoff. I'd read about it in my father's letters. One afternoon. Tears drop from Alice's chin, but she doesn't swipe at them. I don't think she notices them. "You can't believe that would have been worth your life."

"We couldn't even get word to her. Papa's letter arrived after we left. So the next day when she showed up, we weren't there. And the day after that. Until his letter reached her, telling her we'd never be there again." Alice leans forward. "That's what I needed to talk to you about. I want to ask your forgiveness, especially now that you know about Papa. I never imagined . . ."

Her voice trails away in a sniff, and I want to tell her everything. But confidentiality agreements and years of lying and keeping secrets stand between us. I'm no better or, perhaps, no worse than anyone in my family.

Alice swipes at her eyes and her nose. "Can you forgive me?"

"No."

She pulls back as if slapped.

"I didn't mean it like that. I mean, you don't need it." I reach out with my left hand. My fingers sting upon contact with her hand, but I don't pull away. "You don't need it for getting into trouble trying to save your sister and for Opa moving here to save you. I just wish . . . I wish you'd told me."

Now my tears are falling. "You never talked to me. You always pushed me away, then you left. Why wouldn't you tell me? What was so horrible or dangerous here in DC, not over there, about all this that no one could tell me the truth?"

"Guilt. Fear, I guess. And Oma still doesn't know."

"What?"

"She thought, still thinks, Opa needed more work. If she knows about anything more he did, she never connected it with the move." Alice bites her cheek. It tucks in on one side. "I sense he was afraid she'd be angry with me, so he chose to have her angry with him instead."

"What's real, Alice?" I can't keep the weariness from my voice. I'm suddenly so tired. "Seriously. Tell me what is actually real in our family." I'm including myself in that question—not that I can tell my aunt that.

"I don't know."

When I leave, Alice pulls me into a tight hug. Her hug doesn't feel like one from aunt to niece. It feels like a bond between equals, even friends. It feels like sisterhood and home. I rest in it a moment before she pushes me away and stares at me.

I squirm under her gaze. "I feel like I don't know any of you now."

"We can change that. Please. I've missed you." She laughs, something small, sad, and conciliatory. I hug her tightly again as she speaks into my hair. "What will you do now?"

I step back. "Finish reading the letters. I have about thirty more. Then? I don't know."

Taking them to Andrew Cademan at the CIA comes next, but I can't share that with Alice.

It's a family trait . . .

We all have secrets.

CHAPTER 10

Monday, November 6, 1989

Monday morning I wake curled into a tight ball atop my covers. Opa's scrapbook rests open beside me. I try to straighten my legs and arms but find my knees and elbows stiff. They ache as the muscles release. It was the same dream, the one that haunts me at least twice each week and the one from which Oma jostled me awake on Saturday. The one in which I am floating before pain slashes through me. But now I know it's not a nightmare. It's a memory. It's fear, barbed wire, and a fall that stops inches from pavement.

I close my eyes to let it recede, as it always does in the light of day, only to open them again with the recollection of my final discovery late last night.

If my father still lives, he languishes in a Stasi jail.

I say *languish* because that's what it must be. We talk about it at work. Not the codes we decipher or the messages they relay—those are confidential—but the risks those men and women took and the cost they paid to smuggle their missives out. Most of the codes we work were relayed far in the past, but that doesn't mean some of the people aren't still alive. Somewhere. Maybe free, but most likely not.

And the stories we hear about how the East German Ministry for State Security, the Stasi, treated—and still treats—traitors are some of the worst.

The KGB is ruthless. No one denies that. But the Stasi has perfected an art they call *zersetzung* or "decomposition" that, it's rumored, the Soviets work to emulate. It's the careful, studied, and prolonged application of unrelenting pressure from a variety of sources closing in upon the body and mind simultaneously. When applied outside prison, subjects feel they're going mad—their neighbors are watching them, they make mistakes they don't recall at work, they lose their jobs, their housing association calls and threatens eviction for any number of reasons, a friend disappears for a day or two, then returns silent and suspicious. It goes on and on until the subject becomes so broken, nothing is left but the sweet release of confession within a stark interrogation room. Confession to a crime they often didn't commit in the first place.

But decomposition is quite different if the process is initiated post-arrest. Then the subject is given only enough water to slake their immediate thirst, only enough food to churn their stomach for more, and only enough sleep to keep them alive but not sane. The mind and body physically and chemically break down without sleep, so horns and lights accost prisoners at random intervals, and interrogations are broken up only by minuscule breaks. Night, day, reality, and humanity cease to exist until the Stasi has gained everything the subject knows and even a little they simply make up, prompted by suggestions. Once they write a full confession—if they can still write by that point—they get to sleep. Maybe for a full hour or two.

While this approach is effective within the forty-eight-hour period the Stasi can hold a subject without making an arrest, its real power comes after charges have been filed. Then the Stasi can keep a person incarcerated until trial. And that can be a very, very long time.

I suspect, after what I read last night, that the Stasi had ample reasons to arrest my father and file official charges. If so, he's been in a Stasi jail since about the time of his final letter tucked in the back of Opa's scrapbook, dated May 9, 1989. He's been incarcerated, without trial perhaps, for six months.

I spent all yesterday decoding the letters and marveling at my father's transformation. He traveled from devotee of the Soviet system to questioner to dissident to opposition in a matter of twenty-five years for him and within two days for me. As I moved through the letters, I wrote out all the coded messages and dated them, each making its own short letter, and now, rather than trust their safety to the floorboards in my room, I slide them into a manila folder to carry them to work.

I pull into our parking garage in Arlington, Virginia.

Venona II occupies the fourth floor of a medical office building, and we work behind a sign that reads *Fulton, Sales, and Stein, DDS*. Who's going to suspect an off-books CIA department to hide behind the doors of a nondescript dental office?

I fumble with my bag, trying to extract my key card from the usual chaos, made even worse by the letters and Opa's scrapbook. My hands are still tender and ache, but they no longer throb. The swelling has gone down, and the raw colors have faded. Oma came to my room three times yesterday to reapply her salve.

Sitting there yesterday, watching as she gently massaged it into my hands, I reminded myself that Oma's love is expressed in actions and in service. When I was young, she was the one who came to my room whenever I cried out from the nightmare. She was the one who rubbed my back and sang lullabies, threading her fingers through my hair and cooing that nothing could hurt me while she stood watch. The fierce urgency in her voice when she said it made me believe her, and I slept. Some mornings, I even found her asleep next to me, tipped over, fully dressed, and I knew she'd kept her promise and watched over me all night long. It dawned on me that, along with whatever fear she still carries, she was also trying to protect me.

Seated at my desk, I find myself relaxing within the office's usual thrum. It's a quiet place with little stress. After all, we work the distant past without any tight deadlines pinching us. Aside from Carrie's maternity leave, of course.

A tap sounds on my open door.

"Good morning, sunshine, and how was your weekend?" Carrie lowers herself, using both hands as support, into the chair across from my desk. Today she's wearing a blue-and-white-striped sailor dress with a red bow. This and last Friday's blue dress make me think that, if the Diana haircut framing her heart-shaped face didn't already lead me that direction, she's going for the pregnant-princess vibe now. But she's just missing the mark. Poor Carrie is about five foot nothing, and I doubt even the tall Diana could pull off sailor stripes only two weeks prior to her due date.

"Miserable."

"What happened?"

I open my mouth to tell her everything, then stop. I can tell her nothing. I can't share what's in my bag, and I feel the compromising position I've put myself in. All my rationalizations fade in the bright light of reality. I should have called our boss on Saturday.

I huff a large breath through pursed lips. "Nothing. Oma and I fought."

"You? Fight?" Carrie giggles. She actually giggles.

"What does that mean?"

She shakes her head. "I'm not saying you don't have it in you, but I haven't seen it lately." She spreads her hands atop her belly. She does that now, almost like it's a shelf and her hands must rest there. "Why do you think I come here when something undoes me? You're calm. Methodical. You've become the most placid person I know."

"Become?" I lift a brow. This is getting interesting.

"You've changed. In the past year, you've—"

"That's not fair." I cut her off. "Rather a lot changed around me, you know? I have responsibilities now."

She smiles. It's indulgent, almost patronizing. Motherly too. "We all have responsibilities, Luisa."

"Okay, slow down, Mama Freud."

She huffs. "Fine. You asked."

Except I didn't ask.

We stare at each other for a moment. Carrie relents first. "We watched *Married to the Mob* this weekend. You were right, it was adorable. And Teddy sure thought that Michelle Pfeiffer was cute."

"You should see *Ladyhawke.* She's in that too. It's romantic and wonderful." The tape still sits unwatched on my bedside table. I need to return it to Blockbuster this evening. "You'll love it, but Teddy will hate it."

"Which means I'll adore it all the more." Carrie lifts her nose. "Speaking of adore, what's that smell?"

I look around, then realize she's talking about my hands. Oma's ointment. I've grown so used to the lavender this weekend, I'm immune. I raise my hands, both still lightly wrapped in gauze, not so much for protection as to keep the salve in place.

"What happened? Are you okay?" Carrie is up and out of her seat so fast I smile.

"I'm fine. I reached into the fire to grab something Oma dropped and misjudged the timing, the heat, everything really. I got it all wrong." That is as close as I can come to the truth.

"You poor thing." Carrie wraps me in a quick hug. "It really was a miserable weekend." She straightens. "I know just the cure. We'll all go to B & E for burgers today."

"You and burgers. That kid is going to come out a beef patty." I look to my desk and my hands. "These will slow everything down, and I'm not up for it today. Tomorrow?"

"Sure. We'll cheer you up tomorrow."

She's at the door before I remember what I'm to do, what I need to do. "Andrew's light is out. Is he not coming in today?"

Carrie turns. "He's at Langley today and tomorrow for some meetings. Why?"

We often joke about how little we know or need our boss. I shrug. "Just curious. I haven't seen him in a while."

"Jessica had a sighting last Tuesday. She said he's growing a beard." Carrie laughs and turns to go.

I call her back, willing a casualness into my voice. "How are you coming on your Berlin Letters? Think you'll get them done this week?"

She twists back. More like makes a wide turn. "Thanks to you. I hope to have the whole packet on Andrew's desk Thursday."

"He hasn't seen any of them? He doesn't know about them, the infinity symbol, nothing?" Something sparks within me. Questions regarding how much my boss already knows.

Carrie's eyes flash in question, but I keep my expression blank, and whatever she's thinking passes without articulation. "Nothing. Not yet. They're nothing unusual, other than they stumped me. Are you okay?"

So much for casual.

"I'm tired and feel frazzled. Sorry."

"Of course you do. Go slow today. As we always say, none of this is urgent."

Except some things are.

Carrie waves goodbye and heads across the hall to her office while two diabolical thoughts fill my mind. One, my boss isn't here. So even if I wanted to give him the letters, I cannot. I have to wait and that is not my fault. And two, each Monday we four analysts usually go to lunch together. It was Carrie's idea last year, and it was a good one. It keeps us close and builds friendships, as despite working side by side, we interact little during the day. That means today, everyone—except me—will be at B & E enjoying burgers. Our office will be empty at noon.

Specifically Carrie's office will be empty at noon.

I listen as the office clears for lunch. While the receptionists out front will switch off lunch hours to make sure the front is covered until Carrie, Jessica, and Amy return, the risk of getting caught here in the back is low. Especially as our offices aren't even those new cubicles that are becoming all the rage. We each have our own room—once dental examination rooms—so if I can pass through the hallway without being seen, I should be safe behind Carrie's shut door.

I click my door shut behind me. Who am I, and what have I become in the last two days? Because as much as I pushed back on Carrie this morning, her assessment of me was spot-on. I feel it. Something has changed within me, but not only since Opa died.

If I could put my finger on it, and it feels like I can, it started over seven years ago. I was so certain I had what it took to become operational within the CIA, and discovering I didn't was shattering. My senior year in college, I scored great on the entrance exam. Following graduation, I sailed through all the tests and the training. When assigned for clandestine training at the Farm, I thought I'd hit the jackpot and was prepared for that too. But then I got "sent down" without explanation and I was devastated. Beyond devastated. That was the moment everything shifted, for me and within me.

Daniel and all my class tried to cheer me, because only about half of any class actually graduates from the Farm anyway. They figured I was just the first of many, and there was no shame in that. But there was. I shunned them all—especially Daniel, who'd become not only my best friend, but sparked in me an electric desire for more. I was the worst to him actually. I was humiliated to be weak in front of the one person I wanted to view me as strong, beautiful, alluring. Some of the dismissive things I said still make me cringe. I even skipped out on my own farewell party: brats and brews at a local pub.

I can't say that event broke me; I'm not that dramatic. But such a shift can feel destabilizing. I felt like I'd misread myself and misunderstood who I was at a fundamental level. Moving back in with Oma simply solidified the shift. The soft ground hardened around me. Maybe Carrie is right and I've given up.

But this weekend . . . It's like I can suddenly see and feel through the fog. Like a dormant flame has sparked and either I can go on with my life as is and it will fade away, or I can fan it with one, two, three courageous actions and reclaim me. After all, how can one truly know oneself when everything around them is a lie? I hadn't realized that's how I've been living, but I have. And as the pieces of my world slowly sharpen into focus, so much of my life, my family, even my choices, make more sense.

This is the last piece of the puzzle. After talking with Alice, I'm 99.999 percent sure, but there's still a sliver of doubt that I could be wrong and that the whole truth continues to evade me. I need to know for certain that Opa is the author of Carrie's Berlin Letters. And if so, then I see the straight line to teaching and training my father.

I slip into Carrie's office, flip on the light, and cross the room to her safe. We each have one set within the right side of our desks. Protocol demands that any codes we are not actively working on stay filed within our safes. Once finished, we turn over the entire file—original documentation and our decryption work—to Andrew and move on. At any given time, I'd say we each have about three to five active files stored inside.

On the surface it's a secure approach. But we're an office of code breakers, and each safe has only a four-digit combination. Technically, that's a daunting ten thousand possibilities. But humans hold biases. We aren't random. That cuts the ten thousand down appreciably.

I sit on the floor in front of Carrie's safe and pull my list out of my pocket. Despite telling myself to stop it at least a hundred times, I worked on it all morning. It's every detail I know about Carrie reduced to four-digit numeric codes. Her birthday. Wedding date. Due date. Her initials interwoven with Teddy's. I even estimated Carrie's start date and what dates might have been important at that time versus dates that have only emerged recently. After all, two years ago when she started working here, she didn't have an anniversary date or a due date. While protocol also demands we change our lock combination monthly, we—again, being humans—don't. Odds are we each set it the day we arrived and forgot about it.

I start tapping through my options. I get a little nervous when the obvious numbers fail. Even her dog's name converted to digits fails. Second to last on my list is the day her sister died. I remember it because it falls on Aunt Alice's birthday. December 14. 1214. The safe clicks open. Rather than feel a sense of relief or victory, I feel guilt, as if I've used Carrie's pain against her, to deceive her.

I take a breath and shut down the chaos in my brain. I have a job to do.

Inside I find one file. She really has done a great job clearing everything out before her maternity leave. Opening it, I discover she's already filled out some of the batch assessment form. The correspondence spans from September 1945 to July 1961, and Carrie has, to date, identified eleven different nonstandard acrostic patterns within them.

Eight listed are identical to ones used by my father. I also note that my grandparents arrived in Berlin in July of 1945. If I give Opa a few months to settle and reach out to the CIA, or a few months for American troops to arrive, which they did not until August that year, the timing works. On both ends. My grandparents moved from the Soviet to the American Sector in July 1961, and he would not have been called upon by any East German government office for electrical work after such a "betrayal."

I page past Carrie's notes to the actual letters. How had I not noticed it Friday? Opa's handwriting is beloved and distinct. He was the only person I know who made a swirl at the edge of his lowercase *p*. I pause, missing him so much my heart aches.

I then scan Carrie's decryptions. Alice was right about Opa. He was meticulous and professional, and his messages are lists of the names, dates, and locations of implanted listening devices. I'm impressed. In March of 1961, he planted a device in spymaster Markus Wolf's office. I fleetingly wonder if it's still there until a noise outside reminds me to hurry. I put everything back in Carrie's file and shut the safe's door.

The lock clicks and resets. And I sneak back to my office.

Suspicions confirmed.

I can't sit. But I can't pace around this office all day either. I feel like I'm suffocating. I can't go to Langley and find Andrew. I can't—

There's so much I can't do and only one thing I can. I grab my bag and head down the hallway and through the reception area. To leave out the back door will only raise questions later. Lorna, our receptionist, looks up as I pass.

"I completely forgot a doctor's appointment. I'm not sure I'll be back today."

She smiles, and with her "See you tomorrow" following me out the door, I step out of our office and into the building's lobby. Once in my car, I resist pulling out the letters and the scrapbook. I know there's more to this story, and I suspect Opa has left me all the answers. I simply need to piece them together. Because while my father might have thought he was simply telling Opa stories and facts about his world, using his letters to let go of what he couldn't carry, Opa was a spy, and spies spy. He thought differently than his son-in-law, used information differently, and never would have let intelligence go to waste.

I shove my bag away from me to avoid giving in to temptation. Cameras are mounted all over this parking garage. The other medical offices probably don't know about them, but we do. If I want to spend time digging through all this, it can't be here.

It can't be home either. Oma will freak out if I walk back in our door before my usual time. I pull at the floppy silk bow on my high-necked blouse. What looked classy this morning now feels tight and stifling. Wilted too. I've been so on edge the silk sticks to me.

My stomach reminds me it's lunchtime, and without thinking too much about it, I soon find myself at Opa's favorite deli with a turkey and swiss on rye in my hands. I cross the street to Lacey Woods Park and plop down at one of the picnic tables.

It feels like the safest place in the world right now. With my bag resting on the table in front of me, I look up through the canopy of trees to a bright sunny day. The warm sunshine has taken all the chill from the air, and the temperature must be in the low seventies. The chirping birds remind me of my mother. Rays of sunshine bounce off the leaves and branches above me to scatter drops of liquid gold within the shadows. I almost feel like everything is and will be okay.

Almost.

I pick at my sandwich and stare at my bag, as if once again it's a boa constrictor about to devour me. I crumple the sandwich's wax paper wrapping and concede it already has. I reach for my bag and slide out the manila folder in which I've placed all the letters. I look at my father's handwriting, the breaks in his paragraphs, and I cast back to what I've just seen in Carrie's safe. The two men are so different. Opa's notes were precise. They betrayed no emotion. It was all strictly business.

Not so with my father. Tracing my finger over his words, I sense his anger and despair in the slope of his handwriting, the stray watermark on the page, the tight, almost nonexistent spaces between the letters of that very first letter. His paragraphs lengthen throughout the late sixties into the early seventies as if he's grown more comfortable. Then his Stasi interview in 1978 sends the letters chasing one another across the page. And his discovery in 1982 has him so terrified, the letters sit square and squat with heavy ink deposited on their points, almost as if he has to force the knowledge out of himself.

I can feel him. I know him. I understand his wanting things to be different, his needing an outlet to share them, his frustration at what his life has become.

I close my eyes, fully aware I'm conflating my issues with his, and I wonder how different they truly are. At a basic human level, we both want to thrive—regardless of what is swirling around us. I shake myself back to the job at hand and come to his final letter.

After decoding the contents late last night, I was surprised by his penmanship. I would have expected the angst, fear, anger, even distress to be evident in his penmanship. But instead I found a steady hand, flowing ink with few breaks, and long, eloquent sentences. He was in command. He had accepted his fate.

> Glaring mistakes can be made in any job, I suppose. Sorting them out is often the bigger problem. Correcting them, too, is challenging. Are you right? It's hard to ask oneself that question. But one must if one wants to grow.

ARREST

Paging back through the letters, I strike upon a word in an earlier one. *Hockensperren.* I recognize it as referring to metal shards that filled the trenches within the Death Strip, what my father called the "Buffer Zone." From his letters I gather that if the first wall didn't get you, or the electric fence, or the guards, then those metal shards would tear you apart long before you reached that last ten-foot wall on the western border.

I freeze, catching another name for the shards on the letter's second page. Dragon's teeth. It's such an unusual descriptor, and this is not the only place I've seen it. I pull out Opa's scrapbook and page through it, looking not at the photographs, notes, and memories, but at the newspaper articles.

I find it in 1972.

It invaded my musings without my even realizing it.

> If the first wall didn't . . . the dragon's teeth, metal shards dumped within a ditch, would tear you apart long before . . .

The final puzzle piece drops into place. My thoughts had even conjured the same words—all because I'd read them before. Over my lifetime, probably many times before. I page farther and confirm that the letters inform the articles, which often employ my father's original words, simply translated to English. Opa didn't pass the information to the CIA—or perhaps he did that too. After he passed it to a newspaper.

To Bran Porter of the *Washington Post*.

CHAPTER 11

WASHINGTON, DC

Monday, November 6, 1989

I shove everything into my bag and head to the *Washington Post* building. I don't have to look up the address as it's a huge structure one can hardly miss off Scott Circle with flags and *The Washington Post* scripted in its cursive masthead right over the double doors.

I park in a garage nearby, tuck the letters and scrapbook under my car's passenger seat, and walk toward the building. As I cross the street, still a block away from the newspaper office, I sense someone following me. I try to laugh it off as I've felt that way all morning. Perhaps everyone who is doing something wrong feels that way, but now it's so powerful I turn to look.

There is a tall man behind me. His brown hair, though cut short, curls at the edges. He looks about my age, but that's hard to tell as his focus isn't on me but on a pad of paper in his hand. He looks up, notices me, and his brow furrows. Then, within a step, he does the same—he looks behind him, to see who I must be looking at.

I walk on. I cross the street. He's steps behind me.

I turn the corner. He's still there.

I reach the door, open it, and stall within the large lobby.

He enters behind me and pauses as well.

I can't take it anymore. I spin to face him. "Why are you following me?"

He pulls his neck back, clearly startled and vaguely annoyed. "You're blocking the doorway. Do you mind?" He steps around me and I catch a flash of a press badge clipped to his belt.

"Sorry."

Without acknowledging my apology or looking back, he strides toward the reception desk. Smiling, he waves to the women sitting there as he passes by on his way toward the elevators. I almost laugh at my paranoia, then pause in a moment of unwelcome self-reflection. Is this what the field officer saw? Was I too jumpy then, or have I become jumpy now?

I walk to the first woman in a row of four at the reception desk.

"I'd like to speak to Bran Porter, please."

"Do you have an appointment?" At my headshake, her eyes narrow. "What's your name?"

"Luisa Voekler."

She rests her hand on her telephone, fingers gripping the receiver, but she does not pick it up. "Wait over there, please." With her free hand she waves to a set of benches across the entire lobby. I glance around and note there are much closer benches. Nevertheless, I obey with the suspicion she does not want me to hear her conversation.

She picks up her phone only after I am seated.

A group of schoolchildren enters the lobby. They are loud and jostling and entertaining enough that I don't notice the receptionist waving at me until she stands.

I pop up and cross the lobby.

"I thought I was going to have to whistle for you."

"Sorry about that. I—"

"Take an elevator to the fifth floor. You'll be met right as you step off."

"Thank you," I offer, but she's already moved on to her next task.

The elevator opens on the fifth floor, and like she said, a man is waiting for me. I start to step out, then stop. I know this man.

"I wondered if you'd ever come find me."

Images flood my mind with his voice. It's deep, confident, and carries the same notes of gentle teasing it did when I was young.

"It's you." I step back. "We played chess."

"You were quite good. Do you still play?"

"Not since—" I stop. "I only ever played with you or Opa."

He nods and spreads his arm toward the newsroom. It's chaos in an open floor plan. There are at least fifty people yelling over each other, calling out demands, requests, or just exclamations. Desks are piled high with books and files. One desk's stacks are so high they lean precariously over the edge.

My eyes widen and he laughs. "Not here. We'll never hear each other. Follow me." He turns to the right and along the wall is a series of small conference rooms with glass windows inset into the walls. The third is empty. He steps inside and shuts the door behind me.

The din disappears. I look out the window back into the newsroom. "Is it always like that?"

"This is a quiet day." I feel him step behind me. He's tall enough to peer over my head. "See that woman in the red sweater?"

I sense rather than see a finger pointing over my left shoulder. I keep my eyes on the woman.

"Right where she's standing. That's where Ben Bradlee stood when he yelled, 'Stop the presses' as Watergate broke."

I pivot to face him. "Who's Ben Bradlee?"

"You've been raised poorly."

"I'm kidding. I've seen *All the President's Men*." I smile. "How'd

Robards do?" I refer to the actor who played Bradlee in the Oscar-winning film.

"He was spot-on. The yelling. The desk thwapping. All of it. Even Bradlee was pleased with the performance. The role won Robards an—"

"An Oscar," I interrupt, then press my lips tight so as not to do it again.

Bran's mouth turns slowly into a smile as if he knows more about me than I know about myself. "It was a great movie."

He lifts his gaze above my head again, and I face the window once more. "See the guy in the blue sweater vest? That's where I was standing when I heard about my first Pulitzer for one of my articles informed by your grandfather's information. It was the first of many."

A glance reveals Bran's face is soft with memory and, absent of animation, I suspect he's in his midsixties. He's probably a few inches taller than I am, heavyset but not heavy. He reminds me of a younger version of my grandfather in many ways. It's in the eyes. Intelligent, assessing, yet caring too.

"We were a good team," he continues. "I respected Walther very much, and I like to think we did some good too. We let people know what was going on over there at a time when few others were able to do it."

Bran glances at his watch. His face fills with a tight concerned look. "This is unexpected, Luisa, and I want to give you more time, but I have an interview with a senator in about twenty minutes and I can't be late. I'm sorry, but can we set another time to talk?"

I gulp. I have so many questions. More than I had even a half hour ago when I first realized I needed to speak with him. "I should've called."

He blows a quick exhale as if to say I am not to worry about that.

"I'll tell you what. Let's meet at my club for lunch tomorrow. We can talk there. The University Club on Sixteenth Street Northwest. Say noon?"

"Thank you."

"You are welcome." He reaches out and squeezes my arm just below my shoulder. "It's good to see you. I'm glad you reached out. There are things to say."

"Yes." I nod, feeling small and confused because now I remember him. I remember afternoons in the park, ice cream cones, and chess games. All of which ended when I was around eight or nine. It wasn't anything major or even spoken about. Opa simply quit taking me to the park. We did other things together on the weekends but never with Bran again. Those afternoons disappeared without my noting it.

I step toward the door.

"Luisa, did you come because he told you about me before he died? Did he tell you about our articles?"

"No. He put them all in a scrapbook and read them to me over the years, but I thought it was because they were about home for him. Then this weekend I found my father's letters. I pieced together the connection to you only about an hour ago."

"I'm sorry." He pauses. I sense the sentiment covers far more than that discovery and this moment. "That was just about the only issue over which your grandfather and I fought. We became good friends over the years, and I thought he should have told you everything long ago."

"Why didn't he? Why was he so against it?"

Bran leans against the conference table, and for a few tense seconds I don't think he'll answer me.

"He was afraid he'd lose your love and your trust. Afraid Haris would never get out and you'd be left in limbo. You'd already lost your father, you see, so Walther contended if you knew Haris was alive, you'd be forever in a state of losing him. If that makes sense."

"It does. I think."

"It did to me, too, though I still thought it was wrong. It was your choice, not his, how you dealt with that information." He glances at his watch again.

"Thank you. I'll be at the University Club at noon." Hand on the doorknob, I twist to face him once again. "There are details in those letters, intelligence not really meant for the public. How did you know what you could print and what you could not?"

"I vetted everything with the CIA. I'd been around long enough even at our beginning to know I needed to do that."

"Could you tell me who you worked with?"

Bran tilts his head as if I might be crossing a line, but then with the minutest shrug, I sense him relent. "Come to my desk. I was assigned a new man a few years ago. I've got his card."

He opens the door and the chaos of the newsroom grabs my attention again. We stop at a desk on the edge of the room, and Bran reaches into a packed Rolodex. He flips through A . . . B . . . C . . . and pauses. "Better yet, I think it best not to surprise him. Let me reach out, and if he says it's okay to pass along his name, I will."

I open my mouth to protest, but he stops me with a raised hand. "If it comes to pleading, I'll do it. I want you to get your answers, Luisa, but I need this contact. I can't jeopardize it."

I nod.

"I'll call if he gets back to me tonight, and if not, I'll still share everything else I know with you tomorrow at lunch. Sound good?"

It did sound good. Not great, but good.

Again, I nod. "Thank you."

CHAPTER 12

Haris Voekler

EAST BERLIN

Thursday, September 23, 1971

I'm a babysitter now?"

"You are what I say you are." Koch stares at me. Something flickers in his expression. "Schneider is new and raw, but he'll make a good reporter. He must."

It's that last short sentence that clues me in that *Neues Deutschland*'s publisher, Dietrich Koch, is on the line as much as I am. If this young Manfred Schneider "must" succeed, it means he "must" have friends in high places.

"It's an awfully big story." I push back one more time, certain it will get me nowhere.

"And it's his. So you'd better help him make it a good one."

It's a thinly veiled threat, of course, but that's what we're reduced to. Koch, me, anyone and everyone who needs to get something done and has to rely upon others to do it. Because if they fail, we fail, and if you are the publisher of the Party's newspaper, the cost for failure can be extremely high.

As a country, we are at an inflection point. After years of hard-line Soviet-Stalinist policies, a new reformer—with a gentle boost from Moscow, Koch told me—deposed General Secretary

Walter Ulbricht in May's elections. The new general secretary of the Central Committee of the Communist Party, Erich Honecker, is full of promises for transformation and cultural diversity. Already he's loosened some of the travel regulations. Those with family in West Berlin can accept visits now on predetermined days. He's also reduced the restrictions on radios. One used to risk arrest if their radio antenna pointed west. No longer.

Objectively, these reforms are good for us. But Honecker has also demanded a full series of articles to promote both them and him. That worries me. If the reforms are real and true and the first in a path toward reform, why push them on the public? The public will scoop them up and love him for them. Yet perhaps these gestures are all Honecker will pursue, and he needs us to make them feel larger than they are. My growing suspicion is that he believes we'll be satisfied with so little substance if seasoned and served with a bit of propaganda.

After all, as secretary for State Security, Honecker served as Ulbricht's right-hand man when the wall went up in '61. He was directly in charge of the logistics required to surreptitiously buy such vast quantities of barbed wire from abroad and in such small and diverse orders that no one suspected anything. He was calculated, precise. I would say he was diabolical. He also voted, within the Politburo, to increase the Ministry for State Security's budget annually every year he served in office.

Bottom line: I bet anytime Honecker gives something with his right hand, he will use his enlarged and improved Stasi, controlled by his left hand, to snatch it back.

And this is my chance to find out.

Today's interview isn't with Honecker. We've had several of those, and he's got his pithy statements down pat and delivers them with aplomb. No, today *Neues Deutschland* was "asked" to send a reporter to interview Stasi Chief Erich Mielke. A glimpse into Mielke's priorities will, by extension, clarify Honecker's mindset, mandates, and intentions—if the right questions are asked.

And Koch, chain-smoking and fidgety, is sending a twenty-one-year-old kid to handle the interview.

"Perhaps if we go toge—" I cut my final plea short at Koch's glare.

"Give up, Voekler. You know you can't get anywhere near Mielke or Stasi headquarters." He sighs as if we've covered this trodden ground far too often. "It's been years since your in-laws left and maybe time could have softened the Stasi. But the letters, Voekler. There's no getting around those."

So many thoughts fly through my brain at once. First, I must school my expression. And second, I must remind myself it's not the codes he's referring to; it's simply innocent letters to my father-in-law in America. Granted, I knew—everyone knows—the Stasi reads almost all our mail and certainly any post we send abroad. But the fact that Koch, my boss, has been informed or kept apprised of my actions is new. Part of me is horrified, another part shocked, and the most significant part is impressed—it's quite a show of power for Koch to reveal knowledge of my most intimate affairs.

"She's my daughter. What am I supposed to do? I love her. Wouldn't you write?" I pitch my voice as if pleading, implying that I write to Luisa. But I'm a liar and I pray he doesn't know enough to call me out on it.

I don't write to my daughter. She doesn't even know I'm alive. And I'm too much of a coward to tell her the truth now. What would she think of me? What would she think of who I've been and the lies I've told? Would she blame me for her mother's death?

So many questions keep me awake deep into the night but never flow from my pen. I'm too terrified of the answers.

But I want to know about her. Reading about her days and accomplishments constitutes the best part of my life, and I wait for each of Walther's letters like a man dying of thirst. Through his words I envision my sweet daughter's smile, her laugh, her little hand holding her pencil, or her little legs pumping her bicycle pedals. She's thirteen now and just won a math competition, but she's still little to me. She is two, three, and finally four—the age she was when I last saw her. Walther doesn't send pictures. I've asked him not to. To see her grown might prove too painful.

Yes, I'm a coward. I haven't the fortitude to tell her I'm alive, see her picture, or answer all the questions she'd ask if she knew me. I can't imagine how many she would have if she knew even a portion of my story. Isn't it funny I assume she thinks like me? And, like me, I believe she'd have questions to ask and answers she believes she deserves.

Koch shakes his head. It tells me that while he may feel pity for my situation, it hardly matters. He gestures to the door. "Prepare Schneider for the interview, then help him write it up when he gets back. I want it to run tomorrow. First in a four-part series."

I leave Koch's office and I go do my job. Young Manfred Schneider sits waiting in a chair he's pulled up to my desk, full of the same energy, drive, and commitment I wore like a gold star fifteen years ago. I drop into my chair and shift it forward. The metal legs squeal in protest against the linoleum floor. Heads bent over Schneider's notepad, we spend the next hour reviewing his interview approach. I cull out the obvious and mundane questions and wonder if Mielke will dare to answer the subtler ones I add. I then send Schneider on his way, like a boy in shorts called to the principal's office on his first day at school.

Four hours later Manfred returns wide-eyed and pale. "They took my recorder."

"I warned you they would." I flick an impatient hand at the chair he left next to my desk. "Did you at least take notes?"

He flexes his fingers. "Tons of them." He slumps into the chair. "You've never seen anything like it. The headquarters are so grand. So great. They gave me a full tour. You haven't been, have you?"

"No."

"There's a cinema, restaurants, shops, a large grocery store, a barber shop . . ." His eyes widen farther. "There are over forty buildings laid out in concentric squares."

"You can't write any of that."

I don't tell him the Stasi would not allow their inner structure, or extravagance, to be published. I also don't tell him that's how the Stasi forge unity and commitment. Stasi officers shop, eat, and enjoy amusements together. They vacation together. They live in neighborhoods together. They are purposely inserted into every aspect of each other's lives so as not to step outside them. In fact, working for the Stasi is generational too. Sons follow fathers in a never-ending thread of commitment. I narrow my eyes. Considering Koch's demeanor this morning, Manfred must have insights or knowledge into at least some of this.

I venture a test. "How is this new to you? You have family in the Stasi."

"My uncle and cousin have always worked abroad."

I keep my expression bland. It's all Manfred offers and I don't ask for more.

He looks around the newsroom and lands his gaze back on my desk, and his brow furrows. I sense he's just noticed that we are sitting at my desk and not his. I may be older, but by what he's seen and heard—by what he's been allowed to see and hear—he knows he has eclipsed me. His star is rising fast. The first glimmers of pride and scorn dance in his brown eyes, and he refocuses his attention on me. Our next discussion will take place at his desk. The power dynamic between us shifted quickly. Two days on the job, and in one look, he's the senior reporter now.

I glance down, conceding his position in our hierarchy of two. It's a small price to pay for the answers I want. And he's not wrong. If what I suspect is true, Schneider has been groomed for this position his entire life. A Stasi uncle living abroad, powerful enough to pull his son along with him—because it must be a son—is most likely not Manfred's highest connection. I now suspect a Politburo or cabinet-level father here at home.

We review Manfred's notes and select the best quotes. Mielke has given him canned answers promoting a friendlier Stasi and a stronger state security to support our people and the Party's "Unity of Economic and Social Policies" platform. He also spoke of new initiatives and programs, new "streamlined procedures."

Which means he has been given an increased mandate and more funding.

"He said this number?" I point to Manfred's notes. "Are they really hiring that many new officers?"

"Not this year, but over the next several."

I merely nod as if such a fact is neither good nor bad, but simply a fact. The truth is, I'm crushed. Everything Manfred learned confirms my worst fears. Yes, the Soviet-Stalinist policies were stifling and soul-crushing, but they came at you head-on. You saw them before they hit you. Honecker is giving with one hand, tempting us to relax with reforms we will relish, but rather than taking with the other, he's clearing the board. The Stasi was never created to support our people—the Ministry for State Security was created to protect the Party *from* our people. And he is enlarging and expanding it beyond reason.

"They are also expanding the *Inoffizielle Mitarbeiter* program, but that's not for print."

I can't stop my eyes from widening, but I keep my mouth shut. Mielke must trust Manfred a great deal to be so open. The *Inoffizielle Mitarbeiter*, or snitches, are made up of ordinary citizens who are either coerced or "invited" to spy on friends and neighbors for the Stasi. Some people, of course, do actually volunteer for that duplicitous job as well. I check my judgments with a soft, still voice and the admission that there was a time long ago when, if asked, I might have volunteered too. I shake my head to bring my thoughts back to Manfred and his article.

He continues talking, unaware my focus faltered. He is so young and so pleased with his knowledge, and proud to convey it. "The goal is to have at least one informant in every apartment, group, club, office, and factory. It's very impressive."

"Very."

After Manfred has shared almost every word of the interview, we decide his lead and layout before I send him back to his desk to write it up. He'll bring it back to me for editing and a final check, like the copy editor I suspect I've become. Then I'll send it down to be typeset for print in tomorrow's morning edition.

At day's end I walk home, as I do most days. Rain or shine, and always alone. Manfred left before I did today. Another power move, but I don't mind. I prefer it, really.

It wasn't always this way. Not my days. Not my life. There was a group of us living on Rheinsberger Strasse who walked the same route home each night. We'd wait for each other and tread the blocks together, chatting about our work, our families, and our wives. And even when we walked in silence, that felt good too. We'd grown up together. They were my best friends.

Now I feel most free outside and alone. We've scattered across the city—all of us moved from the old neighborhood when the wall went up and the Buffer Zone was created. A couple of us escaped. Another died trying. Sometimes I wonder: Do Jakob, Oscar, and Emil walk home alone now, as I do, or do they keep in touch? Are they happy? I could ask. I could reach out. I could find them. But I don't. I walk on.

Usually I watch my feet. I cover miles step by step and tell myself it's so I don't trip on the uneven pavement. Really it's because I don't want to see the buildings and the old neighborhoods. I don't want to see the ghosts, the rubble, and the work left undone. I don't want to see the new buildings and the work that has been done.

When we first married, Monica and I would walk the city together. We'd leave our apartment early on a Saturday morning and head to our favorite bakery on Friedrichstrasse. If it was a fine day, we'd amble for hours hand in hand. I loved Berlin and I loved sharing the city with her. I still love this city, though our relationship has changed without Monica to share in it.

Back then, I'd stop and point at the buildings, almost as if introducing her to old friends, and tell her where my father grew up or my grandfather, and tell her about my big plans, my great dreams, and where I would take her to live one day.

"You belong in the bel étage." I looped my arm around her and pulled her close one morning and pointed to a late-nineteenth-century building's second floor. I felt so smart and worldly at her lost look. "It's the beautiful floor. See? The apartments on that floor, the second floor, are off the street's dust and noise, but below the city's rising heat. Look . . ." I curved my hand and gestured to the plaster arches above each window. "The windows are longer and more ornamental, and the ceilings inside are higher too. All that detail lets you know that's the place to go, the place to aspire to, the beautiful floor."

Now I walk alone, head down, and that is why it took me far too long to recognize the ornamentation chipped away and the very notion of the bel étage being destroyed. I saw only what I wanted to see—in my memories. It wasn't until seeing jackhammers three years after they began that I figured out they were tearing off the ornamentation, not to update the buildings, but to make us believe in their new way of thinking and living. Every floor was equal. We were equal. We could not dream. We were not self-determining, and we could not aspire to the bel étage if there was no bel étage.

The State's new buildings all look the same too. Every apartment identical, as every man, woman, and child is identical in its estimation. The new buildings are also situated on the streets at odd angles. It took me a while to figure out the thinking behind that—it's to keep us from the life of the street and a sense of continuity. The angles and interior focus keep us watching each other. They uproot our homes as they uproot both our individuality and our communities.

The walk home to my new apartment off Karl-Marx-Allee is a couple miles longer than my commute to my long-ago home on Rheinsberger Strasse. My ankle aches. I'm forty now, so I suppose it's inevitable. My dark hair is streaked with grey as well. In many ways, I am starting my own long and slow crumble. Just like my home.

I turn the corner and the warren of buildings sits before me. Mine is the second building to the left, set at a diagonal behind this one at the corner. Seven buildings make up this complex, all identical prefabricated concrete monstrosities with central heating, warm water, and private bathrooms. At least that was the promise. Though my building is only a few years old, my water is rarely warm and my unit was so cold last winter I wore two pairs of socks and a wool cap to bed. I feel surrounded and watched all the time. A fish lapping around a small bowl. It's why I walk until I can't and I must go home to eat, rest, and start the day again when the sun rises once more.

I climb the stairs to the fifth floor. The elevator broke two months ago. I open the hall door to a cheery voice saying, "You're home early."

I glance at my watch before addressing my neighbor Peter. He's right. I walked faster tonight and meandered less. I narrow my eyes. "You're early too."

Peter Sauer is an office manager for a division of Siemens, and his factory is situated right outside the city. He's not usually home at this hour either.

He laughs. It's become a game to point out each other's "bad" behavior. "We shut down production early for the quarterly review. What's your excuse?"

"I'm just good. I got all the work done."

Peter laughs again. He does that and it's infectious enough to make me smile. "Do you have dinner plans?"

My smile broadens. Peter's wife, Helene, started a campaign a few weeks ago to feed me better. It's a plan I like very much. "Give me a few minutes to settle in." I assume the invitation and Peter nods confirmation.

"Come over whenever. She's already started cooking." Peter winks. "Helene was home early too."

I walk two doors past his, and as I insert my key, the door at the end of the hall opens. I acknowledge Frau Hemmel, but rather than broaden my smile in a true greeting, I narrow my eyes. She stares at me, then closes her door quickly. Ever aware of my comings and goings, but not overly friendly, I doubt she's spoken more than a dozen words to me since I moved in over a year ago. Now, after my talks with Manfred today, my feelings toward her have skewed toward paranoid. The article isn't even printed, the new quota on snitches not even met, and it's already effective. My heart quickens with a wariness of Frau Hemmel as I guess at what rewards she might receive for agreeing to spy on me.

I open the door to my apartment and stand for a second inside without moving. I don't switch on a light or even shut the door behind me. I simply stand and absorb the empty, dark, and quiet space. It feels like what I deserve.

Still without light, I cross the living room to the bedroom. In the corner I have placed a small desk. I pull out the central drawer and reach up to the folder I've taped there. Inside is my current letter to Walther. It's been seven years since I started writing to him and since he started writing back to me.

During the first year of our communication, he taught me how to hide messages. In his very first letter, he described how Luisa loved dot-to-dot drawings and admonished me to try one too. His sentences were so oddly warm, especially as Walther never liked or missed me, that I simply stared at the letter. I stared so long I finally found the dot. It took several hours more to figure out what to do with it. But once I did, I read within,

> We miss you. Everything is going well. Luisa loves dot-to-dot drawings. Can't you just imagine her happy face as she finds the completed picture? Oma tries to help. Me, I let her be. Eventually she finishes the picture and is so proud.

WELCOME

That was his most basic code, but he didn't stop there. Every letter for the next year offered a new cipher to break before I could read his hidden words and they became my lifeline. Between my long walks and the ability to write my real thoughts to someone, I don't feel like I'm losing myself anymore. I'm not drowning. I'm not who I thought I'd be or who I want to be, but I'm no longer disappearing.

I review what I've written and add what I learned today about the Stasi and Chief Mielke. It hardly matters to my father-in-law that the Stasi have a barber and a grocery store within their complex, but it is indicative of their size and power and the pervasive hold they have over their officers' lives, and therefore the country. Living in America, I sometimes wonder if Walther cares about any of this. But that's not why I write, so I keep at it, and I suspect he knows that too. He doesn't need to read it so much as I need to say it.

A knock sounds on the door and I slide my unfinished letter back into its homemade sleeve. I survey the desk to make sure everything is put away properly and give a final check of the entire apartment to confirm nothing looks out of place.

Peter leans against the wall across the hall. "I was beginning to wonder if you'd gone out."

"Nein." I look back into my apartment. It's sterile, empty. I can't say I was cleaning or sorting or anything. There's so little of me there. "I got distracted."

"You need a wife." He laughs. "Come on. Helene has outdone herself tonight."

Our friendship is fairly new. A year old, but even that feels new. Or maybe I'm simply more guarded and quiet. Whatever the reason, I haven't told Peter and Helene about Monica or Luisa. It's time.

After a good dinner, we laugh at their boys' antics until they are called off to bed. Dirk, the older dark-haired one, is thirteen, Luisa's age, while the younger Traeger is just a year behind. Watching them makes me miss her. I can almost feel what strength her arms might hold if she hugged me tight. But I know, especially when watching these boys, that she might refuse to hug me at all. Just like these two, she probably complains about homework, laughs loudly, and has opinions that do not originate with her grandparents. Just like these boys, she is entirely separate, perhaps exasperating, and might deny a hug simply because she can.

Walther wrote that Luisa rides her bike to school each day and refuses to stop, even when snow falls, which I gather is a rare occurrence where they live. He also wrote that she was up and riding at his first push down the street. What a wonder! I never could get the hang of riding a bicycle. Monica used to laugh at me for it, but I grew up here in Berlin. Life was a game of survival and the city in turmoil much of my life. There was no time to learn, nor did we have the smooth pavement to make learning easy. At least that's my excuse.

Luisa is also good at math. Another wonder. Numbers are not my forte either, but I have no ready excuse for that one.

The boys bathe and come back to the living room to tell their parents good night. No hugs are given, despite Helene's requests. As the boys trudge off to their room, the clean scent of them hits me and my mind drifts back to my daughter. Does Luisa smell like sunshine and soap? Is her soap different from what we have here?

I hear their door click shut, and I tell Peter and Helene about Monica and Luisa. I have felt dishonest lately not sharing my family with them when they have welcomed me so warmly into theirs. Poor Helene is in tears within moments.

Peter leans forward, hands steepled on his knees. "I can't believe I said that to you, out in the hallway before dinner."

"You didn't know."

"I still apologize." He sits back. "Did you try to leave, after she gave Luisa to her parents?"

Helene's eyes widen. These are not subjects one talks about. But sometimes friendship takes risk.

"I did. For Monica. She'd given up on life and I believed that was the only way to save her, but I couldn't find a way." I leave it at that. I don't say I tried for a time to get us both out. That is more than anyone needs to know.

A couple hours later, I leave their apartment and I feel lighter. I feel like someone other than Walther carries a little of my story. As I put my key into my door, Frau Hemmel opens hers again.

"Is your heat better now? I am so cold."

I stand with my key in the lock. Her tone is unexpected. It's open, almost pleading, and frail. It takes me a moment to get past chastising myself for suspecting her to start processing her question.

"My heat?"

"The workmen who came yesterday." She points a finger, swollen and red with arthritis, at my door. "They said they installed a new heater, but refused to do the same in mine. Can you ask? You must have connections to get one. I am afraid of winter. It was so hard last year."

"I will check." I turn the key, push open my door, and glance into my dark apartment. "Yes. I will ask. I will try to help you, of course."

She thanks me and disappears into her apartment once more. I enter mine and close the door behind me. As before, I stand there assessing the space, but that is all that is the same. Instead of feeling still, bored, even slightly depressed, I find my heart beating so hard it pulses in my ears.

It takes me a full minute to calm before I can flip on the light. I look around. My eyes canvass the couch, the chair, the oven, and the counters in the kitchen. I cross to the doorway to my bedroom. I see the desk. I stare at it and wonder what, if anything, I missed earlier, and if that *one* thing would be the thing to get me arrested.

I cast back to coming home. Was the letter exactly where I usually paste it to the top of the drawer? Did the paper slide out ink up and upside down as I always put it away?

As I tear each of Walther's letters into tiny bits, then drop them in trash bins on my way to and from work, I don't fear anything from his letters. I fear something being found within my own.

I cross to the kitchen and pour myself a glass of water. I choke trying to swallow it. I rest my palms against the counter and try to think. What would they do? What could they find? I look to the closet right next to the front door. I don't want to approach it. I don't want it to be true. I turn the knob with so much dread that an anxious laugh bubbles into my throat. It's as if I expect a dragon to be crouched within. There is no dragon, but there is no new heating unit either.

I stare into my main room again and remember a conversation

with an interview subject years ago. Back when I was *Neues Deutschland*'s top reporter and Party bureaucrats, VoPo, and Stasi wanted to talk with me, sharing insights in hopes I'd quote them, give them publicity, and elevate their status. One told me the best place to hide listening devices was in outlets, because they are virtually undetectable—who takes apart their outlets?—and are wired to a perpetual power source. No batteries required.

I pull a screwdriver out of a kitchen drawer and twist off the small screws of the outlet by my front door. I find nothing strange inside.

I open another on the far wall. Nothing.

I open the living room's third and last outlet. Inside I find a small, black, rectangular device with a mesh side and a single thin wire threaded into the electrical wire.

I'm no longer worried about Koch knowing I write to my daughter or Manfred eclipsing me at work. I'm worried about *zersetzung*, the Stasi speciality of decomposition, and if this is just the beginning.

CHAPTER 13

Luisa Voekler

WASHINGTON, DC

Monday, November 6, 1989

As I leave the *Washington Post* building, I glance at my watch. Four o'clock. I can't go home and I can't go back to the office. I find myself driving around to kill time, then realize it's too much time to kill driving.

A sign for *The Fabulous Baker Boys* catches my eye, and I'm reminded of Carrie's comment this morning about Michelle Pfeiffer. I turn into the cinema parking lot and decide to catch her newest film.

But it's already started. I'm left with a choice between John Travolta's romantic comedy *Look Who's Talking* or the Shakespearean drama *Henry V*, starring Kenneth Branagh. War, intrigue, blood, and death feel more up my alley tonight.

With dinner in hand—a large bucket of popcorn and a Sprite—I settle in for the show ready to let my weekend, the letters, Oma, Opa, Alice, and Bran Porter go.

And I do, quite successfully, until Branagh makes me pick everything up again.

I am not sure what I expected. I never read *Henry V* in school. While I didn't expect a romp like *A Midsummer Night's Dream* or *As You Like It*, which I did read in tenth grade, I certainly didn't expect such a violent battle or such a powerful call to courage, to brotherhood, to arms, and to a virtuous fight. I didn't expect his rousing St. Crispin's Day speech to put me on the edge of my seat, my heart expanding as I eagerly digested every word. I certainly didn't expect a movie to ignite a lightning bolt of conviction that tells me no matter the struggle, no matter the cost, I need to get my father out of that Stasi jail.

What?

The credits roll and I'm left staring at a black screen with the magnitude of this realization weighing within me. A shuffling teenager with a broom finally asks me to leave.

I gather my trash, swipe my eyes, then drop to my chair again. I had no idea I was crying. But I was. I am. I sit ashamed at how I've been internalizing these letters, as if all this was directed at me, for me, and yet they were kept from me.

None of it was about me. Or not just me. Opa and my father, even my mother when she told Haris Opa's secret. Oma and Alice. Bran Porter. They are all part of a much larger story than how it affected one small girl growing up. One woman with a host of questions now.

And my father is in prison! A Stasi prison! How have I been living with that thought and not viscerally registering its horror?

I drive home with endless plans cycling through my brain. Harebrained schemes that have no hope of working because I have no idea how to put them into action. My mind dashes back to my few months at the Farm, and while much of what we learned was about honing instincts and acumen, a great deal was about planning and preparation. I need to slow down, assess my assets and liabilities; I need to find allies. At the very least, I need to get myself to West Berlin. Fast.

From there . . . who knows?

I pull into the driveway. Oma has left the light above the back stairs on and I note she has planted her peas and oats. The raised beds are no longer churned but patted smooth. Dark lines show where she has watered.

I open the back door slowly so it won't squeak and walk with careful steps to the refrigerator. The popcorn wasn't enough and my stomach demands real food. My heart softens at the sight of a full dinner on the second shelf. A steak. A sweet potato. Broccoli. I pull out the food and wish we had a microwave oven. But they're expensive and Oma doesn't trust anything that cooks food in less than a few hours. Rather than turn on the oven and wait, I sit at the table, remove the plastic wrap on the dinner, and dig into it cold. That's when I notice the hall light is still on. It's our signal for me to check the pad by the telephone. It means I've missed a call.

Call Bran Porter.

Next to his name she's written both his number and a question mark. I smile. She's not questioning if she got the number right; she's asking if he's a prospective suitor or a "nice young man" I should consider dating. As if that's what keeps me from dating—I'm too picky.

That answers one question. Oma does not know Bran Porter.

I lift the handset off the cradle and stretch the twenty-foot cord into the kitchen. It comfortably reaches the table, which is why I bought the cord for Oma last year. She never tells anyone who calls that she's in the middle of lunch or dinner or a cup of tea. Until this long cord, she simply stood in the hallway listening to whoever called her, letting life in the kitchen grow cold.

"Porter speaking."

"Hi, Mr. Porter. It's Luisa." I pause, unsure what to say next.

"I'm sorry to call you tonight, but this couldn't wait until lunch." He, too, pauses and I almost interrupt, but he starts up before I can. "I called my contact at the CIA. He wants to meet you tomorrow morning at Langley, 8:00 a.m. Have you ever been there?"

"Yes. I can find it."

"Good. Go to the main entrance and ask for . . . Do you need a pen?"

"Oh." I jump from the chair and step to the hallway where Oma and I keep a small pad of paper and a jar of pens and pencils. "I'm ready."

"Great. 8:00 a.m. Ask for Andrew Cademan. C-A-D-E-M-A-N. You got that? Cademan. And here's his number if something comes up or you have any trouble."

I'm frozen. I can't think. I can't write. I can't speak. He recites the number, but I don't hear a digit. I don't need to.

I know my boss's phone number by heart.

CHAPTER 14

LANGLEY, VIRGINIA

Tuesday, November 7, 1989

I don't sleep. The world blurs around 2:00 a.m. so I do crawl into bed, but I don't sleep.

This morning, I'm the one downstairs early enough to make the coffee. I'm almost out the door when Oma enters the kitchen. She looks at me warily as if unsure how to approach me. I'm too tired to engage, so I simply pour her a cup of coffee.

"Did you work very late last night?"

I rinse my cup. "A little. I'm sorry I missed dinner, and I need to head to work early this morning." I pick up my bag and stall. There are things I should say. I have no idea what they are, but they're poking at me.

"Yes." She nods as if nothing needs to be said. I appreciate that. "Work is important. You should put the rest behind you. Maybe it is best if you destroy those letters."

I close my eyes. That was not quite what I was expecting. I set my bag down and try for honesty with her as well. "Like you tried to destroy the scrapbook? I can't do that, Oma. These letters are a big deal."

"You must." Her lips tremble. Actually tremble. "They'll come for you."

"Who will?"

"The men. The men with the badges. They knock on the door and they ask all sorts of questions. They came before and asked about Opa, about me, and about you. Whatever he did, he put you in danger and now you've opened it again. It's never over, and if you keep asking, they'll come back. They'll take you away."

I reach for her, but she pulls away. I step forward and reach again. "Sit, Oma. Come sit down."

Only when she is seated and I am sitting across from her do I ask her to explain again. In broken words and in as close to a state of sheer panic as I've ever seen her, Oma describes two men coming to our home once when Opa was out working and grilling her about him, me, and herself. The questions went on for over a half hour.

I'm almost in a panic myself when something she says cues another memory. Right before I got transferred from budgeting to Venona II, my best friend, Susie, called me up. "Two men with badges came around asking about you today. All very cloak-and-dagger, Luisa. What's up?"

I laughed it off and didn't think about it again. I knew about the first round right after college. It was only Opa home that time and he believed my story about it being a normal process for all government employees. It never occurred to me that they came to my house again for another round of background checks when I joined Venona II. "When was this, Oma? A couple years ago?"

She blinks. "Yes."

I hold both her hands in mine. Lightly. Mine are still raw and tender, but holding her feels important despite the sting it causes. She looks down and unclenches her fingers within my hands. "It wasn't anything Opa did. That wasn't about him. It was a security check for my job. I do the accounting and budgeting for several government departments, and they needed to make sure I am honest."

"Of course you are honest." Her quick defense broadens my smile.

"And that's what they determined."

"It was you? Not Walther?"

"Not Opa. I promise. It was a standard checkup about my character. I'm sorry they scared you. What did Opa say?"

"I thought it was like Berlin. We had so many secrets there. I—" She swallows and her eyes fill with tears. "I never told him. I thought if he found out he might do something. Something that could make it worse somehow."

I pull her into a hug. "I'm so sorry, Oma. I'm sorry you didn't know."

Moments later I hear a sniff, I feel her stiffen, and I know she's pulled herself together. Time to get on with the morning. I kiss her cheek and head out the back door.

I haven't been to Langley in a couple years now, not since I moved from budgets to cryptology. As I turn off Route 127 and the main building comes into view, I am again awed by the sheer mass of it and devastated all over again at my rejection. That's what it was, what it felt like, and it was far worse than any of those "let's just be friends" notes from long ago.

As I drive through two security gates, I wonder where my classmates are now and who made it into clandestine service. Who got cut? Who has left altogether? I think about Serita, a year older than me, with dark hair, the most innocent face, and the most brilliant mind. I think of Daniel. Tall, strong, with eyes so observant and a mind that could bend around problems instantaneously. Good looking too. And shoulders . . . I stop myself there as that's a pointless road I cannot travel again.

I find a spot in the visitors' lot and head to the front door. Technically I suppose I could use the side employee entrance, but that doesn't feel right. Technically I'm not supposed to be here now and find it interesting Andrew has summoned me here rather than meeting me at our offices.

After I push through the main doors, the crest on the floor stops me cold. It's a huge circle of black-and-white marble with *Central Intelligence Agency* arced across the top that meets *United States of America* arcing up from the bottom. The words encircle the eagle and shield. Swamped by that same corrosive mix of unworthiness and shame, I almost can't bring myself to walk over it, then think how silly I'll look tiptoeing around it.

I step forward and a security officer directs me with a two-fingered motion to the right side of the lobby where a receptionist sits, fully aware of my every step. I slide her my badge and request to see my boss, Andrew Cademan.

She nods, directs me to step back, and taps on the largest phone board I've ever seen. She says a few soft words into her headset before she lifts her face to me again. "Mr. Cademan will be right down, Ms. Voekler."

Within seconds Andrew crosses the lobby toward me. "Well, Luisa, seems we need to talk."

I say nothing.

He lifts a brow, then gestures past the security guards, inviting me to walk in front of him. I lead the way past the guards to the elevator bank. Inside he pushes the button for the third floor. We pass a series of doors in the hallway that have five-digit combination locks on them rather than doorknobs and stop at the first doorknobbed door we come to. Andrew opens it into a small conference room. It features a large wood table and six leather chairs on casters surrounding it.

He pulls out a chair for me near the end of the table, then once I'm seated, he takes the one next to me at the head of the table. "So you found Bran Porter. How?"

"I found the letters first."

"I see . . . And now you're after either answers or your pound of flesh. Which would be more satisfying, Luisa?" He holds up a hand, clearly believing I am about to interrupt him. I have a tendency to do that. But I can't. I have no words. He continues. "None of it happened the way you're imagining, I'm sure."

"How did it happen?" I'm not even sure what "it" is.

"Initially my predecessor kept loose tabs on Walther's family. He was an asset in Berlin after World War II and stopped when he moved his family between sectors. Then, if I remember correctly, as I haven't reviewed the file in a while, his daughter got into some trouble and we whisked the family—including you—out in 1962. When your family arrived here, his new handler, Montrose, thought all was said and done. Your grandfather had already stopped with his West German handler a year earlier. Then one day Porter called Montrose and it seemed Walther was back in the game."

Andrew leans forward and presses his hands together at the fingertips. It's a calm, measured move. "Then Montrose discovered he wasn't in the game, not really. He wasn't creating the intel; he was receiving it. Not only that, he refused to talk to the CIA. Didn't want any part of it. He would only deal with Porter. That's how Porter stayed in the middle. Walther said it was something about one reporter to another. That only made sense once we zeroed in on Haris Voekler as the source."

He stares at me like he expects me to speak. I stare at him unable to form a coherent thought, much less a word. With a minute nod, he continues.

"We played along as there was no reason not to. Porter brought us Walther's notes, and we used what we needed. We also let Porter print what we determined appropriate. That served the added purpose of getting the public a little fired up over atrocities in Eastern Europe, and as Porter never broke the rules, it worked remarkably well for all parties."

"And my father?"

"To this day, I suspect he doesn't know what your grandfather did with his intelligence. I got the sense he truly believed he was writing to your grandfather for no other purpose than to share his life. Maybe expecting Walther would share it with you." Andrew's eyes soften. "I don't think Walther would have told him any more than that, Luisa. Your father's position would be far more precarious if he knew what your grandfather did with his embedded messages."

I lean forward. "How can it get more precarious? He's in jail." I state it because I assume he still is. If he wasn't, there'd be more letters.

"Yes. He is. But it can still get a lot worse for him." Andrew's cold calm surprises me.

"Worse? How?" I shake my head. "Wait. Regardless of what he knows or doesn't know, he's an asset. He works for you. For the CIA. You need to get him out."

He shakes his head, but it's not the frantic thought-clearing motion I made. It's long and slow. "We cannot do that, Luisa. We will not get involved."

"Not get involved?" His nonsensical statement starts a movie reel of moments and memories leading me to this one. Andrew following my Opa's every move, my father's every move, my . . . "You already involved me."

"I did." He stares at me. "Your grandfather trained you well."

My childhood riddles, ciphers, and treasure hunts are cast in a new light. My training and that final day take on a new hue. "Did I fail the Farm?"

"It was impossible." I feel my lips part like goldfish, but he taps the table to stop me. I wasn't going to say anything. I hardly have the "little grey cells" to think anything. "Look, Luisa, I'd taken over from Montrose a couple years before you came to the CIA. It surprised the hell out of me when you applied, but it never occurred to me that you'd get to clandestine training. I couldn't have you working in Europe, stumbling across your father, or even getting involved in anything in the Eastern Bloc. There were too many variables at play, not the least of which was you thought he was dead."

"Did you—?"

"No. I had nothing to do with that lie, but I wasn't going to put you or anyone else in jeopardy when or if you stumbled across the truth. So, yes, I did what I had to do to secure one mission—your grandfather's—but you can't complain. You've gotten to do good work. Work you are trained to do. You can't deny that."

"You didn't give me a choice. I thought I'd failed."

"You did remarkably well, actually."

I open my mouth to speak. I shut it. I open it again. I find I still have nothing to say.

Andrew spreads his hand on the table as if breaking the plane between us. "What's really bothering you, Luisa? That your grandfather didn't tell you?"

"That. And—" I fall silent again. There is so much more, I can't begin to name it all, and "bother" is far too mild a word for this distress, this chaos, this— What do I call this?

I skip to the one relevant point. "But you never leave a man behind." It sounds trite, but I want it to be true. So I say it.

"This isn't the Navy SEALs, Luisa, or a movie. I hate to remind you of this, but we leave men behind all the time." He raises his hand. Clearly he believes my brain is firing a whole lot faster than it really is. "Do you have all of Haris's letters? Every single one?"

"I expect so. How can I know for certain?" I believe I do, but I sense Andrew is heading somewhere specific and I should leave myself an out.

"Then there are things you know."

"As does Bran Porter."

"Yes. Porter has signed so many confidentiality agreements, we own him. I must remind you we own you too, though you're going a little rogue presently. I need to caution you, Luisa. These are dangerous times."

I blow out a long, steady breath. He's referring to the letter from 1982. He may be referring to more, but he doesn't have to. That letter alone could set the world on fire, and until I learned my father is in jail, it had filled my every thought. Funny how our minds shift when someone we love is in danger.

I don't confirm or deny I've read the letter. I work to keep my face impassive.

"I need those letters now. I had assumed Walther—"

"Of course," I interrupt.

"I had assumed he destroyed them. You need to bring them in."

"I understand and I will. I've kept them confidential. I haven't talked about them." I fold my lips in as I determine where to go next. "I still want you to help my father. His intelligence warrants some support from us."

"Luisa." Andrew's voice falls with a sigh. He's as much warning me as he is exasperated with me.

"I'm not holding the letters hostage. I simply can't accept there's nothing you can do."

Andrew presses his hands together. I get the sense I'm about to receive a lecture. "On May 2, Hungary's new leader, Karoly Grosz, dismantled the barbed wire between Hungary and Austria."

He pauses and I know I'm right.

"Thousands of Eastern Europeans, a huge chunk from East Germany alone, started flooding west. The Iron Curtain sports some sizable holes these days. On October 2 there was a riot in Leipzig with over seven thousand participants. East German protesters actually crying out to Gorbachev to save them. Can you imagine that? 'Gorby—save us!' That's what they were calling to him. Then a week later, on the GDR's birthday, that seven thousand grew to over fifty thousand. And two weeks ago, Minister Egon Krenz ousted GDR General Secretary Erich Honecker and opened the border to Czechoslovakia, trying to placate his people, but twenty-three thousand East Germans fled immediately. They can't plug this hole, Luisa. And if all that wasn't enough, three days ago, on Saturday, seven hundred thousand gathered in Alexanderplatz in East Berlin to protest the government. East Berlin. It's the first protest in the capital since Soviet tanks rolled in, back in June of '53. It's unprecedented, unfathomable, and we have direct orders *not* to get in the middle of it." His eyes soften. "When things settle down, we can talk."

Something crosses over Andrew's eyes. It's quick and gone before I can fully process it, but I trust I saw it. "What?"

He shakes his head.

"Please." My sigh matches his from moments ago.

"It's too late, regardless. Diplomatic negotiations take time and they're in free fall over there. We'd never get a hearing. They're moving all political prisoners from Berlin. They don't want them adding to the tension." He narrows his eyes. "We got word last week your father is being transferred Friday to Naumburg Prison. I'm sorry, Luisa."

"Sorry? Why?"

"It's a tougher facility. A bit of a black hole, really. It's not a good sign."

"Then you have to help him."

Andrew presses his lips together. "My hands are tied."

My heart races. I pop up and hold my hand out to him. "I don't have the letters with me, but I'll bring them into work tomorrow. I—" The lie comes easily to my lips. "I don't feel so well."

He stands and takes my hand. He holds it a moment longer, as if he's offering me condolences or some sort of gift. I resist pulling away. "Take the rest of the day. We'll talk first thing tomorrow. Back at our offices."

"Yes, sir. Thank you." With that he escorts me back to the lobby. I stay calm and I keep my steps measured.

Until I'm out of his sight.

CHAPTER 15

Haris Voekler

EAST BERLIN

Tuesday, October 18, 1978

"Voekler, I want a few lines. The Catholics elected a new pope." Koch yelled that demand yesterday morning. Considering this is a fairly rare and worldwide event, I expected all action around me to stop, but nothing changed. The hum of typewriters and conversations continued.

I headed his direction. "Are you serious?" My heart leapt at being given this story, one I couldn't believe we were covering at all. I had carried my radio into my bathroom the night before, as that bug still transmits from my living room outlet, and listened as this new pope's first papal statement was carried across Radio Free Europe.

At one point he said, "Be not afraid. Open the doors for Christ. To his saving power, open the boundaries of states, economic and political systems, the vast fields of culture, civilizations, and development." My breath caught. For a city languishing behind a wall, this was revolutionary. For a people wanting freedom, it was a lifeline.

"How many words? Should I include his whole speech or select a few quotes?"

Koch looked at me like I was crazy, and I sensed I betrayed something best hidden away.

"You give it nine words for the back page. *New pope elected under the name John Paul II.*"

"But—"

"There is nothing more to say. Is there?" Koch's last two words came out slow and measured.

"Not that I can think of. I'll get it to typesetting." I stepped back and dropped into my desk chair.

Manfred perched in the now-permanent chair stationed beside my desk. "It's not your fault. He's furious. Everyone is."

"Why?"

"Why do you think? The man is a menace. Only elected a day and he's already signaled the waters are going to get worse, not better."

That was the instant I realized how much I've changed and what a danger I've become to myself. I hadn't felt the incongruence yesterday before talking to Manfred nor two nights ago listening to the radio. I'd felt only hope. I hadn't processed how this man's ideas threatened the very power structure surrounding me. I simply hadn't seen the dichotomy because it wasn't an epiphany. It didn't come like a shot in the night, reorienting me, crashing into me, transforming me. I savored the pope's words, and they sifted softly through my defenses without me once recognizing I'd lowered them. At some point in my life, such ideas would have enraged me.

That was the epiphany—I'd *already* changed.

Manfred kept talking yesterday morning, which I appreciated as my mind and soul wrestled with this new reality. "My uncle's in Kraków now. My cousin too. They both left this morning with hundreds of others. They've also sent plenty to Rome."

Manfred leaned closer. I did the same until our heads were only centimeters apart. "They say this pope won't uphold Ostpolitik.

No détente and go-along-to-get-along for this man. That could mean Moscow loses its hold over Catholics in the Eastern Bloc. It's a disaster."

As Manfred straightened, I smiled and nodded my thanks, as if delighted to be given the inside scoop. He has taken to sharing all his family-gleaned information with me over the years. In the beginning I believed he did it to show off. Yesterday, for the first time, I wondered at his motivation. He doesn't need to show off anymore, and he knows it. He has eclipsed me in every way. Even this historic event was only given to me because it commanded a mere nine words on the last page and not a single mention above the fold on the first.

Manfred sauntered back to his desk, and I lowered my head to the page before me. I didn't want anyone to see my expression as I thought through what he'd said and what the new pope had said in his speech the night before. Deep in my heart, I knew it was for us. Well, for Poland too, as he's Polish. But it was for us—and it changed everything.

I wrote my nine words and I walked home last evening. The day's revelations exhausted me. I didn't expect all I'd heard to ignite such a passion in my heart. I didn't expect Manfred's confirmation that it was real and powerful and that what I heard as liberating music soaring high, Moscow heard as a dirge. Anyone who can evoke such emotions, can create such a powerful call to courage, to brotherhood, to a virtuous fight and hope, is someone to watch. I didn't expect to be pressed against my radio all night or to be struck by the lightning bolt of realization and conviction today that convinced me that no matter the struggle, no matter the cost, I needed to do more. I needed to *be* more.

All that energy and hubris—that's danger stuff. It can make you do impetuous things.

I climbed the stairs to my apartment last evening and found Peter standing outside my door.

"I have a favor to ask. Are you busy this evening?" When I didn't reply, he continued, "I need to go to Friedrichstrasse Station tonight. I hoped you'd go with me. I need to carry my aunt's things and—"

He stopped, noticing my expression. Visiting Friedrichstrasse Station, or Tränenpalast—"The Palace of Tears"—is never a good idea. As the last stop in and out of East Berlin, it's one of the most well-surveilled stations in the city. If you're spotted there, you are sure to be recorded, assessed, and perhaps brought in for questioning. And if you've been lucky enough never to have had a Stasi file created for you, one stop at Friedrichstrasse Station and it's a done deal.

"My aunt got one of the last visas."

That was another move by General Secretary Honecker in his pattern of giving and taking away. He lightened the visa regulations, then pulled back when too many people applied. Yet, in a clever gambit, he approved the vast majority of pensioners' requests: it's a boon to our economy to have another country care for them and pay for their pensions.

"Please. I've never been there before." Peter rested a hand on my forearm.

I resisted shaking it off. "I really don't think—"

"Please." He cut off my protest, not with a whine, but with a firm demand upon my friendship. "I can't ask Helene. My aunt is the last of that generation on both sides of our family. Helene's not handling this well."

I knew how hard it had been on Monica when her parents moved across town, then across the ocean. I knew how hard it was on me when I lost my daughter, then my wife. Peter has become my best friend, perhaps my only friend. If I could make this easier for either of them, I needed to do it.

"Give me a minute." I slipped into my apartment, calling myself every kind of fool. Considering all I've been sharing with Walther over the past fourteen years, handing myself to the Stasi was about as stupid a move as I could make. Yet a half hour later, I was helping Peter lug a trunk up the station's stairs. It took only another fifteen minutes to see his aunt off, and we were walking back toward our building.

"I appreciate this."

"Don't mention it." I threw him a glance. "Seriously, don't mention it."

He chuffed, then fell silent. "I wonder how she'll find life in the West." He looked to me. "I've never been."

"Neither have I. I grew up here, went to University here, and there was never a chance or a reason to leave. I clearly ran around before the city was divided, but I was a kid back then. Heck, I spent most of the war years in hiding." I glance to Peter. "My parents were killed early in the war, and as they were opposed—"

"You don't need to say anything. I understand." Peter smiled his assurance.

I tried to shrug away the memories of fear, deprivation, and the promise to myself never to put myself so far out on a limb as my parents did. I promised myself I'd survive back then. Now a small voice asked me, *At what cost?*

Peter nudged me. "You still with me?"

"Oh. Yeah. Sorry. I was just remembering something." I dug my hands into my pockets. Such memories and thoughts could not be shared with even the closest of friends.

"About Luisa?"

I pulled up short. "Luisa? Why?"

Peter looked confused. "Because we were talking about the West and she lives there. I figured that's where you went just now."

"I'm with her more than I care to admit." I smiled and grabbed on to the offered story. "She'll be twenty next month, and I can't see her as a baby in my mind anymore. I miss that."

"Do you ever regret it? Not following her over the wall?"

I told Peter and Helene years ago about Monica passing Luisa over the wall. I also told them I tried to get Monica out, to save her life. But I never shared the full details of my desperate search for a way across for both of us. That I carried alone. Partly because it was and remains dangerous to admit, and partly because my inability to do it, the scorn that met me, still pricks at my soul.

We spent the rest of our trip back to our building in relative silence. I suspect we were both thinking about the West, his aunt, and loved ones lost. She cried when Peter helped her onto the train. Not sobs. Not like the ones I've heard about when family members come and go, tears that gave the station its nickname, but a steady flow of tears I suspect will last many months.

It felt clear to me that leaving wasn't her first choice. I suspected her first choice would have been like mine. To stay home with those you love and live well and safely there. Watching Peter and his aunt made me realize I don't want to leave East Berlin. I don't want to leave the DDR. Like my father before me, I want my hometown to change so it is a place where I can live, and thrive, and make choices, and share with my family and friends. Father's opinions cost him his life. I wonder if mine will cost me my life too.

Because this isn't enough. I want my daughter to be able to visit me. I want to visit her. I want no barriers between us. I want to be me. I haven't felt like me in so long, I hardly recognize who that is anymore. But I got a sense of it two nights ago, crouching in my bathroom with my ear pressed to the radio. I got a sense of it yesterday, listening to Manfred's gossip. And I got a sense of it last night walking back from the Tränenpalast with Peter.

Back at our building I was about to unlock my door when Peter thrust his hand before my face. I stepped back to shake it.

"Thank you. I didn't want to do that alone. My aunt's four kids, my closest cousins, were all killed young in the war. She was it. The last of my family." He nodded to me as if he finally recognized something he should have said earlier. "We've lost a lot, haven't we?"

"We have." I pulled him into a quick hug, then entered my apartment, glad the night was over.

But it wasn't. It isn't . . .

This morning, I find a small white envelope on my desk at work. It holds a simple note. Brief and to the point.

> We request a meeting at 2pm October 18 to clear up some matters.

The address listed below the sentence is not that of my neighborhood's local Stasi office, where such "conversations" usually take place, but of headquarters itself. It feels ominous and I check my watch all morning. Time crawls at an interminable pace.

When 1:30 p.m. finally arrives, I head to both the longest and the shortest street in East Berlin. I try to laugh at my own joke, but I cannot. A summons to Stasi headquarters on Magdalenenstrasse is always a dangerous thing. The street is only three blocks long, the length of the Stasi complex, but it can take one years to get out of it.

I ride the S-Bahn to the Magdalenenstrasse Station and walk up the steps. It's only a couple kilometers from my apartment, actually, but it feels a world away. Two blocks and I'm at the headquarters' outer gate. I can see the central building from the security gate and recall Manfred's awe after his interview with Stasi Chief Erich Mielke years ago. The blue upholstered furniture, the sleeping quarters next to his office, the three secretaries positioned right outside his door, and the private kitchen adjacent to that. I recall Manfred recounting a grocery store, a barber, clothing shops, and more, and by the size of the place I can believe it. It's overwhelming.

"Haris Voekler." The guard checks my name off a list, and he gestures to another guard who steps forward.

"Follow me." He leads me to the closest building on the left. It's two stories tall and cement like all the others. Inside, I'm ushered into a small room with only a central table and four chairs. I sit. The guard leaves. I wait.

A small man with circular glasses enters. His suit is rumpled and papers spill out of his hands. He looks so clumsy and disarming, I suspect a ruse. *Stop being so paranoid, Haris!* Then I remember where I am and become paranoid again.

One minute in and the mind games begin.

The man chats about his day, his commute, and he cites all sorts of random statistics and facts before he lets drop a single word that shatters the camaraderie between us—at least the camaraderie he tried to build.

Republikflucht. Defection.

Panic washes over me. The Stasi can keep people for only forty-eight hours without filing charges, but I've heard stories about how horrific those forty-eight hours can be. Even though you know it's a short amount of time, they bend it in such a way you're confirming any lie they tell you just so they'll let you go. If this man wants to talk about defection, I'm here for the full forty-eight hours and only getting out if they are super pleased with all my answers, or believe I'm sufficiently broken.

My heart races and just as I'm about to regurgitate every word spoken between me, Peter, and his aunt Agatha—because they were all innocent—a sentence Walther said years ago comes to mind. I hadn't processed it then, as it was so different from my own father's choice to simply say "nein" and let the enemy take him. Walther said, "*I fought tooth and nail to stay, until the day I needed to leave.*"

I hadn't known Walther well then. He hadn't liked me and I hadn't liked or understood him. We've become closer over the years, but not because he's changed. Because I have. That's not fair. The Walther of old never would have been as patient as he has been with me over the past few years. That's not fair either. I was arrogant, young, and so sure of myself when we lived blocks apart that anything he might have offered, I was above receiving.

In that moment, as the bespectacled interrogator blinks at me, I wonder how many times Walther found himself in this situation. After all, his name would have been on every Stasi list after June 16, 1953. He was there that fateful day at Potsdamer Platz. The event I cut my teeth on with my first series of articles.

"Event"—that tells you right there how far apart we were. That day saw Walther's leg clipped by a Soviet tank as they rolled in and over two hundred protesters in a brutal suppression of dissent. That event made my career, at least for a while.

Walther was lucky to keep his leg and only suffer a slight limp afterward. But once he read my article and all the propaganda I offered up to justify it, he barely spoke another word to me. The platitudes I spewed, the lies I wrote even though I knew the West hadn't sent spies to the Soviet Sector to start the riot. I also mentioned the increased work quotas that had really gotten everyone out and angry that day—after all, every good bit of propaganda carries a sliver of truth—but I twisted it. I wrote that we were fine. We were happy. Rather than threatening to break the workers' backs, our new quotas were easy and within reach, and we were collectively building a new future. The West was simply trying to thwart our good efforts.

Then right before he moved Gertrude and Alice to the American Sector, Walther looked at me and said, "*I fought tooth and nail to stay, until the day I needed to leave.*" He said nothing more. It was the last time I spoke to him.

I face the man before me and realize, once again, I don't want to leave Berlin. I don't want to live in fear. And I certainly don't want to throw my hands up and let them take me. This is my home and I need to start fighting for it. Although I never wanted to be between the Stasi's crosshairs, I am now. And the fact that I am—for helping out a friend—shows how ridiculous the system is.

I straighten and I go on the offensive. "Don't use that word with me. I went to Friedrichstrasse Station last night to support a friend as he said goodbye to his aunt, who had an authorized visa to leave the DDR. No one reported to you that I did anything more than stand by his side and walk back to our neighborhood immediately following, did they? You bring me in here for that?"

"Well, there are other issues."

"Such as?"

"Your letters."

I slam my hand on the desk. "Enough with my letters. This has been between us for years. Koch told me long ago." I receive a curious brow raise for that tidbit, but I don't stop. "I cannot stop writing to my father-in-law. He is my only connection to my daughter. A daughter I did not send away. My dead wife did, so that, too, was out of my control. But she is my daughter and I love her. And I want to tell her about my days so she might know me. Have you found anything in my letters to warrant this scrutiny? This treatment? I am sure you have read each and every one. And has my father-in-law written anything in reply that concerns you? Do the articles I write for the paper concern you?"

"Nein." The man blinks. "Nein."

"Do you have kids?"

The man pales and opens his mouth to reply.

I cut him off. "I see you do. And you love them. Then I will leave?"

It's a declaration wrapped in a question so he can retain both dignity and authority. I'm not trying to make an enemy here. I'm trying to avoid becoming one.

I finish more softly. "I am still trusted at my work. I still command bylines on the front page. You read what I write. I am loyal and I deserve better. We all have hardships that come our way, don't we? She is my daughter."

"Yes, of course."

I walk out of the office and stride double-time to the exit. I may have gotten away miraculously easily this time, but it won't be my last trip to Magdalenenstrasse. I have moved up their list.

But in this fight, I have lists of my own to make now too.

CHAPTER 16

Luisa Voekler

Tuesday, November 7, 1989

Outside Langley, the day has grown cloudy and it feels personal. Dark clouds hover above me, against me. I keep glancing in my rearview mirror and forcing out strange stiff laughs, hoping they will dispel my sense of foreboding.

"No one is following you," I say aloud. Then I glance to my rearview mirror again, unsure if it's true. Fairly certain it is, I nevertheless drive around looking in my rearview mirror for almost an hour, taking random turns and watching who follows. No one does. I force another laugh, and it doesn't feel any more genuine than my first attempt.

Logically I know following me is not worth Andrew's energy. I may interrupt a lot, but I am trustworthy. He knows I will bring the letters to him and, I believe, trusts I have not revealed anything I've learned within them. Yet he's been there all along. That's what I can't shake. It leads to so many questions about my career, my work, my life, that I do not have time to confront right now.

I drive to the University Club. I've certainly heard of the club with its membership spanning the entire Who's Who of DC, but I've never been there. I park in the reserved lot in the back, walk around the building to the front, and stop. It's a massive red-brick structure with two wings pressing forward like the ends of a U. The white-painted window frames and detailing make it look both old and impressive, new and fresh. Either way—both ways—it's formidable. I look to the right, straight at the White House. Yes, formidable. Once I'm led to a small table for two at the back of a red-painted library, I'm even more impressed.

"Mr. Porter telephoned that he's running a few minutes behind schedule."

I smile. The man's "schedule" carries tony English "shhh" sounds too. I barely have time to place my white linen napkin in my lap before Bran pushes through the library's double glass doors.

He calls from across the room, probably since I'm the only one in it. "I was putting to bed yesterday's interview. It was gold. Sorry I'm late." He sits and waves to a man I didn't even know had entered behind him. "Iced tea, please." Bran looks to me and gestures.

"Same. Thank you."

The man leaves and Bran settles. There's an infinitesimal pause, so I fill it. "I know you're busy, so I thank you for this."

His long fingers wave in a nonchalant "don't mention it" way before I can say more. "I have wanted to see you again for many years. This is the most important appointment of my day. I'm sorry I was late."

I take a breath and release it, willing myself to relax. Finally. Someone is willing to talk to me. My conscience chastises me as soon as the thought blooms. Aunt Alice was willing to talk to me. Sure, it felt late. But that didn't make it any less real.

"I hope you don't mind I requested to sit in here. It gives us more privacy. There are big ears, as you can imagine, all over this town and especially here."

"Not at all." I look around the large room, the shelves upon shelves of books, the leather couches, chairs, standing floor lamps. It is lovely and carries a gravitas that calms me for the first time since Friday night.

Bran picks up his menu, glances at it, then sets it down and stares at me. I decide to order the first thing that catches my eye, a Caesar salad, and set mine down as well.

"You look like him. Not completely. I expect there is some of Haris in you. Perhaps your eyes, but you have Walther's square jaw. His determination too, I expect."

"Aunt Alice shares it too."

"He wanted to protect you. You and Alice. Gertrude too. There were so many things he wouldn't do for fear of hurting any of you. That included sharing who he truly was." Bran raises both eyebrows as if to say "there you have it," and I sense he understands more about Alice, my grandfather, and that long-ago event than I'll ever know.

He slides a hand across the white linen tablecloth. He's not reaching for my hand; rather I can tell he's reaching for understanding. From me. For Opa. He continues, "I believe he felt he was honoring all Monica sacrificed by bringing Haris's letters to me and by sharing what truly happens within a totalitarian regime. He thought, because your father was—" Bran tilts his head in question. "Is?" I nod. He continues, "Because Haris is a journalist, he'd want to get the truth out. Walther felt both Haris and Monica would want that. But Haris doesn't know. You need to understand that."

"Haris doesn't know what?"

"That your grandfather ever showed anyone his letters. Walther sensed Haris believed he was simply writing to your grandfather like one might write into one's journal. It was Walther's decision alone to invite me into this, and I had no option but to include the CIA."

"Andrew Cademan said as much this morning."

"Yes. You met with him."

Bran's sentence draws long in question, but I don't bite as it's too complicated to address, and as Andrew reminded me, I've signed countless forms.

We order, and as soon as the waiter leaves the room, Bran resumes talking. "I know you're mad he didn't tell you, but he did. He could have destroyed those letters. In fact, I'm a little surprised he didn't."

"Me too. All things considered."

"You've deciphered them." Again, it isn't a question so I don't answer. He's got a good interview technique, however, as his confidential tone and pregnant pauses have even me on the brink of spilling everything.

"What do you do, Luisa? For work?"

I rearrange my silverware and stall. I always feel it's better to deliver my false occupation alongside a distracting gesture. "I work in accounting and budgeting for the Labor Department."

"My goodness . . . You're CIA." Bran's voice lifts into a question this time. In epiphany and in wonder too.

"What?" I almost choke as I've never had anyone reply like that before.

"Luisa, I've been a reporter in this town for four decades, and it's full of accountants for various departments, none of whom actually know anything about accounting. They need a new cover for you all. Besides, considering what I know about your family, I'm calling your bluff."

"I am a certified CPA."

"Good for you. That at least helps the lie." Bran opens his mouth to speak, then shuts it as we catch the waiter crossing the library with our salads.

Once he is gone again, Bran asks, "What did Cademan tell you this morning? Only things you can reveal, of course."

"That all Eastern Europe is in turmoil and there's nothing he can do to get my father out."

At his furrowed brow, I realize I need to backpedal and give more context. So, between bites, I start at the beginning and walk him through my weekend, ending on the realization that my father is in a Stasi jail and Andrew's update that he'll be moved soon to a more precarious and dangerous situation in three days' time.

"He says to wait a few months and see how things settle over there, but there isn't time. My father will be transferred Friday from Berlin to Naumburg Prison. I trust Andrew—" My use of Cademan's first name elicits another knowing look. I ignore it. There isn't time for games anymore. "This morning he basically said a move to Naumburg is the end."

"Do you have half a million dollars?"

"Excuse me?"

"That's all I can think to do. Buy him out. That's the going rate for a private citizen to 'negotiate' release of a prisoner. It's easy to do, actually, as it's a huge source of income for the GDR. But it takes time. Less time than formal negotiations, but still more time than three days."

Bran takes a bite of his own Caesar salad and, while chewing, carries on an internal conversation. I can tell by how his head bobs back and forth as if weighing pros and cons.

"Now, if you could get someone official involved, that price goes down two-thirds at least, and you could get higher up the food chain faster, but if Cademan turned you down, I'm not sure who you could involve, but . . ." He lets his sentence fade away as if he's considering other options.

"Would someone take less?"

Bran's brown eyes round with empathy. "I'm not sure it's a viable solution, Luisa. I just don't know of any others."

"But would someone?"

"I suppose. I know a few reporters you could contact over there to ask. They could at least tell you what's happening on the ground right now. But Cademan's right. It's chaos over there. Poland. Hungary. Czechoslovakia. Austria. Now East Germany. I'm not sure how much material reporters or anyone can provide with the ground shifting like it is."

"Please. I'd like to at least call and ask."

Bran slides a small soft-sided notebook from his coat pocket, pulls a scrap of paper from another pocket, and retrieves a golf pencil from a third. He pages through the notebook and writes comments on the scrap paper.

A couple minutes later, he passes me the paper. It's full of names, numbers, and notations. "Three reporters in Berlin. Fichman has been there longest. I'd contact him first. In fact, I'll reach out after lunch and tell him to expect your call. I'm not sure he'll talk with you otherwise. He's been 'in country' for a long time now. The other two will help, but their networks won't stretch as far, both above- and belowground. Fichman is your man."

"Thank you."

Bran holds both hands up. "I'm giving you this, but I'm not recommending you call anyone, Luisa. Hear me on that. This is into-the-belly-of-the-beast kind of stuff and nothing to mess around with. If Cademan told you to stay out of it, that's the CIA of the United States government telling you to stay out, and I suspect you know the weight that carries."

He stares at me a moment before his eyes soften again. "Some of the stories your grandfather told me . . ." He whistles a breath from pursed lips. "Let's say I never heard the like."

Bran sits back and picks up his fork again. He doesn't snag a bite of salad, however. He waves its tongs at me. "You should be proud of your dad too. I know, I know . . ." He lifts his hand as if I'm about to interrupt him, and I realize how often people do that. I barely know this man. Do I give off some sign that I don't let people finish their sentences?

"He was all in as a young man, but you can't blame him for that. He hadn't experienced what your Oma and mother endured. Walther described him as some scrappy Berlin orphan that neighbors hid in their cellars during the war. Then the Soviets came in and took him seriously. Gave him a job, an education, then promotion after promotion. Even your grandfather understood the appeal of all that flattery and material security. Then? Well, let's just say your dad has certainly put all those smarts and ingenuity to good use. Thanks to Walther."

Those few lines churn up a whole new batch of questions, but I squelch them down. All but one. It keeps rising in different ways. Oma. Alice. Stories that start and never get finished. Looks of fierce pain and terror.

"What you just said?" I pause, unsure of what I'm really asking. "About Oma and my mother? What did you mean?"

Bran drops his attention to his salad. "I'm not sure how much you know about history, but the Soviets were raging mad as they stormed across Germany to Berlin. They wanted revenge, retribution, blood. They wanted the Germans to pay for their losses at Stalingrad and beyond."

He pauses again, and I feel a glimmer of where his story might be going. My stomach churns but I don't comment. I don't interrupt. I need to hear this through.

"It is estimated they raped over a hundred thousand women and girls in those few months alone. Many were raped multiple times. I knew your grandfather for twenty years before he shared that with me . . . I'm sorry."

I press my napkin to my mouth. I'm speechless. I'm horrified. I want to hug Oma.

"I'm not sure I should have told you that, but I also don't think lies and secrets have done you any good. Walther and I argued that point lots, but as you aren't my granddaughter, I rightfully lost every time."

"No. Thank you." I shake my head. "I'd rather know."

"But your father didn't know. Walther believed Monica never told him, and he didn't see the Soviets like your mother and her family did. He was a kid and already in Berlin at the time. Most of what I described happened on the Soviet's march west. Haris, on the other hand, probably worked as a runner for the officers after they'd arrived in Berlin. That's how they employed a lot of German youth. They were trying to win over new young soldiers. Haris didn't understand what he was up against until later. And once he did, he was the first. His intel, buried in his letters to Walther, was the first good stuff out of the GDR. And because Walther wanted to work with me, the CIA couldn't cut us out."

Bran sets down his fork. "Now we've got tapes, even video, coming out almost every day, smuggled out in the trunk of a car, or in the steering column or some such place, and we shoot it back in through the airwaves. But it wasn't like that in the sixties or most of the seventies. It was your dad. That made both your dad and your granddad vital to the public's understanding of what was going on over there. You can't underestimate the significance of that."

I drop my hands to my lap. I see the bandage still circling my right hand. I remember Oma's care and feel I can and should forgive my Opa's secrets. My head, heart, stomach, even my arms sag, overwhelmed and heavy.

Bran continues to share stories of my grandfather and their talks over the years, and it's as much a story of friendship as it is of passing information. It makes me realize that while I didn't know this aspect of my grandfather's life, I did know him. I laugh at Bran's spot-on impressions of Opa's grouchy exclamations when someone didn't listen well enough and his deep belly chuckle when something struck him as funny.

Bran ends his stories with another fork wave to my salad. "Eat up. I suspect you'll need the energy."

I finally take another bite, right as he asks a question.

"Leaving all that aside for a minute. Humor an old man. How'd you find the letters?"

Between bites, I tell him about the space under my floorboards and about all the riddles and ciphers Opa created for me as a kid. "He was always preparing me, for my job and for this. I didn't know that, of course, but I'm beginning to suspect I've wasted a whole year by not finding the letters or catching on sooner."

"You can't think that way. We can all get lost with could-haves and should-haves, and they are dead ends." He quirks a small sideways smile. "Walther bet me a beer once that I couldn't crack one of your dad's letters. It's the only one I ever saw. We sat at a picnic table for two hours with me racking my brains over that thing and him smirking the entire time."

Bran nods as if anticipating my next question. "This was after he stopped bringing you to play chess. He was afraid you were getting old enough to notice more than the chess and would start asking questions. Anyway, I never did find a thing odd within that letter, and Walther even gave me his word-for-word decryption to set next to it. My German's not that good, but still the letters were right next to each other. I should've found something. That day cost me a beer and a little pride."

I laugh. I can see Opa's smirk and that glint in his eyes. He was close to that challenging with me as a kid. "That's because you didn't grow up cracking codes to find your birthday gifts. But don't feel bad; even I have never seen anything like these letters."

We talk on and soon I'm able to relax enough to finish my lunch. I find I'm actually hungry.

As we stand in the lobby to say a final farewell, Bran pulls me into a hug and whispers close to my ear, "There's a letter from 1982."

I stiffen.

"That's the one." I feel him nod against my cheek. "Burn it. Don't let Cademan know you've read it. He'll think Walther destroyed it, and that's for the best."

I step back and make a decision. "Could you wait here? For just a minute. Please?"

Bran looks confused and concerned. "Yes."

I run to my car and unlock it from the passenger side. I rarely use this door and the key doesn't slide in the lock easily. I yank open the door and pull my bag from underneath the passenger seat. Resting it on the seat, I sort through the manila folder and slide out the 1982 letter and my notes. I shove those under the seat. I then tuck the other pages back inside the folder, lock the car, and dash back to the club's main entrance.

Upon entering, I gesture to Bran and head straight for the library in which we ate lunch. Though our table is now cleared, no one else is in the room. The double doors shut behind us before I hand him the folder.

He takes it, but he doesn't open it. He taps the folder against his other hand. "The letters. You're going to Berlin, aren't you?"

"I have to. Would you please take that to Andrew? It isn't breaking any trust or confidentiality agreements. You already know everything that's in them. Though, at your suggestion just now, I did remove the problematic 1982 letter."

"I can't endorse this plan, Luisa."

"I'm not asking you to. I'm simply asking you to take the letters to Andrew. The rest is on me. Please."

He presses his lips into a long, thin line, and I wonder if he has granddaughters of his own. Finally, he nods. "I'll call Fichman and make him meet with you. It's the only way I know to help."

"Thank you." I turn to leave and spin back. "One more favor, if you don't mind. Give me tonight. Andrew isn't expecting that file until tomorrow morning. I need until then."

"Tomorrow morning then. And when you get back, I get the story."

I smile. "Yes, sir."

CHAPTER 17

Tuesday, November 7, 1989

Emptying one's bank account is both easier and harder than one might expect. Emptying one's grandmother's bank account, however, is gutting.

That's part of the plan I didn't tell Bran. I am taking money—all the money. Perhaps I really can find someone who, for about twenty-five thousand dollars, as that's all I can gather, will help me. I didn't tell him because he wouldn't support that. Who could? Other than a few of Opa's stocks that can't be sold immediately, I am stealing my grandmother's financial security. The security I promised to protect. And for what? I'm not even sure. Bribes that will go nowhere? Perhaps. Money seized by guards at a checkpoint? Maybe. I just know that if I don't do something, don't try every angle possible, I'll regret it for the rest of my life.

With the money tucked deep into my canvas bag, I head to the next part of my plan. A military surplus store.

I wander the aisles. I have no idea how large my father is. I don't know his height or his weight. Only his age. And fifty-eight is indicative of nothing. I start to make assumptions. Oma says I'm built like my mom. Petite. Five foot seven. But I've seen pictures of my mom and get the impression she was slightly taller, more willowy, almost fragile looking.

Therefore my father probably isn't a tree. I'm guessing no taller than five-eleven. And he's been in an East German prison for over six months. He's got to be thin.

I reach for a generic olive-green American service uniform and the salesperson confirms it's for "average height, average build." I pay her and drive to my next and last stop.

The travel agent gawps. "You want to travel to West Berlin? Tonight?" She glances above my head. "It's already five o'clock."

I force myself to nod. One might think emptying the bank accounts would make this real, or buying a military uniform for my father to wear as we walk across Checkpoint Charlie, but it's actually this moment. I have never purchased a ticket nor have I ever flown on a plane. I've rarely ventured beyond Virginia—one trip, actually, to Disney World in Orlando, Florida, when I was ten.

But despite that, I do have a passport. I've had it since I became a naturalized American citizen at eighteen. Opa marched me into the post office and paid for me to get a passport as soon as the paperwork came in. When I asked why I needed one, as we traveled nowhere and I was going to college nearby, he simply replied, "Because you can. Never take for granted that you can go anywhere you choose at any time." So when it expired three years ago, I renewed it.

The travel agent's hands fly over her keyboard. "Only Lufthansa flies to Tegel now that Pan Am has pulled back." She taps her huge monitor. Her nails click against the glass. "You're in luck. There are two flights tonight." She looks up to one of the several clocks on the wall again. This time I twist to see what she's staring at.

Each displays a different time zone and features a small placard. London. Paris. Rome. Mexico City. Washington, DC. Berlin.

"You'll never make the 7:00 p.m."

Two hours from now. "Are you sure?"

"Considering you need to be at the airport at least an hour before an international flight? Yes." She peers over the top of her glasses at me before returning her focus to her computer monitor. "There's a 9:00 p.m. If we work super-fast, we can make that work. Do you have your passport?"

"Not with me."

"Don't forget it. They'll need it at the airport and you'll need to be there at least two hours early since I can't input that information now. When are you coming back?" Again, her fingers fly.

"I don't know. I—"

She cuts me off with a wave of red nails. "We'll leave your ticket open-ended. You'll have to see a travel agent when you're over there or call the airline directly, but you don't need to know that date right now."

"Good. Thank you."

"Alright. I need a check." She fills out a form and passes it to me. I gulp at the price.

"Cash." My voice cracks. "Do you accept cash?"

"You have that much cash on you?" Her neon-shadowed eyes bulge. "Yes. We take cash."

I reach into my bag and pull out the amount. She takes it and walks to another desk to make change. She returns, hands me my change, then after a few more clicks, she prints my tickets.

"Try to get there around 7:00 p.m. if you can, okay?" One full eyebrow lifts in concern. "And good luck, honey."

"Thank you."

Now to head home . . .

I find Oma sitting on a small stool in the backyard. She isn't poking at her garden or planting more seeds. She is merely sitting.

Looking at her, I'm swamped with guilt over all I've never understood, over what I've done and what I'm about to do. I find myself gripping my bag to my side as if her Superman vision can see straight through the canvas.

"Are you okay?" I stand in front of her.

"I am tired today." She looks up at me, and I sense she feels more sad than tired. But sometimes it's hard to tell the difference. Her eyes drop to my hands and she reaches out.

With infinite care, she looks at the fingertips of my left hand and the still-wrapped palm of my right. There was no keeping bandages on the fingertips, and they are fine without them. The skin is still swollen, red, and incredibly tender to the touch, but the salve has kept the blisters from bursting. They and the pain have diminished to the point I barely notice them.

She lifts an edge of the gauze across my right palm. That hand is not as far along in the healing process. "It is much better now." She looks to me. Her eyes are filled with sadness. "This has not been good between us. None of this is good."

"I know, Oma, and I'm really sorry." I sit on the edge of one of her raised garden beds. The brick makes for enough of a perch that I can balance. "It's going to be okay. I promise it will." I wait a moment, then realize I don't have any time to wait. "But not yet."

She tilts her head up, but before she can speak, I press on. "I need to go on a short trip and I'm going to ask Aunt Alice to come stay with you."

"Why would you do that?" Her tone hardens. "I am perfectly capable."

"I agree, but I'm still going to call her. Please, I need to do this for me." I kiss her cheek and head up the stairs and into the house before she can protest further or ask any questions.

I don't want to lie to her. There have been too many of those. But I can't tell her the truth either. I can't tell her I am going to the one place on earth that still terrifies her, to save the one man she's not sure she can trust—after all, it's only been a day since, I think, she loathed Haris Voekler—and I certainly can't tell her that I'm probably breaking a whole lot of rules—and not for the Labor Department.

Furthermore, I don't know what will happen. I could be back in a couple of days, but if I'm not or if something bad does happen—after I lose all our money—I need Aunt Alice here. I need to know Oma will be okay, and I sense on some level Alice needs it too. She needs to be okay and she's not yet. Opa kept secrets from me, yes, but he actually kept Alice living a lie too. That seems a high price to pay for a teenager who was only trying to save her sister.

As I walk up the stairs, I realize Oma hasn't called me back and she hasn't followed me. I feel another twinge of guilt. I've defeated my irrepressible Oma.

I unplug the phone from the hallway and replug it in my room like I used to do in high school. I press the buttons to dial Aunt Alice and hope she's home from school. As it's five thirty, she just might be.

She answers on the first ring but isn't so quick to say yes to my request.

"Please. I don't want her to be alone."

"But I don't understand why. What aren't you telling me, Luisa?" she asks softly.

I hear it in her voice. A plea to be honest, to tell the truth, and to trust her. "I'm going to Berlin to find my father. I may have to cross into the East and—"

She releases a soft gasp. "I'll be right over. Do what you need to do and I'll take care of Mama."

"Thank you. I'm packing now. I'll be gone before you arrive."

"Then be safe—and, Luisa?"

"Yes?"

"I love you."

I hang up the phone and pull my suitcase from the back of my closet, and after folding the uniform inside the Dr. Scholl's shoebox, I set both into the suitcase. The box takes up most of the space, so I fill the little remaining with only a couple shirts, a wool skirt, tights, underwear, and an extra sweater. While I don't know for certain, I expect November in Berlin will be much colder than it is here in DC.

I open the door to grab my toiletries from the bathroom and find Oma standing right outside my door.

"Where exactly are you going, Luisa?"

CHAPTER 18

Tuesday, November 7, 1989–Wednesday, November 8, 1989

I board the plane and find my seat. It's a window seat in a row of three. There are four seats in the middle and another row of three on the far side of the plane. I'm a little unnerved by the sheer size of it all. How is something this massive going to fly across the ocean?

I settle into my corner and shove my canvas bag under the seat in front of mine. I can't let it out of my reach, even though looking at it makes me feel ill. With a foot pressed firmly on it, I close my eyes.

One thought shines through darkened lids. I have stolen from Oma. I have taken everything Opa left her for her future. I have taken everything from those who gave everything for me. Despite the hidden truths, lies, and secrets of these last few days, that fact remains—my grandparents raised me and gave me every opportunity and every bit of love that was in their power to give.

I open my eyes and hold my hand out in front of me. Still burned, still pink, and still tender, I am no longer angry about my hands or about Oma trying to burn the scrapbook. Bran helped me understand her better. He helped me understand a lot of things better. They are healing. They will be fine. And they are shaking. I clench them into my lap once more.

I try to eat the meal they offer. I try to watch the movie *Working*

Girl playing on the drop-down ceiling screen four rows ahead. I try to sleep. I try a lot of things during the eleven-hour flight, but nothing separates my mind from those initial thoughts.

I check my watch as the flight lands. It's 2:00 p.m. Berlin time, which makes it 8:00 Wednesday morning in DC. Right now or within a few minutes from now, Bran will call Andrew. And before two words are said, Andrew will know what I've done and where I am. He's not stupid. Then he'll fire me, if not charge me with who knows what. So if I'm not incarcerated, I'll be *asoziales Verhalten*, as Opa called it. Criminally antisocial.

Opa had lived almost twenty years in the States when I graduated college, yet he was so scared I wouldn't find a job it made him sick. Unemployment carried dire consequences in East Germany. In the US, now that I've blown my savings and all of Oma's retirement money, it'll have dire consequences for me too. There I go—full circle again.

The plane pulls to the gate and the race begins.

I follow the crowds through West Berlin's Tegel Airport and security. Once outside, I follow the people around me again to the taxi stand and head to the only monument I can name, the Brandenburg Gate. I drew a picture of the eighteenth-century neoclassical monument for a tenth-grade report. All I can recollect as the taxi driver zips through the city streets is that it is located in central Berlin and is presently trapped within the Buffer Zone, or the Death Strip as it's commonly called.

The cab pulls to the edge of Tiergarten Park, and I am shocked by what's before me. The Wall is nothing like what I've imagined. Somehow on television it seems smaller and less imposing. I always thought it a little stark in its height and strength, and interesting with its colors, paintings, and graffiti. But up close it looms larger, more solid and obdurate, and you can sense the living anger in the art. Anger that doesn't translate, I suppose, across an ocean and television pixels.

I carry my suitcase and head west from the park deeper into West Berlin's central district. The city bustles with energy. The cars that zip past are smaller than at home, and the noise from their exhausts reverberates off the buildings at a higher pitch. There is a faint whiff of industry about me. I can't tell if it's gas, coal, or bakery goods, but the city smells different than DC.

I stand at the corner of Potsdamer Strasse and Lutzowstrasße and let West Berlin move around me. I try to organize my thoughts and the afternoon. It's already three o'clock, so the first order of business is to find a cheap hotel. I accomplish that within minutes off Grossbeerenstrasse, and I leave my suitcase in my room. I carry my canvas bag tucked close to my side and head back out.

Next, I need to call one of Bran Porter's contacts. Not one of the three answered last night when I tried telephoning each, but perhaps Bran had better success.

Fichman is my first choice. Balancing the coins, a piece of paper, and a pen to write down anything he might tell me, I make the call from a pay phone outside my hotel. A gruff voice answers, which warms perceptibly when I mention Bran. We agree to meet at a café within the half hour.

I find the shop on the map the hotel manager gave me and order a coffee. It's cold and cloudy with the breeze carrying in more clouds, but in my paranoia I recall Andrew saying Berlin is "spy central," so I choose to sit at a table outside. I want to see who is coming and going. I want to see who might be listening.

A swift knuckle-tap to the table startles me. "Luisa."

I answer yes, though it was not a question, as he looks me over. He seems vaguely disappointed. "I need coffee. Be right back."

He returns within moments and pulls his chair tight to the table. "What can I do for you? Porter sent you? I heard I missed a call at the office from him yesterday, but I didn't have a chance to call him back."

"He didn't send me, but he was calling you about me." I glance around. "I want to get someone out of a Stasi jail and Mr. Porter thought you might know who I could talk to, or bribe, or . . ." I run out of words, not knowing if I'm saying too much, too little, or all the wrong things regardless.

Fichman bursts into laughter—and not the jovial, welcoming kind. "Is this a joke? Is Porter setting up *Candid Camera Europe*?" He looks around as if searching for a cameraman hovering nearby.

"No." I bite my lip to keep tears from forming. I'm beyond exhausted and I sound foolish. I hate sounding foolish.

"You're serious." Again, not a question. But it is full of shock and tinged with sarcasm.

I nod. I don't trust myself to speak.

"And once you get over there? Say I can get you in and you find just the right person to pay off. How do you get your person out?"

"I thought if you . . ." I reach my hand out in a gesture of supplication. "I brought a uniform for him to wear."

"And you have papers?" He takes a sip of coffee. "Identification papers? Good forgeries for either an American serviceman or a VoPo? Which uniform did you bring anyway?"

"American. I thought that if I got him to Checkpoint Charlie, I could explain, and—"

"Are you five?" He sets down his cup so forcefully coffee splashes across the saucer and onto the table. He swipes at it with his napkin. "I'd expect better from my grandson. More creativity and ingenuity, at least. He's five."

The tears fall. "He's my father. I just found out about him and he's being moved to Naumburg Prison on Friday. There wasn't time for anything more."

That changes Fichman's expression and elicits a low-pitched whistle. "I'm sorry. That's rough. That's deep into the GDR and . . . It's just rough." He sits back. "What you propose is ridiculous."

"I did a report on several successful escapes employing a military uniform when I was in high school." After his child comment, I blush at my own sentence. But it's all I've got, so I press on. "There were two in 1962, then two more reported in 1974."

He's smiling now. I can't tell if he is going to laugh or pounce. There's something almost sinister about the way his lips curl. "And you think the Stasi learned nothing in the last fifteen years?"

"No. I—"

"Let me explain this to you. The Stasi is world class. We've got nothing like it in the West. Even the KGB comes here when they want something done systematically and thoroughly because the Stasi will get their hands deep into the muck. Whereas the KGB likes to stay a little cleaner. Getting deep into the muck means examining every angle, exploiting every weakness, and enhancing every strength. Tell me how many successful military-uniform escapes you reported on post-1974?"

"I don't remember."

"None. There haven't been any." He leans forward to deliver that line, then flops back again. "No car boot escapes since '76 either. But arrests? Let's see . . . Three uniform arrests in '73, four in '74, including one uniform the woman was carrying in a shoebox. She got arrested before even handing it off. American woman too."

I sink a little lower.

"The last one was just three years ago, right in Alexanderplatz.

Another American woman. She's still over there in jail, by the way. Now, as for car boots, one arrest in '77, two in '79, a couple more in '81. Those are the arrests that leaked to the media. Most of the time, they keep them quiet. Strange accidents happen, that kind of stuff, or people just disappear." He crosses his arms. "Tell me you have something else."

"I don't." I feel myself deflate as if all my bones have gone soft. How could I ever have believed I had what it took to survive clandestine training all those years ago?

Fichman narrows his eyes and he can't help but see the pity party play across my face. His face softens and I almost want to yell, "Don't do that. I'm an adult. Don't baby me." But I don't. I sit and wait for him to speak.

"And why are you here with me rather than going to the embassy?"

"I can't go there."

"And I can't help you." He stands in one fluid motion and is gone.

I down the last of my coffee and stand. I sway a little and grip the table's edge until the world rights itself. I need water, food, and sleep, probably in that order. But I also know I can't stop, so I walk to the only other place I know in the city: Checkpoint Charlie.

I stop a woman standing in line. "Are you here to cross into East Berlin?" I glance to my watch. It feels later than 4:30 p.m. She looks at me like "duh," but I don't let it deter me. "What papers do they require?"

"You need your passport to register for a day pass. That's all you can get." She steps ahead.

I survey the line behind her. It's over twenty people deep. I step to the end. I might as well see the process through today, without the uniform, so I can figure out what best to do with it tomorrow. Because, ridiculous or not, it's already Wednesday late afternoon. Tomorrow is my only chance.

An hour later, I've moved up and stand sixth in line. My heart is beating so loudly I can both feel and hear it.

"Luisa!"

Someone calls my name, and I spin around. I see no one. I hear it again and this time, twisting the other direction, I see a man I never expected to see again. Not that I haven't dreamt of it a few times.

Daniel Rudd.

He weaves through the few pedestrians to my right with a fluidity that belies his size. There always was something about him, an electric energy, ingenuity, and deftness. He's only about six feet from me now, and I blink, trying to clear my vision. I know he's here. But I just can't believe he's here. "How?"

Daniel flashes a grin of bright white. I notice how his teeth stand out against his skin. He's more tan than I remember from our first meeting in the Bubble, Langley's auditorium and our first stop for clandestine orientation. Tanner than when I saw him that last day too. Granted, that was seven years ago, and I expect Daniel's been to a lot of sunny places since then.

"Cademan stormed into Moreno's office after talking to you. She let me stay as my clearance is higher than his, and . . ." Daniel pauses and focuses on me. His hazel eyes still have that golden quality I remember, made even brighter by his tan. The tiny scar at the corner of his left eye stands out a little more in contrast. The endearing story he once told about how he got it in childhood returns to me. I miss his first sentence, distracted by the memory.

". . . since I got back to the States a week ago and am due for a little downtime, I figured, why not help out a friend?"

I blink again as Daniel's focus travels up and over my head to the line behind me. He tilts his chin as he steps alongside me and we move up a spot. I'm now number five.

"So, Penguin, what's your play here?"

CHAPTER 19

Haris Voekler

Friday, August 28, 1982

I fold the letter, slide it into the envelope, and lick the glue to seal it. I close my eyes, envisioning the censors steaming it open to read its contents. I pray I'm skilled enough to send this. If I am not, and my buried words are uncovered, I will be killed. Tortured first. Then killed.

I've taken precautions, though. I did not signal the acrostic anywhere in the letter, and I've mixed the pattern within every paragraph. I'm relying on Walther. I'm relying that he can follow my patterns, habits, and thinking. After all, he knows me better than anyone after all these years, and he trained me. We've only ever used about eight different styles. Cycling through each, he'll solve it. He must.

I lean back and stretch my spine. The rickety wood chair groans and shifts in protest. I drop the front legs back to the floor again. The sound of splitting wood signals one of the legs might break. It has threatened that for years.

Outside my bedroom's one window the sun rises. I should be exhausted, but I'm still wired. The morning light's pinks and oranges refract off the dust in the air and find their way around billows of coal smoke from heaters working against the chill of our first truly cool night. Fall is coming. The days will grow short and cold soon.

I walk across my apartment to fill a glass of water at the kitchen sink. The window there faces more westerly. I think of Manfred and hope he's gone. If he succeeded and got through, over or under the wall as he planned, I feel certain he'll write to me. Somehow he'll let me know.

I suppose I'll also find out if he fails.

I can't simply ask. I can't ask because Koch would note and convey my interest. That alone would prompt questions. I can't ask because Manfred's family won't be told, no matter how highly they are positioned within the government; they'll be watched. Usually when someone is caught or killed attempting to cross the wall, their family is told some innocuous story. A car accident or other random occurrence happened. But when they are forbidden to hold a public funeral, they suspect. And when family members get called into the local VoPo office on the most spurious excuse for questioning, they know. *Neues Deutschland*'s obituary writer has backed away from enough private funerals to get a clear picture, and downs enough beer nightly to have shared that and more with me.

Manfred turned out to be a good reporter. Maybe too good. His job was to uphold the Party line just as the Stasi's mandate is to protect the Party. But Manfred asked real questions and he searched for answers. He had an insatiable curiosity and a sharp mind. We never talked about when his thinking changed, and his outside demeanor never did. But I sensed a change within him as surely as he sensed it within me, and we became friends.

Yes, he was the Party's man when he first started at the paper, but I estimate they'd lost him by 1980.

Manfred was fascinated by the unprecedented world events that started to unfold that year. They were of such a magnitude even

Neues Deutschland could not avoid them, and Manfred was the star reporter tasked to cover them all.

At first Koch wanted the paper to give only a couple inches to some of the biggest stories of the century. Pope John Paul II. Solidarity. Lech Wałęsa. "We don't want our people dwelling upon them."

Our job was to give a glimpse to the outside world but to keep readers focused on their daily lives and work. One step in front of the other. There really is something so small about the Communist vision. Look at your feet. Never look around. Never look up.

But Manfred disagreed, and by 1980, he had the clout to be heard. "If we don't exhaust each and every detail across our front page, we will look like fools or, worse, conspirators. There is a way to present these movements without seeming to endorse them or fear them."

Koch was offended by the unflattering implications in Manfred's statement but was willing to concede to the judgment. It was Manfred's use of the word *fear* that got him. I saw it in his eyes. It's the compelling force of our lives, but it's verboten to state it aloud.

Yet Manfred's subtle manipulation got him pages of newsprint to cover a shipyard strike in Gdańsk that grew into a movement that swept through Poland; an assassination attempt against the "leader of the free world," US President Ronald Reagan; and, weeks later, an assassination attempt against the leader of the greatest numbered group of Christians in the world, and probably the most electrifying man in Europe, Pope John Paul II.

The articles framed all three events as well beyond our purview—one an unjustified and illegal protest, one the act of a crazy American obsessed with a Hollywood star, the last the act of a singular, perhaps also crazy, Turkish citizen. The Party was happy with the coverage, pleased with the emotional distance Manfred's choice of words created, and delighted that our feedback was disdainful of such violence and chaos. He conveyed a certain sense of "other" within his articles that pleased both Moscow and our Party—earning him several promotions and raises.

But Manfred printed only a fraction of what he learned. He grew into a brilliant interviewer and often learned far more than his subjects knew they'd revealed. He learned from a watch salesman that Solidarity grew from inception to over ten million members within a couple weeks just by chatting about work times, output, and quotas. This led him to track down more Polish informants, samizdat—the underground newspapers—and tune in to Radio Free Europe at all hours of the night.

He noted every move the Polish government made, including the imposition of martial law in December of '81, and studied Solidarity's resilience and resurgence despite the draconian measures to eradicate it. He analyzed the similarities between the faltering Polish economy and our own. He learned of massive numbers of Soviet troops gathering at the Polish border for an invasion, not unlike their answer to the Hungarian Uprising in '56 or the Prague Revolt of '68. And when the Soviet forces suddenly stood down—instantly went silent and fully retreated—Manfred believed he discovered the answer to that too.

"The US president was shot."

We were walking to a bar that evening to meet coworkers. I had noted, over the years, that more and more of our conversations took place outdoors on such walks. I never said it, though. Some things you don't call out.

"How does an American shooting his own president have anything to do with the Soviets invading Poland? It's half a world away. You're reaching." I scoffed and started planning a different discussion in my head. A lecture on how he would get in trouble soon if he wasn't more careful.

"When their president was shot, the US opened all their missile silos. Their military went on high alert. War ready. The Soviets feared a war-ready United States might intervene if they moved on Poland. Call it coincidence. Call it Providence. But that's what happened. Half a world away."

I stopped. "How on earth did you hear any of that?"

"My best friend is Wolf's right-hand man."

I gulped. I had things to hide, yes, but here was a man whose best friend worked with Stasi spymaster Markus Wolf.

"Manfred, this has to stop." I gripped his forearm so forcefully I brought him swinging around to face me. "You need to be more careful. What if he catches on that you are too interested in these issues?"

"I can't and he'd never betray me." Manfred's eyes rounded. A vulnerability lingered in them that I hadn't seen before. "Understanding all this, the truth behind this culture of lies, and the larger world scope, is all that keeps me sane."

"Manfred." My heart sank. It was worse than I'd thought.

We walked on. Both of us were too much in our own heads to speak again. I put another restraining hand on his arm as we approached the bar. "You can trust me. You need to know that. But I can't think of anyone else. Not at work, at least."

"There is no one. And I've known you're trustworthy for a while."

With that we dropped our masks back into place and went to share beers with friends.

Then a few days ago, Manfred headed to Stasi headquarters

to gather talking points for a new series of articles. Koch wanted a puff piece on DDR stability. "Solidarity has gotten every government, especially Moscow, twitchy. The people need reassurance."

I expected Manfred to return from his meeting rosy and bright eyed. All those secrets are like candy to the kid. He's about thirty-two now, eight years Luisa's senior, but I still think of him as a kid. He carries youth about him like Luisa must—at least in my imagination. But Manfred wasn't happy at all. He was pale, quiet, and only when we sat down to review his notes did I see his hands were shaking.

"What's wrong?"

He startled as if I'd shocked him. Not metaphorically, but like I had taken a real live wire and poked him. "Nothing. Why would you ask that?"

I shifted my focus to his hand. He looked down, finally seeing and feeling what I had noticed. He clenched his hand into a fist and dropped it into his lap. "I must be hungry."

I sat back in my chair. "Go get food. I can wait."

And I could. Helping Manfred with whatever he needed was my only task for the day. I've been so marginalized over the years, I don't even flinch over my topics and assignments anymore. Last week my top stories covered a litter of puppies and a new World War II monument that opened last May and has become the top tourist destination here in the city. It's a steep fall from covering the only revolt in East German history, the Potsdamer Platz protest in '53, to an usually large—fifteen puppies—schnauzer litter.

"No." Manfred closed his eyes for a moment. His whole body shivered despite our offices being warmed to the point of stifling by the late-afternoon August sun. He opened his eyes and appeared calm and focused. I blinked at the change he'd accomplished. "Let's get through this."

We talked through his notes. We determined the best order in which to address the points both Koch and Stasi Chief Mielke want highlighted. In the end it was a good piece. "*A good piece*," as Monica called it years ago, "*of top-grade propaganda.*"

I sent Manfred off to find food while I had the article typeset. It only took about an hour and then I left too. More depressed than usual. Something had happened that afternoon at central Stasi headquarters and Manfred lost the light I'd come to value in him. Light I didn't know I needed until it was extinguished. I almost expected Manfred to invite me out for beers to talk and work through it, as we often did, without acknowledging that was what we were doing. It concerned me when he didn't.

I didn't walk straight home that night. I needed to be out. And it was a lovely summer evening. Probably one of our last. I headed west, rather than east, and found myself in my old neighborhood. I knew they were torn down a couple years ago, but the absence of the Bernauer Strasse buildings shocked me. Facades really. Bulldozers brought down the buildings in '65, but the facades remained as part of the wall until its latest iteration was finished a couple years ago.

The wall now stands over three meters high with a one-meter-plus lip at its base stretching to the west. I went easy on Walther in my letter describing it, as he's so Americanized now, and let him know that translates to ten feet high with a footprint stretching four feet to the west. It's that lip, or footprint, that will keep the reinforced concrete standing unaffected in the event anyone tries to drive a truck into the wall again. No one has tried that in close to twenty years, and the concrete is so thick, plus reinforced with metal bars, that I'm not sure it could work ever again. But one never knows who will try, I guess.

I stood staring at the wall and realized how circumvented my life has become. Between work and my apartment to the northeast, I don't travel near the wall anymore. I prefer not to see it. Most days I can pretend it doesn't exist. But facing it, it's undeniable. Not only is it tall, but it's now fitted with a cement pipe fashioned along its top to create a slippery and unclimbable surface. I recalled how, a few years ago during its development, I watched as two police officers, both former athletes, were tasked with trying to scale the new design to detect its deficiencies. There were none. Neither athlete could make it over, and I wrote a short article praising the government's ingenuity, while not reminding the citizenry of the reason for it.

My reporting assignments are almost laughable, really, but there is an upside to all this obscurity. I'm not watched much anymore. I have not been called into Koch's office, nor to the Stasi to "clear up matters," in five years. The bug still sits within my electrical outlet, but as I live alone and never entertain guests, it hardly matters.

The sun set and the night grew cool. I had walked too long and had grown hungry. I headed home.

On my way I noticed again the doors to nowhere. It's been almost forty years since the end of the war and older sections of town still remain in rubble. Like those doors that float on the third and fourth floors of buildings because the other part was bombed away. Why can't those be fixed? Why can't they be bricked over and hidden like so much else? They always invite a hopelessness that makes me uncomfortable. I looked to my feet again.

Berlin is like a movie set. My father took me to one when I was very young. Director Henry Koster had fled Berlin by that time, but the set from his comedy *Thea Roland* still existed and was being used for another film. Papa had a job there before the war and took me one afternoon. It was sleek and clean and modern, but when I took one step off the carefully constructed Main Street to find a bathroom, I found a dirty, broken-down, and cramped world inches away. Reality was vastly different from the fiction portrayed.

Karl-Marx-Allee. Alexanderplatz. Those are our movie sets. That's where the government allows the tourists to visit.

This rubble? The doors to nowhere? That's backstage. Tourists can't see it and we can't escape it. It's where we live.

Manfred didn't show up at work the next day, or the two days following. I fact-checked and filed a couple of articles he'd written in the past to fill his quotas and asked no questions as to his whereabouts. Office gossip told me he was home sick with a fever. I was relieved as it explained the tremors, the startle, and all the odd behavior. Everyone, including me, believed his illness was real.

Then, last night, I got a surprise outside my building.

"Haris?"

I narrowed my eyes. It's harder for me to see in the dark now and I couldn't differentiate between tree and shadow. But I recognized the voice. "Manfred?"

"Shh . . ." He stepped closer. "Can we talk?"

I gestured toward my building, inviting him to come up. I dropped my hand, remembering the bug in my living room socket.

He shook his head anyway, refusing the invitation, and tilted his head past my building toward the industrial park behind. Without another word, he walked away and I followed him. It took me a few quick steps to catch up, and just as I noted his low-drawn cap, he reached into his shirt and handed me one. I turned it in my hands. It was that kind with the bill that are becoming popular.

"Put it on at the corner."

"Why?"

He glanced to me. "Please."

As we were nearing the corner, I didn't have time to ask another question. I ducked my head, pulled on the hat, and we turned left and kept walking.

"Thanks." He looked to me again. "That was the last street camera. There are no others out here."

"How do you know that?" I told myself long ago to stop being surprised by all that Manfred knew, and yet I still was.

"That friend at MfS." Manfred pressed his lips tight. "He's dead."

"Who's dead?"

"My best friend. Wolf's assistant." He said the words slowly. "There will be no funeral, no announcement."

"Hmm . . ." I offered nothing more. Manfred didn't break the silence as we walked on. Eventually I did. "You haven't been sick?"

He didn't answer me. Instead he looked back to see how far we'd walked, then ahead to see how far ahead we could go. Only then did he speak. "We were viewed on camera talking near Magdalenenstrasse Station after my interview with Chief Mielke. They had questions for me."

"Wait." I put my arm out. "You've been in Stasi custody for the past two days?" I took in the circles around his eyes, his cracked lips, and their slight tremor.

"I recounted every word for them." Manfred started us walking again. "Of a conversation we had months ago. It's what saved me. Because it was real. Every detail stayed the same despite their best efforts to change it."

"How many times did they ask?" I'd heard how they wake you with bright lights every fifteen minutes just as you doze off, deny you food and water, apply pressure, pain, and prompting in order to get new answers to incessantly repeated questions. They bend time. They compress time. They bend and compress you too.

"I lost count." Manfred lifted a shoulder in a half-hearted shrug—in exhaustion, not nonchalance.

I scanned the emptiness around us. No one was in sight, yet . . .

"How are you here? Why? You'll be followed for a while, won't you? He was your best friend."

My work and my letters to Walther came to mind, and I'm ashamed to admit I felt panic over my own situation despite the obvious raw need in front of me.

"I lost them miles ago. We're safe for now."

I glanced to him. It felt as if he'd read my thoughts—perhaps because that's how we all think whether we're doing something wrong or not.

He continued, "I've done this for years. As kids, my friends and I located all the cameras throughout the city and tested ourselves as to how long we could stay out of view. It was our form of childhood rebellion and the cameras never change."

I didn't expect that from Manfred and sensed I'd underestimated or misunderstood his discontent and how far back it might stretch. I was also impressed by his ingenuity.

"Why are we walking, Manfred?"

"I need to tell you something. I am sorry. I shouldn't, but if I die, someone must know and I trust you. My best friend is dead."

I closed my eyes for a step, finally realizing he hadn't told me his friend's name. It's such a small detail. But if I was to be arrested, it would become exponentially larger.

"Why?" I pushed back. This was suddenly deeper than I anticipated. My heart started pounding.

"I've heard about your family, your daughter. I've watched you over the years at work. You may not agree with all that happens here, but you endure. Even to the point of obscurity. I also know you visit the Church of Zion on weekdays. I know what you do."

My heart dropped to my stomach, and I wondered if I'd be sick. There's only one reason anyone visits a church on weekdays—to participate in the opposition events that take place in their basements. I took a different path almost every time I went and was sure I'd never been followed over the years. But clearly I had been.

I faced Manfred. There could be no pretending between us anymore. "What do you want?"

"I need you to know something. You don't have to do anything about it. I don't know what you could do anyway. But someday they have to be made accountable. Someone outside their ranks needs to know. It will bring down the world."

"Whoa." I stepped back. "Stop. I don't want anything like that. What are you talking about? Is this some kind of joke?"

My own words reminded me of long ago as I frantically searched for someone who would risk helping Monica over the wall. Everyone first asked if I was joking, then pushed at me, afraid I wasn't. No one would help. No one trusted me. I pushed at Manfred's shoulder in much the same way. He looked up and I saw my long-ago desperation reflected in his eyes.

"What is it?" I conceded. "You can tell me anything."

We walked on and he told me things that were—just as he said—big enough to bring down the world.

He called it *Operation Papst.*

I felt sick at the very name. Nothing good could come from a Stasi operation titled Operation Pope.

Manfred let the name sit in silence between us until I couldn't stand it any longer. "What is it? Just tell me."

He went on to say that despite the KGB disinformation campaign to keep the world's eyes fixed on the lone Turkish gunman, Mehmet Ali Ağca, as responsible for the pope's shooting, that wasn't the whole story. Rumors were beginning to circulate globally. Rumors that Moscow had to squelch.

"What rumors?" I shook my head, trying to think back to everything I'd read, not in our paper, but in the samizdat. Nothing. I'd read nothing other than a fierce commitment to the one-gunman theory.

"It wasn't one lone man. It was planned and highly organized," Manfred whispered. "By the Soviets."

"What?" I stopped again. "People are saying Moscow ordered a hit on the pope? Aloud?" I couldn't believe the questions flew from my mouth. I clamped my hand over it as if that could turn back time and stop them. It's one thing to poke the bear in one's own country—all the "bears" in the Eastern Bloc are mere cubs. But Mother Bear is another beast altogether. Even asking the question felt dangerous.

"That's because they did."

I shook my head. It was more of a swing motion really, a physical and cognitive denial of information I was not prepared to absorb. My hand gripped the sides of my jaw so tight I flinched with pain before realizing I was the source of it.

"No . . ." The words escaped me in a whisper, a breath, a sigh.

Manfred continued, both walking and talking, as if not hearing me at all. I stumbled forward to catch up.

"The Stasi, under Markus Wolf's division, has been tasked to create another, better disinformation campaign to shut down all rumors. There's already a known thread tying Ağca to the Bulgarians, so their security service can't handle it. They have to keep quiet now. But Moscow wouldn't task them with that anyway. Disinformation is what the Stasi does best."

I cast my mind back to 1978 when Manfred first mentioned Moscow's reaction to the pope's election. He said the KGB had tasked the Stasi to analyze the possible effects this new pope could have across the Eastern Bloc. If the KGB wanted information and analysis, they came to the Stasi. An assassination, I gathered, sent them to the Bulgarians.

"The operation is incredibly detailed and thorough. It will send rumors and press bites all around the world. It has to. The order to kill the pope came from the top."

We stopped walking again and he stared at me with such intensity, I couldn't look away. "Moscow to the Bulgarians, who commissioned Ağca and a team to carry it out. The Bulgarians have already rounded up the other players. Now the Stasi's Operation Pope is to shut down any remaining questions. Can you imagine what happens if they don't succeed? Something like this could lead to World War III."

I folded at the waist. I felt like I was about to throw up, but Manfred wouldn't even give me that moment. He grabbed my shoulders and pulled me straight. "I'm trying to get through tonight. There's no way they'll let me live. Even if he hadn't said anything to me, they can't risk it. I didn't know it at the time, but they let it slip that my friend was seen on camera opening the operational file, despite it being marked *Streng Geheim*, then he walked me out the door moments later." Manfred shuddered. "What else are they going to think?"

"Nothing other than he told his best friend everything."

Manfred sighed. "He wanted to be a teacher."

I felt sorry for Manfred. For all of us. Because it didn't matter if his friend wanted to be a teacher, a dentist, or a bricklayer. If his family was Stasi, he was always going to be Stasi.

"How'd they do it?" I whispered. There was no need to whisper.

It simply felt more respectful, and I couldn't draw breath for anything louder anyway.

"His mother called. Suicide. But—no. Just no."

"How are you going to escape?" I thought of all his Stasi and Politburo connections. How could he manage it so quickly? Who would ever risk helping him?

"I haven't worked it out yet." Manfred stared into the distance. I knew he was imagining the wall. I was doing the same. "But that's not important. That doesn't need to endure. What I've told you does. Please."

"What am I to do with it?" I heard the sarcasm, the fear, and the anger in my voice. "The West already has sanctions against the USSR for Afghanistan, the rhetoric out of the US is vitriolic, Moscow is growing its army . . . Where do you think you are right now? We're the epicenter. You remember what Khrushchev said? 'Every time I want to make the West scream, I squeeze on Berlin.' Nothing's changed. When they go to war over this, and they will, it will be nuclear and we'll be the center once more. If you don't survive, this is on me? The greatest secret in the world is my problem?"

I couldn't breathe. I folded over. This time, Manfred didn't grab my shoulders and haul me up. He crouched beside me.

"I'm sorry." His face dropped into my field of vision. "I just needed someone to know. If I get out, I'll be responsible for it—I promise, it's all on me. But if I don't, I couldn't let the truth die with me. You don't need to tell it, just endure it."

I straightened and he pushed up from the ground to stand in front of me again. We took a moment to assess each other. He was right. Someone needed to know. Even if a word was never spoken, it still mattered that someone knew.

I put a hand on his shoulder, sorry that I made him feel selfish, sorry that I didn't realize right away the risk and the burden he had carried these last few days—and will carry for the rest of his life. I will now carry it, too, and I, better than most, understand how heavy some burdens prove to be.

"I am sorry," he repeated.

"Don't be." I left it there. I didn't share about my letters to Walther; I didn't share about my work at the Church of Zion. I simply let him know in two short words that I was on his side. I gestured behind us. "You need to get out of here. Even knowing where all the cameras are can only buy you so much time. Go. I'll be fine." He stepped away and I grabbed his arm. "Be safe."

He walked one way and I walked the other. I made a long circle around my complex, and when I reached the nearest corner to my building, I pulled off the hat and stuffed it into my shirt. I then walked up to my apartment, saying a cheerful hello to everyone I passed.

Once inside, I passed into my bedroom. I said nothing for the benefit of anyone listening, though I suspect they gave up monitoring me years ago. Nevertheless, I didn't sigh. I didn't hum. I didn't cough. I didn't do any of the things I often do. I simply pulled out pen and paper to start the most important letter of my life.

August 28, 1982

Dear Walther,

I have much to atone for. Only too late did I understand the consequences. I never should have let work define me. Please tell Luisa of all my regrets. If she knew me now, she wouldn't recognize me from the man I was in her childhood. Everything has changed for me. And continues to change. Recently I was walking along our old street. Memories came at me so fast, I almost buckled with their impact. Always Monica and Luisa. And me, never the man I wanted to be. Too many regrets, Walther, fill my days and my dreams. So many I can't breathe sometimes. I can, however, ask for her and your forgiveness. Please tell her. Only don't tell her what I once was. You were right to never trust me then. Now I think you could. Please share that with her and share about my work too. Only yesterday I wrote about a litter of schnauzers. Puppies so small and adorable, eyes not yet open, all I wanted to do was cuddle them. Eve, the owner, offered to let me take one home . . .

I leaned back and looked at what I'd written. It was just a beginning and I didn't signify the code in any way. I just had to trust that cycling through the eight iterations we usually employ, he'll find it.

I chuffed. This letter was going to be long. All night long. It took me that whole paragraph just to begin . . .

O P E R A T I O N P O P E

CHAPTER 20

Luisa Voekler

WEST BERLIN
Wednesday, November 8, 1989

Penguin.

I see from Daniel's eyes he's recalling a great memory. Memories of the two of us and not our real code names during training, but the ones we gave each other outside a bar our first week of training. I was dubbed PENGUIN. It seems I flap my arms while running. While not exactly flattering, SUNBEAM's and TARCAT's imitations had me almost peeing my pants in the middle of Wisconsin Avenue. Daniel's code name was GRASSHOPPER. He jumped over a car. I'm not exaggerating. We were searching for a cab after late-night drinks, and SUNBEAM and TARCAT started running like flappy crazy people, making fun of me.

Daniel took off after them. They started a cat-and-mouse game to evade him, but rather than run around a parked car and lose time in catching them, he jumped over a Jetta. Completely over it. Only one hand touched down on its roof to propel him fully across. He vied for SUPERMAN as his moniker. We assigned him GRASSHOPPER.

But as fun as those memories were to make, I don't consider

them great to recall. They're tainted by what I thought was my failure. Now, after speaking with Andrew, I'm not sure what it was, but whatever it is doesn't feel any better. Not yet.

Daniel catches my expression and loops an arm around me as if seven years haven't passed between us. "None of that." Without another word he uses that same arm to twist me out of line and back down the street.

"Hey." I glance back over my shoulder. His stride is so quick, Checkpoint Charlie is almost a full block in our rear before I protest. "That was part of the plan. I want to see how they record passport information and how long day passes last."

"A day. They expire every day at midnight. And your name would be on a list, and the instant you stepped over that border, you'd be photographed and followed. You're better than that."

I stop. "What if I'm not?"

He steps in front of me and crosses his arms over his chest. He's still six-two, but that's all that's the same about this man. He was a thin twenty-four-year-old, loose, lanky, sharp as a tack, and strong, but still coming into his own at Langley. We all were.

At thirty-one he's strong and his chest is broad. He's still loose and lanky, to a degree, but there's a chiseled-ness about him, an edge to his cut, his actions, and his demeanor. I once called his brain sharp. Now I would call all of him sharp.

"Enough," he whispers, but it sounds like a bark.

I raise a brow. He does the same. It's a standoff. Until I break first.

"We both know that's not why you were cut. I've seen your scores too. They were excellent."

"You have . . . Wait, how long have you known?"

He toggles his head as if backpedaling through time. "Six years?

As soon as I got clearance high enough to see pretty much anything I wanted to."

"Are you serious? And you didn't tell me?"

"Stupid questions. Of course I couldn't, so I didn't. But it wouldn't have mattered." He lifts his chin. "You cut me out so thoroughly, I bet you wouldn't have taken my call if I'd tried."

My gaze falls to my feet. He's right. But his posture and words tell me he thinks it was some great offensive move on my part, not the act of a coward who was too heartbroken and downtrodden to show her face. I was beyond embarrassed. I felt ashamed, and I simply "cut" my friends before they could cut me. And they would have—I was out of the jokes, the shoptalk, the adventures, the acronyms and inside lingo, the shared experiences, and the camaraderie. I was instantly on the outside of all of it, and I couldn't bear the inevitable conversational shifts, pitying glances, and canceled plans.

"I'm sorry."

Daniel's finger presses against the bottom of my chin, lifting my face. "None of that. I'm here now. How can I help?"

Zing. Everything I once imagined I might feel for this man—once we graduated from the Farm—is back. But just like the Farm, this is not the time or the place to consider or feel any of that. Besides, I'm not that girl anymore.

"How exactly are you here?" I return to my earlier question.

He smiles again. "As I said, Cademan went to complain to his wife, who's the branch chief of the Southeast Asia division, and I happened to be sitting there innocently drinking my coffee."

I huff a tiny laugh. I should have known. Honestly, the CIA is much smaller than people realize once you include all the marriages. At first the number surprised me; then I realized it makes perfect sense. All those inside jokes, acronyms, crypts, and experiences . . . If you don't want your spouse to be "outside" your life, you marry someone on the inside.

"That's where you're operational?" I lift my voice, fairly sure he won't answer. He merely shrugs. "So you decided to just help out an old friend? No one sent you? No one stopped you?"

"Who would?" He starts us walking again. "Let's just say I've thought about you a lot over the years, but nothing ever changed. I carried secrets you couldn't know—about you. And now I don't. So, yes, the minute Cademan left, I told Moreno I needed a week and grabbed a jump seat on a Navy jet out of Anacostia. I've been here . . ." He glances at his watch, a big-faced, chunky military thing. "Twenty hours." He smiles down at me again. "What took you so long?"

"No way." I stop walking. "You can't have expected this. I hadn't even worked out I was coming until after my lunch with a *Washington Post* reporter, hours after talking with Andrew."

"Please, Penguin."

I catch the note within his voice again. It's the same one that snagged me minutes ago when he first met me in line. It's not my code name he's saying, it's not something just anyone could use; it's a name only he can use. Somehow in one note it's his. I'm not sure what it means or even if he notices it himself. I just know I like it. Very much.

With a hand to my back, Daniel nudges me forward again. "I told you years ago. I know you better than you know yourself. You were always coming here."

I have to take two steps to every one of Daniel's.

I'm about to ask where we're going because it's clearly somewhere specific as he doesn't miss a beat leading us down Franz-Klüh-Strasse for a block before turning right on Lindenstrasse, but he starts talking before I get the chance.

"It's crazy here. Hungary, Czechoslovakia, Poland—it's all coming down. A few months, and we'll be in a whole new intelligence game. Where I've been, there's flux, incredible flux, but this will be wipe-the-board-and-start-over kind of stuff."

"You sound excited." I barely get the words out at the pace we're walking.

"I am. What an adventure. The best kind. The protests are growing, Luisa. They're talking almost a million in Leipzig alone. That's a third of the population protesting with hundreds of thousands fleeing. The country won't exist soon if it doesn't change. With reforms implemented all around them, the pressure will be relentless, for East Germany and the entire Soviet Union. Can you imagine where all this might lead?"

Three more blocks and the cacophony of neon street signs and chaos morphs into older buildings and broader avenues. They aren't quieter, per se, but they feel less frantic somehow. They feel more settled, older.

Daniel opens the door to another coffee shop. He lets me proceed him through the door, but not knowing what I am to do, I stop inside. He sidesteps and brushes past me, gesturing to the back corner. I glance that direction and find a man watching us. He's not heavyset like Fichman. He's medium size, medium build, with short brown hair and wire-rimmed glasses. Despite everything about him that looks conservative and ordinary, there's something flintlike in his eyes that makes him almost dangerous. All Fichman's size and disdain earlier didn't give me the sense of control, power, and even cleverness this man conveys in a single look.

Daniel pauses and I step back into the lead. For better or worse, this is my show.

The man motions for us to sit. "Robert Watson."

"Luisa Voekler." I gesture to Daniel, who introduces himself as well.

"Welcome to the Jungle," he says to us both. To me he adds, "Is this your first time in West Berlin?"

"Is it obvious?"

"No. Which is good." He gazes past us out the window. "I'd say this is how it always is here, but there is no always in Berlin. It's part of the nature of this city. Nowhere in the world is as mercurial. But even for Berlin, we've felt the increased tension of these past months."

Robert shifts his gaze to us again. "A week ago Krenz, the new GDR general secretary, tried to institute travel reforms to quell protests on his side of Berlin. He actually put in writing that East Germans could leave the country for holiday one full month of every year, but the GDR Parliament rejected it. Then all the members of the Council of Ministers and Politburo resigned. I'm beginning to wonder if the Soviets aren't going to come in again, except Gorby doesn't seem interested in military interventions these days. As I said, it's tense. Something will break soon. The question is, what?" He taps a pencil against his napkin and levels his focus on me. "I have heard what is basically your intention here. Are you sure you don't want to wait awhile?"

"I can't."

"Then let's start with what you have in mind."

"I brought all the money I have." His raised brow asks the amount. "Twenty-five thousand dollars. And I brought an American services uniform. It's all I knew to do."

"Probably in a shoebox, no less." Robert chuckles.

I part my lips a fraction.

"You didn't? You did." Robert glances to Daniel, and my face flushes with heat. I must seem so young and so naive to these two. But I'm not—at least I haven't always been. Ugh . . . I hate this feeling.

"Okay then," Robert continues. "Let's go with what I've developed. I can't guarantee it won't get you caught and arrested, but it sure has a better shot of succeeding than that."

He explains his plan. I sit wide-eyed and shocked.

Taking in my expression, he chuckles again. "It's about attitude. Desire. They'll take care of the rest. Either you want this or you don't. Are you in?"

"What about going through as a member of the press? They don't get searched," I offer.

"But they get followed. Every journalist is tailed by the Stasi from the first step in to at least several hours after their last step out. There's no leeway there." He glances between us. "Have I wasted my time?"

I shake my head. "I was only surprised. I can do it."

Robert continues, "You got lucky with the lineup tonight. Außenseiter goes on at 10:00 p.m., so it's not too late. Get to the club no later than midnight so you can see who they are. The place will be packed, which is good for you too, as Eintüzende Neubauten goes on after."

"Is that a person?"

"It's the most popular band in West Germany." He raises a brow, basically chastising me for getting lost in ancillary details. "When Außenseiter exits the stage around 12:30, you follow them to the back. You'll have about a half hour with Willow until their bus heads across the border." He narrows his eyes. "You'll need to look like her. Do you understand? Exactly like her. I don't want her mother to be able to tell the difference."

"Got it."

"Good, 'cause she's a good kid."

I hide my surprise at his comment and let him continue. "When you get on the bus, you do exactly what the band tells you. Their lives are on the line here too. They'll tell you they've all been arrested and interrogated and it's no big deal, but don't believe them. Every interrogation, every body cavity search, every Stasi intrusion into your intimate affairs is horrific. The part that they've all been through it is true, though."

"What about Willow?"

"She'll be you and hang out with Daniel until you get back."

I glance to Daniel before returning my focus to Robert. "When will that be?"

"That's up to you." He shakes his head like I am a huge disappointment. "I can get you through the border and I've got a contact for you tomorrow morning. A Stasi guard whose integrity sells for cheap. You'll get the details later as they're not fully sorted yet."

He stares at Daniel. "You gave me little time."

"It's all I had," Daniel replies, low and calm. "It'll work. She's the real deal."

Robert tilts his head as though he's not quite sure and looks to me. "I'm afraid, on the other side, you'll rely more on your ingenuity than my planning. I got the band and the guard, but anything can happen in between."

He slides his chair back to stand. Both of his hands grip the table. His fingers are strong, his nails cut short. "Best of luck to you. This is all I could do with the time allotted."

"I understand." I say the words, but I actually do not understand anything. I feel like I've been led into a haunted house with no path or exit plan. Surprises lurk around every corner. "Thank you."

"Don't thank me too soon."

With that he's gone.

I shift in my seat to face Daniel. He looks so relaxed, leaning back almost lazily in the chair, I want to thwap him, but I don't. Back in the day, his tell was the tapping of his index finger on any hard surface. He'd controlled it by our third week in, but we all noted when extreme stress brought it out. His finger is beating the table's corner quadruple time.

"I'm not sure I can do this." My vision sweeps the café. It appears so calm, so normal, almost like any café in DC, though greyer. I lift my coffee to my lips. My hands are shaking. Too little sleep. Too much coffee. No real food in hours. I set down the cup and rub my forehead so hard, it feels as if I'm scrubbing off skin rather than trying to help my mind clear. I need to think straight.

"Of course you can. It's a good plan actually." Daniel pulls at my hand. "Stop that. Come on. Let's get some shut-eye, then we'll grab dinner before we head to the club. It's going to be a long night."

We catch a cab back to my hotel. Daniel studies the room's twin bed. "Floor for me?"

"Up to you." I'm too tired and too wired to care. I scrub my face and teeth in the bathroom's tiny sink and, unable to do more, simply curl under the bed's covers and press myself close to the wall.

Daniel vacillates. "You sure?"

I point to the floor. It's some hard surface I can't identify with a thin area rug like office carpet. "It's either that or with me. You choose."

He drops onto the bed and I remember nothing more until he's shaking me. "Are you okay?"

I squirm, twisting into him under the covers until I'm free and sitting. "Did I scream?" Heat climbs up my throat and suffuses my cheeks.

"Moaned more like."

I explain to him the ubiquitous nightmare that's really a memory. I find myself sharing more than I usually do.

"You just learned all that? About your mother?"

"On Saturday." I lift my hands. "Same morning I burned my hands."

"That makes for quite a weekend, Penguin." He tucks a strand of hair behind my ear with such tenderness, I lean into his touch. "And this is quite a week."

He gives the strand a playful tug, then climbs off the bed. I do the same and start digging through my suitcase to give me something to do. Tension, fear, emotion, anxiety, and even a hint of desire all war within me. How can one person feel so much simultaneously? It's like I'm about to burst from the pressure of it all.

I glance to Daniel, who sits in the room's only chair. He points to the window and I notice, through the thin curtains, that the light has changed.

"It's eight o'clock. We should go."

Out on the sidewalk, he orients himself to my map and points to the left. "A friend gave me a restaurant suggestion off the beaten path. Do you like Turkish food?"

"I've never tried it." We take a few steps before I ask, "A friend?"

"A colleague. Class ahead of us at the Farm. Not sure you'd know him."

I don't reply. Part of me is pleased with the answer I got. It's more than I deserved. But part of me is a little hurt too. It's what I dreaded all those years ago, being on the outside. Daniel probably has lots of stories about this "friend" and a much clearer picture of him he could offer—to someone with clearance.

As we walk deeper west and the city continues to darken around us, Daniel explains that Berlin received an influx of Turkish immigrants right after World War II, but that the population never fully assimilated and their neighborhoods, not being hot spots for protests, aren't as assiduously surveilled. Therefore we are about to get great food and, most likely, not catch anyone's attention in the most watched city in the world.

The restaurant is small, warm, and crowded. We are met with smiles at the front door and led to two spots at a long table in front of the grill. Three chefs, who look to be a father and his two sons, work quickly and efficiently in front of us. Although I can't understand what they are saying, I get the impression it's more chatting, fun, and even teasing than it is instructional or anything to do with the orders the waitstaff slide to them on small slips of paper.

Daniel and I both point to our menus with questioning eyes. The waitress, perhaps the mom of the whole crew, laughs at our consternation, takes away our menus, and gives us the distinct impression she'll simply take care of us. Her kindness almost makes me cry, as I don't have the energy to make a single decision right now.

A variety of small plates soon arrive. While I can't name a single one, from one that looks like pale peanut butter to what I suspect are pickled onions and olives in tomatoes to something grilled brown and incredibly flavorful, I try every one.

One of the chefs pours batter onto the grill, and I think he is making a pancake. The pancake rises to the size of a football and is only slightly deflated by the time he slides it over the counter to us. I watch the couple next to us and soon know to pull the bread apart and dip it through our many dishes.

The atmosphere works a kind of magic. I feel full, energized, calm, and even hopeful as our meal progresses. Our conversation turns from the night ahead to the past and what brought us to this point. We cover college courses we never talked about when we knew each other, friends, boyfriends, girlfriends, professional achievements and disappointments (the ones we can share), and what we want from our futures.

"Do you love it?" I ask.

Daniel gives me a small smile, one sincere but full of other emotions as well. I sense regret, even disappointment in it. "I do. It matters. But it doesn't come without sacrifices. I didn't realize how many back then."

The meal ends with a dessert unlike anything I've ever tasted. Our waitress calls it baklava and it's heaven. Like a hundred layers of heaven made of pastry dough with nuts between the layers and oozing with a honeyed syrup. It takes all my willpower not to lick my plate clean.

Daniel's indulgent laugh lets me know he's well acquainted with baklava.

Around 11:00 p.m. we pay the bill, and after our hostess-turned-waitress hugs us goodbye, we find ourselves standing on the sidewalk on a cold, dark, windy night. I glance to Daniel and can tell by his clenched jaw, he feels it too. Reality.

"Come on." Daniel, hands shoved deep into his pockets, points a shoulder down the street. "It's time to get to the club."

SO36, Robert told us, is one of West Berlin's most famous clubs—and even I know that's saying something. West Berlin is a city with hundreds of clubs and no closing times. A city that never sleeps and where the party never ends.

We walk several blocks and soon find ourselves crossing Oranienstrasse. The sign for SO36 glows blue above a black double-wide opening into an old building two blocks down and across the street.

We stand on the corner and stare at it. After our next step, there is no turning back.

Daniel faces me. "We should cover a few things before we go inside. We won't be able to hear much in there. What's the band leader's name?"

"Panzer. And I'm swapping places with Willow, the drummer. But is that his real name?" I can't imagine a mom, no matter her nationality or loyalties, naming her son after a Soviet tank.

"None of them use their real names, not even with each other. It's both a sign of a new identity and protection. You can't rat a guy out if you don't know his name."

"Good point."

"Now remember, only Panzer and Willow know about this. None of the other band members do and one of them could be a Stasi snitch. Willow will be with me, so you only talk to Panzer when you get over there, got it?"

"Daniel, I got it." I can't decide if I find his nerves endearing and oddly reassuring or patronizing. But as I'm not sure I really do "got it," I appreciate his care. He's seen and done things over the years, honing every instinct, and, as I've come to realize, I've fallen asleep at the wheel of life.

"Take this." He hands me a slip of paper. "Tuck it someplace safe."

I unfold the small corner of paper. It's a long series of numbers, but I'm not sure what they mean.

"It's a phone number. Those are the exact numbers you dial. Don't add a country code or anything. It'll get across the Wall, I promise, and I'll be on the other side. While you find your dad, I'll work on a way to get you out."

I tuck the paper in my bra. I want to ask what he's got in mind or who else he can tap without official CIA cover, but before I form the full thought behind any question, much less ask one, he pulls at my arm.

"Come on. Showtime."

We hear the pulsating music a full block away. Once we're outside the open doors of the club, it's so loud I can't hear the people talking around me. As we're about to enter, Daniel pulls me close and yells in my ear, "You ready?"

I'm not sure I am, but I nod anyway.

"Okay then," he yells again. "Let's get you punked."

CHAPTER 21

Wednesday, November 8, 1989

It takes time for my eyes to adjust. It doesn't take time for my ears, however. They are accosted at a decibel I've never encountered before, and I pray they simply shut down before they're damaged for life.

Daniel smiles down at me. He says something, but it's lost in the noise. He pulls me behind him and leads us forward through the packed crowd. The club's center is a mash of people jumping and twisting to the music. It feels claustrophobic with everything crowding in—sound, sweat, heat, people, pressure, with the black walls and the low black-painted ceiling broken up and lit by a single flashing neon white light.

At the far end of the room on a low stage I find Außenseiter. The band's name translates to "Outsiders," and I'm learning that it's the defining aspect of punk. To be outside.

I look at each of the band members in turn.

Panzer, the lead singer, is huge, and I guess that's why he chose a tank for his moniker. He looks to be well over six feet tall with his jet-black spiked hair towering another solid foot above him. His black eyeliner streams down his cheeks as sweat flies off him.

I glance past the other three band members in ripped black

clothing and crazy-colored hair to land on Willow, the single girl, seated behind the drums.

She looks a little taller than I am, though it's hard to tell with her sitting, but she's definitely younger. A lot younger.

I yell into Daniel's ear, "I look nothing like her."

"You will," he yells back.

I gasp, though no one hears me, as the crowd starts to throw beer cans at the band. The bass guitarist dodges the flying projectiles and, against one hurling can, swings his guitar handle like a baseball bat and sends it soaring back into the crowd. The place roars its approval.

"Why doesn't anyone stop them? Someone could get hurt." Although I cup Daniel's ear with my hand, I still yell.

"They'd be more insulted if cans weren't thrown." He does the same, using both hands, but I sense he's not yelling.

"I don't understand."

Daniel merely shrugs. We watch for a few minutes before I feel his hands around my ear again. "Remember, they're an East Berlin band. It's rage, discordance, anarchy, and destruction. It's meant to be all that, as well as angry and alien. Punk in Eastern Europe is nothing like what you hear out of London, New York, or even here in West Berlin. This is political opposition aimed straight at the dictatorship."

I want to ask why the government lets them out if they're so oppositional, but I can't as Panzer releases a final growl, screams a last high, searing note into the microphone, and then proceeds to smash his guitar to flying shards of wood against the stage floor. The crowd goes crazy—again.

We stand at the edge, pressed against the wall with our feet sticking to the floor. My head is near exploding from the strobe lights and the horrible smell of sweat, marijuana, alcohol, and who knows what else. It's cloying and suffocating. But through the smoke and frenzy, I catch glimpses of the band shuffling to a rear door behind the stage.

I pull at Daniel's sleeve and tilt my head to the stage. He notices too and nods.

We push our way forward and body-slam open a metal side door. The contrast to the club blinds me. I close my eyes, then start to blink slowly and methodically to let my eyes adjust. Bare bulbs hang from the ceiling, and the unpainted cement walls feel sterile and glaring. But it's quieter and that's a relief.

There's an open doorway several feet away with shouts spilling into the hallway. I head that way, assuming it's the band congratulating themselves on a great set. The crowd certainly seemed pleased. Turning into the room, I find I'm right. They are clustered together high-fiving, screaming, slapping at each other in a kind of frenzy. All motion stops the instant one of them notices us. They stare.

"This is her?" Willow looks to Panzer.

"Yes."

Close up, I see how young Panzer is. He looks around twenty years old. From a distance I thought his clothes disheveled and crude, but close up I see how much care has gone into each item. Although ripped, his leather pants have been stitched in bright threads. His jacket, torn, has been carefully reconstructed with both safety pins and staples. The chains between his buttons and pockets have been secured by clips and thick threads.

Panzer and Willow step toward us, leaving the other band members feet behind them. They continue with their celebration, hovering around a table laden with bottles.

"Are you sure about this?" he asks in German. He's not speaking to me. He's speaking to Willow, standing only a few feet away and staring at me with unblinking eyes. She nods in a single minute motion.

Panzer snaps his fingers at me. I don't know what he wants until Daniel nudges me. Money.

I reach into my tights and pull out the five thousand dollars I agreed with Robert to pay them. I slid it down the left leg of my tights back at the hotel room. Fifty one-hundred-dollar bills. It feels oddly light and unsubstantial in my hand. I'm afraid Panzer will demand more.

He doesn't. He tucks the money into an inside pocket of his jacket and gestures to a side door.

"Get going. The rest of us will load the equipment onto the bus. Schmidt will be here soon." Panzer turns back to the band. "We got about a half hour. Move!"

Daniel puts a hand to my back and we follow Willow through the door. She can't be more than a teenager. Perhaps a little over half my age. She shuts the door behind us. The room is quiet and empty with a mirror and a sink but no toilet.

"It's not about the money, and he'll use it to print samizdat," she says in German. I cast a glance at Daniel, wondering if he understands. It's not the time to ask and I suspect he does anyway.

She talks on. "We're doing this because we've all been there. Arrested. Our parents too. Both of Panzer's parents lost their jobs when he turned punk. The Stasi pressured them and they wouldn't snitch. My parents . . ." She doesn't finish her sentence as she pulls off her jacket and holds it out to me. "I hope you find your dad."

"Thank you."

Without the bulky jacket hiding her frame, I realize Willow and I are about the same size. She's a few inches taller, but her clothes will fit me and mine her.

"Do you want me to wait outside?"

Willow startles as if she'd forgotten Daniel. "Better not. Panzer told Splinter, but Fuzz and Dragon don't know what's really going on."

"*Ich werde bleiben*," Daniel replies. *I will stay.* It's formal but correct and flows off his tongue with ease.

I throw him a wide-eyed glance. He bats it back with a smirk.

Willow pulls off her skirt and tights. I do the same, handing the rest of the money tucked within them to Daniel to hold. I pass Willow my new black tights, and she hands me a fishnet pair with runs all throughout. I struggle not to make the runs worse as I put them on. I then slide the remaining money into the waistband before zipping up her tiger-print skirt.

I speak because I find the silence terrifying. It allows me to imagine all the things that can and probably will go wrong. "How are you allowed to be here?"

"We earned an *Einstufung*." Willow narrows her eyes at my brown wool skirt, a new one I bought at Ann Taylor only a month ago. "It's a government license that allows us to play in public. A lot of the older punks say we're sellouts for applying for one. They call us traitors and lots worse, but there are other ways to fight than write lyrics so dangerous they'll only get you arrested."

She sets the skirt aside and yanks on my tights. "It was Panzer's plan. Tamp the lyrics down a little, earn a license to play in the West, and get our message outside the Wall. Let the world know what's going on. This is our third concert over here. I think the Ministry of Culture keeps sending us in hopes we won't come back."

"They'd let you go?"

"They want us to go." Willow steps into the skirt. "It would save them five headaches and probably a lot of Stasi man-hours spent following us. But we don't want to leave. That's not what we're after. We want our own home to be better."

I remember a line from one of my father's letters, the encrypted version. "*We shouldn't have to flee. Home should be better.*" What does he think of punk?

Willow stares at my white blouse for a moment with almost as much disdain as she regarded my skirt, before she slides her arms into the sleeves and starts buttoning it up. I keep myself from staring at her mustard T-shirt with the same expression. I shrug on her leather jacket and stand for inspection.

She smiles at me and Daniel nods his approval. I can't help but match their expressions. Despite the danger, there is something funny about this moment, empowering even. I feel like we're Jodie Foster and her mom in that old *Freaky Friday* movie, and despite some hilarious mishaps in the middle, all is going to turn out well—just like the movie.

"Here." Willow grabs a slip of fabric off the sink's edge and shoves it into my hand.

I uncurl it. It's a black glove with the fingers cut off. For my left hand.

"It's soft so it'll work on your other hand. I usually wear it when I play, but it got so hot tonight, the drumsticks were already slipping in my hands at warm-up. You can wear it to cover that." She points to my right hand, still wrapped in gauze.

I wiggle on the glove. The fingers don't quite line up, but she's right. It's soft, workable, and hides both the gauze and my burns.

I move toward the door.

"Not so fast." Daniel's voice holds a teasing note that feels incongruent with what's about to happen.

I look to him. He circles a finger at my head. "The real work begins."

He reaches into the messenger bag that's been slung across his body all evening and pulls out a long blonde wig. I almost reach for it, but he hands it to Willow. "You'll need this to wander the city with me until Luisa returns."

He reaches back into his bag and pulls out a can of black shoe polish.

"What else is in there?"

"Wouldn't you like to know?" He winks.

"You're keeping it secret?"

"Not everything. I just thought knowing the extent of this transformation might derail you." Daniel has the decency to look sheepish.

I scrunch my nose but say nothing. I can't get angry because I'm not sure he isn't right. I look to Willow. My guess is her hair is about chin length. It's hard to tell as it's spiked up in about thirty points that cover her head. The tip of each is dyed black. Hence the shoe polish. I now suspect the order of events. "You're kidding."

Willow reaches to the sink, and that's when I notice the scissors. Not nice thin scissors, but huge cutting shears.

"You're using those on my hair?"

"Unless you want to." Willow waits for me to reply.

After a pause that feels like forever, I simply shake my head.

She hacks at my hair. It takes only four cuts and ten minutes with a can of shaving cream to make my hair almost look like hers. The numerous spikes are at least eight inches high each. Daniel dabs his fingers into the shoe polish and coats each one. He stands so close I smell the coffee and baklava from dinner and the starch of his pale blue Oxford shirt.

"Is this going to work?" I whisper to him.

"You have to trust it will."

While Daniel applies the finishing touches to my hair, Willow washes her face in the sink. When she finally lifts her head and turns back, she is scrubbed pink and looks so very young that I almost don't see Willow in this girl any longer. Her eyes are wide and clear blue. I want to hug her, but I resist. She may be young, but she is tough and independent.

"Your turn." She holds up a thick black eye pencil.

I take the pencil and press close to the mirror. She stands next to me and guides my work. I'm grateful for the help, as I wear little makeup normally. Lip gloss, powder, a hint of pink blush, and mascara and I'm out the door most days.

"Thicker on the outer part." She taps my temple with a light finger. "And the lower line needs to go out to your temple. All the way to here."

In a few minutes, I hardly see myself in me either.

We all nod to each other and Daniel opens the bathroom door.

Only Panzer and, I think, Splinter are in the room. Panzer gestures for him to leave. He obeys without question. "Fuzz and Dragon are almost finished loading the equipment. They can only occupy Schmidt a few minutes more."

The way he spits out "Schmidt" catches my attention. "Who's Schmidt?"

"He's from the Ministry of Culture. He always comes with us when we cross the border, but as he's the only one who does, I suspect he's Stasi too. He'll be on the bus. Don't look at him, don't talk to him, nothing. You let us load you on the bus as if you're too drunk to see straight. Borderline passed out. Got it?"

"Got it."

Panzer looks to Willow and his expression softens. "Never thought I'd see you look like that again."

She blushes. "It's for a good cause."

His eyes narrow and his expression changes as he turns back to me. "You're missing something. Something that'll get you arrested. Willow too."

"What?" I glance between us.

Panzer steps toward me. I feel his bulk and his breath and I struggle not to step back. He reaches up and black-painted nails rush at me. I think he's about to hit me when his trajectory changes and he tugs at my ear.

"No." I gasp. Willow's right ear is pierced three times with large buttons in each. But her left ear is pierced from lobe to top at least ten times. She wears small rings in the top holes and a silver chain dangles between the topmost ring and a bottom button.

Willow waves her hand in front of my face. It takes me a moment to register as I feel cool and faint. She slides off five of the small rings. "See? They're just clamped around my ear, not pierced."

I gulp air with relief.

"But these"—Panzer steps between us and gently taps Willow's right ear—"Are pierced and we're running out of time. Schmidt won't let us hang out in here forever."

Willow grips my arm. "I'm sorry. They have the more permanent details of our appearance recorded. They may not catch the ears, but they could."

I ask, "What does that mean?" just as Panzer nudges Splinter, who has walked back into the room. "Get vodka." Panzer flicks two fingers to the back table.

Splinter swipes off a bottle and hands it to him, who hands it to me. While Panzer pulls a safety pin from his jacket's shoulder, I lift the bottle. My throat is on fire at first gulp, but I keep going.

"Hey." He grabs for it. "You were to hold it. Not guzzle it."

"I thought it might help." I choke out the words.

"A little, maybe. But our heads are on the line here. Yours needs to be clear."

Willow pulls out all her button earrings and lays them in her palm. Panzer pours vodka over them. He then pours it over his safety pin, and, standing so close there is no room between our bodies, he whispers, "Don't move a muscle."

I close my eyes and feel Daniel's hand slip into mine. While I keep my face perfectly still, I squeeze Daniel's hand so hard, I feel his finger bones roll over and across each other. I don't let up the pressure and he doesn't pull away.

I want to cry out with the pain, but I don't. I do, however, feel tears seep from my eyes. What'll they do to all that black eyeliner?

"Ice and a rag," Panzer says to Splinter. I feel two more stabs in one ear before he grips my jaw and turns my head to move on to the next ear. Daniel steps behind me. One hand holds mine and the other grips my waist, keeping me standing steady.

Panzer finally steps back. Splinter hands me both ice and a grey towel. Daniel doesn't move.

"Is there blood?" I dare to ask.

"Not much. Hold the ice against them." Panzer gestures to Willow. "Help her clean up. I'll go check on Schmidt."

Panzer and Splinter leave the three of us alone.

Willow gently dabs at my ears. "My papers are in my inside right jacket pocket. They will ask for them at the checkpoint."

"And then?" I twist to look to Daniel.

"Panzer's got your contact's information. He may still be waiting on some details, but he'll let you know." Daniel runs a hand over his jaw. I raise a questioning brow. He shrugs. "Nothing. It just doesn't feel like a good enough plan anymore."

There's a crack in his confidence, and he must hate it or even be surprised by it. But, oddly, it brings me peace. It lets me know I'm not too far behind, that this is the big deal I think it is, even to a consummate professional, and that he cares. I'm not jumping ahead and wondering how much or in what way he might care. I just feel assured he does. And that's enough.

"It's the one we've got and it'll be fine." My calm delivery surprises me, and by Daniel's expression, I can tell it surprises and pleases him too.

Maybe it's Daniel's vulnerability. Maybe it's the vodka. Maybe it's the focusing of pain. Maybe it's the fact that seven years ago, I actually went through CIA training for just this kind of work. But it dawns on me that no matter what has happened since those days, I was good at that job once upon a time and maybe I still am.

I shift to face Willow, who is still dabbing at my ears. While I feel willing and ready to take these risks, looking at this girl, I'm ashamed anyone has involved one so young. "I'm sorry."

"For what?" Her eyes flicker with confusion.

"This could cost you a lot and you'll be here waiting on me. If something happens and I get arrested—" I stop as I don't want to imagine what might happen to her. Would she be forever separated from her friends and family, certain to be arrested if she tried to go home?

"That's what punk is, you know?" Willow cuts across my dark imaginings with a small, sad smile that is way beyond her years. "It's letting go of what you're supposed to be doing for whatever comes your way. It's about creating a future of our own making, not accepting the one they shove at us. And it's all risk. Every breath in every day."

The door opens. Panzer looks between us before speaking. "It's time."

Willow walks to the dressing room door where she and Daniel will hide until we're gone. Daniel pulls me back.

"Remember that phone number, okay? And if something, anything, feels wrong, find a place to hide and call me. I trust Robert, who trusts Panzer. We'll see you to safety." He stares at me as if trying to imprint each word into my brain. "You can do this."

I walk one way and he walks the other. Before I meet Panzer at the door to the hall, I hear the click of the dressing room door shutting.

I am Willow now.

And while I appreciate Daniel's care and his advice, I cling to Willow's wisdom because there's no "safe" from here on out.

It's punk and it's all about risk.

CHAPTER 22

Thursday, November 9, 1989

Panzer looks me over, and I can tell he's not displeased with our work. To say he's pleased might take his assessing expression too far. But he's not growling so I take it for a win.

"Lean on me. You're drugged, drunk, something."

Rather than answer, I let my lids drop to near closed and slump into his arms. I feel rather than hear him chuckle as he takes on my weight.

We stumble me toward the bus.

"What now?" The voice is strident, aggressive, and plainly sober. It's older too. I assume Panzer is shuffling me past Stasi Schmidt.

"She probably mixed her vodka with tranqs again."

"Get her seated." I get shoved to the right. "Not there. I don't want her to throw up anywhere near me."

Panzer yanks me up and pushes me to the back of the bus and flops me against the cold vinyl seat. My head bounces off the bus's metal side wall.

I crack open an eye and whisper, "You could be a little gentler."

"Get Willow arrested and you'll see how gentle I am."

It's a good reminder. I close my eyes again.

The ancient bus grinds into gear, lurches forward, and we're on the move. Someone clicks on a cassette player and a super-fuzzy version of what I think is a Sex Pistols song starts to play.

After several turns and pauses, at what I assume are stoplights, we slow to a halt and wait. Panzer calls out and I suspect he's doing it for my benefit. "How's the checkpoint line so long? It's almost 2:00 a.m."

"There must have been some problems," Stasi Schmidt calls back.

"Protests more like," another voice calls out. Since I heard Splinter's voice earlier and it's not his, I assume Fuzz or Dragon just spoke.

"That's enough from you." Stasi Schmidt's voice is clear, low, and almost menacing.

The bus inches forward, stops again, and I hear the door open. The music clicks off. I then hear a bench creak and footsteps. Someone is walking down the bus aisle toward me. I keep my eyes closed.

"We're stopped for a few minutes." Stasi Schmidt talks as he walks. "If any of you want to get out and leave, I won't stop you. I don't care." *Step. Step.* "Now is the time."

No one on the bus moves. Like doesn't move a muscle. The plastic seats don't creak. No metal shifts. Nothing.

I don't dare open an eye, but I sense Stasi Schmidt stands in the aisle right in front of me. Finally, I hear the faint sound of movement. A bench creaks and Panzer's words come close and soft. "You're not throwing her off," he says calmly. "Don't even think about it. She's going home with the rest of us."

Schmidt doesn't reply. He doesn't say anything. After what feels like forever, I hear the footsteps retreat and the bus door close. The bus inches forward and someone clicks the cassette player on again.

The bus continues its stop-and-start motion for so long, I have to shift to stop my head from hitting against the wall. I slump to lying across the bench. Finally, the cassette player is clicked off again and Stasi Schmidt calls to the back, "Grab her papers. I'm not coming back there."

Panzer, I can tell by the smell of him, leans over me and reaches into Willow's inside jacket pocket. I don't move as he pulls out the papers and heads to the front of the bus.

The door opens and someone gets on. He, I can tell by his voice, and Stasi Schmidt share a few congenial comments before a bright light makes its way toward me. I see the dancing white beam through closed lids. It hits my face full-on. The insides of my eyelids shine bright yellow-orange. I work to keep from tightening any muscles or shifting away.

"What happened to her?"

"Got into something. She does that sometimes. We'll take care of her. You've got her papers."

I hear papers shuffling and the light retreats. Moments later the bus door shuts again. As the bus rolls forward, I feel Panzer hover over me. This time he's shoving Willow's papers back into her pocket. "Good job," he whispers. "I underestimated you."

I keep from smiling, but his praise matters to me.

The bus makes a series of slow sharp turns, like we're driving a high school driver's ed course, before it picks up speed in a straight line. A few more minutes and it grinds to a halt again.

"Home again, boys and girls," Stasi Schmidt jeers. "Grab your pay as you step off."

Panzer hauls me up and pulls my arm across his shoulders. We bash against bus benches as he half carries me down the aisle. "I'll take hers too."

Panzer releases me, probably to grab Willow's check, and I teeter between the need to stand up straight and the directive to keep semiboneless. Thankfully, his guiding arm returns before I fall too far.

We shuffle from the bus to the cold night to a room only slightly less chilly. From a distance, I hear the bus grind into gear again and pull away.

I open my eyes.

We are standing in a large and plain lobby with a laminate tile floor and walls painted some shade between off-white and dingy yellow. Huge cement pillars break up the space every twenty feet, serving as support beams to hold up what I suspect is a massive building.

Splinter, Fuzz, and Dragon tease and jostle ahead of us. Still drunk, still high, they climb the four flights of stairs, taking two at a time while singing and yelling at the tops of their lungs.

Panzer follows slow and silent behind me. He puts a restraining hand on my arm as we reach the fourth-floor exit. "When we get inside the apartment, act wasted again. You can open your eyes a little, but keep your head down so no one really sees you. I'll put you into a bedroom to sleep it off. Most are fine, but there's no way there's not a *Spitzel* among them."

A snitch. I remember Oma telling me stories growing up, how the Stasi, despite employing a seemingly countless number of agents, still recruited on average one snitch, one *Inoffizielle Mitarbeiter*, per eight people. That would mean statistically, sitting in a room with seven friends, you'd be confiding your secrets to a Stasi informant. Join an opposition lifestyle, like punk, and I bet that ratio is much higher.

Panzer opens the door to the fourth-floor hall. The others are gone and it's empty. It's also equally as stark as the lobby. All the apartment doors are shut except one. Loud music—I think we're back to the Sex Pistols—pours into the hallway. I almost trip over an open box of cassette tapes inside the door. There are at least a hundred, all with handmade labels. The Sex Pistols, X-Ray Spex, The Stranglers . . .

Panzer kicks the box out of our way. "Fuzz taped all those off Radio Luxembourg. Endless music." He pulls me tighter to him, and I loop an arm around his neck. Half stumbling, half carried, I shuffle into the hallway.

People yell for him to join them in the main room at the hallway's end. We stop at a door midway down and he calls back, "Let me set Willow down. She's out of it."

No one comments or comes down the hall to help or inquire. Panzer opens the door to a bedroom and we stare for a split second at two people making out on the mattress on the floor. He yells, "Out. Now."

Once they push past us, pulling on clothing as they scamper, Panzer motions to a bag tucked against the mattress. "I got the call only a little before we left. It's the best I could do. Put all those on before you leave. And be out by six thirty or you won't make it on time."

"Where am I going?"

"It's all in the bag."

I glance to my wrist and realize I gave my watch, the Ebel that Opa gave me for college graduation, to Daniel in SO36's dressing room.

Panzer reaches up his sleeve and draws down a gorgeous antique watch. He hands it to me. It's heavy with a cream background, gold trim, and the lowercase word *ruhl* written in a blocky script across the face. The band is a fine worn black leather.

Unable to hide my shock, I look from him to the watch and back again.

"It was my father's and his father's before him. He loved that watch and gave it to me when . . ." Panzer lifts his chin. He looks young and vulnerable. "Don't get arrested. I want it back."

"Yes."

He gestures to the bag again. "I also scribbled out a map to your meeting point. It starts when you exit the building two over. Don't go out this lobby. Take the stairs one flight below it and walk two buildings down. There's only one way to walk. Dressed like you will be, anyone watching won't associate you with us. But still, it's better to exit a couple buildings over."

"This is not a popular look?" I pluck at Willow's jacket. It's a rebellious look. A turbulent and jarring one. It's a dangerous look, and a courageous one too. I've never met more courageous kids. Angry, loud, and chaotic, yes, but courageous.

Panzer catches my tone and smirks.

I clear my face of all humor. "Thank you, Panzer. And if I don't see Willow again, please thank her too."

"Just be smart." He's not joking now either. He backs out of the room and shuts the door behind him. The pitch in the living room rises a notch as the throng welcomes him.

I pace the tiny bedroom's few feet of treadable floor, unable to sit, unable to rest. I pick up the bag and sort through the contents. There is a hastily drawn map on scrap paper, another pair of tights, a long dark green wool skirt, a dark-toned patterned blouse, an equally dark thick sweater, and a knit scarf. I'm still wearing my own black leather boots. Neither Daniel nor Willow thought anyone would notice they weren't her clompy Doc Marten-esque ones.

I check Panzer's watch: 2:30 a.m. I have four hours until I must leave.

I sit on the mattress. I stand again. I sit again. Three hours crawl by before I change my clothes. I slide the money down each leg of the wool tights and pull on the long skirt and top. I leave the thick sweater on the bed. At 5:30 I poke my head out of the bedroom and look down the hall. All is quiet and I see black-clad figures sprawled out asleep on the main room's floor and furniture. I spy a bathroom across the hall and a few steps closer to everyone sleeping. I tiptoe toward it.

I stop halfway and stare at the bold black letters spray-painted across the white wall. *Don't die in the waiting room of the future.* I smile. There is nothing complacent about these guys. No waiting rooms for them.

I step into the bathroom and shut the door.

I'm a mess. The eyeliner, never precise to begin with, has traveled halfway down my cheeks. I look like a panda bear. My ears, though not exactly bleeding, are red and swollen, with little threads of blood peeking from behind each button.

I start with the earrings. I first undo the rings and carefully remove the chain from my left ear. I then brace myself and begin to pull out each button. They stick and pull at the congealed blood that has fused them against my ears. Tears spring to my eyes, but I make no noise. Once all are out, I scrub them clean with the small bar of soap on the sink's edge and rest them on the windowsill.

I then work up a weak lather between my palms and start to scrub my face. I scrub my eyes, my cheeks, my ears, and even as much of my hair as I can get into the sink. My hair morphs into a gooey mess with the shoe polish slicking it into a dull grey before it eventually becomes pliable and clean in my fingers.

I emerge like Willow did in the club's dressing room—scrubbed pink and clean. My hair hangs in wet clumps against my face and my eyes and ears are bright red from the rubbing. I dry myself as best I can with the dingy towel hanging on the back of the door and try not to think about where it's been or how long since it's been washed.

Gathering up Willow's earrings, I return to the bedroom and place them within her jacket's inside pocket. I almost take her papers. If stopped, I'll need something. I hold them in my hand. I can't. If caught, I won't implicate her trying to save myself. She's taken enough risks. I tuck the papers back into her jacket pocket, place everything within the plastic bag, and pull on the brown sweater. The wet collar of the blouse feels scratchy now beneath the wool. I tiptoe my way back into the hallway and out the front door.

Five floors down I emerge into a cement corridor. It's wide and lit by a series of bare bulbs. If I understood Panzer correctly, this is the passageway that connects the buildings underground.

I pass a door with *Ausfahrt* painted in black stenciled letters. *Exit*. One building down. One to go.

I stop at the next metal door and pause before opening it to let Panzer's admonishment cycle through my brain once more. "The moment you step outside that hallway, you will be watched. By the VoPo, the neighbors, the street vendors, everyone. You keep your scarf on your head and you don't break a slow, deliberate, almost bored stride. Look like everything around you."

"Be the opposite of you?" I quipped.

"Yes. You like the future they offer you. It fits you just right. Act like that."

I secure the scarf around my head by crossings its ends under my chin, then tossing them over each shoulder. I open the door and climb the stairs one flight to the lobby. Within minutes I'm outside in the darkness. The sky looks a little lighter than when I stumbled off the bus those few hours ago, but not by much. I figure I have about another half hour at least until sunrise.

I turn to the right and walk straight for the three blocks until my first turn. I hope I've memorized Panzer's map correctly. I don't dare stop, however, to examine it and draw attention to myself. My training returns like a soft refrain, reminding me that having few people on the street makes standing out worse rather than better. Anything out of the ordinary is more easily noticed with fewer distractions. Anything out of the ordinary takes on an ominous nature when not buffered by the security of crowds. You notice, and report, what doesn't belong.

Like an errant ink mark on a letter.

CHAPTER 23

Haris Voekler

EAST BERLIN
Thursday, August 13, 1987

It's been five years since Manfred's death. My head is getting crowded with the people dead and gone I think of daily. My parents. So many friends. Monica. Luisa. Manfred. While there are others, those three absences haunt me the most. Monica, who I couldn't help and will love till the day I die; Luisa, who is forever out of reach and who I can never love enough; Manfred, who was the kid I once was and, like me, woke up and couldn't return to sleep. I also wonder every day if there was something I could have done for him that night. That's hubris—there was nothing anyone could have done. But after all these years, I still wonder—about him, about Luisa, and most especially about Monica.

I never had to wonder about what happened to Manfred, however.

The morning after we talked, I posted my letter to Walther on the way to work. I couldn't leave it at my apartment for one second longer than necessary. Someone would come around asking questions, and considering I knew Manfred well, it meant nothing was off-limits. Not my person nor my apartment. Granted, the letter would be read somewhere. But it was best to let it be read by the censors with quotas to fill and thousands of letters passing their desks each day than a Stasi code breaker with time on his hands and superiors to impress.

It was a good thing those thoughts directed my actions, too, because that very evening, minutes after I returned home, a knock sounded at my door.

They delivered the standard line. "We need to ask you a few questions, clear up some matters."

"Can it wait until morning?" I yawned.

There was no answer to that question, just a hand toward me, inviting me to step out of my doorway and join them. I obeyed.

The next part was unexpected. It wasn't the forty-eight-hour experience I'd heard of or the brief but aggressive questioning I received a decade ago. The agents who addressed me at the neighborhood Stasi office, not at headquarters, spoke calmly and the atmosphere was informal, almost congenial. I suspected, even in death, Manfred had friends high up whom no one wanted to embarrass. To implicate Manfred in something disparaging could be a problem. Yet no stone could be left unturned either. My attention wavered for a moment after twenty minutes as I wondered what "accident" they had concocted to tell his family.

"What? Wait—" I brought myself back to the discussion in a jolt as I realized they were lulling me into a whole host of assumptions. Assumptions I should not, could not, have or make on my own. "Why are you asking me all these questions? This isn't making sense." I tapped the table in an effort to wake both mind and body. "Ask Manfred Schneider. He's been out sick, but you can visit him at home or come to the paper. I'm sure he'll be back soon. There's no point asking about him; just ask him directly."

"He's had an accident."

"Is he dead?"

"Why would you assume that?" The stockier of the two leaned forward.

"The way you said it, and I didn't assume. I asked. And by your reaction, I can tell he must be. How horrible for his family. And the paper. He was our best reporter."

"We want to know about his interests, his articles. You two worked very closely. He was recently tasked to write an article on Chief Mielke."

I shrugged as if those were the most boring questions in the world. Then I took a few hours to walk them through Manfred's work and the glowing things he always put in his Mielke articles, as proof for why he was given such honored topics. I wrapped up my monologue with the article I'd finished polishing that very afternoon, which would be featured in the next day's Sunday edition.

I extolled Manfred's writing, his loyalty, his work ethic. I even denigrated myself—which wasn't hard to do—and explained how writing to my daughter kept me from the top stories, but what was I to do? My in-laws had taken her to the United States and there was no legal recourse as my deceased wife had given her to them . . .

I droned on and on. Soon, even they couldn't stand the litany of things that had happened to me, that I wasn't responsible for, that I'd fallen victim to.

They asked me to leave.

As I walk home from work tonight, that memory fills me. It often does, as do so many memories about Manfred. I miss the honesty we shared. I miss having him for a friend. I stop at the street corner. Cars pass. Countless "Trabbis," as the Trabant is about the only car one can purchase anymore. A yellow one sits at the side of the road blocking traffic. I suspect it's out of petrol.

Prices have gone up a great deal in the past several months. Seeing cars at the side of the road is becoming increasingly common and they are clogging traffic. I look around. I don't want to go home yet. I turn and walk the few miles toward Bernauer Strasse to dwell on other memories. I am in just the right mood to punish myself tonight.

It's been two years since I've been here, but this evening the light is soft with the sun just dipping to the horizon, and I can almost feel Luisa and Monica with me. Luisa is asleep in my arms. My dear wife laughs and says something witty as only she knows how to say. I smile at them and am awash with love, with hope, and with the promise of our future.

The wall was raised twenty-six years ago today. Twenty-six years ago today, I lost my daughter. Then I lost my wife.

I stand at the inner wall and, rising up, look out across the Death Strip. The auto-firing guns are gone. It's been two years, but I haven't been close enough to the wall in that time to actually see the empty metal stanchions. The government needed cash. The government always needs cash. That time, I learned from Koch, West Germany refused to grant the one-billion-mark loan our Politburo requested until the guns were gone.

I shift my gaze down the block and feel the loss of the Church of Reconciliation. It was a beautiful church, built in 1894. It had sustained damage during the Allied bombs but still stood at the end of the war. And despite being situated in the Soviet Sector, its Protestant parish remained stronger than most. Many from the French and American Sectors would come over for Sunday services. We went to church there—when Monica insisted we go—and a few couples would join us occasionally for Sunday lunch afterward. Those were fun days. None of us had kids back then, and we ate and drank for hours. The church and those lunches embodied, for me at least, the closest we came to true reconciliation and happiness in Berlin after the war.

But, as it sat on Bernauer Strasse, it was too close to the border. For twenty-four years, the Church of Reconciliation sat as an empty and decaying ironic symbol within the Death Strip. Honecker and his cronies grew furious every time a Western news agency splashed pictures of the forlorn church across its front page as an indictment against us and the Soviets who kept us imprisoned. So, while planning celebrations for the wall's twenty-fifth anniversary, they tore it down.

It was probably for the best. It would have been a true embarrassment this summer and been torn down anyway. Why delay?

This summer is Berlin's 750th anniversary, and celebrations were planned and have been executed across two full months, spanning the entire country. Most are wrapped up by now, but what crowds we saw. We invited the entire world to visit us. USSR General Secretary Mikhail Gorbachev traveled throughout the country, along with a host of Soviet Politburo members, and for the full two weeks surrounding his tour, East Berlin was alight with events, parades, galas, and gatherings.

US President Reagan was in West Berlin as well this summer, as celebrations were planned for both sides of the wall. He, of course, stayed in the West, but we did hear he gave a very provocative speech.

The day before he spoke, Radio Glasnost reported that over fifty thousand gathered to protest his visit, claiming he wanted war with the Soviet Union. Snippets of his speech were then broadcast into East Berlin the day afterward, and commentators drew out certain words and themes to confirm this belief. But I heard the speech in its entirety on Radio Free Europe and didn't agree with all their conclusions. I sensed a deeper meaning to Mr. Reagan's words, even in his call, "Mr. Gorbachev, tear down this wall!"

Though it was aggressive, it was said in the context of seeking peace and freedom, not underscoring a threat of war. In fact, his words before that exclamation directly appealed to the very programs Soviet General Secretary Gorbachev promotes—peace, openness, and freedom. Those are the direct translations of his *Glasnost* and his *Perestroika*: "openness and freedom" alongside "restructuring."

Bold ideas, especially when they come from both the East and the West. Bold ideas that are taking hold across Eastern Europe. That is, everywhere but here. Our government works double-time to bar them from our borders. The entire situation, to my mind at least, took visual form this summer during our celebrations as I trailed Gorbachev's entourage around the much-anticipated new museum, *Topographie des Terrors*—the Topography of Terror—which opened only days before his visit.

The new museum is a tremendous and remarkable space, with both indoor and outdoor exhibits that stand on the very land that held the Reich Security Main Office—the home of the Gestapo—from 1933 to 1945. Of course, those buildings are long gone. They were first targeted by the Allies in 1945, and anything they didn't decimate was razed by the Soviets soon after. Opening night we all toasted and congratulated ourselves on how humane we were and how successful we've been at purging Nazism from within our borders.

It's an odd thing, though, this monument to decry past horrors. I stood there as Gorbachev ended his visit, jotting a few last notes for my article, and realized that for all the money we spend on memorials to prove we are nothing like the Nazis, we opened that museum to celebrate an anniversary Hitler himself created.

Berlin is, in fact, quite a bit older than 750 years. Hitler picked that year because Berlin's original founding date didn't fit into his propaganda calendar quite so conveniently. The Berlin birthday he chose and we still celebrate is actually about seventy years off the city's original founding.

Also I noted that day that the Topography of Terror Museum runs along Niederkirchnerstrasse. The wall runs along Niederkirchnerstrasse as well. So for the entire length of the museum's property, the eye travels in a single sweep from a museum condemning Nazi terror to our ever-present reminder of Communism and Soviet aggression. We are not tortured, I conceded that day and I concede the point now—unless the Stasi gets you—but we are not free in any sense of the word either. It led me to wonder if history will be kind to this chapter in Berlin's story.

Standing here looking across the Death Strip now and the empty hole left by the Church of Reconciliation, I think not.

I turn to amble back to my apartment. I almost head toward the Church of Zion, but I stop and redirect my steps toward home. I am too tired to drum up the energy to visit the church, and I am much too tired to stay up late tonight.

Because if there's one thing I've learned over the past few years, it's that working with the *Ostpunks* always requires energy and always keeps one up late.

I have a letter to write to Walther. I'm not even sure why I do it anymore. For years, telling Walther the truth of our lives, restrictions, and deprivations was enough. But I've created a new outlet—admittedly a more dangerous one—but one that satisfies me more too. With my letters to Walther, I was simply getting the words out and, most of the time, didn't care if he even read them. It's perhaps selfish to admit, but he was the recipient of a journal and little more. But now I am no longer simply conveying the story; I am trying to change the story. Like one of those mottos these young kids say, I refuse to die in the waiting room of the future.

It's remarkable, really. Over the past few years, doors previously shut to me, as a mouthpiece for *Neues Deutschland*, opened wide. I can't tell if this is because people are fed up and willing to take risks or if I, somehow, have signaled my willingness to listen. The punks say I should leave my job, step into their dress, their rebellion, and their world, and simply be punk. They laugh as they say it, of course, but it's kind of them to think I could. I'm much too set, too staid, probably too scared, and certainly too old.

Besides, there are stories to tell, both at *Neues Deutschland* and in our samizdat.

For one, as I wrote to Walther a few months ago, the trees along many of the main thoroughfares in the central city died this past winter. When it was discovered in spring, as nothing greened or bloomed, they had to be excavated. After pulling the first few trees from the ground, the VoPo had to clear the streets. Citizens became anxious at the site of the trees' black and shriveled roots. They had clearly not died a natural death.

While I reported in the paper that they'd been stricken with a rare but entirely natural blight, my article did leave open a few questions. Questions that I hoped would lead others to ask for more information, even demand proper and logical answers. But I could not hint at the darker truth a civil engineer gave me. The trees died, and more will continue to die, because of the city's leaking underground gas pipes. City workers patch them as best they can, but they make little headway as the old infrastructure crumbles faster than funds for repairs can be generated. Our ground is saturated with gas.

After a few beers, that same engineer also told me that over a third of the lakes in East Germany are too toxic for summer bathing because of the government's constant deals with West Germany. We take their toxic waste and fill our lakes and landfills because we so desperately need their cash.

Over a walk and cigarettes another night, a city economist explained why we need all that money. We've run a deficit for years now and are on the verge of national bankruptcy. The Soviet Union is no better off, so they can't support us any longer. He also added that maintenance for the wall alone truly costs over a billion marks each year.

And just yesterday, a punk told me what he'd learned about last year's bombing at La Belle discothèque in West Berlin's Friedenau district. That was a horrific bomb that killed a Turkish woman and two American soldiers, injured 229 others, and incited the US to bomb Libya in retaliation. Yet this punk learned it could have been avoided—if it had served our interests. He heard from a friend, who has a cousin in Poland's security service, the SB, that our Stasi—while not responsible for the bomb—knew every detail of the entire plan a full week before the explosion and did nothing to stop it. That makes the Stasi culpable and the world needs to know.

What started years ago as flirting with opposition has become my lifeblood. I hadn't realized I could stop my slow descent into apathy, depression, even madness, by making one proactive effort to change the world around me. One step then led to another and another. And that's how I discovered my unlikely group of comrades wired the same way. Walther's "*I fought tooth and nail to stay, until the day I needed to leave*" has become my rallying cry. I don't want to leave. So I fight. With kids.

It astonishes me most days. My closest friends and staunchest allies are a bunch of twentysomething kids. Strangely dressed twentysomething kids too. But if someone is going to be heard, it will be the Ostpunks. These young kids have created enough noise and become such an embarrassment and a threat that Stasi Chief Mielke himself has declared war on them.

And the war has only made them stronger.

The Ostpunks offer their arrests, even torture, as a mirror against the brutality of the government, and their numbers grow. Not quite the numbers we hear about in Poland's Solidarity movement. But these kids are no less courageous, and they are willing to make incredible sacrifices to change the system rather than flee it.

I once asked why they protest on every level, positing that it would be easier if they dressed more like ordinary citizens, talked like ordinary citizens, and then got to work. A sixteen-year-old kid named Panzer replied without pause, "Everything in a police state is political. So we attack every aspect of it."

Panzer is younger than Luisa. She's twenty-nine years old now, and I would guess he's only just reached twenty. What would she think of him? Could she understand, or are our worlds so different she couldn't even see what these kids see or feel what they feel? These kids, some as young as fourteen, already recognize they have no voice in their own lives—down to where they will live, what they will do for work, where they will shop . . .

So they rebel at the most fundamental level. They show up for school wearing what they are not allowed to wear. They rip their clothes to symbolically break the system, then sew them back together because they actually need clothes. They know they need a social structure to support them, so they create one because they will not abide by the one in charge, as the notes they pin to those resewn clothes attest. *Down with the State* and *Stasi Stooges* are two of my favorites.

And these kids are clever . . . Like me, they found the churches.

It's an odd reality, but after World War II the churches carved out a remarkable degree of legal autonomy from the State. The years of Ostpolitik diluted the Catholic Church's oppositional fervor—though it's gaining traction once again under their Pope John Paul II. But the center of Solidarity opposition remains in Poland. Here in East Germany, however, it was the Protestant churches that fought for their autonomy and made good use of those legal provisions on a spiritual and political level. Granted, the atheist Communist state did its job well too, and only about 3 percent of the population sits in any pew, Catholic or Protestant, for a Sunday service. But that autonomy stretches into the week, and that's when the churches are packed. With punks. Presently they form several of the largest and best organized oppositional groups in the DDR, and they found the churches for their meeting grounds. Mielke is not wrong to worry about them.

I worry about them too, but I worry about their safety. Yet even that is eclipsed by my respect. I'm continually impressed by these kids. Other than the music, the drugs, the partying, and the general lack of good hygiene, I commend them. I'm fifty-six. I can hardly be blamed for noting a few things they could improve. The music gets me the most—it's not music. It's screaming, screeching, discordant, and ridiculously loud. But I've seen a few pages of sheet music, before they get hidden away, and their lyrics are good. They have to be hidden, of course, in all that screeching chaos because they are subversive, visceral, and condemning toward the State.

"Why don't you sing so people can hear these words? At least at some venues?" I asked one night. They laughed at me. I suppose because their generation can actually hear the words.

But they listen rather than laugh when I start talking about how to get our paper distributed or how to work the ancient printing press in the church's basement. They need that samizdat; we all do. It's the way we share the information we glean from across the entire Eastern Bloc, and it's how they advertise their concerts. It's through the concerts, and swapping information with other punks, that we learn some of the best stuff. It's a delicate powerful circle, and for our opposition group, I sit in the center hub of the wheel.

We're not the only oppositional group, of course. Several groups' papers have gotten so popular that we all print on an almost twenty-four-hour schedule now. There's too much going on to stop the presses, as a true newspaperman might say. All around the Eastern Bloc, protests are growing and these young people talk to each other with an honesty and candor my generation is fearful to approach. The word spreads, along with the courage, and the protests gain momentum.

Solidarity in Poland has grown to count the vast majority of the populace within its membership, despite all measures to squelch it. Even the horrific murder of the pro-Solidarity priest Father Popiełuszko, by three agents of the SB, didn't slow its growth. In fact, more than two hundred fifty thousand people, including Solidarity leader Lech Wałęsa himself, attended Popiełuszko's funeral. That's a mighty large protest. And while *Neues Deutschland* didn't print that news, we did out of the church's basement printing press. Four thousand copies passed and passed again, reaching over thirty thousand readers.

We've also printed helpful tips for the masses moving to East Berlin. Tips about how to participate in the growing shadow economy. Tips about how to secure squatter housing. It's necessary as people can no longer eke out sustainable lives in the villages. All those years I feared being charged as *asoziales Verhalten* are behind us. The State can no longer enforce the laws as black-market trading and the shadow economy have grown too robust to shut down. Change is happening even though General Secretary Erich Honecker denies it whenever he opens his mouth.

I pass through Alexanderplatz and head down Karl-Marx-Allee. Another couple kilometers and I turn into the warren of buildings that create my neighborhood.

"You're late tonight. I was hoping you'd come by and watch the football match with me." Peter opens his door as I unlock mine.

"I will. Let me find some dinner first."

He tilts his head into his apartment. "Come in for dinner. Helene made plenty. She expected Traeger to come over, but he canceled."

I willingly follow him into his apartment and smell rosemary, pork, and something sweet. Soon we are enjoying a few beers and Helene's excellent cooking.

"Did you hear about the Ministry of Security's hiring freeze?"

I raise my brows. Peter works in a plastics factory now. "No. How did you?"

"Our resident officer was complaining about his workload. I gather his request for an assistant will be denied."

"That makes for an interesting statement about the state of things. No one will know, though. The paper certainly won't report on it. Without Manfred, we barely cover the security service anymore."

"Was he the reporter killed trying to escape?"

I nod. "Five years ago now."

We drink and the conversation moves on. Even among friends there are things best not talked about. Because even though Mielke was forced to put a freeze on all new hiring within his Ministry for State Security, the Stasi remains more pervasive and powerful than ever.

After dinner and a good football match viewed on the Sauers' snowy black-and-white television set, I return to my apartment, pull out paper and pen, and write to Walther.

I may doubt the necessity of writing him anymore, as it's not my only outlet, but I can't deny I enjoy the camaraderie. Even if he doesn't read my letters or doesn't care about happenings in his old country, he does write me back. He shares Luisa's life with me. And throughout these years, he has become my closest friend and my truest confidant.

One should never discount the necessity or power of a good friendship. So, yes, there are stories to write for the official Party paper, more stories to write for our samizdat, and letters to write to Walther.

CHAPTER 24

Luisa Voekler

Thursday, November 9, 1989

The sun rises as I make my way toward Karl-Marx-Allee. The sky has an eerie brown quality, heavy and leaden.

I turn the corner and stop. I glance back. I turn forward again to confirm what I'm seeing is true. I'm standing at the edge of an imposing and glorious promenade; there's no other word for it. Behind me, the streets feel crumbling and shabby in comparison. It reminds me of my one visit to Disney World when Oma lost her purse and we left the park's shiny thoroughfares to find the security office back in the littered alleyways and run-down office spaces.

The neighborhood I just walked through was crumbling, quiet to the point of somber, and poorly lit. This broad avenue is lit with gas streetlights and lined with green space and trees. There's a huge swath of lawn and foliage running down the center of the divided road. Massive white buildings flank either side of the boulevard. Two towers rise high on each side as well, as if proudly announcing my entrance to the city. I feel like Dorothy approaching the Emerald City in Oz, and for the first time, I feel the true sheer magnitude of the government, the ideology, the power that built this place, and keeps it running still.

My eyes shift from the buildings around me to straight down the Allee. Miles away, and perfectly centered in the distance, I see Berlin's iconic television tower, the Fernsehturm. I start walking toward it. For while the Fernsehturm is centered on the Allee, it also constitutes the center of Alexanderplatz, my map's next marker.

Once in the plaza, I turn left and walk south toward the Reichstag, which sits near the Brandenburg Gate—neither of which I'll actually get close to, as one sits in West Berlin and the other in the Death Strip. The walk takes about a half hour, and I am surprised by how much of the city I see. I started in a warren of uniform and massive buildings, set at odd angles from each other, traveled through the daunting showcase of Soviet and East German power and architecture of Karl-Marx-Allee, and am now walking through the tightly packed central-city neighborhoods, some of which are clearly over a hundred years old.

Numerous empty lots litter this part of town as well, tucked between the buildings, and it takes me a moment to look up and realize they were most likely created when parts of the original buildings fell during World War II bombings. Doors are still fixed and visible in the walls three, four, even five flights up, as if it doesn't matter that the building is no longer there. I stand staring. What do these doors to nowhere look like from the other side?

I walk through the business district as shopkeepers unlock their doors or dust inside display cases. I'm surprised there are none of the neon signs or billboards so prevalent in West Berlin. Then I realize it's a planned economy. There is no need for advertising.

I make what I think is my final turn and see the street sign ahead of me. Reinhardtstrasse is clearly marked in both Soviet Cyrillic and German. As instructed I step into the shadow of the building across from number 156, a cutout into the cement forming a sort of outdoor lobby entrance. I wait.

There's an alley to the side, and I glance down it to make sure I haven't missed a detail or anyone waiting for me. It's empty. I step back to the street side and stand pressed against the building, watching as the sun continues its march into the sky. The light is soft and diffused, yet there isn't a cloud in the sky. The haze's eerie brown tinge reminds me of one of Bran's articles. He reported a few years ago on the environmental horrors being perpetrated in East Germany and in East Berlin: trees dying along main streets due to leaky gas pipes, buildings coated in brown soot from the coal furnaces used for heating, and a number of lakes too poisonous to swim in because of toxic-waste dumping. He even reported on a series of secret deals signed between West Germany and East Germany—East Germany agreeing to dispose of West Germany's toxic waste, with no questions asked and no limits set, for cold, hard cash.

A single ray of sunlight breaks through, and it looks like a solid, beautiful beam. I stand mesmerized until a shadow blocks it. Startled, I step back. *Focus!* My head bumps the cement wall as my attention lands on a man shifting from foot to foot in front of me.

"It really is you," the man says. "I see him in you." The man's German is soft and his expression is kind.

"Excuse me?" I look around. My "contact" shouldn't know anything about me. And he should be a Stasi guard. Panzer's note clearly stated he'd be wearing the grey uniform of the Ministry of Security.

"I'm Peter Sauer." The man steps toward me, hand outstretched as if we are old friends. I look from his hand to him and am unsure what to do. "I was your father's best friend." His mouth drops open for an instant. He snaps it shut. "I apologize. Not was. Am. I *am* your father's best friend."

My mind whirls. Again, I look to his hand, to his eyes, but I still cannot lift my own hand to greet him.

"Yes, of course." He pats his chest, searching for something, and steps back. He pats his trouser pockets and pulls out a note. He holds it out to me. "I got this only a few minutes ago. You were to meet someone here." He raises a brow like he knows who it was, but is too discreet or wise to say it aloud. "But Panzer just learned your contact's schedule changed. The protests have everyone scrambling now, and he won't be on duty here until 5:00 p.m. tonight."

"Panzer?"

Peter shrugs. "Yes. Though I don't like his methods. This is dangerous stuff. Notes under my door. But it was your name, and so few people know your name, and it's for Haris." He looks down the street one direction and then the other. "Please. We must go. We will be noticed here." He looks up at the building behind me. "They closed this office for security reasons. Again, the protests. Come."

With that Peter flaps a hand at me and starts to walk away.

I hesitate. I was to meet a bribable Stasi guard at this corner, pay him, and get my father in return. I expected it would all be over within a few hours. How, I didn't know, but that was the basic plan. Now I'm being asked to trust a man named Peter, who claims to have been sent by Panzer, who knows my father, and who asks me to follow him who knows where. Behind the Iron Curtain.

I stay put, unable to move, until I remember Willow. Panzer would not lead me astray with Willow in jeopardy. She is safe as long as I remain safe. I think of Daniel, who took off from DC without a moment's hesitation to set all this up, and know he'd expect me to trust my instincts and employ my training, no matter how long ago it was or how dusty and rusty it feels. I imagine my father, penning all those letters, asking about me, wondering if I am well, begging Opa to tell him how much I'm loved. My father, who still doesn't know Opa never told me he was alive. My father, who faces certain death, perhaps beginning tomorrow. There is too much riding on this moment for me *not* to follow Peter.

I rush to catch up with him and match his pace for one block, then two. We don't talk. We don't look around and we don't rush. At a short stone building several blocks away, he stops and pushes open a heavy glass and wood door. The building looks like something from the 1920s. The stonework is ornate, but the mortar is old, dry, and covers the stonework like dust. I notice a huge hole, stone nicked from its side, as if someone took a bite from a wedding cake. I suspect it was created by an Allied bomb, as there's an empty lot next to this building as well.

We start up the stairs at the back of the black-and-white-tiled and wood-paneled lobby. On the second floor, his hand on the doorknob to the hallway, Peter turns to me and whispers, "It's the third door down to the right. Don't say a word. Keep your head down and under your scarf until we are inside."

I obey and, once seemingly safe behind the closed door, I breathe again. The apartment is small and clean. It has a wood floor and wood paneling up to the chair rail in both the small front hallway and the living room to my right. The curtains are drawn across the room's one window, and a faint tang of cleaning vinegar reminds me of Oma.

"Is this her?" A woman emerges from the living room.

"Yes." Peter steps back and stares at me.

I stand, looking between them, unsure of what's going on. Then, suddenly, I'm engulfed in a tight hug. The woman has one hand around my back and the other at my head, cradling it as if I'm a child. She slowly rocks us back and forth, and I can't tell if she's laughing or crying.

"Who are you?" I whisper with the last air she hasn't squeezed from my lungs.

She jumps back as if I've shocked her and swipes at her eyes. "Forgive me. I shouldn't have done that. It's just— We never thought we'd meet you."

The woman looks to Peter. I do too.

He places a hand on his chest. "As I said, I'm Peter Sauer and this is my wife, Helene. We lived across from Haris for many years. Then he was arrested and we were moved here." He waves his hand. "One had nothing to do with the other. It was just the way of those things."

"You look like him." She touches my shoulder, then turns to her husband. "She looks like him."

"Yes." He nods. "That's how I knew it wasn't a trick."

I furrow my brow.

"One does not follow notes delivered under one's door. Anyone could write them."

His repetition of his earlier sentence and his tone make me laugh. "No, I suppose one shouldn't."

It breaks the tension between us. Their stiff postures relax, and I practically slump against the wall.

"Come in." Helene pulls at my arm. "Let's get you some tea, then you can sleep a few hours. I can't imagine what you've been through. You must tell me how you got here at all."

Peter stops our progress to the kitchen. "I need to go to work. Will you be okay?" He speaks to Helene alone.

She looks from him to me, a broad smile filling her face. Wrinkles circle her eyes. "We will be just fine. I'll send her off on time."

Peter nods. He opens his mouth to say something more but closes it again. Instead he steps toward me and rests a hand on my forearm. "Tell your father I'll see him soon."

Just as quietly as we entered, he is gone.

I pull the scarf off my head. The apartment is warm and the radiators knock with trapped water.

Helene's eyes widen at my hair.

I put a hand up to it. It's cold and still wet. A few hacked strands are stiff at the ends with ice or perhaps the remnants of shoe polish. I can't imagine how horrible it must look. I feel self-conscious and note that I'm patting my face and my hair. "I'm sorry. I'm a mess. I had to cut my hair to impersonate a punk to get across the checkpoint."

Helene smiles again. "That was very clever." She gestures down the short hallway. "Come have some tea and a little breakfast. Then I expect you need sleep."

"Do you know what happens after that?" I follow her down the hallway.

"Peter didn't tell you?" She fills a worn metal kettle from the sink and places it on the stove. Using a match she lights the burner. "The man you're to meet will be there at 6:00 p.m. during his first cigarette break."

"And Panzer wrote you this?"

Questions arise as to why Panzer would reach out to them when he knew exactly the route I was walking and my precise timing. Why not just find me?

"He knows Peter from the church and also knew you'd need a

place to wait until tonight. Hanging out with the Ostpunks is not wise. They are watched and, I expect, more than a few have been forced to snitch for the Stasi."

Her words make sense and I'm so very tired. I lift my head to find Helene staring at me.

"How long is it since you've slept?"

"What is today?"

"Thursday."

"Then four days really. I caught a couple hours yesterday afternoon, but I've not had a full night since last Friday . . . I never sleep well. I just—" I sigh. "I'm just awake. A lot."

"That won't do." Helene hands me a cup of tea. "You can eat later. Drink this and let's get you into bed. You have nine hours until you need to get ready, and you're safe now. Okay? You can sleep."

I sip the tea and savor how it warms me all the way through. A sliver of peace comes with an exhaustion beyond anything I've ever felt, and after sipping only half the cup, I follow her to a bedroom and let myself get tucked into one of the room's twin beds. Again, the curtains are already drawn.

The last thing I hear is a soft lullaby.

CHAPTER 25

Haris Voekler

Friday, May 19, 1989

The wall . . . will still be standing in fifty and even a hundred years' time."

That's what General Secretary Honecker said. He said it aloud and it was transmitted around the country and around the world, on both the television and the radio. I closed my eyes that January day several months ago and willed myself not to fall into despair. The thought that everything I dreamed about and worked for was for naught was painful. But the knowledge I would be stuck behind this wall for the rest of my life and never see my daughter was unbearable.

I'd held greater hope last summer, back in '88. That July, American singer Bruce Springsteen came to East Berlin for a concert. They set up a stage in a giant meadow in the Weissensee district, and he sang for four hours. Over three hundred thousand people flooded the field that night, and I stood on the crowd's edge, listening to "Badlands," a song I suspected might be about our country, "Born in the USA," and "Chimes of Freedom." The kids around me told me the song titles as he started each one. But I didn't need them to tell me anything more. I picked up on Springsteen's messages. I heard the freedom in his lyrics. It opened for me, for all of us, a wellspring of hope.

Then came winter and Honecker's statement this January. Defeat.

Then came spring and our election victory. Hope again.

It all started with Panzer punching a hole in the church's basement wall last March. We were discussing the upcoming general elections in May and how the Party cheats to win, each and every time. But as no oppositional candidate ever makes the ballot, the outcome is—and always will be—inevitable.

"Or is it?" I asked.

"What do you mean?" Panzer stilled.

"What if the outcome isn't inevitable?" I shared with him a series of articles I was tasked to write to celebrate the DDR's fortieth anniversary coming in October of this year. While the articles are to be a typical propaganda piece, sharing our country's 1949 creation and extolling our prosperity and peace, the research was extensive and had revealed surprising results.

"I've been studying our constitution." I perched on a crate in the church basement's corner. "We don't need someone to run against the Party; we just need to show they didn't win to the degree they will say they won."

"What do you mean?" asked another kid, whose name always escapes me.

I glanced around. All charcoaled eyes and spike-topped heads were turned to me. "What percentage do they say win in an average election?"

"It's 98 to 99 percent of the vote. Never less." Panzer sneered.

"And do they?"

He shrugged. "I can't imagine how."

"Then let's find out." I watched their confused expressions almost a full minute before explaining that our country's constitution not only guarantees free elections—they sniggered at that statement—but also gives the right to every citizen to monitor those elections.

"What do you mean?"

"It means we can see with our own eyes if the Party wins by as much as it says it wins. We watch as they count the votes. And if the Party doesn't win by that margin, it's election fraud."

The room erupted into chaos. Everyone started talking at once about the idea's lunacy. The Stasi, which guards every polling location, would never allow it. We'd be arrested. It'd be a lost effort. We'd lose ground putting resources to it.

"Wait." I tried to calm the chatter. "This could be it. If we discover the SED only wins 70 or 80 percent of the vote but announces the usual 99 percent win, then we have them. Election fraud is a constitutional violation. It's the stuff of headlines, major headlines, the kind that bring down governments. Those journalist friends of yours can smuggle the real data to the West, and they can pipe it back in over the radio to our own people. Protests and riots here. Global pressure out there."

It took time for everyone to settle. A few yells by Panzer helped. Then I explained how I thought we should go about it. A "no" vote could not be formed by writing a single *X* across a ballot, as people usually did when they were frustrated and wanted to show they were against the Party. We had to somehow let people know to write "no" or to draw a little *X* over each individual name. If they did that, their ballot would be marked as "against" the Party rather than as an invalid ballot to be thrown away.

We got to work.

Within three weeks, we—joined by several other oppositional groups—printed enough pamphlets to distribute all over the country. The kids took them to their concerts, their friends, and their underground networks. Each flyer explained how to properly lodge a dissenting vote. We even provided examples of names with small *X*s beside them.

Within eight weeks, we signed up over three hundred volunteers to monitor the polling stations. That meant we could place two or three people at every East Berlin polling station, and many across the country as well. While we couldn't monitor the full national vote, we believed our coverage was enough.

On May 7, Election Day, we were ready. I didn't admit to any of them that I fully expected the Stasi to arrest or, at the very least, harass our volunteers. But it didn't happen. Not one single officer addressed or laid a hand on any of our volunteers, who stood watching the elections all day and remained to monitor the count at each polling station later that night.

Early the next morning, our volunteers either showed up at the church or called in their numbers for each polling station.

20 percent. No.

38 percent. No.

25 percent. No.

28 percent. No.

It was unheard of. The SED, the Socialist Unity Party, had reported winning at a 98 percent margin or better for every election across the past thirty-plus years. We wondered if the polls were dramatically different this year or if the Party had been lying all along. We suspected the latter, but we also couldn't discount the growing opposition and dissent all across Eastern Europe.

We were stunned and whispered among ourselves as if a loud voice would burst the bubble. "What will they report? What will they do?" A few got discouraged, sure the Party would tell the truth and win. After all, they knew we'd been watching and a 70 to 80 percent vote in favor was still a win.

I hurried straight from the church to my office that day. I remember it so clearly. May 8 was a clear, cool day—a hopeful day. I had to rush because I was already late. I'd lingered at the church for the numbers to come because I wanted to know the truth before I heard the Party's official announcement. But I needed to get to the office for the official proclamation and to put the finishing touches on the Party's announcement declaring its win. As the Party never lost, the article was already written, edited, and typeset, save a title and a quote from General Secretary Honecker.

We usually received the official word from the party by 8:00 a.m. in order to make the afternoon edition. But by the time I arrived, Minister Egon Krenz, General Secretary Honecker's deputy, had already called. Koch glowed as he told me the news—an impressive Party win that had secured 98.5 percent of the popular vote.

My hands trembled as I wrote the headline *SED Party Wins!* Koch, perched at my shoulder, crossed it out immediately. For a moment I thought he was going to acknowledge what it seemed everyone sensed—at least everyone I knew sensed it. This was a lie.

Koch sat with his pen poised on the edge of the page. I waited. Then, in a flourish, he wrote *An Impressive Acknowledgment of Our Policies of Peace and Socialism* and slid the paper back to me. "That's a better headline, don't you think? It shows what the Party is about and why the win and the vote of confidence are so important."

I nodded. "Ja. Very impressive."

We had our proof. Not only that, but the Party and its official newspaper were doubling down on the lie by announcing it to the world.

The next day, we printed our samizdat at the church and passed along a template to all other opposition groups. It outlined the charge for election tampering and fraud and the math behind our analysis. A few math geniuses on our side had stayed up all night and calculated that even though we didn't have the entire country under surveillance during the election, we had enough to guarantee our numbers within a 98 percent confidence interval. The best math minds in the DDR assured us our calculations were irrefutable.

Then Panzer got the information to a reporter friend from the West. He rolled the datasets and our analysis into film canisters and ChapStick tubes because even though reporters don't get searched, one can never be too sure.

It got out. And that night, over Radio Free Europe, it got back in.

I couldn't hide my excitement. I wanted to celebrate, sing, dance, shout for all to hear. But, as I am truly too old to keep up with the punks, I had to settle for writing a quick note to Walther and sharing the news with Peter over cigarettes and beer.

He tapped the neck of his bottle to mine. "That's huge. You pulled off the win of a lifetime."

"Not just me." I was feeling magnanimous and a little drunk. "There's nothing they can do against us either. It was legal. Not a single law was broken. No dissenting opinion expressed. We simply printed facts and have the data to back them up."

We continued our celebration over one of Helene's outstanding dinners and a bottle of wine, and I went to bed happy for the first time in twenty-seven years.

Over the following days, as the news started to fuel protests, I knew it was just the beginning. The first rumblings sparked in Leipzig and the winds of discontent blew the flames higher and across the country. The fervor that had seized Poland for years had finally crossed our borders.

At the end of that first week, I found a summons in my postbox at work instructing me to report to Stasi headquarters on Magdalenenstrasse immediately "to clear up some matters."

No arrests had been made. No one had even been brought in

for questioning. But I knew. As one knows deep in their bones when something horrific is about to occur. I was about to enter the shortest street in East Berlin for the longest time.

Risking everything, I didn't race home. I didn't wait one second. I opened my desk drawer right in the middle of the *Neues Deutschland* newsroom, pulled out a pen, grabbed a piece of paper, and wrote quickly, quietly, intently.

I hadn't heard from Walther in six months. But we'd gone through stretches of silence in our writing relationship over the years. It didn't worry me. But—just like Manfred's information about Operation Pope—he needed to know.

Someone somewhere in the world needed to know where I'd gone, and why.

May 19, 1989

Dear Walther,

Glaring mistakes can be made in any job, I suppose. Sorting them out is often the bigger problem. Correcting them, too, is challenging. Are you right? It's hard to ask oneself that question. But one must if one wants to grow.

ARREST

CHAPTER 26

Luisa Voekler

Thursday, November 9, 1989

I shoot to sitting, unsure of where or even when I am. My head is heavy and foggy and the days have blurred together with too little sleep and frightful dreams when sleep comes. But it wasn't my usual nightmare that startled me awake this time; it was Daniel being harmed. He was in pain, far away and yet close, and it was my fault. I put him wherever he was and I let my enemy grab him, wound him, and leave him bleeding. While Daniel is beyond capable, in my dream he was caught by surprise and I was clearly responsible.

I scrub my eyes, imagining him and Willow and who might be following them and what danger might be lurking. Is anyone following me? Does anyone truly care about this small drama at all? Because Andrew was right—the tension in the air is palpable on both sides of the Wall. Eastern Europe feels like it's breaking apart. I suppose I have no way to know if it's the usual tension, but I can't imagine it is. How can one live day by day in this charged, electric, fraught atmosphere?

I swing my feet over the side of the bed as one of Opa's many quips comes to me. He always had "words of wisdom" that sounded clever at first but grew tedious at the twentieth, fortieth, or hundredth recitation. "*Just because you're paranoid doesn't mean people aren't after you.*"

I remember laughing at that one when I was ten and stopping sometime around age fifteen when I could better interpret tone. That was when I realized Opa was very serious about that particular pearl of wisdom.

I flip on the light and Panzer's watch tells me it's four thirty. I calm after calculating that it took only twentyish minutes to walk here this morning, so if I am to be back there at six o'clock, there is time. I'm not late.

I take a deep breath in hopes it will prepare me for all that's to come.

I slip on my boots and pull the thick, scratchy sweater over my head. The neck is tight and pulls at my short hair. I open the bedroom door. Down the hall, I spy Helene's feet tucked under their kitchen table, her body just out of sight.

She smiles as I step into the room. "You slept well."

The calm assurance in her voice soothes me. "I'm surprised I slept at all. That's unusual for me. I had some pretty crazy dreams."

"You're under a great deal of stress."

I settle into the kitchen chair across from her. "It's so dark. I thought I'd missed my meeting at first, but—" I tap Panzer's watch to assure us both of the time.

"The sun sets just before five o'clock now. In December it sets near four o'clock. That's a lot of darkness and I find it depressing after a month or two." She pushes back from the table and stands. "I made *bigos* for you."

I lift my nose, noticing the smell. It's warm, sweet, rich, and earthy. Fully awake, I examine her kitchen more carefully. It's a small space with grey-painted cabinets and a square table pressed against the wall. There are marks dug into the wood as if kids did their homework at this table, created art projects here, even had temper tantrums here.

Beside the sink there is a knife and cutting board, clean but resting as if ready for use.

My eyes travel up to the room's only window. It's centered above the sink at the narrow end of the kitchen. Checkered curtains are pulled across it. I glance back to the living room behind me. Its window is covered as well.

Helene follows my gaze. "We can't risk anyone seeing you. We have two boys. Though both are grown and married now, someone would pay attention to a young woman in our apartment who is not either of their wives."

Helene pulls out a bowl, fills it with the fragrant stew, and sets it before me. She then pulls a loaf of bread from a bread box very similar to Oma's and cuts a slice.

"What is this again?" I inhale the steam.

"Bigos. We also call it hunter's stew. It would be easier to tell you what's not in it than what is. I had all the ingredients because I was planning to make it this weekend, as it's best simmering on the stove all day, but then I had this day suddenly free." She smiles and sits across from me again. "And I thought you probably haven't eaten in a while."

I take a bite. It's delicious but foreign. I've grown up on German food, but I've never had this. "What am I tasting?"

Helene glances over to the large pot resting on her stove top as if peeking inside. "Your Oma probably makes her own version. It's a very regional dish and mine is heavier than most on the caraway seeds and apples. The prunes too. I think they deepen the sweet tartness you get from the apples nicely."

"Didn't you need to be at work today?" I recall the *asoziales Verhalten* laws that used to worry both Oma and Opa so much.

Helene fakes a tiny cough into her hand. "Much too sick today. I believe I'm running a fever."

Two bites in and I'm ravenous. I lean over the bowl, and only when my nose practically dips into the soup do I realize how rude I'm being and how ill-mannered I must look. I sit straight. I slow down. "I'm sorry. It's been about twenty-four hours since I ate."

"Please don't apologize."

I still try to slow further and be polite and make conversation. "You mentioned sons. How old are they?"

"From what Haris told us, they're both near your age. Well, Dirk is. Traeger is about a year younger than you."

"You know my birthday?"

"Haris talks—" Helene stops and resets herself. "Talked about you a great deal. He received letters from your Opa, which he would share with us, and we celebrated your birthday each year. My kids were teenagers, as were you, by the time we met Haris, but who doesn't love an excuse for a night of cake and celebration?"

"He's still alive."

She presses her lips together and regards me for a heartbeat. "I hope so and I apologize for that, but I have found over the years that I fare better being surprised by hope rather than being fooled by reality." She reaches out and touches the table between us.

"I understand. In fact, you're helping me understand my grandparents a great deal more. It's funny how easily you can convince yourself that the people you live with see the world like you do." I survey her kitchen again. "But I remember nothing about living here, and they haven't forgotten a moment of that life. In many ways"—I tap a tender finger to my temple—"Oma is still here, and that's something I need to remember and better respect."

I look to the stove and imagine Oma standing at a similar one cooking her own hunter's stew. I can almost see her feeding my mother dinner or Aunt Alice snacks and monitoring homework at a table just like this one. I imagine her telling her daughters all the ingredients she included in her stew that evening. I imagine—

"I hope you find this is all a mistake." Helene looks at me curiously, as if surprised I'm not following her. "Haris's arrest? He's been questioned before—most of us have at one time or another—but not arrested. He's a good man and a good reporter for *Neues Deutschland*, the Party's paper. He's respected. He's loyal. There is nothing he could have said or done to warrant this."

"I'm sure you're right."

"Then why are you here?" Something in me quickens. It's a legitimate question, but not one anyone else has asked. Everyone, from Bran to Daniel and the punks to Peter, seemed to accept I needed to come. But looking at Helene, I'm not sure how to explain without sharing about the letters and the codes. And that I cannot do. If by some chance I can't get my father out, I certainly won't add to the charges against him. Anyone could be a snitch, after all.

"With all the protests, I learned that things would—" I pause, searching for the blandest and most innocuous phrase. "Could get worse for him in jail. I simply want to contact him." I wave a hand toward the window. "I gather the protests are making the government more reactionary right now."

"You want to help him escape."

I take a bite and force myself to chew slowly and reply casually. "I suppose if it's possible."

"I expect it is." Helene, too, looks toward the covered window. "We've not seen the likes of this week here. The Party made travel concessions, though, so perhaps that will quiet things down."

"I hope so." To keep the conversation from returning to my

father or my motivation, I point down the hallway. "May I use your bathroom?"

"Of course."

I step into their tiny bathroom and assess myself in the mirror. Was the thread of tension I detected in the kitchen real or imagined? My words to Helene come back to me and placate me. As with my grandparents, I cannot assume she thinks or would act as I do. And I must be putting her, Peter, and even their boys and their wives in grave danger. She should ask questions. She has a right to be wary of me.

I shift my focus from internal to external and groan at what I see. I'm a mess, an absolute mess. The dark circles around my eyes are all mine now. Willow's black eyeliner is long gone. I look overly pale, almost ghostlike, and the stiff, jagged ends of my hair still carry a black tint from the shoe polish. I glance away with the determination not to look in the mirror again. There is no reason for such torture.

On the sink I find soap, toothpaste, and lotion. I sense Helene has set them out for me, so I use them. My right forefinger makes a good toothbrush, and after washing my face, the lotion feels like heaven on both my hands, which feel tight as the skin heals and hardens, and my face, which remains chapped from this morning's scrubbing. Though tempted, I don't look in the mirror again to see if any of it has helped my overall appearance.

Helene is standing at her kitchen counter when I return. She's drawing something on a piece of paper. "Here." She beckons me over with a waved pencil. "This is our apartment. Once you open our door, you must cover your head and walk straight away. Soft steps, but not like you're trying to hide anything. Frau Jäger next door is too curious for anyone's good. I suspect two others in our building snitch for the Stasi as well, but she has the best hearing."

"How can you live like this? Doesn't it infuriate you that your neighbors spy on you?"

Helene's expression falls, and I open my mouth to apologize. I'm not sure why it's necessary, but I sense it is.

She rests a hand on my forearm to stay my words. "It takes time to understand, but you can't be too angry about those who snitch because you never know why they do it. Most don't do it for money or privilege, though some do. Most are coerced. They are threatened—and often not with harm to themselves, but with harm to their loved ones. For instance, parents might do anything to keep their children from arrest because they did something stupid or even, conversely, do anything to help their children walk a smoother path in life. No one has a smooth path here."

I open my mouth to ask a question, but close it as I can't find a way to frame it politely.

"I sense Frau Jäger has a good heart. I want to believe that if she is a snitch, she does the bare minimum to stay safe and not to harm others. Here . . ." Helene slides the map she's just drawn across the counter toward me and proceeds to trace every step I need to make until I've reached the meeting spot once more.

"Thank you," I say after I've memorized the drawing.

I feel like I've said those two words more in the last few days than I've said them in my entire life, and like I've never meant them more. Inside I'm an odd amalgam of gratitude and shame. I'm not sure I would risk so much to help a friend, much less a stranger, in such circumstances.

Helene smiles. It's soft and full of memory. "For Haris? For you? This is nothing." Her smile fades. "How much money do you have?"

"Seventeen thousand dollars." I paid Panzer five thousand and left three thousand with Daniel in the hotel room in case he needed it for an emergency.

Her eyes narrow.

My heart sinks. "I know. It's too little."

She holds out a hand and taps her fingers against her palm. Does this gesture mean something different in the GDR? Because in the US it means "hand it over." I step back. If Helene notices, she doesn't react.

"Come now. Hand it to me. We need to divide it up. You cannot give a guard so much. He will not expect it, and greed begets greed—and bad behavior."

"I was told it would take hundreds of thousands to release my father, and—"

"Officially perhaps. But you are dealing with ordinary people with small needs who wouldn't see that much money in years, much less in a day. You must be more prudent."

As I dig the three bound stacks from my tights, she leaves the room and returns with a small cloth pouch dangling from a long string. "I use this sometimes for safety. There are gangs all over the city now." She reaches her hand out again. "Please. Give me your money."

I hand her the bundles with a quick prayer that I'm not being robbed. Each stack is about pencil-width thick. Helene counts out the hundred-dollar bills onto the table with fast fingers. She puts ten thousand into the pouch and drapes the string over my neck. "Tuck that into your sweater and blouse. Do not mention it or gesture to it. You will not need it and you mustn't pull it out. Promise me?"

I nod.

She holds the remaining seven thousand, divided into two piles.

One in each hand. "Keep these separate. You don't know if you'll need to use this two thousand until you meet him." She waves the smaller stack. "This one." She waves the other stack. "Five thousand dollars should be sufficient. Pull it out first and don't mention more until you see how he reacts."

Helene hands me both, and I slide them into my tights, one at each hip.

"It's still too much, but we'll leave it." She clasps my arm and leads me toward their door. "I can't go with you. I can't even walk you down the stairs. I would draw attention to you, at least here in the building." She reaches into a closet by the door and pulls out a wool coat.

Oma has one coat. She has several skirts, a few more blouses, and a variety of sweaters and dresses, but only one coat. "*Who needs more than one?*" she used to ask when I showed her new styles at the department stores. I thought she was unnecessarily stingy. Now I see when you grow up with little more than the necessities, you take care of them, and you don't put your happiness into more. And one really doesn't need more than one winter coat. Especially in DC.

"I can't take that."

"You must. It's very cold and you will be noticed without a coat."

"No, I'll be fine."

She drapes it over my shoulders and starts to maneuver my arms into the sleeves. "You are so American." She laughs. "Your father loves movies and gets tapes sometimes. He didn't have a television or cassette player, so we watched them at our apartment. Americans are always fine, they always do it themselves, and they always 'get their man.'" She deepens her voice in imitation of such an American. "But we could not survive like that here. We may have snitches, but we also have friends we rely on, we must rely on, with our very lives. And you'll be noticed without a proper coat."

I don't resist any more. "Thank you."

"Remember to keep your head down and walk fast, as if you know where you're going. People don't like trouble and anything suspicious can get reported. Everyone is on edge now and might feel safest in snitching."

She hugs me tight as if she'll never see me again, which is probably true. She releases me. "Are you ready?"

Unable to speak, I nod.

"Then go." Helene widens her eyes, opens the apartment's front door, and gives me a little push.

Almost silently, the door clicks shut behind me and I'm on my way. I walk down the stairs, marveling at her practical wisdom and her generosity. I am also swamped with guilt over the question that was on the tip of my tongue, so close to slipping out, so unwarranted, and so insulting.

"Is that what happened to you?"

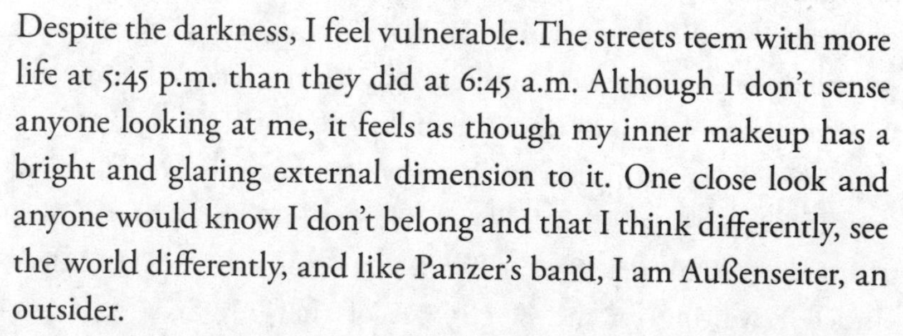

Despite the darkness, I feel vulnerable. The streets teem with more life at 5:45 p.m. than they did at 6:45 a.m. Although I don't sense anyone looking at me, it feels as though my inner makeup has a bright and glaring external dimension to it. One close look and anyone would know I don't belong and that I think differently, see the world differently, and like Panzer's band, I am Außenseiter, an outsider.

I visualize Helene's map and turn right, left, then right again. But at the next street corner, the map vanishes from my mind and I'm left standing lost. I can't remember the next turn or even the shade of pencil on the page. The heat of panic rises within my borrowed coat. I turn to the woman waiting on the corner next to me.

"I need to find the corner of Reinhardtstrasse and Luisenstrasse?"

She looks to me and without a word points to the left.

I walk away quickly. Looking back, I note she crosses the street with all the others who surrounded us. None of them glance my direction, and I suspect no one is thinking about me at all. I almost laugh. This cloak-and-dagger stuff, or my version of it, has clearly gone to my head. I was barely in the game before being booted out, and since then I've watched too many movies, read too many books, and now I'm seeing enemies where I have only met friends.

I again feel guilty for the instant of doubt I felt toward Helene.

At the next corner I glance across the street and note something I didn't see this morning. There is a sign above the building and the GDR flag waves at the top. It's a government building. Perhaps it's a Stasi building. I know it's not the main facility on Magdalenenstrasse. My father wrote Opa about that facility and it's an over-forty-building complex. But could my father be here? Right across this street in a neighborhood office jail? Is that why I am to meet my contact here?

I step into the alcove and again glance down the alley opening to the right. A single light bulb hangs within a recessed doorway. Smoke, probably from a cigarette, billows in the light.

A man steps out from the doorway, just enough, and stares at me. His expression is cool, bland. He appears bored, but something deep in his pale eyes tells me that's not the case. He's alert and he's waiting for me. A glimpse of the grey Stasi uniform beneath his brown greatcoat confirms it.

I approach.

When I'm only a couple feet away, he shifts to face me. Leaning against the building, he draws out his "*Ja?*" bored and lazy. It says to me, "I'm on my cigarette break. Why are you bothering me?"

It's now or never. This could be a trap, a feint, a deceit, or this is legit. Regardless, here it goes . . .

"Haris Voekler . . ." I say my father's name and my words die away. In all of this I have never once thought what to say in this moment. Do I ask for this guard to help him escape? To accept money for information? Do I say, "Take me to my father"? No, that's ridiculous. Then we'd both end up in jail. Do I ask him to set off the smoke alarm or something in hopes they'll bring all the prisoners outside?

I freeze.

He stares.

The guard holds his hand out. I notice this a moment late and only after he shakes it in front of me. It says "nothing paid, nothing offered," so I open my coat and reach down my skirt's waistband into my tights, praying Helene is right about the amount.

The man's expression doesn't change, as if he's seen this maneuver a hundred times. Perhaps he has. I pull out the bound five-thousand-dollar stack of bills and slap it into his palm with a confidence I don't feel.

He remains unmoved.

I look around. No one is in sight. I speak softly in German. "That's five thousand US dollars, all in one-hundred-dollar bills." Though my voice is barely above a whisper, I do speak with conviction, forcing each syllable to stay low and slow, as if I know what I'm doing.

He tries unsuccessfully to hide the sneer of victory. I breathe again. Helene was right.

"Haris Voekler." I simply state the name again in hopes this guard will have the plan I do not.

He opens his coat and slides the money into the pocket of his uniform. "You are too late. You missed him."

"I just paid you."

"For information. I am giving you that information." He mashes his cigarette out against the brick wall and lets the stub fall to the pavement. "He was transferred by van an hour ago for a train to Naumburg. The last of the political prisoners are being shipped out of the city tonight."

"Why not tomorrow?"

"The schedule changed." The guard shrugs. "It happens."

It's hardly a helpful answer. "What do I do now?"

"Visit him at Naumburg Prison. He will be registered by tomorrow." The man steps past me, his shoulder brushing mine with enough force to knock me off balance.

Before I can fully process what's happened, the Stasi guard is out of the alley and gone.

I follow him for a few steps and, standing at the alley entrance, watch him walk—in a stiff German kind of saunter—across the street toward the government building. I don't take my eyes off him until he has opened a side door and disappeared inside the large block building.

I am alone.

I retrace my steps to the Sauer apartment. Just as I'm about to push open the outer door, I back away. I cannot enter. First there's the issue of Frau Jäger and her excellent hearing, but something else dances across the back of my mind that I can't let go. I've been chewing on it, telling myself I'm ungrateful and paranoid. But Helene's "Then why are you here?" and her explanation of snitches play over and over through my mind like a song on repeat. It was not the question. It was a legitimate question. It was not the explanation. It was a legitimate explanation. It was her inflection, her intonation. It felt—I shake my head at my own paranoia—almost sinister yet confessional. I shift my gaze down the street and wonder if I can remember . . .

Over thirty minutes later, I'm both congratulating myself for finding my way back to Panzer's building and almost sick with dread at what he'll say when I knock on the door. I retrace my path through the building two over via the connecting cement hallway. By the time I've climbed the stairs to his fourth-floor apartment, I'm sweating inside Helene's wool coat.

I lift my hand to knock before remembering all the warnings about snitches infiltrating punk bands. Panzer was very clear that only he, Willow, and Splinter know about me. And even Splinter doesn't know the whole story. I try the doorknob. It turns easily.

I walk to the living room, passing the bedroom in which I stayed along the way. The door is cracked open and two people lay sprawled across the mattress on the floor. In the living room, another dozen people are lounging, chatting, eating, probably preparing for a big night out.

Panzer notices me and stands immediately. He strides toward me at such an angle I suspect he's trying to block me from everyone else's view.

"Who are you?" someone calls out.

"A friend's older sister," Panzer replies before I can say anything. He takes me by the upper arm and marches me back down the hallway. He tucks us both into the tiny bathroom before he speaks, growls really. "This was not the plan."

"I'm sorry. The guard I met said I missed my father. He's been transferred to Naumburg Prison already."

Panzer lets go of my arm. "That's a nasty place."

I slide down the wall. We're packed so tight my knees press Panzer's legs. Until his confirmation, I hoped. *I hoped* . . . I'm not even sure what I hoped. Maybe that Panzer would have a great idea. Maybe that Naumburg Prison wasn't a nasty place but more like those cushy prisons DC politicians go to when they embezzle their campaign funds. Or maybe that this was, as Helene thought, just a big misunderstanding and, somehow, Panzer now knew that.

"I'm sorry." He crouches next to me. He's pressed tight between the toilet and the wall, but it doesn't seem to bother him. "But that was hours ago. Where have you been all day?"

"What?" I twist toward him. Our faces are inches apart. "You sent me to the Sauers. They got a note from you. Peter Sauer came for me."

"Who is Peter Sauer?"

CHAPTER 27

Haris Voekler

Thursday, November 9, 1989

Six months.

I've been here six months and there is no end in sight, especially now.

The worst of the interrogations ended quickly. I can't tell what amount of time it truly took, but it couldn't have been that long because I wasn't terribly thin when it ended. I was a little beat up, but I'd lost only enough weight to see my ribs and that hollow spot right below the collarbone. There were all the elements I'd heard about—the bright lights, the wakings, the endless questions, the lack of sleep, food, and water. But then it was over.

I think it ended because there was nothing to tell them. They knew what I'd done and where I'd done it. It took me a long time to work out how they discovered it all, but I finally got there last month. A guard let something slip and it clicked into place.

Peter Sauer.

For all his and Helene's talk about Frau Hemmel, he was the snitch in our building. Maybe they both were—and still are. Conversations over the years played back like a movie before my eyes, and I couldn't believe I'd not noticed before.

Our meeting the first day their family moved in. How he sought me out and created a bond over food, work, unspoken dissent. Never agreeing with me but implying, teasing out my opinions, encouraging my confidences. The dinner invitation the night I discovered the bug in my apartment rather than a new heating unit. The movie nights. My first call to Stasi headquarters the day after my trip to the Tränenpalast. The words the interrogator had used. He'd been so prepared, his notes so detailed. How could I have been so stupid not to realize that such preparation had to have been the work of months, not a mere day? Now I suspect Peter took me to the Tränenpalast on purpose because it provided the perfect excuse to bring me in for questioning. I'd never suspect it as everyone who goes to the Friedrichstrasse Station runs that risk. I doubt Peter even has an Aunt Agatha.

Then there was Manfred. Sure, there were other hints, but that conversation alone should have alerted me. And it did—at the time and finally, in its fullness, last month. Over beers Peter asked if Manfred had been the reporter who'd died trying to escape. I shot back yes without thought. I remember, at the time, something discordant striking my mind, but I couldn't name it, pin it down. Only last month could I see it clearly—I never told Peter about Manfred, and no one but the Stasi or the VoPo could.

I've rested in this cell for the past few months berating and consoling myself. The berating is justified—I was an idiot. I let my guard down. I was a fool. But gentle consolation comes with the next thought, and that is real too—it's only me here. I never gave them any actionable intelligence. I never gave up any of the punks' names. Heck, I don't know their real names.

And I've never heard from any prisoners coming or going that more arrests surrounding the elections have been made. And I gather they'd know. The elections became the talk of the city, the talk of the country, and even six months later remain top of mind.

It seems I'm the election scapegoat, but as long as the others are safe, that's fine by me. I rest in that fact, even when my trial gets delayed or I get tossed into solitary confinement for no good reason, again.

Then a few days ago, a guard announced I was getting transferred to Naumburg Prison. I've heard stories of that place. There are two prisons in Naumburg, one for the men and another for women, and both are equally terrible hellholes. You don't go there to await trial so much as to disappear without one.

"When will my trial be scheduled? When do I go to court? What's going on . . . ?" I yelled after the guard, but he never turned, much less answered. The prisoner in the next cell did.

"They've canceled all the hearings in East Berlin right now. The riots are growing too fierce. That's why they're moving the political prisoners. They're worried you lot will stir things up further."

"Who are you? How do you know this?"

"It's all over the streets. Everyone knows it. You'd be shocked at what's being talked about these days. Secrets spilling all over the place. Protests. Riots. It's coming to a boil, I tell you."

"Riots? Are they about the elections?"

"The elections are long past. They're about freedom now."

My legs lost strength and I dropped to my cell's metal bench, stunned. *Freedom?* The word has consumed me since that moment.

I glance to the clock as an officer comes to my cell. It's six fifteen and I haven't gotten dinner yet. I almost comment, but he's sporting a twisted smirk that puts me on guard. He hauls me off the bench and cuffs me. "You've got some friends about, don't you, Voekler? Got money too, not that it helped you."

"Peter Sauer?" I keep saying his name to the guards in hopes it'll get back to Peter. I want him to know I know. I want him to feel that prick in his conscience if he can.

"No." The guard sneers. "A pretty young thing. Do you have a daughter?"

I twist to face him, but he holds my hands tight. "Who?"

"A German girl. Blonde. With big blue eyes."

What is Willow or Tiny up to? They're the only two blonde punks I can think of, and I hope neither is trying to do something stupid to help me.

"No daughter." I return to the guard's question, hoping the girls are long gone. "I don't have a daughter and no one would help me, so leave it alone."

"That's what I thought. Told them it was too late anyway."

"Too late?"

"We're moving you tonight. Get going."

With that, he pushes me so hard I stumble out of the cell toward the building's loading dock.

CHAPTER 28

Luisa Voekler

Thursday, November 9, 1989

"*Who is Peter Sauer?*"

I slump back against the wall and try to untangle what was real, what was imagined, and how I might have messed it all up. "He and his wife said you sent them a note that the guard wouldn't be on duty until tonight. Then he was there, at 6:00 p.m., and I paid him. For nothing."

I open my eyes and clutch Panzer's arm so tight, I feel the stiff skin on my palm split open. "What if it was a trick? What if the right guard really was there this morning, but I walked away? I just handed five thousand dollars to a fraud."

I stop. Why not all seventeen thousand? If Peter and Helene were in it for the money, they could have taken all of it. And who told them about Panzer? How did they know? My mind reels off into the ether until Panzer brings me back with a snap so close to my nose I feel it.

"Focus. We'll figure this out later, but now . . ." He taps the back of his head against the bathroom's tile. "We've got to get you out of here. Your safety matters most now."

His care brings tears to my eyes. I swipe them away. "How do you live like this? I've only been here a day."

He chuckles. "Maybe it's worse here. I don't know. I've never been anywhere else, but doesn't one find conformity, complacency, and even persecution of the outsider everywhere? Rats and snitches too?"

His questions surprise me. I was asking about police, regulations, and authoritarianism. He's examining human nature.

"I suppose."

"It's humanity at our most basic level. You go along until they come for you. Then you find out what you're made of."

"You and Willow and all of you"—I wave my hand toward the bathroom door, then swipe it across my damp face—"are made of good steely stuff. I'm not sure anymore about Peter and Helene Sauer."

"You don't know they weren't being honest. That could have been your real contact."

"But how?"

He shrugs. "I have no idea, but you'd be surprised at how small this city is and how much everyone, if you just scratch the surface, knows about each other."

He smiles, trying to fill me with encouragement, and again I am struck by how young he is beneath all his black leather and makeup, beneath his wisdom too.

"I'm done here, Panzer. I missed my chance. I need to go back so Willow can come home." I reach down the neck of my sweater and pull Daniel's scrap of paper from my bra. "Do you have a telephone?"

Panzer holds up a "wait here" finger and, using the toilet for leverage, pushes himself up. He steps over me and whacks me with the bathroom door as he leaves. He's back in under a minute carrying a black rotary dial telephone, dragging the long cord behind him. "I'll keep them talking in the other room, but keep your voice down in here."

I nod and take the heavy phone from him.

I dial the number and am surprised when Daniel answers on the second ring. I was almost expecting everything to have fallen apart, on both sides of the Wall. "Luisa? Where have you been? I expected to hear from you hours ago."

"He's gone. The guard wasn't on duty this morning like he was supposed to be, or so I was told, so I had to wait. But I met a guard tonight and paid him, and he's gone. My father was already transferred out of the city."

"They're moving political prisoners because of the riots. Have you heard the news?"

"I've been walking across this entire city, Daniel." I stop. That's not true. I was asleep. The oddness of that strikes me again, but I push it away. "I've heard nothing. What's going on?"

"Wait there. Stay at that phone. You'll get a call. This is a little out of my hands now."

"You can't call me back. I don't know this num—" I lift the phone. The plastic holder for the number card is empty. But it doesn't matter; the line is already dead.

It rings seconds later. I pick it up, too shocked for pleasantries. "How'd you do that? And what do you mean it's out of your hands?"

"Good evening, Luisa."

"Andrew?" I choke on my boss's name.

"Listen carefully and don't interrupt."

I glance around the bathroom as if my boss is somehow here, looking over my shoulder. "How do you—?"

"Luisa," he barks. "What time does Panzer's watch say?"

He's right. I do interrupt. "It says 6:41."

"You have only an hour and the streets are going to start filling. The news won't air until the 7:00 and 8:00 p.m. broadcasts, but it's seeping in regardless. You need to move fast. Do you understand me? You need to run. Don't take the S-Bahn as I'm not sure what they'll do to those lines and the VoPo monitor them well. You're best on foot. Running. Let nothing stop you. Your father's train leaves at 7:48 from the Friedrichstrasse Station. Not up where the S-Bahn trains travel aboveground, but below. Platform 6. Repeat that last part."

"7:48. Platform 6. Friedrichstrasse Station. But why will the streets fill? Is there another protest?"

"There's no time for that. First you need to get your father. The rest—it'll become clear. Pay attention." He pauses as if giving me time to prepare myself not to interrupt.

I nod. Then I realize he can't see me. "Yes."

"There is a door as you enter the station from the southwest stairwell. You have to go up to go down. It's marked *Employees Only* and it's the most watched door in East Berlin. It's a regular party at that door. All the agencies on both sides watch it as it's the VoPo and Stasi entrance to the trains below. It's how they move people, officers, and prisoners. I can't say that tonight will be any different. You need to go through that door and don't let anyone stop you."

"Yes."

"Below there will be two guards. You talk to one named Beck. If you have to ask his name, ask. There's no time to be subtle. Call the number after you get your father and we'll go from there."

"We? I thought the CIA couldn't help me."

"Of course they can't and we never had this conversation, but considering Daniel's involved, I'm sure he'll think of something."

"Thank—"

"Thank me later, Luisa, when I don't fire you. Run."

Again, the line goes dead.

I put the receiver back in the cradle and open the bathroom door. "Panzer," I bark just as an "older sister" might.

He comes striding down the hallway.

"Friedrichstrasse Station? I have to go on foot."

He pushes me back into the bathroom and stands against the wall beside me rather than in front of me. I'm about to interrupt him when he starts moving his hands to the left and right. I see he's working out directions as if walking the route himself.

He points ahead of us, as if he can almost see the parks and building I will pass. "You go straight through Alexanderplatz. Straight. Because on the other side, you'll start getting street signs. You're only a few blocks from the station at that point and every corner is marked with an arrow. It's not the fastest way, but it's not that much slower and you can't mess it up."

"I need the fastest." I look at his watch. "I only have an hour."

"It's over six kilometers. You can't make it."

"I have to make it." I undo his watch and shove it into his hands.

He pushes it back. "You need it."

I shake my head. I can't take anything more from him, and certainly not a treasured family heirloom. Besides, I don't need it. I either run my fastest and I make it or I don't. Pausing to count down the minutes isn't going to help. I kiss Panzer's stubbled cheek in thanks and race out the door and down the building's stairs. This time I do not go to the basement and walk two buildings away. I crash through the lobby and start to run, just as Andrew told me to.

I run to Karl-Marx-Allee, turn right, and run the couple miles straight to Alexanderplatz. I try to continue across the plaza, as instructed, but it's packed tonight. People fill it with more pouring in every second. They're not organized. I don't see any signs signaling a protest. Instead I get this odd feeling that no one knows what's going on but they need to be out and about to be a part of whatever it might become. The size of the protests all across Germany that Andrew recounted in our meeting at Langley was staggering, and Daniel's update eclipsed those numbers. Perhaps tonight will be the granddaddy of them all.

The deep chime of a bell reverberates off the buildings. I look up, bumping into a broad man as I do, and notice a large clock atop a red building to my left. Seven o'clock. I stumble around him, catch myself, wave an apology, and race on, seeing nothing until a firm grip on my arm lifts me off my feet. My body spins midair and lands facing the green uniform of the Volkspolizei.

"Papers."

I have no papers and I have no time.

"He just started screaming."

I remember hearing that line as part of a story Splinter was telling on the bus. He was describing how a friend evaded forty-eight hours of Stasi questioning by simply screaming his head off in public. Embarrassed by the commotion, the officer simply let him go. Stasi Schmidt didn't laugh at the story, but all the other band members did. Even in my pretend comatose state, I smiled at his friend's creativity.

I twist, trying to break free of the policeman's grasp, and start yelling at the top of my lungs in German. "I've done nothing wrong. He's hurting me. Help mc. Help me."

People turn toward us. The crowd presses close and everyone's attention focuses on us. No one says or does anything, but they don't have to. The policeman lets go at my first yell, and I push through the throng and sprint away.

I finally reach the end of the square—which I decide is more of a rectangle—and my lungs are on fire. A horrible cramp has seized my left side and I can't pull in air. I dig my fist into the soft space above my hip bone and start running again. Panzer's advice was good. I have no sense of direction and barely a coherent thought in my brain, but each street corner is marked with a sign for Friedrichstrasse Station, both in Russian Cyrillic and in German. I simply need to follow the signs.

Within several minutes I catch my first glimpse of the massive train station. I stop, grab my side again, and close my eyes, trying to envision a map of East Berlin in the hopes I can discern what corner I'm approaching. Starting up again, I pass the closest stairwell and run under the tracks, suspecting the southwest corner is on the other side. I pray I'm right as I climb the stairs. My legs are jelly so I grab the rail and half pull myself up the double flight.

At the platform I gulp in air and relief. A door marked *Nur für Mitarbeiter*, Employees Only, sits exactly where Andrew said it would be. I spot a few men loitering nearby but don't give them time to approach. I yank open the door and descend a dim stairwell that's at least twice as far down as I climbed up moments before.

The door at the bottom opens to an underground station. Not for city commuter trains, but larger ones that travel greater distances. The platforms aren't as full as those above, but plenty of people are milling about. I search for signs and find the placard for Number 6 is one platform away.

The train sits ready to depart, and with each step I expect it to pull away. It doesn't. I round the back of it and head toward the boarding crowds, afraid I've once more missed my father. My heart pounds so loudly it feels like my whole body pulses with its beat, especially my ears.

Across from the train's open doors and the people lining up to enter them, I see a row of men sitting on a bench. It's their greyness that captures my attention. Everything about them is the same color. Grey shoes. Grey clothes. Grey hair. Grey faces. Grey expressions.

Two Stasi guards, dressed in a sharper iteration of grey, stand beyond them. I walk toward the guards, unable to pull my eyes from the line of men. Every instinct tells me one is my father.

The train's whistle blows and the sound pierces the air around us. Nevertheless I hear, as if spoken to my heart rather than to my ears, "Mäuschen?"

Little Mouse.

It's soft. It's a question. I pause and find that the second-to-last man in the row has his eyes fixed upon mine.

One look and I know he's my father. We have the same eyes.

CHAPTER 29

Thursday, November 9, 1989, 7:36 p.m.

I minutely shake my head and keep walking toward the guards.

"Beck, I need to speak to you." My German carries a bravado to signal I know what I'm doing and know who will answer me. Shouting my command from a few feet away forces Beck to step toward me. I tuck my hands in my coat pocket to keep their shaking from giving me away.

I stall and Beck closes the distance between us, making it so the guard left standing behind him can't quite hear. Not that he could regardless. The train engines are ramping up.

"I want Haris Voekler." My voice carries such confidence my eyes widen in surprise. I tilt my head toward the line of men to hide my expression. I also straighten myself to my full five-foot-seven-inch frame. After all, in the movies moxie means more than size every time.

"What are you offering for your Haris Voekler?" The guard's voice is low, oily, and I silently thank Helene. If I'd had my way, I wouldn't have any money tucked down my shirt for this moment. I dismiss the two thousand in my tights immediately. I need to wow this guard and, I sense, there will be no second chance to do so.

"Ten thousand US dollars. Cold. Hard. Cash."

Now Beck's eyes widen. He glances to the train. "Here? Now?"

"It's now or never."

He looks back to the other guard, and I use the moment to pull Helene's pouch from inside my blouse. I want him to see the money. I want him to be so enthralled by it he can't say no.

He turns back just as I'm opening the pouch. His lips part, his tongue runs over his lower one, and he reaches for it, his hand covering it and tucking the money back inside the pouch. He slides the whole thing from around my neck, out of my hands, and into his pocket in a single fluid motion.

"One hour."

I reach for his arm as he turns away. "What do you mean one hour?"

The other guard calls his name and he steps back, his eyes still fixed on mine. "We need to board the prisoners now. One can get lost and it may take a full hour before we notice. After that, we must report it and begin the search."

He doesn't let me protest or reply. He turns and walks to the line of grey men. They stand at his call, and while the other guard leads the line to the train, Beck stands back to follow at the rear.

The other guard gives me a cursory glance as he walks by but doesn't break his stride. He climbs the three steps onto the train and the prisoners follow until, at the last moment, Beck yanks my father from the line and pushes him toward me.

I don't wait to be told anything else. I grab his sleeve and dive into the press of people still waiting to board the train at the next door.

"How are you here?" he calls above the noise. In English. "You are Luisa, yes?"

It makes me smile. Does he think, considering where I've grown up, that I don't speak German?

I stop and reply in German. "Ja. But we don't have time to talk now. We only have one hour before they'll start searching for you."

He's smiling at me. It's broad and joyful, as if he didn't hear a word I said or maybe as if he only heard my yes. My breathing skips pace. It's a wonderful, beautiful, once-in-a-lifetime type of smile.

"Luisa." He sighs. "Maüschen."

"Yes," I say the word again. Then I yank his arm again. We have to move.

"Luisa?" he calls, and I stop at the panicked note I hear within his voice. He lifts his chin to my neck. "Your scarf." He wiggles his hands slightly between us. His sleeves tip back and I see the glimmer of handcuffs. I pull off my scarf, wrap his hands within in it, and grip his sleeve once more.

"We've got to get as far away as possible."

"I have friends who will hide us."

"Peter and Helene?" I slow as the crowds press us near the stairwell.

"Nein," my father barks. His hands fumble from beneath the scarf as he tries to grip my arm. "You have met them? They know you are here? What do they know?"

We climb the stairs side by side. We're both speaking German and hopefully blending into the crowd around us. "They helped me this morning, but they know nothing. They knew about my first contact, but that all went wrong."

"They probably made it wrong."

I stop. "I wondered about that."

A man bumps us from behind and my father shakes his head to signal silence and says, "Later," so softly I barely catch it. I nod and start us climbing again. We reach the top of the stairs, descend the second set from the platform to the street, and pour out onto the sidewalk along with all the other people leaving the station.

"There are others we can trust." He points down the street. "We must get to the Church of Zion. We will need papers and can print them there."

I follow his gesture and step in front of him, trying to clear a path in the direction he wants us to go. But within seconds, I know it won't work. I look to my father and see he senses it too. Our way is blocked. Not by a barricade or anything official, but by a wall of people surging into the streets and all of them walking toward us rather than the direction we want to go. We can't make any progress.

It's the strangest crowd too. It's not excited or angry. It carries with it a timid jubilance, almost wonder. People greet each other as if they've woken from some collective dream and are trying to discover if the other person remembers it too and has done the same. No one says stuff like that; it simply feels like that.

I step in front of my father so he can use both hands to grip my coat from behind. Because no matter what this is or where these people are going, we still need papers and our time is ticking away.

Five steps and we get pulled apart by people pushing around and through us. They're not trying to; it's just that the sidewalks are so packed, we're all crashing into each other. I turn, lunge for my father, and again grasp his sleeve. The crowds have spilled into the street as well. Cars are moving at a snail's pace, but drivers aren't honking in annoyance. Again, a strange, almost silent thrum carries everyone along.

"We're not getting anywhere." He pulls at his hands, which

drags me with them, and we step aside. Pressed against a building, we let people swarm by us.

A man stops and pounds his hand onto my father's shoulder. "Don't look so glum. Come on. It's open."

"Open?" my father asks, but the man is gone.

Standing with our backs against the building, we finally listen and examine what's going on around us. Some people are crying, but not out of anguish. Tears run down their cheeks and get lost within smiles and laughter. The chatter is starting to rise, hitting a new emotional note. The crowd's demeanor is changing right before our eyes. Most are beginning to talk in excited voices, saying words I can't fully grasp, and their eyes are wide with disbelief. The crowd's buoyant energy seems to intensify even in the short time we stand studying it.

I face my father. "They say the Wall is open. That's what they're saying."

He rolls the back of his head against the brick as if trying to knead reality into his brain. "Don't believe them, Luisa. Honecker would never allow it. It's impossible. We must go. We'll need papers to get out. We need a plan." He looks to me. "Do you have a plan?"

"Honecker was ousted. Last month. Egon Krenz is general secretary now."

My father pales from grey to bone-chilling white. I grip his arm, worried he's having a heart attack or something. I berate myself for surprising him. I should have kept my mouth shut.

"We need a plan. We still need a plan." He repeats the sentences like they are lifelines.

"I have a phone number that will become a plan, I promise. We just need a secure telephone."

My father's hopeless expression makes him look frail and vulnerable to me, even more so than when I first noted him sitting on the bench in the train station. He wants to hope but can't, and I fear that if we fail it'll destroy him.

I push against the crowd, holding fast to him, and start again. Panzer's phone is the only safe one I know about. Any pay-phone line could be bugged.

We press on in the same direction we've been heading, and it takes an inordinate amount of time to travel even one block. I sense our hour is almost gone, if it's not gone already.

"You're going the wrong way." A young woman smiles at us. "Turn. Come on."

"Why?" My father stops. It feels like he's challenging her to repeat the same lie we've heard again and again.

"They're opening the Wall. It's over."

Now I'm shaking my head too. It can't be true. After all, in January of this year, GDR head of state Erich Honecker declared the Wall would stand for fifty or a hundred years more if the West was, well, still the West. Although Honecker is not in power any longer, Egon Krenz hasn't done or said anything to defy that. Loosened travel restrictions, yes, but papers are still required. Bringing down the Wall? I'm as hesitant to believe as my father.

"It's true." The young woman is practically laughing at our befuddlement. "They announced it on television at a press conference tonight. The border is fully open."

My father and I exchange a glance. Only knowing him for a minute, I'm surprised at all that can be said between us in a single glance. Yes? No? Finally, we both accept we must simply give up trying to struggle against the tide. Either they are right and we are going to be fine, or they are wrong and we end up no worse than we are right now. Our hour is gone, and at this rate, we'll never reach Panzer's apartment.

We let the crowd push us west.

The crowd grows to a massive size at Bornholmer Strasse. Everyone is talking about Politburo member Günter Schabowski's statement.

"He did not look like he knew what he was saying."

"But he said it."

"It's all around the world. They can't take that back."

Words bounce around us like pinballs in a machine. Everyone is saying the same thing over and over as if trying to convince themselves it's true, that the barricades are down, that the Wall is effectively no more, and that they are free.

I glance over at my father. The streetlights catch tears streaming down his face. I say nothing, as I don't sense he fears getting caught anymore. I sense he believes them.

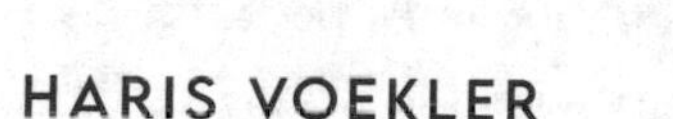

HARIS VOEKLER

7:36 p.m.

I notice the young woman, and at first I think I am seeing a ghost, I am dying as I deserve, and Monica has come to haunt me. But then *it* comes with a flash. I tamp it down and yet I can't stop it from escaping: "Mäuschen?"

It was my name for Luisa. Only mine at first. I asked Walther once to continue it, hoping in some small way she might remember me, but I'm not sure he did or, if so, that he's used it in recent years. It may be a memory of a dream I alone carry, because there is nothing small or mouselike about the beautiful woman who glances my direction.

My eyes widen as if I'm looking into a mirror. Hers do as well—she is real and she knows. My heart stops, then starts beating double-time, triple-time. I no longer worry about hallucinations; I fear a heart attack.

I want to reach out. One touch. But she keeps walking forward. I want to stop her. She cannot understand what these men are capable of. But I sit still. I am ashamed. I am ashamed of my weakness, my impotence. I am ashamed that I am here, that I am chained, and that she is here and has seen me like this.

She speaks. Officer Beck sees her now too, and I worry for her. It takes me a few gulps of air, as I haven't eaten well for months and I've only just recovered from a rough bronchial infection, to realize that I can't stop whatever is about to happen. It's real and it might harm my daughter. I repeat this to myself, as my head has been so full of the hallucinations of the sleep deprived, I sometimes wander the thin line between reality and my dreams.

The young woman . . . Luisa? Is it possible? . . . She walks with purposeful confidence. Her stride is long. She must be Luisa. She is not Monica. She moves nothing like my wife did. There is something unique in the carriage of this woman, the way she strikes out on the ball of each foot, the way she carries her head high.

Beck speaks to her and, after a few moments, returns to load us onto the train. The woman stands to the side as Wagner yells for us to embark, and Beck circles around to flank our rear. Just as I'm about to step forward onto the stairs, there is a jostling in the line ahead and Beck pushes me aside.

The woman grabs my sleeve and pulls me into the press of people still waiting to board the train a few feet distant at its first-class compartment.

"How are you here?" I shout in English. I feel my voice give way. It's not strong enough yet. I'm getting so little air. Walther wrote they only spoke to Luisa in English as she was growing up. They wanted her to fit in. They even hoped she might forget her life here. I couldn't blame them and I never wrote how sad it made me, because she deserved the gift and freedom to forget.

When she doesn't answer, I call out again, "You are Luisa, yes?"

She stops and turns back. "Ja. But we don't have time to talk now. We only have one hour before they'll start searching for you." Her German is flawless. It carries a little of Gertrude's eastern notes. I almost laugh as it seems Gertrude wasn't as resolute in Walther's forgetfulness campaign as he assumed.

I smile. It feels light and bright, unfamiliar, and a little painful on the edges. I don't remember the last time I smiled. My cheeks are unused to the stretch. But it grows and grows to the point I think my whole face fills with it.

She hiccups, almost as if she, too, has suffered bronchitis and can't fill her lungs with air.

"Luisa." I simply want to say her name again. "Maüschen."

"Yes." She nods in a stiff, decisive motion, and once again I am reminded of my mother-in-law. Before I can comment or laugh about it, she tugs at my arm and sets off through the crowds at a pace I can barely meet.

"Luisa?" I muster enough air and energy to call again. When running, my handcuffs rattle and can be seen as my shirt cuffs pull back. It's only a matter of time, seconds even, before someone notices and reports us. We are rule-followers; we are a fearful people.

She stops and turns, but I don't have enough air to speak again. I lift my chin to her neck. Her eyes flicker with question and I croak, "Your scarf." I shift my hands between us. Her gaze drops and she understands. She pulls off her scarf, wraps my hands within it, and starts off again, pulling me along by my sleeve. "We've got to get as far away as possible."

We are side by side now. "I have friends who will hide us."

"Peter and Helene?"

We slow with the pace of the crowd as we all climb the stairs to street level.

"Nein." My voice breaks. Panic seizes me. How can she know about the Sauers? What have they done? I struggle to free my hands from the scarf. I need to touch my daughter, make sure she's okay, and make sure she hears me. "You have met them? They know you are here? What do they know?"

We climb the stairs side by side and the people pass around us. I can't keep pace. She continues to speak in German and that is best. English would get us noticed, especially with how close the crowd presses. I do not remember any street, station, or stairwell ever being so busy.

"They helped me this morning, but they know nothing. They knew about my first contact, but that all went wrong."

"They probably made it wrong."

"I wondered about that." She stops and a man bumps us from behind. He swears at her and moves around us. I shake my head, murmuring, "Later." We cannot talk here.

We reach the top of the stairs and, like pressure released from a clogged valve, spew onto the platform of the elevated trains. Luisa pulls me to the stairs and we descend, this time even more slowly, as I'm having trouble with all the chaos around me. My cell was a much quieter place and my brain doesn't adapt well.

I expect relief when we reach the sidewalk and are out in the open, but none comes. The sidewalks are crowded. Too crowded for nighttime. Are they here for the protests the man in the next cell mentioned? What's happening, and how much have I missed in the last six months? I wonder about the protests in Leipzig. I wonder about the elections and if the Party was able to sweep it all under the rug. I wonder what General Secretary Honecker stated about the uprisings across Europe or even about the horrific revolt in Tiananmen Square in China that we heard whisperings of within the prison walls.

I shake my head. It is heavy and fuzzy, but I must stay focused. "There are others we can trust," I say, gesturing with my bound hands down the street. "We must get to the Church of Zion. We will need papers and can print them there."

I pivot to the east and she follows. Then, within a step, she steps in front of me to take the lead. She blocks me from the crowds. My daughter protects me. It ignites a battle within me. Pride for who she has become. Shame I am not capable of protecting her. Yet I am not. I am too weak. I can barely keep my weary fingers clasped to the back of her coat.

But it's not helping. We are making no headway. The crowds are growing by the second, and we get pushed back a half step or more for every step of progress. Something has gone horribly wrong. People must be seeking safety. My first thought is that the Party is locking us in tighter. My second thought is that Soviet tanks are moving in as they did in 1953. My mind casts to the incongruence of that thought as Gorbachev had been promoting reform and peace before I went to prison. But who knows? He could be ousted by now. He could have been replaced by someone more of Honecker's ilk. Anything could have happened and I would not know.

My city suddenly feels foreign and frightening to me.

The crowd separates us and I try to cry out, but my lungs flare and I end up coughing. I feel myself stumble back and fear I will fall and be crushed by the crowd. But I see her . . .

A hand yanks me upright. Quite strong, my little mouse.

"We're not getting anywhere." She looks around frantically. I want to push her away, tell her to save herself. If we only had an hour, then seeing her was worth it and I will go back to prison a happy man. But she must not get caught with me. She must go free.

I shake my head and try to convince myself to say the words I do not want to say, because I don't want to let her go. I am selfish and she is life to me. She pushes me against a building and we stand side by side, momentarily safe from the crowd's crush.

"Don't look so glum. Come on. It's open." A man's heavy hand slams upon my shoulder. I feel my whole body crumple with the weight of it.

"Open?" I ask, but he is gone.

I watch the crowd, trying to make sense of what I am seeing. No one is rushing, calling out in fear, or hurrying to safety. They are moving quickly, yes, but not in frantic haste. It's almost as if something happy is driving them west. Some are crying, yes, but almost in disbelief or pleasure. Excited voices reach me. I see eyes wide with anticipation and disbelief. Has Bruce Springsteen come back to town? I have only seen such crowds at his concert, such jubilance too.

Luisa shifts against the Wall to face me. "They say the wall is open. That's what they're saying."

"Don't believe them, Luisa." I shake my head. I don't want her led astray. To think such things is wishful and dangerous. "Honecker would never allow it. It's impossible. We must go. We'll need papers to get out. We need a plan. Do you have a plan?"

"Honecker was ousted. Last month. Egon Krenz is general secretary now."

I part my lips. They are cracked and dry. I can't process this change. I can't think what good it might bring. "We need a plan. We still need a plan." I feel frantic. I don't understand the world around me. I don't know what to do.

"I have a phone number that will become a plan, I promise. We just need a secure telephone." Luisa's eyes narrow and her voice calms me. There is such confidence within her I almost believe we'll make it.

We push against the crowd and I notice that even within these few minutes, the tenor around us has changed again. What was questioning and quiet is growing louder and more jubilant, more courageous. They are growing strong as Luisa and I grow weary. We have made it only a few blocks toward our destination. There are at least a couple of kilometers to go. She said we had an hour. I know that is long gone. Her life is now at risk.

"You're going the wrong way." A young woman smiles at my daughter. "Turn. Come on."

"Why?" I reach out to her. I am angry she would lie to my daughter and harm her this way.

"They're opening the wall. It's over." I glare at her and she smiles again, like I'm a small child and not a grown man. "It's true. They announced it on television at a press conference tonight. The border is fully open."

I look to Luisa. I don't know if it's true, but I need to get her to a checkpoint regardless. I don't care about me, but if there is conflict at the border, I believe they will let her through. The Party won't want the press that would come with publicly harming an American in our internal turmoil. And Walther wrote me that Luisa is now, and has been since her eighteenth birthday, a naturalized United States citizen. I am certain her government won't stand by and watch one of their own, if so close and at a checkpoint, be seized.

They won't. They mustn't. While the Americans did nothing to help us in 1961 when Ulbricht, with Brezhnev's backing, built the wall, it's different now. Their President Reagan is more vocal and more active. His work alongside the Catholic Pope John Paul II has been reported over the airwaves for years. And Gorbachev too. He wants increased freedoms. He has been promoting reform. I look to the west. Perhaps it is our only option now—her only option.

We stare at each other and I marvel at how well I know her in so short a time. I concede. She agrees. We let the swell push us along. As we retrace our steps, I convince myself that this is right and trust she will be safe.

The crowd grows to a massive size as we near Bornholmer Strasse, the city's northernmost checkpoint. It fills the entire space, across the sidewalks and the street. A thin line of Trabbis try to move toward the checkpoint, but they can't inch forward at more than a walking pace. The crowds push tight around them. But the drivers do not rush, they do not honk, they do not rail against the rude inconvenience. Their windows are rolled down. They smile and chat with the crowd as everyone moves forward in unison.

I hear one driver yell about Politburo member Günter Schabowski's statement. "He did not look like he knew what he was saying."

A man walking alongside her car laughs. "But he said it."

"It's all around the world. They can't take that back," another calls out.

The calls and camaraderie bounce around us like titling ideas in the newsroom. Everyone is on the same team and saying the same thing over and over, as if needing to convince each other it is true.

I can't speak. And I don't know I'm crying until Luisa looks over and I feel the wetness on my cheeks and chin and, looking down, see the splashes darkening the grey of my jumpsuit.

God help me, I'm beginning to believe.

CHAPTER 30

Luisa Voekler

Thursday, November 9, 1989, 11:00 p.m.

In the distance the guard tower ahead of us stands empty.

The crowd tucks tighter and the momentum changes again. It feels tinged with dark, and the first tendrils of fear creep in. My feet lift off the ground in the crush. I reach for my father, but my hand swipes at another man's shirt. Bodies wedge me in. I can't see. I can barely breathe.

It's almost a living thing, this sense of anger and frustration washing over the jubilance and disbelief of moments before, and I struggle to create space in the press.

"Open the gate. Open the gate."

I hear shouts from ahead, and as they ripple back through the crowd, they get picked up by those around me. The chants go on and I am suspended in space and time. There is nothing more than the next breath. I wiggle to slide my arms up my body and cross them in front of my chest as an elbow drives hard into my sternum. Stars burst across my vision. I feel the need to protect my heart and lungs.

I catch a glimpse of my father, only two people away. I call for him and push myself in his direction. My foot falls on the top of someone else's, and I use the firm footing to launch. My father catches me with bound hands and pulls me close.

"We were fools. We never should have—"

He stops talking as a new sound emerges. Cheering rises somewhere ahead and, like the stadium wave that started a few years ago at football games, rolls back along the filled streets. Car drivers start to honk their horns and hands go up all around me.

The raised hands free room around me and my feet land on firm ground again. The crowd begins a steady thrust forward. I am one hundred feet from the guard tower. Sixty. Something firm and startling grips me from behind, and despite the crowd pushing me forward, I topple backward. The neck of my blouse and sweater cut off the air in my throat as they are yanked to such a degree I feel the blouse's stitching break against my neck.

My hand still grips my father and he topples backward into the man behind him.

I turn in the crowd to see what's happened and find my father's face first. Shock and surprise dance across his face, then recognition and almost joy, before his eyes cloud in confusion. All this passes within an instant and I stand facing Splinter.

"You're not going anywhere." He lets go of the back of my sweater, which has twisted with me, and secures a better hold on my arm. I grasp his arms with both hands, trying to secure my freedom, but he's strong. Stronger than I anticipated. I see my father out of the corner of my eye pushing people away as he tries to stay close.

Splinter, with a grip sure to leave a bruise on my arm, marches me feet away until I am pressed against a brick building.

My father is dragged with us, pulling at Splinter's arm. "Let her go. You will let her go, Splinter. What are you thinking? What have you done?"

"Nein. We wait. We wait until I figure this out. Panzer was helping her help you escape. I had to stop that." He's shaking his head in a short, twitchy motion. I am not sure if he's on something, coming off something, or just in a state of high anxiety. Perhaps all three.

"You helped us. You can't be working for them. We've been together two years." My father is clutching at him.

"They ruined my father. I had to get his job back. And now—it's all gone wrong. You weren't supposed to be here. You weren't supposed to come back to the apartment."

"Why not?" I push into him. "Where was I supposed to be?"

Splinter looks as if he's about to answer when my father presses between us. Splinter still grips my arm but now around him. I can no longer see Splinter's face as I'm pressed against my father's back, but I can hear his words. His voice is young and frightened. "I don't have a choice. You don't understand."

"I do." My father's voice is calm and paternal. "I understand more than you think, and you've got sisters and a brother. I know that about you, Splinter. You're a good son. I'm sorry they've done this to you, but hurting my daughter won't help your family. If you want to take me, fine. I'll come. I'd do that for your family. But let her go. She's American, Splinter, and I sense your officer will not be pleased if you embarrass him."

Splinter's grip shifts, almost loosens, and I wrench myself free. He grabs for my father.

"No!" I step forward, about to take on this young man, half a foot taller and probably sixty pounds heavier, but my father stops me with a hand to my shoulder.

"Go, Luisa. I'll be fine."

I glance between them. I look to the crowd. It's moving quickly past us now. The cheers only a hundred feet away are growing. Happy sounds. Disbelieving still, but happy.

"Splinter." I turn back. There is no way I'm leaving. "It's over. It's all coming down. They can't hold you, which means they can't harm your family. Please." I reach into my tights. "I've got money to help you get them out if you need it."

I shove my last wad of bills toward him, at the hand gripping my father. I'm not sure if he even wants it, but his reaction is what I banked on. He's distracted, confused, and lets go to accept what's getting pressed into his hand.

In that instant before Splinter realizes what's happened, I yank my father behind me—and straight into Peter Sauer.

"You?" My father pulls back as if punched, yet Peter has made no contact.

He slides a glance to Splinter. "I'll take him from here. Go. Go find your friends." The young man vacillates, but Peter repeats himself. "Go."

Splinter takes off. But not in the direction I expect. He doesn't follow the crowds toward the gate. He weaves and winds his way with remarkable agility against the crowds and heads east.

"How dare you!" My father pushes against Peter's chest. It's weak and Peter barely loses his bearings. A tiny step backward with one foot balances him.

My father continues yelling. "I trusted you. I don't care that I went to jail, but you sent me there. All that time. You did that to me. You were my friend. And you took my daughter? What have you become? What are you?"

"I couldn't get out of it, Haris. I'm sorry, but you had no one. They couldn't get to you because you had no one. But I have Helene, Traeger, and Dirk. I could help them, and—" Peter's eyes fill with tears as he glances at me for an instant. "I'm sorry."

He faces my father again. They are the same height. The same build. They almost look as though they could be brothers. "I'm sorry for what they've done to you."

"Are you taking me back? Is that what this is?"

Peter shakes his head. "It went wrong. Helene called Splinter to follow Luisa after she woke—"

"That's it." I step toward him. "You drugged me. That's why I slept."

"It couldn't hurt you. We needed to keep you there until Haris was transferred. Then . . ."

"They'd come for me too." The words fall from me as his betrayal, both of my father and of me, plays out like a spy show in my mind.

Peter shrugs. "Helene let you go. She didn't want to be the one, so she called the guard and Splinter. She thought you might come back to us, but just in case—" He stops again as the crowd jostles us. "Go. It's over."

I shift to move away, but my father stands firm. "How can I trust this? What about Dirk and Traeger now?"

Peter smiles and it's different. I'm not sure how I know that; I just sense it is. There's something unburdened and free within it. "Didn't you hear? It's over. They are in the crowd with their wives. They are free." He gestures to the crowd again. "Tomorrow, who knows? But you should go too. Now."

I don't wait for another word to be spoken. I seize my father's arm and shove him forward. I want to get him away before Peter changes his mind or fear seizes Splinter and he returns, or who knows what else might happen.

As I push my father ahead of me, the crowd catches us up into its surge. Within seconds we're twenty, thirty, forty feet away from Peter. A few more minutes and we're past the first wall and into the Death Zone. I can barely see over the heads all around me, but I can tell there are no buildings here. There is no light. The crowd feels quieter in this space between the inner and outer walls.

Twenty feet. Ten. And I'm standing beside the guardhouse. That's when I notice the gate, very similar to the red-and-white train guards at home, is raised. There is no barrier whatsoever between the East and West, merely a change in the color of the street's pavement.

People around me are jubilant. I can feel their joy and their wonder. They are quieter here than they were farther away. It's almost as if they, too, wanted to believe it is true and now have to slow down and absorb that it actually is.

As I clutch my father's bound hands in both of my own, we step across the pavement's transition. Cheers erupt around us as West Berlin welcomes us. I hear it, but as if it's in the distance, far away rather than mere feet. The world tilts, almost like a kaleidoscope, one click from clear.

I turn back and nudge my father to do the same. Behind us, people are standing atop the Wall. They are swaying, calling out, waving flags, crying, and laughing. As we watch, more join them. Friends pull friends—everyone's a friend—up the Wall's slick surface and onto the large pipe fitted across the top.

My eyes travel from the Wall to the guards, now lined up next to the barrier. People rush at them, and rather than push them away, they submit to kisses and hugs. They look as bewildered as my father looks and as I feel.

He pulls his eyes from all that's happening in the East and the crowds lining the road on both sides of us in the West and faces me.

Without a word he lifts his bound hands high above his head. Understanding, I step close to him and wrap my arms around his middle. His bound hands drop in an arc behind me, creating a circle to hold me close.

He hugs me tight and cries. I do the same, soaking the front of his grey jumpsuit with twenty-six years' worth of tears.

We are free.

CHAPTER 31

WEST BERLIN

Friday, November 10, 1989

We stand hugging until the crowd around us presses so close, I fear we'll topple over. My father stumbles and I duck out of his embrace to hold him steady and lead him out of the center of the street. West Berliners jostle ten deep on the sidewalks as if cheering along the most wonderful parade. And I suppose they are.

The restaurants all around us have reopened. The bars never closed, but now—although it's a cold night—their doors are wide open, spilling a cacophony of music into the streets, mixing with the calls, cheers, and jubilation. Bottles of champagne pop open all around us. The noise startles me at first, then once I confirm to my own mind it's not a gunshot, it blends into the happy mayhem. Bottles of who knows what else keep getting pressed into my hands as well. I pass them along without sipping. There are plenty of takers all around me to drain the endless bottles dry.

"What do we do now? Where do we go?" My father looks thin, lost, and bewildered. How long has it been since he last slept or ate? Is anything more serious wrong with him? It strikes me how little I know about him or his current health.

"Are you okay? Do you feel faint? Can you breathe?" I don't know what questions to ask, so I keep firing new ones. His hand shakes, and I wonder if it's the cold, low blood sugar, or something worse.

He grips my forearm as he tries to take a deep breath. It wheezes and rattles and sends him into a coughing fit that doubles him over.

I look around. While there are people all around, there is no true help nearby. I make a decision—we cannot stay and watch; we cannot celebrate. While this is a historical moment never to be repeated, the mission isn't finished until my father is safe. Healthy and safe. That's my job and it's time to move on.

I wrap an arm around him and start us walking farther west. "I have a hotel room nearby. We're going to head there and get you some food, then sleep. While you rest, I'll find a doctor. Then we'll figure out our next steps."

He closes his eyes in both exhaustion and acquiescence and lets me direct him.

As we slowly weave through the crowds—there is no reason to rush anymore and my father clearly needs the slower pace—I stop passersby and ask directions. Everyone is eager to engage, and no one drops their attention to his wrists. Everyone is enamored with the world around us. It's friendly, cheerful, and merry; it's neon lights, liquor, and singing. Soon, with only a couple wrong turns slowing us down, I recognize a street corner, a building, a park, and finally my hotel.

I shift us sideways through the throng and feel my father stop next to me. He turns and pulls at my hands. His face is paler and tenser than when we stood hugging only a short time ago. I open my mouth to begin my litany of worried questions when he lifts both hands between us and rests them against me, right below my throat. His fingers reach up to my cheeks as if he's studying my face both by sight and by touch.

He says nothing, but I sense he's struggling somehow and I'm not to rush him. He stares at me with such intention I can't look away. It's as if he's tracing my childhood, my teenage years, my entire life in this one long, searching moment.

"I am sorry. I can never say that enough. I am truly sorry. Please forgive me."

I open my mouth to push back from the request, just as I did with Aunt Alice only days ago. I don't want that. I don't want—I stop, recognizing that my discomfort is worse than irrelevant; it's selfish. I can't push away another's need just because such emotions make me twitchy. Which means I owe Aunt Alice an apology.

My father continues after a long, wheezing breath. "I did so much wrong. I didn't see. And when I did, I didn't act when I should have. I hurt your mama. I hurt you. I—"

"Shhh . . ." Now I interrupt, but for an entirely different reason. Lightning has struck, and if I've learned anything this week—though I've caused hurt by not realizing it sooner—it's to let the past go. It may feel uncomfortable, perhaps unnecessary, or, as I suspect, it may be the most vital aspect of healing: forgive and move forward. Opa. Oma. Alice. Me. Perhaps especially me. And, certainly, my father.

"You're enough, Dad. You are more than enough. Don't go back a single day. You're here now and I love you. I forgive you."

My own words shock me. Yet they are true. He is enough and he is my dad. I taste the word within my mind again. *Dad* . . . It's such an affectionate, loving, and close term, and one I have never used. And yet, without thought, it is simply here and it feels right.

Dad's lips press together in a thin line. His head bobs in tiny nods. He looks like he's about to burst into tears and I know I am. The pressure builds in my nose and my forehead. My eyes sting.

In a surprising shift the pressure bubbles out in laughter instead. One look and Dad's chortling is only a millisecond behind mine.

We swipe at our eyes; I grab his arm. "I didn't know until a few days ago, Dad. I would've written. I would've come—" I stop, unsure where to go or what to say next, so I end with, "I'm sorry."

Again, my dad's face bursts into a radiant smile. "Walther never wrote that he kept up the original lie, but by not writing about it, I knew he had. I always knew." He reaches up again and with his bound hands touches my cheek. "You look like her. You have my eyes." He beams. "But you have her smile. It's a beautiful smile."

"Luisa!" I hear a call close by and look up.

Daniel stands outside the hotel's entrance.

I wrap an arm around Dad and head that direction. Daniel meets us in the middle, and unsure whether relief or love launches me forward, I hurl myself into his arms. He lifts me off the ground and hugs me tight for the briefest moment before sanity returns and I wiggle out of his embrace, embarrassed by my exuberance. He quirks a sideways smile as if he knows the full complexity of what I'm feeling, and I accept that he probably does.

"Daniel Rudd, sir. It's good to meet you." He holds a hand out to my dad, who lifts both his own to clasp it. Rather than shake it, Dad pulls Daniel's hand close to his chest. "Did you help Luisa? Did you help us?"

Daniel glances to me again, and I'm struck by the openness within his gaze. In all our time together, all those years ago, it feels as if I have never seen him so clearly.

"It was her show, sir. I was just along for the ride." He tilts his head back toward the hotel. "Let's get you inside and get those cuffs off you."

We weave through the crowds, and at the hotel's doorway, I realize what's missing. "Where's Willow?"

"Back in East Berlin, I expect. We heard over the radio that the Bornholmer Strasse gate was the first to open. She took off that direction hours ago."

I look to Dad. "I saw that sign. That's the gate we came through."

He nods with a new set of tears streaming down his face. "Willow helped you? She's a good girl. The risks those kids take . . . But it's better now, right?"

"I hope so." Daniel faces east as if considering what's happened and assessing what may happen next. "The gates are all open now. There's no stuffing this genie back in the bottle."

"How is this even possible?" I ask him.

"Call it a mistake. Call it Providence. New border regulations were to be implemented tomorrow, but ones still requiring passports, papers, and registrations. They got misread over the airwaves."

We enter the lobby. Daniel walks over to the registration desk as I lead Dad to the couches. He sinks into a corner and I am again struck by his fragility. I glance to Daniel. Whatever he says to the young man garners a startled look and a shrug of acquiescence. He walks back to the manager's office as Daniel returns to us.

"Politburo member Günter Schabowski hadn't read the regulations beforehand and hadn't attended the meeting. So when he got a note handed to him at the press conference, he clearly had no idea what was going on but still read it aloud. He declared all borders open. A shocked Italian reporter asked him to clarify, actually gave Schabowski a chance to backpedal, but he doubled down instead and said 'open immediately.'"

The attendant returns and slides something across the counter to Daniel, who—without breaking the conversation—gestures for me to come close. "Within minutes all West Berlin was at the checkpoints calling for friends and family to come out. Stunned, East Berlin was about an hour behind them. The guards had no choice.

No official order was given at the gates at first, but it became a do-or-die moment either to let the thousands through or chance what might've happened next. So they opened the gates. Now I've heard that official orders came down and everything is truly and legally open."

He hands me a set of bolt cutters and whispers, "Do the honors?"

I smile at his thoughtfulness and, with Dad's wrists stretched as far apart as they can reach on the coffee table in front of the couch, I cut the thin links connecting them. "I'm sorry we can't get them fully off."

He wiggles his new clanking bracelets. "They're not bothering me a bit." He looks to Daniel. "Will they call people back? Will they shut the gates again?"

"I can't say, Mr. Voekler. The numbers feel too big for that. Thousands are pouring out and all Eastern Europe is breaking apart. But who knows what they might try?" He throws me a glance. "It doesn't matter, though, because you two won't be here."

"What do you mean?" Dad's voice wavers and my heart breaks for the fear I sense within it and the trepidation I see in his eyes.

Daniel tilts his head to me. "There are a few military planes at Tempelhof Airport taking off over the next several hours. My job is to get you on one of them. We don't have to rush, but we do have to move that direction."

"Andrew?"

Daniel nods. "This is not a sanctioned operation, and the faster we end it, the fewer questions will be raised."

"Why'd you tell him at all?" It's a selfish question, as I know that, despite Daniel's status, he put himself on the line for me. But Andrew's knowing can't bode well.

"Insurance." Daniel's confident reply flummoxes me. He chuckles at my consternation. "Cademan can't do anything after the fact if he's officially briefed during. Moreno was on the call too, and she's not about to let me get docked."

"You pitted his wife against him?"

"They will both come out fine. Better than fine." Daniel lifts a brow. "If you hadn't gotten out, maybe there'd have been an issue, but I trusted you, always have. I told them there'd never be a problem." He gestures to Dad. "Besides, your dad is technically Cademan's asset, making this his op. The fact that it was successful, flawless even, looks very good for him."

"But you did this. If anyone should get credit, you should."

"Me?" Daniel winks. "I was never here." He points to a suitcase resting beside the couch. "I hope you don't mind, but I packed for you."

He reaches for it and starts talking to my dad. I'm impressed by the care he shows him. "I'm going to walk you both a few blocks away from here to a larger street that will be outside the crowds. Luisa's boss, Andrew Cademan, has arranged a car for you. It will take you both to the airport."

"Where will we be going?"

"Washington, DC, sir, if you don't mind."

Dad looks to me. "You live there, right?"

"I do." I can't help but grin.

He turns back to Daniel. "I don't mind."

Daniel walks us several blocks farther west to Schöneberger Ufer, while sharing with us the historic and unbelievable events of the evening, who said what when and what followed, all around the world. The crowds thin with every block we walk west, and I soon see a black car waiting in a bus pullout a couple blocks ahead.

Upon reaching the car, Dad immediately climbs in. He settles and closes his eyes. His exhaustion worries me once more.

I pause, sensing Daniel take a step back rather than forward. "Aren't you coming with us?"

He shakes his head. "Now that I'm here, Moreno wants me to check a few things out. This changes everything geopolitically, so I'll be here at least a few days more. It's a whole new game, Penguin. One you might want to get involved in."

He looks at me a long minute, and I find myself unable to move. His eyes carry that same intensity they did years ago, and just like before, I see more in it. I see deeper into him, and I sense that his look, this look, is only for me. It's not the general level of focus he brings to every task; it's something special and intimate. I can't even blink for fear of missing a heartbeat of it.

"Go to dinner with me when I get back?"

I smile and remember that when Daniel got nervous at the Farm, his sentences lost their subjects and his questions came out brief, almost terse.

"Yes. It's a date."

"A date?"

Something deep within me falters for a second. Old wounds rise, but I hush them with a single steady breath. I did not fail. I'm right where I should be. And, even more surprisingly, I know what I want. "Yes. A date. So you'll need to plan a few details to make sure it's memorable."

"Don't you worry. I got you." He leans down and presses a long kiss against my cheek, right below my ear. It's the sexiest thing ever and my face flushes with heat as I drop into the car.

The streets are empty, so it takes only about fifteen minutes to cross what feels like several miles. The car circles the main airport and enters an unmarked entrance off a side road. The huge chain-link gates stand open.

Several planes are parked near a hangar, but only one sits fully lit. The car stops and a Marine steps down the plane's few steps.

"Haris Voekler." He stretches out his hand. "Luisa Voekler." He does the same to me. "Please come aboard. We're ready to go." He looks over his shoulder to the next plane to our left. "Unless you need more time. We're lifting that one off at 0300."

"No. Thank you." I look to my dad for confirmation. He nods. "We are ready."

We board the plane. It's a small jet with the seats lining the sides rather than facing forward. I wonder what the plane has been reconfigured for, but I don't ask. The Marine most likely wouldn't tell me anyway. He directs us with a gesture rather than words to two seats near the front. A few others are seated across from us, but as the engines ramp up and make hearing difficult, we merely nod our hellos.

Dad and I buckle in. His hand reaches over and holds mine as the plane takes off.

I glance over and, still holding my hand, my dad—with his head tilted back and a soft smile on his lips—is fast asleep.

EPILOGUE

WASHINGTON, DC

June 9, 1990

Only six months later and it's a whole new world . . .

Dad works for the CIA now. Not in Arlington, and no longer at Langley, but—as of last month—back in Berlin. Soon after his arrival and debriefing last November, he wanted to "officially" enter the game. His decision was actually surprising as he wasn't too pleased at first to discover he'd already been enrolled in the "game" long before.

"He gave you my letters?" he barked at Andrew the very morning we arrived.

We landed at Anacostia airfield at about 4:00 a.m. DC time on November 10, and Andrew, dressed in a dark blue suit, stood waiting for us on the tarmac. My heart dropped, but he wasn't interested in me at all—not at first.

He whisked us off in a car to Langley where, over coffee and Danishes, he started to debrief Dad immediately.

"Can't this wait until he's rested? Or seen a doctor?"

"I'm afraid it can't." Andrew wasn't harsh, but there were national security issues to address—ones I had not fully comprehended.

Once Dad digested the fact that Opa had shared the information encrypted within his letters and that not only had it informed the US intelligence services but also constituted some of the earliest newspaper reporting out of East Germany, he visibly relaxed. A glow suffused his face, and I got the sense that he felt delight that they had effected change. He had made that difference for good as he'd wanted to for years.

Tears sprang to his eyes as he leaned over and whispered, "I think your mama would finally be proud of me."

We also quickly discovered what "couldn't wait"—Operation Pope.

Andrew cleared the room so only the three of us remained. "Mr. Voekler, that information is too explosive to ever discuss. The US never even conducted an official intelligence inquiry into it because the opposition was too great, both inside and outside the service. Director Bill Casey conducted a private off-books investigation and came to your conclusions, but that report is hidden and its results have not been released. They will never be released. Do you understand? Both the Vatican and the president have agreed on this and have determined to leave the matter alone."

Dad and I sat silent for a full minute before Dad answered Andrew. "No one is to ever know?"

"Nothing more will ever be said. The Italians finished their investigation years ago, and the world's journalists have moved on. For all parties, that event is closed."

"Why? Where is justice in this?" he asked, and I sensed his mind was drifting to Manfred Schneider. It didn't feel like a fitting end to the information he died to preserve.

"Is justice the nuclear devastation World War III will bring?" Andrew waited as Dad and I digested his bald and rhetorical question. He relented and didn't force us to answer. "The Vatican—well, the pope, as the 'Vatican' doesn't know any more than most people—has determined that it is best for the world if nothing derails the extraordinarily peaceful steps toward freedom occurring in Europe. Neither Rome nor the US will push the Soviet Union into an offensive position, as we could be sitting on the edge of the whole thing crashing down without a single shot fired."

The very idea that such a thing could happen silenced Dad, and I could tell he thought even Manfred might be okay with that.

Dad won't work as a spy in Berlin, but as a consultant and envoy for the US as efforts begin to reunite both the city and the country. He expects that's still a couple years away, but he holds great hope for a once more unified Germany.

One upside of being in the "game" since 1964, he declared, was that the CIA had been paying him all along. It seems when Bran vetted his first coded message with Andrew's predecessor, he set up an account for Bran's contact under the code name PRESSMAN. Through Bran, Opa then made sure that the code name and payments were tied to my dad's name rather than to himself.

It was Dad who refilled Oma's account.

It was Dad who paid down her mortgage. "What will I do with all this money?" he asked.

It was Dad who sat me down after work last February and said, "It's time for you to move out and enjoy your life more."

And I am. I work for the CIA too now. Well, I always did, but now—when not abroad—I officially work from Langley. Andrew didn't reprimand or fire me. He put me back in the operational pool where I'd started all those years ago. He even apologized for how he'd ousted me from the Farm. Not that he did it, just *how* he did it.

It took until April for me to move out, though, because I started to really love living at home. Dad took over Alice's room, and the two of us would stay up long after Oma turned in for the night and talk about all sorts of stuff. I learned about a world, a mom, and a life that I had no concept could exist. Dad learned about a way of life outside his wildest expectations as well.

"*You* decided if you wanted to go to University? *You* picked your curriculum? *You* chose your own job?" At first he would repeat everything I said in the form of a question just to make sure it was true. It took a few weeks for that pattern to shift.

We also watched movies. And, yes, I am very much like my father. We both love the movies, and once I introduced him to Jiffy Pop, there was no turning back. Those were some of our best nights. Dad shared with me some of his favorites such as *Casablanca* and *Chinatown* along with *The Rose*, an old German film the Blockbuster guy had to special-order for us. It was filmed in Berlin when my dad was a kid, and his father actually worked for Henry Koster, the director, before Hitler came to power and Koster fled to the United States.

Of course, after that, we had to watch all of Koster's films. I liked *Harvey* with Jimmy Stewart best, and Dad watched *The Bishop's Wife* with Cary Grant and Loretta Young three times before I had to return it.

That was another surprising moment. Dad bought his tapes off the black market and kept them hidden under a floorboard in his bedroom. A Blockbuster video store and the ability to choose, return, and choose again was almost as staggering to him as me choosing my college major.

A new Oma has emerged during these last months as well. She cried a lot at first, but now she laughs more. Alice visits more too. She is truly the friend and big sister I always hoped she would be.

And don't get me started on Oma's garden. Her friends are green with envy at the abundant produce Oma is already gathering.

Daniel's not doing too badly either. He stayed in Berlin a full month after the Wall fell but called me nightly. After a couple weeks, I quit returning the upstairs hall phone to its little table each morning and simply kept it plugged in within my room. It was an incredibly special time because, until all my security clearances transferred from an off-site project and role into an operational one, we could really only talk about ourselves. All those hopes and dreams, fears and vulnerabilities, one rarely approaches without trepidation. He knows most everything about me now, and I know and love everything about him.

Except . . . he says he had a long talk with my dad last night, and neither will share the subject matter with me.

By the time he picks me up for tonight's dinner, I'm so tense I stop on my apartment building's sidewalk halfway to his car. "Just say it. You're going back into the field."

"How'd you know?" Daniel stares at me. "Yes. Two years. Minimum."

I nod. I have just been asked to go to Eastern Europe myself. But Daniel's work is different. Working under nonofficial cover means there's no communication while he's away. He's simply gone.

Tears prick my eyes. I duck my head to hide them. "Southeast Asia?" I ask, but I don't really expect him to answer.

"Eastern Europe."

My head flies up. "But that means—"

"You have no patience, you know that?" he teases.

I nod, afraid to speak, think, or ruin the moment in any way. He steps to me. He's so close I can smell the grass and citrus notes of his cologne and see the small scar at the outer corner of his left eye.

"It means, if you marry me, like I pray you will, we go together."

As I said, one would be surprised how many marriages exist within the CIA.

Once again, I launch myself into his arms. And once again, he catches me, lifts me off the ground, and hugs me tight.

This time, I don't let go. I'll never let go.

AUTHOR'S NOTE

I had an incredible time digging into this fascinating and tumultuous time within history. Of course, I bent it a little for fictional purposes, but so much true history remains within these pages as well. And, as always, any and all mistakes are mine alone . . . But let's peel back the curtain a little.

I was able to travel to Berlin in February of 2023 for several days and walked the city a few times over. I thoroughly enjoyed it. It is a city unlike any other—at least any other I've visited. One author I read for research, Rory MacLean, put it so well: "Paris is about romantic love. Lourdes equates with devotion. New York means energy. London is forever trendy. Berlin is all about volatility." And that's what I found. A city on the edge throughout history, surging between the cosmic—and cosmopolitan—heights and the lowest of lows, with periods of tremendous pain and horror within its past as well.

One thing I found interesting is the speed at which the Wall went up. Without the world realizing it, General Secretary Ulbricht had been stockpiling all the materials and preparing the troops for months in advance. Once he got Moscow's approval, he was ready to move, all in one night. But Bernauer Strasse was a bit of a problem. As stated, the buildings were in East Berlin and the sidewalks—one step out the front door—were in West Berlin. I found it an ideal place to situate much of the story as those buildings were an ever-changing part of the Wall and the city's history.

So while I got to know a great deal about Berlin during my visit and walked it several times over, I still played with its geography. Bornholmer Strasse is not the closest border crossing to Friedrichstrasse Station, but it was the first gate to open on November 9, 1989. Even without official orders, guards—under pressure from thousands of people pressing toward them—opened the gates at 11:00 p.m. I wanted Luisa and Haris to be at that first gate.

Also note that Haris doesn't capitalize the "wall." I chose to let him leave it uncapitalized. He doesn't want to give it too much respect. He believes it already wields enough control over his life. Furthermore, to clear up any confusion, Haris speaks of the DDR, the Deutschland Democratic Republic, which is East Germany or what we, on the west side of the Atlantic, would call the GDR, German Democratic Republic—which one man I interviewed noted, with dark humor, was "neither democratic nor a republic."

There is also a bit of interesting history, posited as true with good supporting evidence, in Paul Kengor's fantastic book *A Pope and a President*. He writes that the Soviet Union was planning to invade Poland, as it had Hungary in '56 and Czechoslovakia in '68, and was hiding that intention under the guise of their extended Soyuz '81 military exercises along the Polish border. However, when US President Reagan was shot, the US—not knowing what kind of threat it was dealing with—put Strategic Air Command on alert, as is standard protocol. Although not intended as a show of force to the Soviets over Poland, that move may have—unexpectedly—stopped an invasion.

Kengor's book, as well as a few others, is also where I learned a great deal about the details surrounding the assassination attempt against Pope John Paul II and where I found the text for John Paul II's quote from his first speech. I highly recommend this book if you'd like to learn more. We may take it for granted today that the Soviets were involved, but that wasn't always the case. While the Italian investigations pointed that direction, as did the research and writings of journalist Claire Sterling, much of the world refused to look at the Soviets. The consequences were too dire. In fact, the official CIA document still remains classified and the Stasi Operation Pope didn't come to light until 2005. To avoid World War III, everyone seemed to feel that believing the disinformation campaign of a single gunman was in everyone's best interests, especially as the Soviet Union in the mid- to late 1980s seemed to be falling apart on its own.

I also want to share two other invaluable resources: Tim Mohr's *Burning Down the Haus* and Paul Hockenos's *Berlin Calling*. Both books introduced me to the young men and women who fought for a freedom and a future of their choosing through dress and music—as everything in a police state is political. Within Mohr's book, I also learned one of their slogans: "Don't die in the waiting room of the future." Basically, don't be complacent.

What happened after November 9, 1989?

There is so much history to explore here and so many good books can help. I have included a list on my website, and I hope you'll enjoy them and the photographs and other details I placed on *The Berlin Letters* page. Germany was reunited, the

Stasi disbanded, and people even started requesting to see their files—and many were shocked at how many of their friends and neighbors had been spying on them for years.

I hope you've enjoyed *The Berlin Letters* and, again, please go to my website, katherinereay.com, for some of my source materials.

ACKNOWLEDGMENTS

As always, there are so many wonderful people to thank for this book . . .

Thank you to Claudia at Folio Literary Management and the fantastic team at Harper Muse—Amanda, Becky, Julee, Kerri, Margaret, Nekasha, Halie, Kim, Laura, Lizzie, Savannah, Natalie, Colleen, Caitlin, Jere, and Patrick. I appreciate all the hard work and your incredible dedication to this story!

Thank you, Ashley and Meghan of UpLit Reads and Laurel Ann Nattress of Austenprose. Also, many thanks to Kathie Bennett of Magic Time Literary Management for supporting me every step of the way.

I also need to thank family and friends. Elizabeth—thank you for your encouragement and loving this story from the beginning. Thank you to all my writer friends, as this is truly a community that supports one another, and in this world that is a tender and valuable thing. And never last, thank you to my family. There are not enough words to express my gratitude and love.

Thanks to all the bookstores and libraries that have generously opened their doors to me. I have so much fun sharing my love of books with you! And thank you, dear readers, for trusting me with your time and your hearts once more! I hope we meet within the pages of a book again soon.

Enjoy!

Katherine

DISCUSSION QUESTIONS

1. How do you feel about Walther's decision to share Haris's letters with a journalist?
2. Do you think Walther should have told Luisa her father was alive? Why or why not? Were his secrets justified?
3. Luisa begins to grasp the fear that continues to affect her Oma's life. Do you think she'll ever fully understand? What does that say or mean with regard to our ability to understand each other?
4. Would you have risked everything and traveled to Berlin? Why or why not?
5. What do you think of Luisa's initial plan? And considering how little information was conveyed over the wall, was she wrong to hope it might work?
6. Did the story change your thoughts regarding punks in Eastern Europe? What do you think about music and dress as a form of protest?
7. How would life feel when, at any moment, anyone, including

your best friend, could be watching and reporting to the government about you?

8. Did you enjoy the split-time scene between Haris and Luisa as they raced away from the Stasi for their "one hour" on November 9, 1989? Do you believe that, despite hearing the same words, two people can perceive things so differently during a single event?

ABOUT THE AUTHOR

Corinne Stagen Photography

KATHERINE REAY is a national bestselling and award-winning author who has enjoyed a lifelong affair with books. She publishes both fiction and nonfiction, holds a BA and MS from Northwestern University, and currently lives outside Chicago, Illinois, with her husband.

Visit her online at katherinereay.com
Facebook: @KatherineReayBooks
Twitter: @katherine_reay
Instagram: @katherinereay

From the Publisher

GREAT BOOKS

ARE EVEN BETTER WHEN THEY'RE SHARED!

Help other readers find this one:

- Post a review at your favorite online bookseller
- Post a picture on a social media account and share why you enjoyed it
- Send a note to a friend who would also love it—or better yet, give them a copy

Thanks for reading!